Don D. Plinton is a retired civil servant. He always had the desire to write but never got around to doing so. Since retiring, Don has written articles but never tried to publish any. Not so long ago, he decided to do something about it. He published his first novel; one could say it was a trial run. The outcome wasn't favourable but not because of him; the publishing was done hurriedly. Don got dismayed and gave up on the idea. However, at his family's urging, he has taken up the baton once more.

At times, one wants to do something constructive, but that get-up-and-go attitude is missing; complacency, and at times laziness, take control. To activate what you know you can do, or should be doing, you need that little urge or a kick up the backside. I was lucky to have someone who did just that—my sister, God rest her soul. She was always on my case. I wasn't always true to my words, and with time on my hands, there was always something to do apart from writing.

When I settled down to write this book, the phone never rang. Mostly, it was her, my sister. She didn't say it, but I knew what she was doing—checking up on me. Now, I don't have to be determined to write; not only does the attitude come easily, but the words do too. Now, it's like a hobby, and I like it. This is what was missing from my life all these years. One cannot turn back the clock, but I wish my sister were alive today. Even in her twilight days, she would still be keeping watch on me.

Don D. Plinton

Don D. Plinton

TALES FROM JAMAICA

AUSTIN MACAULEY PUBLISHERS
LONDON * CAMBRIDGE * NEW YORK * SHARJAH

Copyright © Don D. Plinton 2025

The right of Don D. Plinton to be identified as author of this work has been asserted by the author in accordance with sections 77 and 78 of the Copyright, Designs and Patents Act 1988.

All rights reserved. No part of this publication may be reproduced, stored in a retrieval system, or transmitted in any form or by any means, electronic, mechanical, photocopying, recording, or otherwise, without the prior permission of the publishers.

Any person who commits any unauthorised act in relation to this publication may be liable to criminal prosecution and civil claims for damages.

This is a work of fiction. Names, characters, businesses, places, events, locales, and incidents are either the products of the author's imagination or used in a fictitious manner. Any resemblance to actual persons, living or dead, or actual events is purely coincidental.

A CIP catalogue record for this title is available from the British Library.

ISBN 9781398444317 (Paperback)
ISBN 9781398455627 (ePub e-book)

www.austinmacauley.com

First Published 2025
Austin Macauley Publishers Ltd®
1 Canada Square
Canary Wharf
London
E14 5AA

Mrs M. Beckford – this person was a great help to me in getting the book out. As a person who has worked alongside publishers, her words of advice were helpful.

Ms F. Cole – a young woman who was always going through the things I had written and discarded. Bill, you know you could write a book, as she used to say.

Chapter 1
Tales From Jamaica

This was a time of lawlessness, a time when men with guns ruled. Their homegrown produce of marijuana, and cocaine from South America crippled the country. Money-grabbing unscrupulous officials, some of whom aligned themselves with illegal trades; the government could not function effectively. Gangs fighting for the lion share of the spoil, and with that, killing came easy. Those who could, fled the country, seeking a peaceful existence elsewhere. Tourist that contributed to more than fifty per cent of the country's economy, was no more, the violence saw to that. The Constabulary tried, but too many crooked men run the show; no one could be trusted. Top of the list of bad men was one Harry Wells. In the era he lived, a teenager doesn't become an adult until he or she was twenty-one, however, that criteria didn't apply to Harry. At the age of eighteen, he considered he's a grown man and shouldn't be living at home with his parents, so he up and left for the bright light of the city. His mother was heartbroken; she cried days and nights. For his father, the feeling was different; he was glad to see him go. Harry, his only son, had become an embarrassment. He developed a mean streak, and his temper was uncontrollable.

In the district, it was never a good idea to get into an argument with him; someone got hurt, sometimes quite badly. Some thought him behaving the way he was behaving was on the strength of his father's reputation. Daniel Wells was a self-sufficient man and well respected, not only in the district but beyond.

Old man Wells didn't lose sleep when he discovered his son was gone. Nevertheless, with Henrietta grieving, he made her a promise, he would seek him out and bring him back; a promise he had no intention of keeping. But from time to time, he would be out and about, pretending he was looking. Some were gladdened to see the back of him, those who suffered at his hands. He was extremely unhappy and disappointed with the way his son turned out, constantly dragging the family's name in the mud, and ruining his reputation. Harry was a well-built young man, about six feet two; a handsome individual with good features, but that's where the niceties stop. A man with very few friends, if any, he was mean as a pole cat. After some two years, he returned, but the only person glad to see him was his mother. Since he left home, she had lost the will to live; so, in some respect his father was pleased to see him. Of course, he'd no intention of staying among the good people of Herring Hill; this was just a flying visit. Their only daughter, Marian, was doing well for herself, but she lived and worked away from home. That, however, was of no comfort to Henrietta; her beloved son was home – the world was good again.

It was a very hot night. Harry took part in a dice game, the feature on a Friday night. He had an argument with a fellow gambler that ended up in a fight. Being bigger and stronger, he beat the man to a pulp; while others looked on. Of course, no one was going to interfere, this was Harry Wells. He thought the man was dead, so he didn't tarry; he fled the scene under the cover of darkness without so much as goodbye to his mother. Once again, Henrietta fell back into the dark place she once was.

The man wasn't dead, but was helpless to himself. With little to no urgency, he was taken to the nearest hospital some eight miles away. At the hospital, there was no urgency regarding his condition; he had to wait his turn. That's the way it was here. A man turning up at the hospital suffering from machete wound or gunshot, the doctor wasn't going to make him a priority; he must wait in line like. In some cases, he would die before the doctor would see him. Such was the case for this unfortunate fellow; by the time the doctor got around to treating him, it was too late; he died where he sat. Harry was charged with murder; but he wasn't around. A murder investigation began at his parent's home, but investigations like these were never thorough. After a week or so, the enquiries would peter out and soon be forgotten. Well, some people's lives didn't count for much; the killers and the more affluent would get away with murders, yet there were those who were innocent but charged and sent to prison, or even to the gallows.

Harry's parents were people in their twilight years; they could do without all this bothers, but they were his parents, and as such, questions had to be asked. Old man Wells wasn't surprised to hear of his son's misdeed. He tries to bring him up in a God-fearing manner, but his efforts fell plenty short. A decent law-abiding man, was Daniel Wells, and even though it would break his heart, he will give the police whatever help he could without Henrietta knowing. Devious, one might say, but it's all for the good name of the family and his wife's sanity.

However, he could only help if Harry returns, but why would he? He knows he's a wanted man, and if caught, he'd be charged with murder and most certainly be hanged. The hunt was on, but the way these lawmen seek out their quarry, there wasn't a chance in hell of them finding him. These killers; whenever they committed their crimes, they would hide out in some of the most dangerous and inhospitable places in the country; places no lawmen ventured. As for the government, it was as though law and order weren't a priority, and the way the country was being run, it wasn't difficult to see why.

Sometime later, Harry returned, but under the cover of darkness; it seems he wanted to see his beloved mother once more. Of course, he knew his father would prefer he didn't, and given the chance, he would shop him to the police, so he tied him up, Harry was a powerful twenty-five-year-old; he could restrain an ox.

His mother was in tears looking on, but there's nothing she could do. Old man Wells didn't put up a struggle; he knew it would be futile, he knew how brutal his son can be, even to him. He remained calm, hoping he would be gone soon. He'll get his wish, but before he leaves, he told them why he had to flee the district. Of course, they already knew. It would be sad to see him gone, but at the moment, that's what his mother wanted. It was still dark when he decided to leave.

"So, this is goodbye, Harry?" she asked with tears in her eyes.

"Yes, mum, this is it," he said with a callous look of defiance. He embraced her but her response wasn't receptive.

"Goodbye, mum, dad. I'll say goodbye, and I'm sorry I had to tie you up." But his apologies fell on deaf ears; his father just wanted him gone. On his way out, he turned to talk to his dad.

"Dad, I'm going to untie you, but I must ask you, please, dad, don't go to the police."

Old man Wells, a strong-minded individual, gave him an ultimatum.

"You promise me; we'll never see you again, and I promise you I won't go to the police."

"Don't worry, dad, this is the last goodbye; you'll never see me again." His mother started wailing.

Two days later, Sister Marian came home. When she learns of her father's predicament, she was livid. She knew only too well her brother's brutal nature. This family is in mourning and will be for some time, but old man Wells won't go to the police. He promised he won't, he'll keep that promise. Killings were never out of the news; dead bodies turning up all over the country, and Harry was linked to many, reports *The Gleaner*. One Saturday evening in broad daylight, a man was murdered, shot down on the street while people looked on. The gunman casually walked away, and no one saw anything. That was the way things were and things to come.

Palma, the capital of the island, had recently seen some brutal murder, but things were to get worse. The constabulary had a bad reputation; most of whom wore the uniform were corrupt, including some in government. No one could be trusted. It was believed some were tied in with the gangs and took bribes. It's also evident that the police were no match for the gunmen. As a result, the people were left helpless, so they gravitated towards the gangs. It was said, whenever there's a murder, the police were involved, and any form of investigation was only a sham.

It was becoming clearer that the man behind some of these brutal killings was Harry Wells and his gang. After months of assumed investigations with no result, *The Gleaner* began running articles about the constabulary; they were told to hand off Harry Wells. Was this propaganda? The adage, no smoke without fire came to mind. Well, like other gunmen, Harry wasn't in hiding, he was always about town. One wouldn't think he was a murderer. But if the order was issued, from whom was it given? If the piece *The Gleaner* ran was to believed, the word came from high up in the government. In this city, everyone reads *The Gleaner*, and those who couldn't, would ask someone to read it to them, and they'll tell you this government is corrupt. Apart from *The Gleaner's* reports, very few people were saying anything, and for a good reason. If they protested or talked too much about government's corruption, their lives could be in danger, and not only from the gangs, but from government men too. One mustn't rain on those crooked politicians' parade.

Sometime later, there would be an even bigger surprise; it seemed Harry had landed on his feet. He was seen keeping company with the Nelsons, one of the most affluent and notorious families in the country, and a big landowner. They're supposed to have links with the cocaine cartel, and the police knew that, but some tied in with the cartel. So, what was Harry's role in this family? He's the frontman for the largest gang in the marijuana business; joining forces with a drug baron would make him quite dangerous. He walked about in town like any other citizen; one wouldn't believe this man was at the centre of some of the most horrific killings. Some think he was making a point, let everyone know he runs things around there. He was like a movie star, revered. He was often seen rubbing shoulders with prominent members of government and other VIPs. The man's a law unto himself. On this particular day, there were some disturbances down town, a man was killed, shot through the chest, and a woman was injured. There was nothing new or unusual about that, an almost daily occurrence, except this was someone of repute. The crowd grew bigger and was getting out of control, some wanted answer. The police tried to control the crowd but was of no use, and of course their actions could be just a caper. So, in walked Harry and took control; he quieted the mob down. Of course, his gunmen were always close by.

On that island paradise, lived a few affluent people, they're not too bothered about the rules of law; the law couldn't touch them. They're behind some of the killings; but it never could be proven, the law men saw to that. Of course, when a crime was committed, it was never by their own hands, but by their gunmen. No one ever charged, the police would tell you it's lack of evidence, but that's 'poppy-cock'; the cocaine barons had them in their pockets.

Will the authority position change regarding these cocaine barons? It's hard to see how. Those who wanted to do something about it were known to end up in wells. It's a matter of 'don't interfere and you'll live'.

Harry's friendship with the Nelson was now public knowledge. Whether it was a consensual friendship or one that the Nelsons were forced into, no one knew. He was now driving an American car, a Buick; it belonged to the Nelsons. It was always washed and polished. He would drive right in through the big gate as though he owned the place. He wasn't brandishing a gun anymore, but for sure he carried a pistol on his person.

This strange friendship, Harry and the Nelsons, a friendship some thought must end in tears, or death. They had nothing in common. They were out of his league, so how this killer managed to charm his way into these rich people's confidence? Some think there could only be one explanation; Harry made them an offer they couldn't refused. Well, as the wind shifted, so did their friendship. Harry was now a regular companion of Janet, it appeared he had taken over. This had now become a talking point in the capital, Janet behaving as though she's got a new man in her life. She was no longer seen out with Vincent –her husband. In fact, he hadn't been seen for some time. There were whispers that Harry might have done him in. Later those assumptions were soon realised. One a morning in June, the alarm was raised. Vincent was found dead in a swimming pool, shot through the head, but not his pool, his neighbour's. This was big news, one of the richest men in the country murdered, someone must be held accountable.

It wasn't long before the police arrested someone, but that someone was innocent; he was being used as a scapegoat. If they suspected Harry, and they probably did, they didn't arrest him; they apprehended this poor innocent man. Snoopy – as he was called – was a well-known house breaker, but murder wasn't his style, and in all his years of larceny, he had never burgled the rich people. Those premises were beyond his capability, and there was no record of him ever murdering anyone. This poor petty criminal was innocent, but could be hanged for the authority to save face. *This is an outrage,* reported *The Gleaner*. *Why should an innocent man be charged for something he didn't do, while the culprit or culprits were still at large?*

Along with *The Gleaner*, few protested; but the protest grew more and more with people speaking out. The action was gathering momentum, and fast; soon there were many. People turned up at members-of-parliament's offices to voice their displeasure. The pressure was mounting and couldn't be ignored. Nearly two weeks after he was arrested, Snoopy was released. The police were made to look ashamed. Now they must go and find the real murderer or murderers. However, that was unlikely; Harry and his hoodlums got nothing to fear, if the police wanted him, they knew where to find him. As for Janet, she took it all in her stride; and it could be she contributed to her husband's demise; now she's got a new man in her life.

Chapter 2
Harry Wells

The question everyone was asking was: why was Vincent Nelson murdered? He was supposed to be deep in the cocaine business, and had Harry got anything to do with it? It wouldn't seem likely. These people were the rich elite, if one was to be murdered by a marijuana gang member, there could be a gang war. So, why was he murdered? And did Janet have anything to do with it. Some seemed to think so. She's believed to be the brain behind the cartel, so, did she kill her husband to shack up with Harry? After months of investigations and no one being charged, the authorities were under pressure to find the killers. Will they arrest another innocent man to save face? They couldn't be that naïve. For them to be caught with their pants down once is scandalous enough, but twice would be disgraceful. They had some hard thinking to do, but they seemed to be short on ideas.

Realising they haven't got the means to solve this or any of the country's problems, they were decided to ask for help, but who would they ask, and what would they ask for? Well, the British, and they would ask for help to man the constabulary. The island is independent, but they're still a member of the brotherhood of nations, the Commonwealth, and Britain is still recognised as head of that body; there's was no one better to ask. This requirement however, was never going to be welcomed by the islanders; they believed their internal affairs should be managed by one of their own. But they were naïve, gluttons for punishment. The people who controlled their internal affairs were the same people wrecking the country. However, with all the protests, the government had to do what was best for the country, and fast. As expected, the British Government was quite to comply. Negotiation didn't take long; terms and conditions were agreed; they're sending a man to Jamaica, and he'll be the commissioner of police.

It was on a sunny day in July. Mr Noel Wade arrived in the country. He had visited the island twice before; it was said he was fascinated by it. His arrival was low-key; few saw him arrive, and those who did, booed. After meeting with Home Secretary Mark Burns, he took up his post, replacing Commissioner Don Michael who was found in a well some months later with his throat cut. A day later, he had a brief encounter with Prime Minister Young, sometime later, they'll have a more formal meeting. Back in England, Mr Wade had a reputation to be a hard man. Here, he'll have to be. He'll be coming up against killers and some of the island's most hardened criminals. He'll also be dealing with some of the most corrupt people ever to be part of a government. Among his assignments will be to try to won over the hostile public. They're no friend of the constabulary, and they certainly won't be friendly towards him. However, he was not going to be deterred; a man of strong will, was Mr Wade. "I came here to do this job, and whatever obstacles are thrown in my path, I'm going to get it done." His words. He'll learn later that his boss, Home Secretary Mark Burns, and his deputy, one Mr Miller, were tied in with the gangs. He was told about Harry Wells; he was the big man around town, his reputation preceded him, and most of the locals gravitated to him. Of course, some of the adoration was out of fear, speak ill of Harry and you might get a visit from a gunman. Then what about his affluent sweetheart, Janet Nelson? Where did she fit in with the gang? Well, with her lover being Harry Wells, and her link with the cartel, she could do what the hell she likes.

However, since the arrival of Mr Wade, their walkabouts in town stopped, but the lawlessness increased. Dead bodies being found all over the island, it seemed the gang was stepping up their activities. Some said it was to show the new commissioner his arrival wasn't going to make one iota of difference. Were they right? Not while this commissioner was in charge; their free for all ravaging and killing will have to stop. For a few months, things appeared to be changing – not a lot, but changing nevertheless. After a meeting with prime minister Young and Home Secretary Burns, they made a declaration to root out the bad weeds from the constabulary; the commissioner should make it priority. But it wouldn't be easy; these rats wouldn't grass on each other; but he hoped there were a few that were loyal. This criminal factor ran right through the establishment; some, if identified, would certainly be killed. That is the general pattern, when these crooked people are of no further use to the gangs, they eliminate them. It's been said Britain has the most efficient police force in the world; could the English man buck the trend and rid the island of these killers? Time will tell.

His campaign to win over the public wasn't going too well, but there's no let-up in his effort. He knew if they took him in their confidence, he would be greatly benefited. It's a tough call, some of these people had suffered at the hands of the law enforcers, so they had no wish to co-operate with them. From the offset, there were to be stumbling blocks, cover up and deceptions. Their stories were mostly false – rely on what they said at your peril. Civil servants receiving backhanders to shield whoever they're in with, and supplying information. It was Saturday afternoon, and after a discussion with Miss Scott (the secretary he inherited), the commissioner decided to pay Janet Nelson a visit. The case of her murdered husband was closed, but he would like to see for himself. Janet Nelson, a beautiful white woman of about thirty-seven, soon after she got married, her father returned to England, leaving her the estate. Her husband, a white Dominican, was a mystery. How, he got to the island and ended up marrying a rich man's daughter, no one knows or cares to. His visit to the estate turned up nothing, except he discovered Janet's callous and couldn't-care-less attitude. She and her kind thought nothing of the law, and they considered themselves untouchable. A week later, two police officers were found dead close by. When the news broke, some officers got the jitters, these were those who had ties in with the gangs.

The commissioner hadn't done much since his arrival, but to some officer, his presence was causing concern; they could be thinking he was on to them. Harry was believed to be behind this killing, so why wasn't he arrested? Well, Harry wasn't around anymore; he hadn't been seen for some time. The question that was on everyone's lips was, will this import from England fare any better than his predecessors? Maybe, he's better equipped and probably more honest. But Harry and his killers had a firm grip on politicians and business people alike, and with the locals, some of whom adored and admired him, he could do as he wish. But not anymore; with the arrival of Mr Wade, it appeared he'd gone in hiding. When Home Secretary Mark Burns paid an unexpected visit to PHQ, he assured Commissioner Wade of his full support. The commissioner would be relying on it; his support and co-operation was imperative if they're to clean up the country.

However, there were whispers regarding the minister. He had links with the gangs, and from what the commissioner learned, there could be some truth to it. A few weeks later, he discovered his hunch was right. The minister was tied in with the gangs; however, any case against him would be difficult to prove. In a conversation with a friend, he commented.

"I'm asked to come here to do this job, but it's difficult to work under a crooked home secretary."

"Why don't you expose him?" asked the friend.

"How can I? I've got no proof."

It was a moonlight Saturday night, and the city was buzzing; people looking for entertainment. Because of the action of the commissioner, the gunmen seemed to be keeping a low profile. Before his arrival, at night, it wasn't unusual for gunshots to be heard all over town. Men shooting their guns in the air, having fun. At times, people got hurt. However, that lawlessness ceased, but in that city, one should always be on their guard. The unexpected was likely to happen, and that night it did.

At about midnight, volleys of gunshots rang out somewhere near the Odeon cinema. Arriving on the scene, the police found two men dead, and no one seemed bothered. The gunmen, well, they do what they always did, secretly disappear. One of the dead men was a police officer, again.

Their investigation turned up nothing. No one was going to point the finger. The following day, the commissioner was in for a surprise. About midday, a man called at the office. He told Miss Scott he would like to speak with the commissioner, but wouldn't give his name, and wouldn't say what about. She buzzes the commissioner.

"There's a gentleman here to see you, commissioner."

"Who is he, Miss Scott?"

"I don't know, sir, he won't give his name."

The commissioner didn't tarry; he came out to meet the man.

"You would like to speak with me?" he asked curiously.

The man was standing with his hands in his pockets, looking decidedly uncomfortable.

"Yes, commissioner, I have some information I think you would like to hear."

"May I ask, whom am I speaking to, sir?"

"You don't need to know my name, commissioner, and I won't talk standing out here."

The commissioner could afford to address him as sir; he was an elderly looking man and dressed appropriately. The commissioner took him inside and offered him a seat, but like someone in a hurry, he preferred to stand.

"Now listen, commissioner, about the killings last night…" And from there he related. He said what he come to say, and left in a hurry without the commissioner knowing his name. He'd realise later that the man was a loyal citizen, but wanted to be unanimous. Armed with this information, he would like to go after these killers ASAP. This however would not be a house-to-house search, more a manhunt.

Usually when they committed their crime, they head for the hills; the police never followed, but not this time.

It was early morning when he went to discuss the matter with the home secretary. He didn't want a long discussion, just for him to agree to the use of soldiers for the mission. Since he didn't know the officers well, and there're 'snitch among them', he'd rather not use them. He thought the soldiers were more trustworthy. This was the second time they did business, and the greetings were low key. But the commissioner would soon learn first-hand that he was dealing with a bent home secretary. When he mentioned the use of soldiers, the minister was against it; it's as though they were off limit.

"Are you sure you're not being sent on a wild goose chase, commissioner? It could be a waste of your time and the government's money."

The commissioner was aghast; he couldn't believe such a statement would be coming from the minister.

"Why not the police officers? The soldiers are for the army, and not for chasing criminals."

"Mr Burns, there's a good reason for me wanting soldiers, and I didn't expect you to question my reasoning."

"What may that be, commissioner, if you don't mind me asking?"

"I need men I think I can trust. Men who can shoot straight; I believe the soldiers are more equipped for this kind of mission."

After a lengthy argument, and the commissioner insistent, he conceded.

"Commissioner, I must tell you, it is with reluctance that I'm agreeing to your request, but remember this, we're not at war."

"These men you're going after, they're armed, and you're armed. You're not going after them to bring them back alive; all we can expect are dead bodies, the very thing we should be trying to avoid."

The commissioner could see through this man; he's full of deception, he's not talking for the government, or the country, he's talking for himself.

"Minister, we're going up against merciless killers. I was told some carry MK-47 rifles. Now, sir, would you like me to approach them and ask them nicely to hand over weapons?"

"Mr Wade, I'll pretend I didn't hear that, and I hope you didn't come here to be sarcastic."

"I was merely stating my opinion regarding merciless killers. The only way to deal with killers, is to meet them head on."

At this point, the commissioner couldn't give two red cents for his opinion; he could see where his loyalty lied.

"Tell me, minister, what you think they're going to do when they see us? Bid us welcome? Not at all, they're going to shoot at us. So, I'll tell you now, we're not going to arrest anyone; the men we're bring back, if any, will be dead or wounded."

"That is what I'm afraid of. It appears as though your intention is to start a war; I must ask you not to."

The commissioner had heard enough; he got to his feet but couldn't help showing his dissatisfaction.

"Mr Burns, in future discussions, I do hope we will be able to agree with less difficulties. These gangs are running rampant; you know that better than I, and to deal with them, your full co-operation will be needed, but if we can't have a consensus, then I'll take my case to the prime minister."

"There's no need for threat, Mr Wade. I said I would co-operate, but I won't go along if I thinks there're flaws in your plans."

"Minister, I didn't come to you with a plan. All I asked for is the use of soldier, and for a matter of this importance, I shouldn't have to haggle. I must be clear, I'm here to combats criminals, not to protect your reputation."

"I didn't expect you to do, Mr Wade; there's no need."

He soon realised the commissioner is no pushover, and his link with the gang could be in danger of exposure.

"Commissioner, I promise you my co-operation, but only when I think it is right to do so. We understand each other, Mr Wade?" he asked as though the commissioner should be aware of his intention.

"Certainly, Mr Burns. I will say good day, sir."

The two men were a collision course; and he would try to make things difficult for the commissioner. However, the commissioner's threat would be ringing in his ears; a threat he doesn't like.

Chapter 3
The Man Hunts

By now the commissioner had forged a working relationship with one Lieutenant Dickenson, in whom he's got much confidence. They discussed the situation. The commissioner was ignorant of the geography of the terrain, but the lieutenant wasn't; he'd be relying on his knowledge. He was also depending on the element of surprise, so they decided it was a better option to go at night. Firstly, he must brief the men chosen, aware that among them there could be traitors. The briefing would be less than an hour before departure; that way, no one leaves the premises. At 8 pm, they gathered in the big hall, five soldiers and five police officers. Along with the lieutenant, while briefing them, he was observant, noticing if anyone showed signs of dissent.

"Men, does any one of you know the killer Harry Wells?" There was some show of hands. Of course, they all knew of him, but probably never met him.

"Keep a lookout for him; he's our main target, do we all agree?"

"Yes, sir," they shouted.

The day before this operation, it was reported that three bodies were discovered in a well, in the parish of Mount-

View. The commissioner couldn't do anything about that. He had a job at hand to undertake. It was 9 pm when they set off, according to the information they got a specific location in mind. The terrain was not too difficult, if one knows where to go, and the lieutenant did. They had done their homework, but with the home secretary's words ringing in his ears, they would tread cautiously.

They were in the terrain but moving cautiously, awarded that at any time they could run into the gang. It was mid night when a light was spotted. It was the gang; they could be asleep, and there's no sentry. Apart from the toad croaking, it was awfully quiet; they were oblivious to the law men presence. The commissioner quietly positioned his men in advantageous positions. It's about 1:30 PM when he got on the loud hailer.

"You in there, lay down your weapons and come on out, and no one will get hurt."

Of course, he didn't expect them to do as he asked; no one tells killers like these what to do. In an instant, there was a burst of gunfire. They woke up, and realising it's the law, opened fire. Among the trees, it was pitch dark, but the law men with torches attached to their rifles, could see clearly. The commissioner gave the order to fire. They opened up from all sides; bullets could be heard ricocheting off trees. They tried to fight back but were caught cold. When the shooting ceased, gunmen who weren't killed took to their heels; they disappeared into the woods, leaving trails of blood. It was a good night for the lawmen. Five gunmen lay dead, and no telling how many wounded. Harry wasn't among the dead.

"Lieutenant, I didn't think he would. Man like him don't make their bed among the trees."

"I didn't think so either, and probably has nothing to do with this lot."

By noon, *The Gleaner* got hold of the story. It was one hell of a front page. The bodies of five dead men were depicted. On street corners, on the park benches, people were reading the paper. The main interest was Harry Wells. They were expecting to be reading about him. They suspected that after that night, some officers will be having sleepless nights. It's obvious the gang got no knowledge in regarding to the raid.

Home Secretary Burns requested an urgent meeting; he's not happy about something. The commissioner anticipated fireworks. 1 pm on Saturday, the meeting convened; Home Secretary Burns was as nervous as a man about to face the firing squad. He became irritable, accusing the commissioner of not finishing the job. It was obvious he didn't want loose ends. The commissioner reminded him of his words.

"Are you forgetting what you so rightly warned me of, minister"?

"We're not at war; and we shouldn't avoid starting one, wise words. Are you going back on it?"

"Mr Wade, when you set out to do a job, it should be done thoroughly."

The man was like a chameleon. He changed his stance to whatever suited his purpose. He didn't like to hear some got away. He wanted them all dead – dead men tell no tales.

The commissioner however wasn't going to play his game; he made his bed, he must lie in it. He's not a man to stand on ceremony, so, he put him straight.

"Mr Burns, if you played with fire, you're going to get burn. If you're anticipating reprisal because of the raid, then, sir, you'll have to deal with it."

Deputy Home Secretary Don Miller smiled. He seemed to find the commissioner's comment amusing. A shifty-looking character if ever there was one, why was he at the meeting? Probably to keep an eye on his boss.

"Mr Burns, I want you to know this, if doing this job causes unpleasantness in some quarters, then so be it, but it's going to get done."

He probably thought that the commissioner was on to him, and with nothing further to offer, he was almost at a plea.

"Mr Wade, all that I'm saying is, whenever you do a job, don't leave it half done; the country is counting on you."

A deceptive statement if ever there was one, he's trying to back track trying to hide his deception.

"Mr Burns, I'm not going to thank you for reminding me of my duty; I'm fully aware of it, and there's no skeleton in my cupboard."

"Neither in mine, commissioner, but if you're trying to tell me something, please, let's hear it."

"No, there's nothing to tell. Each must wrestle with their conscience, I'll say. Good evening." The meeting drew to a close.

The commissioner walked away thinking of the two men he encountered, two dishonest characters he had the misfortune to be dealing with. Throughout the meeting, the deputy sat observing, but said nothing. It could be that he and the home secretary shared the same secret.

After months of operation, things were looking up, and the commissioner was becoming popular among some sections of the public. He was working hard, using his public relation skill to gain their trust, and his action was beginning to bear fruits.

The gangs however, were not going to give up their operation in the capital; their most important customers were there. The districts meant nothing to them. Those were places they used for hiding out. However, there's no letting up in the law men action. They kept the pressure on, and gangs were rattled.

Success came, but slowly. Most of the shootings were now outside of town. Some took their operations to the small cities and districts, an act of desperation. For some time now, there was no sighting of Harry or Janet. Were they alive or dead? The lawmen were somewhat baffled. The locals were asking questions, too. They would like to know if the man they revered was alive. When *The Gleaner* ran a piece on him, it was just speculations. They reported he's alive, but had left the country. Some in the constabulary were thinking that way too; but not the commissioner.

They decided to step up their effort to go gunning for the men in the marijuana business. The sooner they rid the country of them, the sooner they can turn their attention to other matters. The cocaine cartel was off their radar; to take them on would be a folly. It was debated in Parliament; the government should ask Britain for help to deal with them, but they decided against it.

Some two months later, there was news of Harry. He was seen in Herring Hill, the place of his birth; rumours or not, it was big news. The paper ran a piece on him. The headline: Harry Is Alive.

The police didn't attempt to go after him; they knew it would be pointless. *The Gleaner* reported the story, so why bother? Instead, the commissioner and the lieutenant paid old man Wells a visit. He didn't appreciate it, and why should he? He wanted nothing to do with his son. His mother was suffering, and all because of him. The lawmen sympathised, but they've got a job to do, and even though these two old timers are feeble, the question about their son had to be asked. It was done as gently and humanely as possible, but they couldn't shine any light on the matter; Harry was never there. The story *The Gleaner* ran was just rumours.

Chapter 4
The Letter

On Sunday when most people were going to worship, suddenly, there was a burst of gunshots; it was coming from the direction of the rich people's quarters. In no great hurry, the police made their way to Janet Nelson's home. A body was found in her pool, lying face down at the shallow end. At first glance, they thought it was Janet, but it wasn't. The deceased wasn't from around there, and no identification was on her person. So, where did she come from? And why did she end up in the Nelson's swimming pool? The commissioner had his own take on the mystery.

"Lieutenant, I heard Vincent's body was found in his neighbour's swimming pool. Do you think they repaid the compliment?"

"That is more than likely, but we're not going to find the evidence to substantiate that theory."

"Quite so, Lieutenant, and as far as things go, we're like little fish in a big pond. We can't touch them; we can't even question them. They treated us as though we were the culprits."

They're not going to waste too much time in the way of investigation; this could only be the work of the cartel.

Janet wasn't at home. Like her lover, Harry Wells, she hadn't been seen for some time, and the general feeling was, she knew nothing about the woman found dead in her pool. The lieutenant had a thought.

"Commissioner, I believe wherever you find Harry, you'll find Janet."

"Why in heaven's name would she abandon her estate to be hiding out with him?"

"Love, commissioner? You remember that word? What people do unusual things for?"

"If that be the case, do you think she'll ever return to her estate?"

"I'm sure she will. Whenever he gets tired of her, he'll send her packing. That said, I think we should keep a close watch on the estate."

At this time, there were copycat killings but mostly out in the districts, and because lack of police presence the police things are getting out of control. The good work done earlier was starting to unravel. It was almost as though a new insurgence of murders appeared on the scene. All this time, they were anxious to know if Harry was alive; they couldn't be sure if he and his gang weren't behind these killings. Of course, there was always speculation about his whereabouts, but that was all it was, glorified speculations.

Monday afternoon, a letter was brought to the commissioner; delivered by Deputy Home Secretary Don Miller. According to him, the letter was for the home secretary, but it wasn't address in his name. The content of this letter was dynamite; it would be a sensation if *The Gleaner* got a hold of it.

But there's a reason for bringing this missive to the commissioner's attention; the Deputy would like the senior position. He knew of his boss's double dealings; he's probably a party to it, but now, he wanted to expose him, so he delivered the evidence.

The commissioner was told what was in the letter, now he must read for himself.

"Kram, this is the only letter you will be getting; we're watching you and your family. Be careful of what you say to the English man. We'll contact you soon in regarding to the transfer of funds."

The commissioner studied the letter. He believed this could be the consequence of the raid that killed five gunmen a week ago. The letter wasn't signed, it was just addressed to Kram, but it didn't take the commissioner long to crack the code. Kram is an anagram the home secretary used to hide his identity. He knew nothing of the missive; if he did, he would destroy it. Now that the commissioner was in receipt of it, he must bring it to the prime minister's attention. It's being whispered that his daughter was kidnapped by gang, some months ago, but he kept quiet about it, probably held the belief she was abducted by Harry Wells. An intriguing situation; but could it be that this young woman had gone off with a member of the gang of her own free will? The commissioner thought so.

They discussed the situation, and the Deputy told what he knew, but mostly to incriminate his boss.

"Mr Miller, once I approached the prime minister with this letter, your boss is finished; I'm sure you are aware of that."

"I don't really want him to lose his job, commissioner, but I'm his deputy. This letter causes me to look bad, too."

The commissioner looked at the letter, raised his head, and looked at him with disdain. He asked, "Mr Miller, you said the home secretary has dealings with the gangs. Are you quite sure? After all, as deputy, you know what he knows."

"No, sir, not at all, there're things he kept me in the dark about."

"So, tell me about the cartel. Do you think he has dealing with them?"

"I can't say for sure, even though I suspect that could be the case."

"You're quite sure of that, Mr Miller?"

"No, sir, how could I? What I said it's just suspicion. However, whatever my thought, isn't the letter proof enough, commissioner?" He didn't respond. He could see right through this fellow; his deceptive and devious attitude was plain to see; the man was more bent than a boomerang.

"Mr Miller, don't try to insult my intelligence; you are here to expose your boss, so you present the evidence, why? You would like to be in his chair, isn't that so, Mr Miller?"

"No, sir, that's not so at all," he said, looking frightfully alarmed.

"As Deputy, it's my civic duty to report anything unseemly, even if it's about my boss, don't you think so, commissioner?"

Not wanting to prolong this conversation, he didn't response. The man was insincere and full of deception; and he had enough of him.

"Mr Miller, I won't throw you out of my office; that's not my style. But I must ask you to leave. Go back under the stone from where you came."

Thinking he has been caught, his attitude changed. He probably regretted delivering the letter.

"Commissioner, you have no cause talking to me that way. I was only doing what I think is right."

Suspecting that his plan was no longer looking too wholesome, he decided to leave, then turned and asked, "Are you going to need me along to see the prime minister, commissioner?"

"Unfortunately, yes, Mr Miller. You presented me with the evidence. I want you there to explain it."

The following day in a phone call to the commissioner, he asked for his name to be kept be secret of any enquires. He was told he's the prime witness, his name could never be kept out of it. But such was the action of a traitor; he stabbed his boss in the back, but didn't want him to know he was the knife man.

The commissioner detested crooked cops, and he held the same disdain for people like this fellow. There's such a thing as loyalty; he despised the home secretary, but he despised this fellow even more. One who 'grassed on his friend or his boss, is a dirty lowlife'.

Two days later, the commissioner had an audience with the PM, accompanied by Deputy Miller. Mr Hunt, the PM's close adviser and confidante, was sitting adjacent to him. When he arrived in this country, he had a fleeting moment with the PM; this will be their first real encounter. The two men had a friendly talk before they got down to business. When the content of the letter was revealed, the prime minister was flabbergasted, it appeared he had difficulty believing his old friend, the home secretary, would involve in such a misdeed. He read the letter again; his countenance taken on a different feature.

"Mr Wade, what do you think about this letter? Could it be a frame-up?"

"I was thinking along the same line, prime minister, but it's hard to say."

He turned his attention to the deputy; he was rather angry looking when he asked, "Mr Miller, are you sure this letter was for the home secretary?"

Deputy Miller seemed unsure of himself; he knew the commissioner suspected him of the foul play, he must choose his words carefully.

"Prime minister, as you can see, the letter didn't carry his name, but I was asked to give it to him. Other than that, I couldn't tell you."

"Then how did it come in your possession?" asked Adviser Hunt harshly, as he got up and went to another chair.

"Simple, it was handed to me by person unknown. I was asked to deliver it to the home secretary."

"So why did you open it? It wasn't addressed to you. It's dirty habit opening other people's letter."

Deputy Miller, a multi-colour man, quite handsome with curly black hair, was strop for an explanation. Being accused of opening people's letter, is a damming inditement.

"I was curious about the name on the envelope; after all, I'm the deputy commissioner. If anything appeared suspicious, it's my civic duty to investigate."

"Was this the first time you suspected the home secretary of underhand dealings?" the PM asked.

There wasn't an immediate response; he was sweating like a pig and it's not even a hot day.

"Yes, sir, but if he's into anything illegal, I believe he was forced."

"So, you believed he's into something, Mr Miller? Do tell us your thought," asked the Adviser.

"I didn't say that, Mr Hunt, I didn't even suspect him of anything."

Realising he's being suspected of foul play, he was backtracking, and trying to cover his track.

"But you did, Mr Miller. Back at the office, you said he's always in contact with the cartel, don't you remember?"

There was no answer; he seemed lost for words. He realised no one believed his story. Now the home secretary must face the music, and soon – only, he doesn't know it yet.

The letter, if proven to be true, will decide the home secretary's fate, which up till then he knew nothing of. The prime minister is still pondering over it. He knows it is true, but he doesn't want to believe it. They had been friends for many years; nevertheless, he must act, and fast. But as a long-serving minister and a colleague, he doesn't want to disgrace him by sacking him; too many questions would be asked. For the PM, it will be a hard decision, but he must decide, the home secretary must go. The meeting ended.

He must now consult with his colleagues regarding, and there's no time to waste. Deputy Miller, well, he was none the wiser in regarding to his position. The question should be asked though: of all the years working together, did the PM have any notion regarding his minister's dishonesty? Well, he should. *The Gleaner* regularly ran articles about corruption in his government, even though no one was named. Then again, who was to say the PM himself hasn't gotten his hand dirty? In this part of the world, it's hard to find anyone who is beyond reproach.

It was Wednesday noon, and the commissioner had a meeting with the home secretary. The two men talked law and order; the commissioner reported his findings on the last murder. But he knew something the home secretary didn't; this could be their last meeting.

The Meeting

It was raining heavily on Friday; Home Secretary Burns is meeting with the PM. When he left home, he thought this was one of their not-so-important meetings. Well, it wasn't the time for their routine meetings. However, when the boss calls, one doesn't ask why. He arrived at the parliament house, but the prime minister wasn't in, but right-hand man, Hunt, was. "Make yourselves comfortable, gentlemen, the PM is delayed," reported Miss Green. But this could be deliberate. A man who was a stickler for time keeping was never going to be late for a meeting of this importance. In conversation with Secretary Green, Adviser Hunt revealed, ever since the revelation of the letter, the PM had been in a foul mood.

The home secretary was uncomfortable; the long wait was making him nervous. But he got no reason to be; he didn't know what the meeting was about. Adviser Hunt occasionally gave him a fleeting glance, observing his behaviour. With his links with the gangs, he could be thinking he's found out. It was a warm day so it's normal to be sweating, but he began pacing the floor puffing away on his cigarette. All this time, the eagle eyes of Adviser Hunt were sneakily watching his action.

The prime minister arrived. He didn't appear friendly; he's a man with problem, and it showed. Normally he would apologise for being late, but not this time; he just sat himself down, looking very sad.

"Take a seat, home secretary," he said while taking document from his ledger. He wasted no time; he went straight to the agenda.

"Tell me about your dealings with these drug men, home secretary," he asked dolefully.

Well, the man may be the PM, but he's well short on diplomacy. The question was asked with his head hung, as though he didn't want to make eye contact with his old friend. The minister didn't respond. He looked startle; it's obvious he didn't expect to be asked such question. The PM raised his head, looking directly at him.

"Home secretary?" he enquired.

The minister now knew he was in deep trouble. His secret was out, but how? He reached for his briefcase and pulled out what looks like documents, and began to quote from it. But the prime minister had no interest in what he was quoting, he knew he was falsifying anything and everything, quoting things totally irrelevant to the question.

The prime minister was now in full thoughtfulness; he allows him to carry on his deception. In conversation with Commissioner Wade, the PM was advised, during the meeting he should refers to him as Kram, mainly to see his reaction. He geared himself up for this approach. He turned to Miss Green and whispered, could be just a ploy. "Now, tell me, Kram, do you…" He paused.

The home secretary, a man fair in colour, now turned red as a sun burnt mango. He suddenly got the jitters, and the ledger fell from his hand.

It was a warm day; it usually was in the tropics, but not warm enough for someone to be dripping sweat the way he was. If he wasn't sure before, he was now, he's been rumbled.

Whatever the PM's lines of questioning intended; everything had now changed, he asked him again, and this time he called him the way he usually did.

"Mark, I know you are tied in with these drugs gangs. Are you're going to tell me about it?" Then there were tears. This once proud man couldn't keep his emotion in check. In a trembling voice, he spoke.

"I do hope you believe me, prime minister. What I've done I was force to, they threatened my family and holding my daughter hostage, what else could I do? Willy, (as he usually calls him) you must believe me; I didn't have a choice."

But the prime minister was in no mood to forgive or to sympathise; whatever the threat, he shouldn't have gotten in bed with these people.

"Prime minister to you, sir, please address me as such." His voice was full of anger. "I expect so much of you, but because of greed, you let yourself down, the government and your country; I trust you can live with yourself."

There was no response; he sat with his hands clasped as though he was pleading for forgiveness. Adviser Hunt sat with a stern look, observing – the government was in trouble, and so was his boss. The meeting dragged on, but a decision was made; the home secretary must go. But to avoid a scandal, they would like him to resign. But the unscrupulous minister had no intention to. He was under the assumption that his old friend would reprieve him.

"Go back to your office, home secretary; I'll talk with you again soon." The meeting ended. Now, because of what the prime minister said, he might be thinking there was a chance of him keeping his job – that was wishful thinking.

During the meeting, Deputy Home Secretary Miller wasn't called to explain the letter, he was deliberately ignored. His fate had already been decided. He'll get a job in the administration, but not to replace his boss. It was a tactful move by the government; that way he might keep his mouth shut. This disgraceful situation must be prevented from getting out.

Chapter 5
The Decision

On Tuesday at two, a meeting was convened. The PM, his secretary and Adviser Hunt were in attendance when the home secretary walked in. They greeted each other like old times. The PM was angry but was trying not to show it. He was hoping his old friend would co-operate without much difficulty. He explained to him he had to resign, but it fell on deaf ears; there were his constant apologies. Even though he was angry, he spoke to him as a friend.

"Mark, how long have we known each other?" He raised his left hand. "No, don't tell me. Over fifteen years, and in all that time, we shared many things. But you must realise your position is un-attainable. You must do the decent thing and resign, for yourself and for the country. But tell me, was it money why you joined up with these people?"

The minister was ashamed; he couldn't look his old friend in the eyes and give an answer. The game was up; the reprieve he had hoped for wasn't going to happen, yet he was making excuses for his treacherous action; the man had no scruple. The PM tried once more to make him see the error of his ways, and even then, the crooked minister wanted to hold on to office.

An angry Adviser Hunt, realising the dilemma the PM was in, asked, "May I speak, prime minister?"

"Go ahead, Jeffery," he said, looking rather dejected.

Without hesitation, the Adviser was direct and to the point.

"Home secretary, you must realise that your position can't be maintained. You have to go, and to avoid much scandal, you must resign. That's the honourable thing to do. That way, it wouldn't look bad on you or the government."

He didn't respond, it's as though he was thinking, but Adviser Hunt's patience was running thin; he wasn't a friend of the man before, and now, he detested him.

"Minister, you know if word got out about your double dealings, it won't make good reading for the government. Is that what you want?" His tone was hostile.

He didn't response. He seemed lost, but Adviser Hunt was not about to waste more time.

"We're sorry to see you go, but you must resign, and you must do it now."

He decided to speak, but directly to his old friend. There was trembling in his voice.

"So, you want my resignation, Willy?" he asked nervously.

"Mark, don't you see I—"

"Where is your decency, man?" Adviser Hunt interrupted. "Were you expecting to hold on to your job after you'd been found out? You aligned yourself with criminals. Think of the scandal if words got out. Do the decent thing, man. Resign," he said with venom in his tone.

Ignoring the adviser, he was making one last plea for mercy.

"Willy, I love my job. You know that. What will I do now?" he asked with his hands clasped in a humbled manner.

"Mark, don't make a scene; do what's right," said the PM. Adviser Hunt, who didn't want to prolong this any further, walked over to the prime minister and gathered sheets of documents already prepared for his signatures. He walked back to the minister.

"Sign here, Mr Burns," he said, handing him a pen. He took time to read it – a long time.

"I have to resign from the government because of ill health, etcetera, etcetera, etcetera." He was reading aloud.

There was a long paused, but eventually he signed. The PM looked on; there was no doubt he had remorse seeing his old friend leave the government. But it was done. Adviser Hunt collected the document and presented them to Miss Benson.

"We'll put out a statement regarding your resignation," said the PM. "You will back it up when *The Gleaner* comes asking question, and they will. I'm counting on you, Mark, to do the right thing."

"You know I will, prime minister. I won't let anything come before my country."

Adviser Hunt looked up to the heavens – in this case, the ceiling – as to say, *it's a pity you didn't think of your country before you got in bed with the crooks.*

"Thank you, old friend," said the PM, with tongue in cheek; he seemed a relieved man. The meeting ended.

Will they ever see each other again? It's more than likely. It was a small country; bumping into each other at times was un-avoidable. There will be a new man at the home office, but it won't be Deputy Commissioner Miller, he'll remains as

Deputy; but not for long, they're not going to forgive him for his part in his deception.

It was only a fortnight since the minister was removed from office, and it seemed he was out of favour with the gangs. There were rumours he was preparing to leave the country, but where would he go that they couldn't find him. There's an adage, 'you can run but you can't hide'. If the rumour was true, he was running away, leaving his daughter; she's supposedly adapted. It appears he was running away to save his own skin; his daughter can take care of herself. It had been months since the assumed abduction and no one made demand. If she was alive, and she probably was, this young woman wasn't kidnapped at all, and the disgraced minister knew it; so he's not too bothered about her.

The Assassination

Wednesday was a public holiday, one of the many holidays the country inherited from the British. To some, they are of no significance, but it doesn't matter, everyone will be out having a good time. It's a beautiful day, and people are gearing up to go off to one of the many fun fairs of their choice. Today, however, will be a day to remember; there'll be an outrage.

At about 5 pm, there was a shooting in Bucks Hill, the area where ex-home secretary Burns lived. Anticipating it's got something to do with him, the police wasted no time getting there. Arriving on the scene, their fear was realised. Mr Burns and his wife were murdered, assassinated in their home. The gangs must've learned about his resignation. They probably wouldn't kill him for that, but when news got out about his plans to leave the country, he signed his own death warrant.

The question was how the gangs knew of his intention? The lieutenant had his own take on the matter; former deputy home secretary blew the whistle.

"Lieutenant, there's some truth in the old sayings; one reaps the seeds one sows. Mr Burns' dirty deeds had accounted for the loss of many lives, now he paid the price."

It was late that evening when the prime minister heard the news. He was distraught, blaming himself for his old friend's demise.

"If I didn't force him to resign, he'd probably still be alive," he said to his wife, Dotty.

"Don't be too hard on yourself, dear, you know he had to go, and if he hadn't resigned, you would have had to sack him."

She was doing what a good wife does, console her grieving husband, but telling him what was the truth. Yet it seemed this honest but naïve man just woke up to the hard facts; the drug people not only infiltrated his government, but the constabulary too.

"How far will they go, and will they ever stop?" he asked grievingly.

If he had doubts before, it should be crystal clear now.

He needs an urgent meeting with the commissioner. These gunmen had to be stopped, and quickly. Before the arrival of the commissioner, the word on the street were, the gunmen ran things, and even though there were changes, the words are still out there. So, what now for the commissioner and his team? The job lying ahead was a mountain to climb, but he's determined to prove his worth.

The meeting was set for Saturday at 2 pm, but it had to be cancelled; the commissioner got a tipoff about Harry Wells; he has been held up in Lincoln Ville', a small town not too far from the capital. He decided to follow it up, but he must inform the PM, so he spoke with him on the phone and asked for a postponement. The PM promptly agreed; the meeting was put on hold. He met with the lieutenant; it called for urgent action; there was no time to send out a scout. At about 5 pm, a team of six soldiers and four officers were called together.

"Men, we're going to Lincoln Ville, the gang is there. But keep a look out for Harry Wells. If he's there, we would like to take him alive; but only if we can."

He was voicing the government's agenda; they would like to make an example of him, hang him openly, to show 'this is what we do with criminals'. The 75 miles didn't take long. They were in the area by 7 pm. The men wore plain clothes; they wanted to be inconspicuous as possible. They circled the area. When the shooting starts, they must avoid killing civilians – this or any mission; kill civilian and it won't be the criminals who get the blame.

It was about 8 pm when the first shot was fired, and a running battle began. It raged for nearly two hours. When the shooting ceased, 6 gunmen lay dead, but they were the drones. Harry wasn't among them. There were no casualties among the law men. The information said he would be there, so why wasn't he spotted? Probably he wasn't. The commissioner began to have misgivings, he didn't like what was happening. There was something very odd about this fellow. He was never where he's supposed to be. *The Gleaner* treats the story favourably on behalf of the lawmen.

Two days later, the commissioner met with the prime minister; he should be pleased but he wasn't.

To say he was dissatisfied would be an understatement. Holding an edition of *The Gleaner*, probably expecting to see a headline about Harry Wells being captured or dead.

"Commissioner, I don't want you to tell me you're doing your best. I know you are, but probably you should look for another approach. Every time you went after Harry, you came up empty. This fellow is causing the country to look bad. Tell me, commissioner, is he that smart?"

Mr Wade's a man who doesn't stand on ceremony, but he's also a man of compassion, he knows the PM is desperate, he would like a quick fix; but neither he nor his ministers have anything to contribute. He was about to light a cigarette but thinks better of it; he puts it back into the pack.

"Prime minister, I share your anxiety and concern, but I must tell you, when I took on this job, I never thought I would come up against so many obstacles. But we're going to get this job done; it will take time, but we'll get it done. However, what we need is manpower; we're thin on the ground. We have to be using soldiers, and they're for the army, I was told by home secretary, Burns."

"Your determination is good to hear, commissioner, but if you mean more men with guns, you should continue with the soldiers."

"I was thinking of my own men, prime minister. New recruits I can train to be good officers."

"Commissioner, I fully understand, but unfortunately this Government can't afford any such undertakings; we haven't got the funds. So, I'm sorry, you'll have to make do with what you got, but rest assured, as soon as it's possible, we'll look into recruitment."

That wasn't what the commissioner wanted to hear, but it seemed the government was not looking far ahead.

"About Harry Wells, commissioner, he must be out there some place. I hope he's your priority."

The commissioner reached again in his pocket, but came up empty. He thought on the PM's statement; it was a bit naive. To make awkward statement served no useful purpose.

"Well, sir, we followed up on every lead, but we never saw the fellow. Apart from captions in *The Gleaner*, I'm beginning to wonder if he exists at all."

"I don't think I like that kind of talk, commissioner. I would rather hear something more positive, like, you'll catch that son of a bitch soon, and bring him in, dead or alive."

There were a few raised eyebrows; they'd never heard the PM speak in such a woeful manner.

"Prime minister, I was only making what is a practical point."

"Yes, but you need to get a move on. Tongues are wagging, and I'm aware of what they're saying, and I don't like it. We cannot allow one man, be it may he's got gang or gangs behind him, to hold the country to ransom."

The man is desperate, and right now, he could do with a bit of a miraculous intervention.

"Prime minister, I'm a man who doesn't believe in maybes and perhaps, but I must tell you, I believe the people are not only shielding this man, but also informing him of our plans. Some in the constabulary, and even in the government."

He sat up straight. He didn't respond immediately. He took from his pocket a tube of Vicks, but he didn't seem to have a blocked nose.

"Are you sure of that, commissioner?" he asked as though he had doubts. But why should he? His ex-home secretary, deceased, was found guilty of deceit.

"Well, sir, as of now, it's only conjecture, but whenever and wherever we turned up, he's never there; the man is like the scarlet pimpernel."

Adviser Hunt smiled. The commissioner's comment amused him. He asked, "Is he in hell or is he in heaven?"

"Yes, Mr Hunt, I do wonder where the hell is he."

The PM however wasn't amused. He gave the Adviser a stern look, as to say, *remember where you're, Jeffery.*

"He was where he's supposed to be. That could only mean one thing, he's being told our business. Whenever we asked about him, it's as though his name was tabooed; no one wants to talk."

"I can see your dilemma, commissioner, but I hope you're not depending solely on the public to help you catch this killer."

"No, sir, but their help would be useful. Aren't they aware of the evil of this man? They treat him like some kind of a Robin Hood, except he's giving them nothing."

The time expired. They had much more to discuss, but they'll meet another time soon, and that meeting will include the new home secretary, who up till then hadn't been named.

Times were hard, and people had to fend for themselves, but they're proud and resourceful. Some worked their own little cultivation; their produce went to market. Others turned their hands to whatever can make them a living. But it seemed they were crying out for a hero; someone for them to gravitate to, hence Harry Wells. Not the kind of person one should be looking up to, but then again, he gave them something to talk about. There was a famous quote from one of his brutal murders. Just before he shot the policeman in the head, he quoted the words that were to become folklore. "Tell the devil not to wait up." The story was told by the dead man's partner; he probably was an informer. People believed stories like that; and loved to tell it. They believed he's got supernatural powers; there're rumours he slept in graveyards and talked to the dead.

"How else could he manage to elude the police so many times?" one woman asked.

"He could be standing here among us at this moment," said another. Of course, they're the converted; to them these stories were no myth.

Chapter 6
The funeral

It was a sunny July morning. Old man Wells was to be buried; his wife had died a few years earlier, for obvious reasons. Harry didn't attend, but the police were of the belief he would. The locals also said he was there, rubbing shoulders with mourners. "He sprinkled dirt on his father's coffin," said one woman. Of course, no one knew how much merits any of these stories had, but they believed it. With devious intent, with six men, the commissioner decided to pay his respect. At the grave site, there were some unpleasant scenes. The police swooped on a fellow wearing what looks like a disguise, thinking it was Harry Wells. The ceremony was disrupted and the mourners were stir crazy. To them, a burial is a secret affair, and for the police to desecrate it, it's un-forgivable. Realising their blunder, the police quickly withdrew, but the commissioner didn't; the people needed apology and an explanation. So, he braved their wrath and tried to explain the situation. His intention wasn't welcomed, but he stood his ground. A man who appeared to be the leader approached him. "Who did you come to arrest, Mr Policeman?" he asked angrily.

The commissioner, a man of sensibility, showed respect for their tradition. He tried to explain. Talking aloud for all to hear, he turned to the man they thought was Harry.

"I must apologise to you, sir, and all you people. What happened shouldn't have, but someone pointed you out, thinking you was Harry Wells."

That comment stirred their anger; there were shouts of, 'who, who did that?'

Secretly, the commissioner gave himself a slap on the wrist. He had just told a great big whopper. However, it did the trick. After some tactical talking, they began to warm up to him. But they wanted to know who pointed out the man to be Harry.

"Harry was never here, Mr Policeman, but tell us the son of a bitch who told you he was," asked another.

"Ma'am, I can't do that; it wouldn't be right. But I promise you this, it will never happen again."

From there, he talked his way out of what was an embarrassing situation; the people, they were angry, but they'll calm down. They made a hasty getaway, leaving the people to mourn their dead. Another of their mission to capture Harry had gone up in smoke. In time, he'll have to explain the situation to his superiors.

The Following Day

It's the day after the fiasco; the Commissioner got up with the incident still fresh in his mine. Later, he's got a meeting with Prime Minister Young. It was 11 am when the meeting was convened. Along with the prime minister were Adviser Hunt and one other person, presumably he was the new home secretary.

"Come in, commissioner, and take a seat," said the prime minister, sounding quite cheerful. He sat waiting in anticipation for an introduction; it was instant.

"Commissioner, shake hands with Mr Walker; he's the new man at the home office." They greeted each other, and then got down to business.

The prime minister was oblivious to the incident at old man Wells' funeral, but the new home secretary got wind of it and seemed eager to tell it. When the matter was raised, the prime minister was none too pleased.

"We should display the use of weapons only when it's necessary. We don't want the people to think we don't care about them," he commented. "At funerals, we should try and avoid any such action; to interrupt a burial in this manner is sacrilege. Commissioner, in whatever way this incident happened, see that it doesn't happen again."

Well, he had his moan; but not in a way to ridicule the commissioner. The commissioner explained the situation and how he dealt with it, and the people's reaction. The prime minister was satisfied.

Then there was a question from the home secretary. It seemed he's anxious to show his worth.

"Commissioner, was it necessary to brandish weapons at the grave site? This man, Wells, was one of the district's leading citizens. He should be shown respect."

The question was loaded with implications. The subject was dealt with, but it seemed the new man was not satisfied. He didn't like his line of questioning, and he certainly didn't like this fellow's tone. He didn't respond to him; instead, he directed a response to the prime minister.

"If I am to clean up this country and rid it of these gunmen, at times some of our actions won't be pleasant."

"Like the one at old man Wells' grave, commissioner?" asked the home secretary. This time he responded to him, and in a manner probably he didn't expect.

"Mr Home Secretary, if you want to look good in the eyes of the prime minister, you should choose your subject carefully." There was no further comment from the minister; probably thinking he had said too much.

But it appeared the prime minister was alert to the situation, and could be thinking the commissioner was right.

"Come along now, gentlemen, we're here to solve the problems facing us, not to make it greater. Commissioner, it's good to hear you talked to the people, and they accepted your explanation. Good work."

"Thank you, prime minister, but we should remember also, the people are the police's main source of information; they tell us, we act on it, genuine or otherwise."

"Point taken, commissioner; it can't be easy looking for a killer without knowing where to look."

The home secretary appeared to go back into his box; he said nothing further. The commissioner, well, he didn't add anything either, probably thinking of the coming relationship, working with his new boss.

Chapter 7
Harry Is on Quay Island

The commissioner appeared to have an ally he wasn't aware of, Adviser Jeffery Hunt. Apart from meetings, they never met, but that was about to change. On a breezy Saturday afternoon, unexpectedly, Adviser Hunt paid him a visit, but why? Could it be the prime minister was having his most trusted personnel check up on him?

"Don't be alarmed, commissioner, it's a friendly call. I was in the neighbourhood and my curiosity got the better of me."

"I'm not, Mr Adviser. Do come in." The welcome was most exuberant. "I hope there isn't bad news that brings to the neighbourhood."

"Not at all, it's more like a casual stroll. It's not often I manage to get out and let my hair down."

The commissioner smiled; he was not totally bald, but there wasn't much hair left.

"Yes, I do see what you mean."

He seemed to like the adviser, and if they trump up a friendship; it could be most useful. Adviser Hunt was a lofty fellow with a very straight nose, rugged looking, but an honest face.

"Pull up a chair, Mr Adviser, and make yourself comfortable."

But he didn't. Instead, he turned to have a look around as though he was browsing.

"I expect you've been here a few times before, Mr Adviser?"

"Oh, yes, but some of memories are best forgotten."

"I'm sorry to hear that, but if you care to talk about it, I'm a good listener."

"Not especially, commissioner, but one day perhaps; over a point I might just do that."

He would like to hear the adviser's account of events of his pass, but he wasn't pressing the point.

"Would you like a drink, Mr Adviser? I'm going to have one myself," he asked while trying to get the drinks out.

Before the adviser could respond, he came up with a bottle of scotch and a bottle of Captain Morgan; it was for the benefit of the adviser.

"I would love a scotch, thank you, commissioner."

"How do you take it? Neat or on the rocks?"

"Neat, thank you," he said with some eagerness.

However, the commissioner will soon learn, drinkers of the island's favourite tipple (white rum) never say no to a scotch. They settle down for what will be a friendly encounter. On this social occasion, they'll probably will be trying to figure out what makes each other tick. But he's got news for the commissioner.

"On my way here, commissioner, I was—"

"Mr Adviser, what is your first name, if you don't mind me asking?" he interrupted.

"It's Jeffery, but why do you ask?"

"Then I'll call you Jeff, if you don't mind."

"Don't mind at all, but what would I be calling you?"

"You can call me Noel; my friends do, and let's hear no more of the formalities."

"Good to meet you, Noel."

"Likewise," said the commissioner. "Let's raised our glasses to friendship." And so it was, they settled down for what was a social afternoon.

"As I was saying, Noel, on my way here, I heard a whisper. Harry is on Quay Island; it was what partly brought me here."

"Quay Island? Where the hell is that?"

"It's about thirty miles offshore. One of the many islets dotted around, and they're all occupied."

"However, if you're considering going after Harry, be warned. Like the people, these places can be treacherous."

"Thanks for the warning, Jeff, but do you think the info is genuine?"

"I would like to think so, but one can't be sure, you know that. If I said it was, you might take me at my word, and find yourself on a wild goose chase." In this friendly encounter, the commissioner would like to find out things from him, but the man's a diplomat; he won't be giving away trade secrets.

"Tell me, Jeff, why it is so difficult to get any sort of information about Harry Wells; the people treat him like some sort of a hero."

Taking a sip from his glass, he didn't respond directly. Instead, he commented.

"Noel, you should've learned by now, these people are no friend of the constabulary; and most turned from the government, and why? I don't think I have to tell you."

The adviser painted a damning indictment of the establishment, of which he's a part of, but he's stating the truth.

"With difficulty, you might get an answer, but it could be misleading."

"The same where I came from, only, here it's much worst."

"A damn shame though, we could do with their help."

His visit turned out to be quite instructive; and they seemed to trump up an understanding. In this job, he needed all the friends he could get, and the adviser's friendship could be most important. He won't decide on the information about Harry until he talks with the lieutenant.

The following day, he's to have his first meeting with new home secretary Walker. If he was expecting a difficulty, he was going to be disappointed. After a warm greeting, the commissioner explained about Harry and the info he received; after a short discussion, they agreed on all counts.

Home Secretary Walker made it clear; the commissioner should act as he sees fit; he'll support his decision. The commissioner was left wondering, the minister didn't put up much of an argument, could it be he wasn't up to the task? Later that evening, he had a meeting with Lieutenant Dickson; he told him of the information he received and from whom; he was a little sceptical.

"So why did he go out of his way to bring you this information?"

"Maybe he thinks it was his civic duty."

The lieutenant wasn't buying; he's wary of everyone, even the advisor.

"So, what are you saying, Lieutenant, you think the adviser would deliberately mislead us?"

"No, not saying that at all, but there's an old saying, trust no shadows after dark."

"Actually, it was about mid-evening when he told me," said the commissioner, sarcastically.

"Very funny man," replied the lieutenant.

"I supposed we'll have to trust someone, but thirty miles offshore is a long way to go; only to find he isn't even there."

"Yeah, that would be a waste of time; however, it's the chance we'll have to take," said the commissioner.

So far, Harry had been leading them a merry dance, chase after chase; regardless of information.

"You know, Lieutenant, the folklore could be true; the man could possess supernatural powers. For a long time, we been chasing shadows. He probably sees us, but have we ever sees him? Never."

"Don't talk wet, man, I do hope you're not going to believe what the glory worshippers are saying."

"Well, the man has either got what they say he's got, or he's much smarter than us. I must tell you, I don't know what to believe."

"Those sort of talk gets us nowhere; he's nothing of what they claimed, we should be thinking positively."

They decide to go after him, but they needed a plan; the commissioner was always wary of his own men; he much rather use soldiers, for this or any other expedition.

"Lieutenant, we'll be needing two boats, will that pose a problem?"

"No problem at all. I'll see to it."

"Another thing, I'm planning on using your soldiers again; do I have to explain why?"

"No, man, just say how many."

They picked six soldiers and briefed them. Some had never been to Quay Island, but they were zealous and raring to go. They'll leave in time to arrive on the island by twelve o'clock dark, counting on the element of surprise.

They landed and were about to move inland; quietly, but someone was in the way, a fisherman. He was sleeping on the beach. This wasn't unusual; fishermen, after a hard day's fishing, would drink themselves drunk, and being intoxicated, instead of going home, they would sleep it off lying on the beach. He was spooked, seeing so many men with guns bearing down on him. He became alarmed. He shouted aloud. "It's a raid! It's a raid!"

Suddenly, the sleepy little neighbourhood became alive, wanting to know what's happening. The raiding party moved in fast, respecting the local privacy; they searched thoroughly but discreetly. No shot was fired, no need; Harry wasn't there. The islanders were furious; they were disturbed from their slumber, and they didn't like it.

When the search was over, the commissioner tried to explain the situation, but whatever he said wasn't going to satisfy them. One woman confronted him.

"You're not here looking for any gunmen, you're after Harry; why don't you leave him alone?"

"Was he here, madam?" he asked. She looked him up and down, scornfully.

"If he was, I wouldn't tell you."

The commissioner got the message; he was talking to the converted. It was two in the morning when they were about to leave, a man and a woman approached them.

"He was here, commissioner, but not for long." He could be one of those who don't side with the gun men.

After hearing that, the lieutenant asked, "Tell me, sir, do you know Harry Wells and his gang. They have killed many people, some of whom might even be relatives of yours."

The man didn't respond, but the woman did. It seems she didn't appreciate such talk.

"Why are you pinning all the killing on him; he has never killed anyone for me, or anyone that I know."

The commissioner shook his head; this woman, it seemed, didn't mind Harry killing a few people, as long as he didn't kill any one of hers.

"Lieutenant, these people belong to the Harry's fan clubs; we're not going to learn anything from them."

"Only because we're too soft," replied the lieutenant.

"Oh! What would you have us do, beat it out of them?"

"Come on, man, you know what I mean, I—"

"I know what you mean, Lieutenant," he interrupted, "and that is never going to happened. We're done here. Let's go home."

The operation was over without a shot fired. They were no wiser about Harry than they ever were. If the man and the women were to believed, the information was good, only Harry vanished like always. But how? This is an islet; one can see from shore to shore, and the place was thoroughly searched. The commissioner had misgivings.

"Lieutenant, I know I said it before, but I am baffled; there something unnatural about this fellow, the locals can't all be wrong."

"I hope you're not going to believe fables; those are mythical tales made up by the fanatics. He's just a man, a man we haven't caught yet."

"I hear you, Lieutenant, but this fellow can't be that smart. There's got to be more to him."

"Listen, man, I hope you are not going funny on me. With that sort of thinking, we'll never catch him."

"There're times, lieutenant, things are more than what meets the eyes. In other words, one can't be sure of what can't be proven."

At the office, he called his team together, the lieutenant and Deputy Commissioner Holmes, the man he inherited.

"Gentlemen, we're here to think Harry Wells, this fellow has got under my skin. He's giving us the run around, and I don't like it."

The lieutenant was just as baffled, but unlike the commissioner, he's not thinking Harry is anything other than an ordinary man; only he kills people. However, he had an idea.

"Commissioner, suppose we run a piece in *The Gleaner*, reading:

"Harry Wells is dead; drowned in the Black River. We believe his body was eaten by Alligators. When he reads it, he might want to prove the story wrong."

The commissioner lit a cigarette; he took one puff and then put it out, he often did that.

"I see what you mean, Lieutenant, and lure him into a false sense of security?"

"Something like that," He paused to light another cigarette, the lieutenant noticed. "You're not really a smoker, are you, Commissioner?" He didn't respond. He just put it out.

"Lieutenant, I think it's worth a try."

He was running out of options. His natural policeman instinct told him Harry would never fall for it, but at present, anything's worth a try. There were more ideas, but nothing they could use. It was two in the evening, and he was about to leave for his appointment with the Home Secretary Walker, but he wasn't looking forward to; it's not a good feeling explaining a failed mission to the minister.

"Wish me luck, gentlemen," he said while putting some documents in his briefcase.

"Wish you luck!" exclaimed the lieutenant. "What the hell you're talking about, man? You're calling the shots, not the minister. You tell him what happened, and if he doesn't like it, he—"

"That will do, Lieutenant," he interrupted. "Remember, he's the home secretary, our boss. Let's not overstep one's position."

"Look, commissioner, I understand all that, but we're out there doing the job, he should ask you and listen. However, if you're going to ask him for something, then that's different. So, tell me, commissioner, what are you going to ask him for?"

The commissioner looked at him with a wry smile. There was some truth in what he said, even though he didn't like it.

"Lieutenant, you sure know how to make a man feel bad about himself; however, funny as it sounds, I take your point."

The Lieutenant must go, he's got a duty to undertake.

"OK, man. On your return, if you want me, you know where to find me."

Throughout the meeting, Deputy Commissioner Holmes sat in silence, observing, but saying nothing. His action was noticed by both men. Could he be the mole? They'll be keeping a close eye on him.

On arrival at the home office, Miss Benson greeted him; she was quite exuberant.

"Good morning, Commissioner, isn't it a lovely morning?"

"You think so, Miss Benson?"

"Yes, sir. Feel that gently breeze? It's good to be alive."

"Of course, you're right, Miss Benson; it's just me being gloomy."

"I'm so sorry to hear that, sir. You'll feel better with a cup of coffee; I'll bring it to you."

"Thank you, Miss Benson, but hold the coffee," he said politely.

"OK, sir. The minister is waiting. I'll bring you a cold drink instead."

"That will do nicely, thank you."

She alerted the home secretary on the intercom; he promptly opened the door.

"Come in, commissioner," he said gratifyingly.

After a light conversation standing, they got down to business, but there wasn't much to say about the expedition, except what happened. The minister didn't have much to say regarding it. It seemed whatever the commissioner said was good enough for him.

"Minister, we've come up with an idea about Harry we would like to try."

"Is this about another one of your shooting matches, commissioner?"

It was all going so well, the commissioner thought. The lieutenant's words began ringing in his ear, *tell the man; don't ask him.* But he's not going to; he'll try to be civil.

"No, there'll be no guns; not this time."

"I'm glad to hear it."

His thoughts were working overtime, but for now, he'll go along with the minister's caper. He handed him the article he wrote; he read it out aloud.

"Harry Wells is no longer alive; he drowned in the black river and probably eaten by alligators, good riddance."

He raised his head; he appeared to treat the article with scepticism.

"Commissioner, what makes you think he will fall for it, and what outcome you're expecting?" *Fair questions,* the commissioner thought, whatever the intent.

"This one we're playing by ear, minister. He might react to it – then again, he might not. What we're hoping for, is to lead him into a false sense of security – then again, he might want to show he's very much alive."

"Surely, commissioner, you really don't believe that, do you?"

"Well now, if I knew that, I wouldn't be using the word like 'hope', would I, minister?"

The commissioner was getting a little irksome; the minister wasn't saying no, but he wasn't helping either.

"Could you get it to *The Gleaner*, minister? As soon as you can."

"I can, but it seems a futile exercise."

"Mr Walker, if you have a better idea, I would like hear it."

By now, both men were behaving quite peculiarly; this discussion was not going the way the way it should have. The commissioner smiled, but it was the smile of dissatisfaction; he needed words of encouragement from the minister. Instead, all he got were doubts.

"Commissioner, don't think I'm throwing a spanner in the word; only I have doubt about the idea, it seems a little far-fetched."

"I have doubt myself, but far-fetched, minister, don't you think you're stretching it somewhat."

"Could be, but that is my thought, commissioner."

Later, he was to ponder the minister's action; having nothing to add in the way of advice, he tried to be difficult.

"I'll talk to Mr Wicket myself about this article, and yes, commissioner, it's worth a try."

"Really, minister?" he asked sarcastically.

"Yes, commissioner, and let's hope it works."

"Well, thank you, minister. I hope so too." The meeting concluded. But he was in for a surprise, as he was leaving.

"Mr Wade, I hope our next meeting will be of a more of an informal nature. We don't have to stick to the script at all times."

"I thought it was just that, minister; informal," he replied sarcastically.

"I'm pleased you find it that way, commissioner, but let's try and make it better next time."

"I'll certainly try, minister, you can count on that."

Chapter 8
Killings at Lincoln Ville

Thursday morning and the first edition of the morning paper was out. It ran an article regarding Harry Wells. A man walked by a police officer; he was brandishing a copy. "You'll never catch Harry; he's too smart for you lot," he said mockingly. He probably belonged to the Harry Wells fan club. It wasn't a flippant comment; but such was the belief of the people. The officer looked at him with weary eyes; he told him to get a move on.

The day after, four bodies were found in the nearby parish of Lincoln Ville. The commissioner sent in two Officers to investigate. He wasn't expecting to learn much in regards to the killings; no one was going to talk, but the police must show their presence. There were no police in the districts, the ones in the parish, were located in the cities, and they're only a few. As expected, the investigation turned up nothing, everyone was tight-lipped.

"I would like to change the way things are done," he moaned to the lieutenant.

"Having 10 policemen overseeing an entire city, not to mention the districts, it's bonkers."

"That's the way it's always been. You'll have one hell of a job changing it."

"Well, lieutenant, we're going to try. It can't go on this way."

But the lieutenant had misgivings. He hoped the commissioner won't go biting off more than he could chew.

"Commissioner, if you want to be a reformer, I think you're in the wrong job. You're not going to change this Government stance on matters like this."

"Lieutenant, I learned a long time ago; for one to succeed, one has to try. We're going to do just that."

"You kept saying we, whom may I ask is the other person?"

"Who do you think? You! You're as much a part of this outfit as I am."

"I don't know so much about that, but good luck, man, but there's a proverb, there's no use flogging a dead horse."

"Lieutenant, those are the words of the defeatist. They throw in the towel as the going gets tough. We're not going to do that."

The commissioner was remembering something the PM said at their last meeting; he was reflecting on it.

"We don't want the people to think we abandoned them, because we didn't."

He didn't sound like a prime minister who didn't care; probably had no idea how to, but he sounded as though he cared. There was something odd about the killing. The victims were gang members. Were the gangs turning the guns on their own now? The commissioner hoped so. But the police weren't wise to the fact, and they're not going to. They murdered two of their own, who cares? They can keep doing it.

The Sighting

April, and although the twelve months of the year were usually the same, this was really the beginning of the planting season. People took no notice, but the characteristics were there. There was a reported sighting of Harry. That was some four weeks after the article was posted in *The Gleaner*. The information told of where Harry was likely to be, and when. The commissioner wasted no time, at 11 o'clock, he met with the lieutenant and Deputy Commissioner Holmes. There was an air of urgency.

"Gentlemen, if Harry is due at this location, I would like to be there before him."

He'd been talking for a while but said nothing of where Harry was supposed to be or when, but it was for a reason. The lieutenant became impatient.

"Commissioner, are you going to tell us where he's supposed to be, or are you keeping it a secret?" Well, he would like to kept it a secret, from the ears of Deputy Holmes, the man he suspected to be a mole, but he'll have to tell them.

"At Lincoln Ville, didn't I say?"

"No, you didn't, but isn't that where the killings took place three weeks ago?" asked the lieutenant.

"It was, and I wondered why he chose to go there so soon after?"

"Well, it could be he fell for the article in *The Gleaner*, and now he wants us to know he's alive and well."

"Or there could be another explanation, like been there before and likes it there."

"You really don't believe that, do you commissioner?"

"No, not really, but who knows how these killers' minds work? However, something about this note that got me thinking. He'll be staying in a boarding house. Why would he do that, when there's a hotel?"

The lieutenant shuffled himself about uncomfortably. *Something doesn't add up,* he thought.

"How is it the informant knew the exact time and place, and why he chose a boarding?"

"Harry likes to live big; a boarding house is not his style."

"Why indeed, Lieutenant, but I guess we'll never know."

"However, let's assume he's not there yet, I think we should get there and wait him."

"I like that thinking," replied the lieutenant, "but we could be waiting for days, and he doesn't show, a wild goose chase' comes to mind."

"Well, since the informer gives the time, we'll work to that time table, but we won't go. We'll have the team on standby, while we send in a scout. Any volunteers?"

Deputy Holmes, who sat listening attentively but had nothing to interject, spoke, "I would like a crack at it, commissioner, I know the place quite well."

But he won't be going nowhere. He's the main suspect, and they got their eyes on him.

"Thank you, Mr Holmes, but I want you here."

He wasn't too pleased, and he didn't argue, but his disappointment was plain to see. The commissioner glanced at the lieutenant as if to say, *what about you?*

"OK, okay, no need to give me the eyes, man, I'll go."

"Are you sure, Lieutenant? I wasn't insinuating anything."

"Yeah, yeah," he replied sarcastically.

"Anyway, I know these country folks quite well, actually, I'm one of them."

"Have you ever done this sort of assignment, Lieutenant?"

"No, but I know what to do. I'm a soldier, remember?"

"OK, Lieutenant, you're the man. Have dinner with me and we'll put this plan together." The meeting ended.

That evening they met at the hotel for their unfinished business. The lieutenant, a married man, did business here before, but that was before the commissioner moved in.

"Lieutenant, it's the second time I think we've dropped a clanger."

"Did we? You'll have to enlighten me."

"Deputy Miller, have him sit in on meeting about Harry. Did you notice the way he sat listening; but saying nothing, to said, but he was quick to volunteer for the mission."

"Yes, and he wasn't too please when told he was told he's wanted here, yes, I noticed."

"Which means, we're wasting our time. If he's in with Harry, he'll get word to him before we can say, Jack Sprat."

"Yes, but we'll do what we've have to do, but fast, and hope for the best."

"I suggest you book a reservation using an alias. If you use your real name, they most likely will know who you are."

"Commissioner, where I'm from, it's a stone's throw from this place. Someone is likely to recognise me, regardless of the name I used."

"You left there a long time ago, you said so. They've probably forgotten about you."

"That may be so, but I doubt it. These people have strong memories, but I like the idea."

But the lieutenant seemed fascinated by what he considered an undercover operation; it's not only exciting, but intriguing too.

"Lieutenant, I do hope you're serious about what you're about to embark on. It could be a wild goose chase, but we need to know, so don't foul it up."

"Don't worry, man; I'll get the job done."

The commissioner gave him a sideways glance, as if to say, *make darn sure you do*.

"So, you see what you've done to me, man? You've turned me into a spy, but it's got a good feel to it. I'll book in using Dalton Moore; I saw this movie once and——"

"Now listen, Lieutenant," he interrupted. "This is not a game. We need to know if he's there, so, be serious. You're only going to be there long enough to see the target; whether he's there or not, you come right back."

"Oh, come on, man, lighten up. Where's your sense of adventure?"

"I have it, I can assure you, but now is not the time to play Mata Hari."

"OK, man, I was only fooling."

"Well, do it in your own time, we're out to catch a killer, or you forget?"

"No man, I don't, but being serious isn't going to get the job done faster, or better."

The Errand

Late that evening, the Lieutenant set off on his errand; he was gone for over a day and there was no news about the target. The commissioner was getting anxious; not hearing from the Lieutenant was causing concern. Another day passed and still no news; he decided to act. He would like to send in a man to make contact with the lieutenant, but who? He can't ask his officer; anyone of them could be an informer. He doesn't know his officers well enough to be sure of who is loyal from who isn't. Once again, he is faced with a tough decision, not exactly a dilemma, but it is causing concern. He's got a brainwave; he'll choose a soldier; someone he has worked with, there is more loyalties in the army than the constabulary.

He went to the barracks and called for the soldier. His name was Albert Reed. He told him about the errand. He's to make contact with the lieutenant, he doesn't know he's coming. He's to get the information from him, and come directly back.

It was noon. Soldier boy Albert sets off to Lincoln Ville; it won't take long, about an hour on the bus. He was gone for nearly eight hours; the commissioner wasn't counting on him to being away that long. He was on tenterhooks; his plans weren't looking too wholesome at all.

Early Saturday morning, there's a knock on his hotel room door. He looked at his watch. It just turned 4 am. He was still in bed; and he didn't get much in the way of sleep. He pulled on his robe and made his way to the door; it was soldier boy Albert.

"Come in, Albert; come in," he said anxiously. "Take a seat and tell me what the lieutenant said."

He settled himself in the deep foam settee; the sort of comfort he wasn't accustomed to, but he was Jady.

"He said you come about eight this evening, sir, but you shouldn't come up the main street."

"Does that mean Harry is there?" he asked anxiously.

"The lieutenant said he is, sir, but I didn't see him."

He sat himself down with a pencil and paper at the ready.

"What else did he say?"

Then, Albert relates, he gave him all the info as it was given to him.

"Did you see anyone of his gunman?"

"There were plenty of people about, sir, but I can't say for sure, but if he's there, his men are there too."

"Good work, Albert, would you like breakfast?"

"Yes, thank you, sir."

Well, the commissioner liked to make the men around him feel comfortable; a way of building up trust.

Breakfast was ordered. He continues to talk about the mission.

"He also said he'll be staying on, sir. Whatever you're planning, you'll have to do without him."

The scamp has absconded, the commissioner jested to himself. *I didn't think he would be a turn coat.*

"Are you sure that's what he said, Albert?"

"Yes, sir. He said he's staying on to keep an eye on Harry, in case he decided to pull out."

Soon breakfast arrived. While he eats, the commissioner took a shower. When he returned, Albert had finished eating.

"Is there anything more you need me for, sir?"

"No, Albert, you've done well, but stay handy. I will need you again."

"OK, sir, and thanks for the breakfast."

11:30 am, he met the home secretary; he brings him up to speed regarding the situation. He explained, the men he'll be using for this expedition will be soldiers. But the minister wasn't too pleased with the idea.

"Shouldn't this be a job for the police, commissioner? What so special about the soldiers?"

The commissioner recalls disgraced Home Secretary Burns. He had asked the same question too, only, he was totally against it. This home secretary wasn't, but stubborn, perhaps wants to show who is boss. But he has to tread carefully, if it was seen as a lack of co-operation, the PM wouldn't like it. The man is a patriot, only the commissioner doesn't know it yet.

He was slow in his decisions; the commissioner thinks he was dragging his feet, he wasn't here for a long discussion, more of a yes or no. What he's got to do must be done in a hurry.

"Home secretary, for this one thing, I'm determined to have my way, because I believe it's the right way. However, if we can't have a consensus, I'm prepared to take my case to the prime minister." A course of action he took with Home Secretary Burns, and it paid dividend.

"Is that a threat, commissioner? If it is, it's in bad taste. I don't know the reason for it, maybe you can tell me."

"Minister, with respect, this operation is for tonight. If it is to go ahead, I must move fast, this hanging about is doing my plan no good at all."

"It could be I was a little slow to respond, commissioner, but there was no need for threats. I assured you my full co-operation, and you have no reason to doubt me, we're working toward the same goal."

The commissioner wasn't bluffing, only he's got the wrong impression of the home secretary, but he got what he came for.

He went to the barracks. He chose ten soldiers, but he felt the need to know if Harry was still there before he sets off. Once again, he called on Albert. Using the commissioner's car, he was sent to get further information from the lieutenant, but he must return before the hunting party sets off. The soldier had to be quick, but he can do the thirty miles plus round trip without too much of a hurry.

About an hour later, Albert returned; he made his way directly to the hotel. The commissioner armed himself before answering the door, but it was Albert. He quickly put the weapon under his clothing.

"Come in, Albert," he said as he said as he opened the door open.

The soldier walked in and handed him a note. It seemed the lieutenant didn't trust him to deliver the message verbally.

The commissioner studies the note; it's a little different from earlier information. He should rendezvous at Lincoln Ville at eight that evening, about two hundred yards from the hotel. He was satisfied with the info, but he hasn't got much time.

He's got no idea as to why the changes, but he's not going to dwell on it; in a couple of hours, he'll be off on the mission.

Cast a Long Shadow

In less than an hour, the news he'll receive would cast a long shadow over the operation. The lieutenant returned in a hurry, bearing bad news. Harry and his gang had pulled out, they just up and went, and he booked in at the hotel, not a boarding house.

"I didn't believe he would, lieutenant, he's always go for the top shelf."

"I wish you wouldn't speak of him that way. The man is a criminal, he should be referred to as such."

The commissioner was most disappointed; he was feeling rather sick to his stomach, once again. All hope of catching this killer was suddenly dashed.

"Lieutenant, another mission went up in smoke. What you suppose happened, someone got to him before us?"

"Most likely, but we did suspect that might be the case, so, don't go beating up yourself. Harry was there, but he must have been tipped off. There'll be other times, he's not going anywhere."

The lieutenant was relaxed about it all, but one couldn't say the same for the commissioner. He's concerned with how often Harry had given them the slip.

"A man like Harry Wells, he will be around to show how bad and daring he is, playing to the gallery, you might say."

"That maybe so, Lieutenant, but he's been leading us a merry dance for far too long, and I don't like it. He's making us look foolish."

"Our time will come. One of the times, he'll let his guard down, and when he does, we'll be waiting."

"Only we haven't got time on our side. The longer this fellow is at large, the more the country gets a bad name, home and abroad."

There was an air of despair. Tomorrow he had to make out a report for the home secretary; this constant bad news was causing an embarrassment.

"Lieutenant, I don't like making this kind of report; it makes us look incompetent."

"You have nothing to feel bad about; tell the minister what happened; if he doesn't like it, that's too bad."

"That, Lieutenant, isn't going to happen. Respect should be given where it's due, and he's our boss, remember?"

"All I'm saying, man, is that our plans was never going to be fool proof, and it could be someone fouled it up."

"Lieutenant, tomorrow we must meet for a chat. This thing has weighed heavily on my mind. Someone is fouling up our operation, and we must find who."

The soldiers were disappointed when they learnt the mission was off. As soldiers, they hadn't seen much in the way of action; they were looking forward to it. However, the commissioner was gratified to learn of their eagerness, and to know they're ready for action whenever he calls on them.

Chapter 9
The informers

The following day, the commissioner and the lieutenant convene a meeting; the agenda: informers. Too many of their missions were fouling up, the rat of rats must be rooted out.

"Lieutenant, there's a mole or moles among us, I'm sure of it, and we must find him, and fast. Harry is giving us the run-around, and it's keeping me awake."

"I'm feeling bad, too, but I'm not letting it get to me, and you shouldn't either. It's bad for health."

"You know, Lieutenant, the home secretary wasn't too keen when I mentioned the use of soldiers for the operation, you don't suppose—"

"Stop right there, man," the lieutenant interrupted. "Surely, you're not pointing the finger at—" He paused. The name eluded him.

"Home Secretary Walker, Lieutenant, you don't think he could? Remember Home Secretary Burns? The man had a good honest face, and so does Home Secretary Walker."

"I'm not a fan of the home secretary, but I think you're barking up the wrong tree."

Of course, he was clutching at straws. There were moles among them, but the home secretary wasn't one.

"Well, tell me what you think, I'm plum out of ideas. When I sit to talk with the minister, I would like something more definite to present to him."

"Listen man, you're too obsessed with Harry Wells, and if you're not careful, it's going to give your a hernia. You shouldn't let him get to you; it will cloud your judgement. Anyway, now that you suspected the minister; how are you going to look him in the eyes?"

"Perhaps I was a little hasty, but only because we're scratching around for answers."

"I hear you, man, but if we're going to catch him, we have to be thinking positively. Some of our operations are going to end in disappointment, like the last one, but that's how we have to play it. The right time will come, and when it does, we'll have Mr Wells."

"You talked as though you're looking into the future. What else you can tell me?"

"Listened, man, I don't like your obsession with this fellow. He's like all the other criminals, let's not treat him as though he's special."

"I know you're right, lieutenant, but the man is making a monkey out of us, and he will until we find the informer. We're not talking to anyone on the outside, so, it's got to be someone in the constabulary."

"I would say we are, there're people out there giving us information," said the lieutenant.

"That is so, but they don't know our plans, and they wouldn't go tell Harry they gave us information about him."

"No, lieutenant. From now on, we're going to concentrate on catching a rat. He's among us."

"Fine with me, but how are we going to set about doing that; have you got a plan, or anyone in mind?"

"I certainly have, but it's only a suspicion, see what you make of this. Deputy Holmes was awfully anxious to run the errand, remember, and—"

"Wait a minute there now, have you given up on the minister?" interrupted the lieutenant.

"No, I'm ruling no one out; I'm keeping an open mind, but Deputy Holmes is my main suspect, the signs are there." said the commissioner.

The Lieutenant commented, "There're other ways he can inform Harry of our plans without running an errand, so, if he's the rat, how do we go about catching him?"

"We—" he paused. "I have a suggestion, we'll wait until we get news on Harry's whereabout; then we convene a meeting, after which we got someone to watch him, if he's the rat he'll trying to make contact with his man."

"Lieutenant, it's a better suggestion than you think, yes, sir. We'll do just that."

The failed mission was one story *The Gleaner* didn't get hold of. The morning after the commissioner arrived at the home office, Mr Walker was waiting. Their greeting was mediocre, well, almost superficial; neither man wanted to appear civil. At their last meeting, the minister suggested he hopes their next encounter would be more sociable. They settled down, the commissioner explained the failed mission, but the minister appeared to have misgivings.

"About these tips off, commissioner, could it be someone is deliberately giving you false info? You must be mindful; these people are friend of the establishment."

"I'm aware of that, minister, but the information was good. Only Harry left before we were able to get there. However, if you're saying we shouldn't follow up on information received – false or otherwise, how are we going to catch this fellow? We haven't got a looking glass."

"There's no need to be abusive, commissioner; I was merely asking the question. But tell me, without the public information's, will you ever catch this fellow?"

A logical question, the commissioner comment was un-called for, he re-thinks his comments.

"I'm sorry for my somewhat loose comment, minister. We'll catch him alright, but you must realise police work depends on a little help from the public."

The minister was calmed, but the commissioner seemed a little rattled, probably because of his misplace comments.

"Commissioner, I want you to know this, I'm working with you, and not against you, but I will quote my opinion, always."

"Hell! I know that, minister, I was just stating the facts."

He tried to be tactful as being forthright, but they calmed down and got through the agenda. One could say it was a matter of keeping a stiff upper lip, something the English men are quite familiar with.

Two o'clock that evening, he summoned the lieutenant and waited for him at the hotel. It was 5:30 pm when the lieutenant arrived, just in time for dinner. Back in England, he would be having supper, but here in the tropic things are different, they dine late.

"I hope you're hungry, Lieutenant, I've ordered dinner for you."

"Thanks, man, as it so happened, I'm starving. I could eat a horse."

"I hate to disappoint you, they don't do horse, but they do a mean curry goat."

"Very funny, man," said the lieutenant.

"What would you like to drink? A drop of the hard stuff?"

"No thank you, I never touch the stuff, but I could do with a cold beer."

"Are you telling me you never drink Captain Morgan?"

"No, I never. I'm not what you might call, a boozer. Anyway, it's far too strong for me."

The commissioner seemed surprised; he's of the belief that everyone on the island drinks rum, why he thinks that? Only he knows. He ordered two bottles of cold red stripe beers.

They're talking Deputy Holmes; the commissioner explained. "He wasn't my choice for the position; I inherited him, my bad luck, wouldn't you say?"

The lieutenant agreed, his action at meetings was suspicious, he never said anything, just observed.

"It is possible he could be the mole, but as of now, it's only conjecture; we need proof, and we're not going to get it unless we catch him red-handed."

They paused; dinner had arrived along with drinks. The waiter set the table, then left.

"Now, Lieutenant, tell me your thoughts. Is there any further suggestions from that of yesterday?"

"Why, weren't those enough?"

"I want to know if there's any further thought."

"Well now, I never thought I would live to see the day, a white English policeman asking a black soldier how to catch a thief. I must be in the wrong job."

"Lieutenant, neither of us are detective, but what we are; we're in it together, and don't you forget it."

"That may be so, but only because you're making me out to be a police man."

"Okay, here's what I think. We stick to the plan, but the question is, who could we trust to watch him?"

"You shouldn't be asking; you've got a man."

"Who might that be, Lieutenant?"

"Soldier boy Albert; you've been using him on errands, he's perfect for this mission."

"Hell, yes. I completely forgot about him; right, he's, our man."

"You're a good man, Lieutenant, your brain is always at work; I like that."

"That maybe so, but the problem you've got—"

"Stop right there," he interrupted. "It's not the problems I've got, it's the problem we have, and don't you forget it. One more thing. When we're alone, do call me Noel, that's what my friends call me."

"OK, man, but only if you call me Dick."

"Then so be it, Dick."

"Nevertheless, Mr Commissioner, you're Noel only when we're alone. One shouldn't be too familiar in front of the men; standard must be maintained."

"Point taken, Dick."

The commissioner was in desperate need of a right-hand man; the present one was of no use to him.

"Tell me, Dick, do you ever get tired of being a soldier?"

"No, but why do you ask?"

"It's what you might call a rogue question. Forget I asked it."

"Come on, man, there must be a reason for asking, and I'm curious. Do tell."

"Well, I was thinking, how would you like a change of duty. You would make a damn good deputy commissioner. You ever think of that?"

"No, man, no need; I'm a soldier, and I like being a soldier. Moreover, I know nothing about police business."

"Come on. The difference between the two bodies is paper thin, and you've been doing police work every day."

"Only because I'm forced, and that doesn't mean I like it."

With a smile, the commissioner commented, "No one forced you, Dick, you did it because you wanted to. You want rid the country of vermin's just as I do. Anyway, it was only a thought, but if you ever change your mind, the job is yours."

"I hope you're not holding your breath; man, I've gotten fond of you."

The time was running late. The lieutenant picked up his staff, and got up to leave.

"Tell me, Noel, does the home secretary know anything about Holmes. That he could be the informer?"

"I don't know, and I can't remember talking to him about it."

"So, are you going to?"

"I will, at some stage, but I don't think he'll believe it. Of course, in your book, he's a suspect," the Lieutenant said sarcastically.

"OK, Dick, don't keep rubbing it in; I didn't consciously believe he was; whatever the man's fault, he's not a traitor."

"That's good to hear. I'll say good night, boss."

"Go home, Dick, you're drunk."

"No, I'm not. I'm as sober as when I first walked in."

As he was about to exit the door, he asked, "Is there any further duty you have for me in the morning, boss?"

"Go along on home, boy; I'll see you in the morning."

Chapter 10
Murder at the Courthouse

It was a beautiful day, but it'll be a terrible day for the judiciary; on his way to the office, the commissioner got a news. A judge and his colleagues were shot, they were trying a case. He hurriedly drove there; the police were already at the scene, but no one else. These killings happened so regularly, no one bothered to notice.

"Tell me, officer, how did this happen; and who did the shooting?"

"Two men walked in as though they were attending court. Suddenly, they pulled their guns and shot the three men. The guns were hidden under their clothing, sir."

"Then where were you while the men were murdered?"

"I wasn't here, sir. I rushed here when I heard the shooting."

"Did you see the gunmen?"

"No, sir, they were gone when I arrived. What I'm telling you is what told me by the usher."

"Where's he now?"

"That's him over there, sir," he said, pointing.

The commissioner walked over to the man; he didn't seem bothered; he could be in with the killers.

"Mister, were you the usher in court today? Tell me what you know about the killing."

"There isn't much to tell, sir, two men walked in as though they were attending court. There were no weapons showing."

"So, what the men look like? You saw their faces?"

"No, sir, I didn't. They wore masks."

He knew the man was lying. Those gunmen had no need to wear masks; they were not bothered who saw them.

"You have a gun, mister, why didn't you use it?"

"I couldn't, sir, they got the drop on me. They took my gun and told me to stand behind the door. That's when they killed the judge and the other two gentlemen."

Knowing the usher's account was all lies. He asked, "Tell me, mister, were these gunmen short or tall?"

"They looked the same height, sir, but I can't be sure."

"You're not telling me the truth, are you, mister?"

"Oh yes, sir, I wouldn't lie to you," he said, trying to looking sincere.

He wasn't going to waste time talking to this fellow; whatever his story, it's certain to be lies. In situations like this, it is hardly worthwhile investigating, unless the gunmen are caught in the act, no one's going to tell.

Mr Walker's Visit

Late that evening, the commissioner had an unexpected visitor, Home Secretary Walker; he was angry and looked like a frightened man.

"Commissioner, I want to see these killers caught and hung," he said as he walked through the door.

He could be referring to the court house killing, but the commissioner wasn't sure. However, it was an odd statement coming from him, he wasn't too eager to support going after the gang using soldiers, but here was, wanting killers to be stopped. *I wonder why?* the commissioner thought. He pulled up a chair; his speech was blurred with anger.

"Have a seat, minister," said the commissioner sarcastically.

The minister however had no time to observe ethics or protocol, he's far too angry. The commissioner was still in the dark regarding his angry, and which killers he wanted to be caught.

"Would you mind telling me why you're here, minister, and why are you so angry?"

"The killing of the judge and his colleagues; those killers must be caught."

His eyes were red with anger. What he wanted was revenge, but revenge he wasn't going to get, in regard to the killers; the commissioner was as much in the dark as he was.

"Commissioner, you need to find those murderers; I can't tell you how to, but you must find them."

The man is a bloody hypocrite, or he's suffering from amnesia, thought the commissioner. *These killer's been killing members of the establishment long before I arrived here. What does he expect? Does he thinks I can work miracles?*

"Mr Walker, I noted your grievance, and I see you're deeply concerned about the killing of these men, but tell me this, do you share the same concern for the many who're being murdered every day?"

He didn't respond; he was in a foul mood; but so was the commissioner. He didn't appreciate him coming to his office, demanding what he wants.

"You know, minister, if everyone would give their full support in regards to law and order, the situation probably could be a lot better. The constabulary desperately short of men; but it doesn't seem to bother the Government; nevertheless, here you're, looking for a quick fix. The people, they could help too, but they won't, and all because of the way this government treated them."

He has his moan; and probably feeling better for it, the minister however, didn't come here to listen to his moans, his friend the judge and his colleagues are murdered; he's concern about them; not the locals.

"It's not the people's job to help you catch these killers, it's the job of the police, so don't go blaming them if you fall short of your commitment."

The commissioner was hurt. This man who is unable to think for himself, unable to contribute anything in regard to ideas, has the gall to accuse him of falling short in his duty. However, he bit his lips and bore it; a slanging match wasn't going to serve any purpose.

"You know, minister, I believe there's—" He paused. He was about to tell him about the mole or moles he believed to be in the constabulary. He remembered something someone said a long time ago, an uncontrolled anger is an easy way for one to give the enemy the edge. He wasn't saying the minister was an enemy, but telling him would serve no purpose. The minister was so angry, he was oblivious to the commissioner's attempted comment. He left a very angry and disgruntled man. The commissioner will learn later that the judge was his brother-in-law, hence the demand for reprisal. He summoned one of his officers; he wanted to speak with the lieutenant; but he couldn't seem to get him on the phone.

"Where would I find him, sir?" asked the officer.

"I don't know, officer, that's why I want you to go look for him," he said angrily.

Of course, he was still seething from his encounter with the home secretary. The officer was leaving, but realising his action, he called to the officer to wait up. As the officer walked back, he appeared a little gloomy; probably, he didn't appreciate the way the commissioner spoke to him.

"What's your name, officer?"

"Daniel Brown, sir," he said, looking gloomy.

"Daniel, I'm so sorry I shouted. I'm angry at someone else. I shouldn't take it out on you. Will you come and see me the moment you return?"

"That's all right, sir, I understand." he said humbly.

"Nevertheless, Daniel, do come and see me. We should have a talk. You don't mind, do you?"

"No, sir; I don't mind at all."

In his anger, he might just make a friend, and it could turn out to be productive.

Sometime later that evening, Daniel returned; the commissioner was going to have a man-to-man talk with him; probably he might learn something about the men he works with.

"Did you see the lieutenant, Daniel?"

"Yes, sir, and I gave him the message."

"Thank you, Daniel, take a seat. I'm going to have a drink; would you like one?"

"Yes, thank you, sir," he said appreciatively, and why wouldn't he? Having a drink with the boss, he could only dream about it.

"What would you like?" he asked, displaying a bottle of Captain Morgan taken from his desk.

"I'll have what you're having, sir."

"Good man, Daniel, how do you take it? With water?"

"Oh no, sir, I never chase my drink, and I usually put this much in the glass," he said, using his fingers to show how much.

Damn cheek, thought the commissioner; however, he smiled amusingly, poured the drink with a little extra and handed it to him.

"Cheers," he said, and the officer returned the compliment.

Now he'll try to see what he can learn from this officer; he might know something about Deputy Holmes.

"Have you ever met Harry Wells, Daniel?"

"Yes and no, sir."

"What do you mean, yes and no?"

"Well, I was in a store one day when he walked in, and everyone stopped and stared."

"Did he talk to anyone?"

"No, sir. One of the two men did the talking; they collected a parcel and went."

"Were you in uniform?"

"Oh yes, sir, they saw me."

Well, that bit of information gives the commissioner food for thought; could this store be a supply post?

"Daniel, I would like you to help me catch this fellow."

"Who, me, sir? What can I do?" he asked with his eyes popping as though he has just seen a ghost.

The commissioner noticed his reaction; it's fear, but what he wants from him is information.

"Have you ever heard any whispers as to where he might be at any time?"

"No, sir, but if I hear anything, I'll let you know."

"That would be helpful, Daniel, and if you know of anyone meeting with him, would you let me know too?"

"Yes, sir, that I'll do."

"Now listen, Daniel. If ever you have a problem, any problems at all, do come and see me."

"Yes, sir, I will, and thank for the drink, sir"

Will his little talk be productive? It has already; he learned about a store downtown, something he was oblivious of.

That evening at his hotel, he waited for the lieutenant who was delayed. When he arrived, the commissioner had already ordered dinner for two.

"What kept you, Dick? Couldn't find your way?"

"I was checking out a lead I got on Harry."

"Oh! What did you learn?"

"I heard he would be at a certain location, so I checked it out and waited, but he didn't show."

"Do you think he might not get there yet?"

"Well, I waited for some time; he could've been there before I got there, and left."

"Well, you done what we must, followed up on the information," said the Commissioner.

"As you weren't here, I ordered dinner for you; the same as you had before; I hope you don't mind."

"Don't mind at all. I'm so hungry; I hope it won't be too long coming."

"Good heavens, man, why is it you're always hungry; isn't your wife feeding you?"

"Funny you should ask. I don't get home too often these days, and before you begin to give me a lecture on matrimonial affairs, I must tell you, we parted company."

"What do you mean, parted company?"

"We said goodbye, what do you think?"

"Are you trying to telling me you're divorced?"

"Don't sound so surprised, man, that's what people do when they fell out of love, and we fell out of love long ago."

The commissioner looked a little surprised; it seemed he's thinking the Lieutenant shouldn't be grieving.

"I'm sorry to hear that; break ups are never easy."

"Don't be, man, I'm not; we had a good run."

"What do you mean, a good run? Marriage is for keeps; till death us do part. Tell me, Dick, do you remember taking those vows?"

"Of course, but it's just words of symbols; doesn't mean a damn thing."

"So how long were you married?"

"Nearly four years, and man, that's a long time being married to Lucille."

"Then, why did you marry her, you couldn't love her?"

"Heaven only knows, man, it was good while it lasted, but even the good things have ending. So, you see, Mr Commissioner, I was out doing your police work; it's only right and proper that you feed me."

The commissioner looked at him, but with a stern face.

"Well, I do hope you find someone soon to feed you. I can't afford to."

Over dinner, the conversation continued. The commissioner couldn't get over the casual attitude the lieutenant took regarding his divorcee.

"Dick, you never cease to amaze me. Four years of marriage and you see that as a long time?"

"A very long time, and I'll let you in on a small secret; she couldn't bear children."

"That's unfortunate, but I hope you didn't leave her because of that."

"I love children, and I'll say no more about it."

"So, what about the meeting with the home secretary, how did that go?"

"That man, Dick! At times he irritates me so much I could punch him in the kissers."

"Oh no, you mustn't do that; that wouldn't do. You would be on the first plane back to England. Anyway, you said he was the wrong man for the job, you shouldn't let him get to you."

"He hasn't got to me, but you have to have both tolerance and patience to deals with that man."

"You know, Noel, there's a proverb, 'do unto others as they would do to you', only you do it first."

"Dick, you should be a diplomat. Sometimes I'm slow to react, but only because I try to be even-handed, but thanks for your concern; it shows you care."

"Well, don't you go telling anyone that."

The conversation turned to Harry Wells. The commissioner wanted to see if they can come up with any plan to catch him.

"About Harry, we are no more the wiser about him then anytime time before. We know he's the boss for more than one gangs, but how many, we don't know. We don't know he's also blamed for most of the killings, but I don't see how or why."

"I can't either, unless he controls all the gangs. Then, there's the cartel. They're killing people too, but hardly ever blamed."

"Listen, you said we could do with a little help from the locals, but we're not going to get it, why, we're too damn soft. We should be leaning on them a little, isn't that what you guys do back in England?"

"No, we don't. Whatever gives you that idea? you must be watching too many crime movies. If you mean going around using the law to rough people up, that's never going to happen."

"That's the problem with you, man. Too damn nice. Anyway, it was only a suggestion; I know you wouldn't have the stomach for it."

"I have the stomach, but you've lost sight of who we're: the good guys, that's us."

"Listen, nice guy doesn't get things done, not with these people. At times, to get result, one has to act tough. If you even have to pretend, you can pretend, can't you, man?"

"I think if you were a policeman, you would be a nasty piece of work."

"Listen, we're going to get Harry; but without leaning on anyone, so put that thought right out of your head."

The lieutenant mumbled something. He's not happy with the commissioner's ways of doing things, but there'll be no dissent.

"Did you say something, Dick?"

"No, man, I swallow too quickly; the food went to the wrong throat."

"Well, you shouldn't eat while talking, bad habit."

"Don't talk to me then, let me eat in peace."

"How can I? I want to tell you about a chat I had with one Officer Daniel; don't talk, just listen."

"Who the hell is he?" The commissioner had a lengthy pause looking at the lieutenant, as to say, *I told you not to talk.*

"He's the fellow that brought you the message."

"Oh him, what about him?"

"Do you know this officer, Dick?"

"Not really; he's just someone I saw around from time to time."

"Well, he promised to keep his ears peeled, and if he heard or saw anything, he'll tell me."

"Do you think he will?"

"Doesn't matter what I think, I've got nothing to lose, he said he will. He also talked about a store down town, we should keep a close watch on."

"He said that too?"

"No, what he said was, he saw Harry with three men. They walked in and collect a parcel, now, what do you think was in that parcel?"

"It wouldn't be clothes, you can bet on that, and it certainly doesn't take three men to collect one parcel; more than likely cocaine."

"But I thought Harry was only into marijuana, so now he's in cocaine too?"

"We're assuming it was cocaine, Dick, but it could be something else."

"Like what? It's either cocaine or Ganja, and there's no need to parcel up Ganja."

"So, what's your intention, are you going to talk with the store owner?"

"We've got to do something, but we must think how to approach it. We don't want to tangle with the cartel."

"You could stake out the place, see who comes to do that sort of business, but it could be a dangerous undertaking if we were to arrest someone and it turns out be the cartel."

"Quite so, and the way Daniel said they entered the store and did their business, it could well be."

"OK, we'll do a stake out; but only to see if Harry revisits."

"I can't argue with that. If you can't win a fight, why start it?"

"The other matter is Deputy Holmes; this information you got regarding Harry; do you think we could use it to convene a meeting?"

"As I said, I checked it out, but he didn't show; probably, the info wasn't genuine, I think we should wait." It was agreed upon.

Chapter 11
The Execution

Today's Wednesday. Tomorrow two men are to be executed. They'd been on death row for over a year, waiting on a decision from the privy council. Their hope for a reprieve was denied. Tomorrow at 11 AM they'll be hanged. An execution is like a fanfare; activities outside the prison will be at fever pitch. People will be doing business, making money out of these men's demise. But for the men to hand, the authority must find an executioner, and it won't be easy. The money is good, but it's a dangerous undertaking. The last two suffered an ill fate; one was hacked to death, and the other was maimed; he died from his wound. But in a country where it's hard to make a living, there's always someone to risk it for the money. The sun was out and the breeze was gentle; one could say it's a good day for a hanging. The people gathered, but they won't be seeing the hanging. They were doing business of all sort, some enjoying the razzmatazz, some were praying for the souls of the condemned. There're those who consider these people's actions barbaric or immoral, but it's their way of life, a tradition handed down.

The time is getting close; and there's no hangman in place. If it's gone a minute pass the appropriate time, these men cannot be hanged. Home Secretary Walker came up with a plan. If they find a man who is willing to risk it, they would dress him in disguise and bring him in. But they have to be wary of those inside too; no one can be trusted. It wasn't too difficult to find a man, once he was told of the plans and the money on offer. A man was found, but they have to move fast, time was running out. People outside and all around the country got their eyes on the clocks; they don't want to miss that vital moment. Outside the prison, Lieutenant Dickson and his men were on duty; it wasn't unusual for a group of desperados to do something to disrupt proceedings. However, nothing was going to stop this hanging; the place was like a fortress. Inside the prison, everything was ready, all eyes are on the clock.

Outside, however, there were rumours. It was said the men granted a last-minute reprieve. The rumour spreads fast and people were jumping for joy. One could ask why? They're the same people doing business, enjoying themselves, waiting to hear the bell toll. They had no mercy or showed no sympathy, so why are they jumping for joy? It boggled beliefs. They wait to see the men walk free, but they were in for a surprise; the bell began to toll; it signalled the execution was over; the men hung. Outside there was pandemonium, the crowd was stirred crazy.

"They hung these innocent men," some shouted. "Murderers!" shout coming from others; they were less than civil with their comments.

But it's all over, justice in these parts was never always as it should; the dead men could be innocent. *The Gleaner* ran an article regarding the hanging, and the legality of it. They were doing just that before the final verdict, and they'll continue for some time. But who are they to tell of the men's innocence? They could well be, but at times, the good has to suffer for the bad.

The commissioner turns up, he wants to talk with the lieutenant, but his talk was interrupted by one of his officers; he brought news.

"There is a sighting of Harry in his hometown; he is visiting his mother's grave, and this wasn't the first time," reported the officer.

"How do you know that, officer?"

"The man that brought the news told me, sir; he's from the district."

"This man, where did you meet him?"

"In the market. He came up from the country to sell his stuff."

"I see, thank you, officer; I'll look into it, and officer, any further news of Harry, do let me know."

"Sure thing, sir, you'll hear."

Soon, he raised the matter with the lieutenant; anything about Harry was treated as urgent.

"What do you think, Dick? You think Harry would visit his mother's grave?"

"Quite possible. There're no police there, and the locals aren't going to bother him; they're probably glad to see him."

"Should we go after him?"

"I don't think so. It's only a visit. By the time we organise a party to get there, he'll be long gone."

The commissioner agreed. They're not going after him, not this time.

"You know, Dick, I've seen barefaced killers, and barefaced convicts, but this fellow takes the biscuit. When we catch him, I'll probably shake his hand."

"Only because you tend to believe all the myths the locals brandish around."

"Listen, man, Harry is just like any other man; cut him, he bleeds. Don't go making him out to be something he isn't."

"Come on, Dick, you must admit, some of these stories are fascinating, even if it's not true."

"No, I do not. What's the matter with you? It seems as though you want to join the Harry Wells fan club. You've begun to worry me, you know that?"

Business at the prison is over, and the crowd drift away, the soldiers apart from those on guard duty gone back to barracks. The lieutenant went with the commissioner to his hotel, whatever else they have to discuss will be done there.

The Hang Man Is Murdered

Later that evening it began to rain lightly and it continued. In town, the night was hot. The heats from the asphalt raised the temperature. The hangman is going home. He leaves it this late hoping there'll be fewer people about. Thinking his identity wasn't known, he sets off home. It was just after mid night; the alarm was raised; a man was found dead on Fenton Street. No one was concerned; they're accustomed to these killings. It's a miserable night, so the police leave their investigation till morning. He was found lying face down in the sidewalk; knife through the throat and his night earning gone. Where he lay was stained with blood, running down the water table. When his identity was known, some walking by took one look and spat on the body. That's the kind of treatment they dished out to anyone who took on the job of a hangman. The investigation was over as quickly as it had started. Well, no one is going to point the finger, even if they knew the killer.

"You know, Dick, this is not good. A man does a job and gets killed for doing it; it is so wrong."

"Maybe, but that's how it is here. He knew the risk; he just couldn't turn his back on the money, greed you might say."

"So, what are you saying, you agreed with it?"

"It doesn't matter what I think; that's how it is. He's not the first, and he won't be the last."

"As I said, Dick, you never cease to amaze me."

The morning after, the day was gorgeous; the cool breeze blew gently; people from all corners of the country came to town, bringing their produce to market. Some travelled long hours to get here. Here, they get the best price for their produce. The streets are congested, it always is, and that when the pickpockets do their business. If you're smart, any money you're carrying should be somewhere secure, like in your shoes or on your person, but never in your pockets or handbags. The spot where the hangman was killed is still stained with blood, and probably will be there for a while. It will serve as a reminder to those who want the job as a hangman, they could suffer the same fate.

Chapter 12
The Surprise

Monday noon, the commissioner arrived at the home office for his weekly meeting. When he walked in, the welcome was somewhat exuberant; the minister was in a jovial mood.

"Pull up a chair, commissioner, and take to load off," he said looking bright eyed and bushy tailed. *Whatever has come over the man?* the commissioner wondered. He took a look around in a sarcastic manner, as though to see if anyone else was there.

"Now then, commissioner, what can I get you to drink? And don't say a cup of tea, that I haven't got."

"That's a shame; I could do with a cuppa."

But even though it was a flippant comment, the commissioner could really do with a cuppa. Back in England, whenever the weather is hot, that's exactly what he would be having. He wasn't sure the minister understands he was just being facetious, so he asked.

"Have you ever had tea this time a day, minister?"

"Good lord, no. I never touch the stuff, but why do you ask?"

"No particular reason, call it curiosity."

"So, what can I pour you?" he asked, looking awfully pleased with himself. The commissioner was still at a lost. He'd never seen him in this mood before.

"Well, I'll have whatever you are having, or recommend something."

"Well now, if you're sure you want to take a chance on what I'm having, then you're most welcome."

I hope he's not talking about some sort of a homemade brew, thought the commissioner. But the home secretary was only fooling. He knew what the commissioner liked. He's got word; he's partial to Captain Morgan, so he's got a bottle prepared.

"I'm having Captain Morgan, how about you?"

"That will do nicely, minister."

"Do you take it neat, or on the rocks?"

He didn't respond. He was thinking. Could this be the same man with whom he couldn't get an agreeable word pass between them? He was flabbergasted as he was pleased, but could there be an ulterior motive.

"Oh, I'll have it neat, minister. How do you take yours?" he asked for no particular reason.

"Oh, I take mine neat too, but when the weather is hot, it's best taken on the rocks."

There was time for small talk, and even though the commissioner can hold his liquor, he had only two, and for the first time in their encounter, there was a friendly aura. On principle, he wouldn't be drinking the man's liquor, but the minister showing willingness to change; he thinks he would be lacking if he didn't comply. Sometime later, however, he was to discover the minister was acting under orders. A few days earlier, he'd met with the PM. It appears word had gotten out about his unwillingness to co-operate. The PM probably had words with him, hence the change of attitude. Now they begin what is a sham relationship, trying to get along, but this will later blossom into a genuine friendship.

The social was over. Now they were talking Deputy Commissioner Holmes, but the minister found it difficult to believe he would align himself with Harry and his gang. The commissioner reminded him of his predecessor, Mr Burns; the Government thought was true to the cause. After that example, the minister seemed to have second thoughts.

"I seem to have my head in the sand," commissioner. "I stand corrected."

Playing the leading role, the commissioner wanted a consensual agreement to carry out his operations according to how he saw fit. The prime minister actually said so, but he's not going to remind him. It was so agreed, they shook hands and parted company.

Meeting the PM

It was Friday and the birds were out in numbers, birds of different species, but the noise of the city blotted out their tweets. Nothing unusual was happening, but the city was buzzing, the boys with their foot carts were out looking for a business. Those who're browsing were mostly from the country. There are no tourists; they stayed away on account of the violence, and that's where the locals lose out. On a day like today, they would be busy helping foreigners and earning a living.

2 PM, they arrived for their meeting with the PM. Miss Green shows them in.

"Make yourselves comfortable, gentlemen; the prime minister will be with you shortly."

It wasn't long after the PM walked in, followed by Adviser Hunt.

"Good day, gentlemen, good to see you, commissioner," he said as he walked in. But the same compliment wasn't paid to the home secretary; probably there's no need, they're parliamentary colleagues. The meeting convenes, and sitting next to the prime minister was Miss Green. When he asked about Harry Wells, the home secretary jumped in. The question wasn't asked directly of him but he tried to explain. A question he should have left for the commissioner, but probably wanted to show his worth.

The commissioner took a wary glance in his direction; *the man is digging himself a hole*, he thought. The prime minister feels he was babbling; but might have decided not to be too hard on him.

"Dave (his first name), I need to see result. The country is waiting for results; hearing you're doing your best gets us nowhere."

His comments might sound as though the onus was on the minister to produce result. But he was running out of patience; his government was looking as though they cannot handle the situation, while the gunmen continued to run rampant.

"Tell me, commissioner, is there any progress in regard to catching Harry Wells?"

"Honestly, prime minister, no, but probably if we didn't have a 'snitch' among us, things might be different."

Adviser Hunt sat up straight. He took note of the commissioner's comment and he asked. "A 'snitch', commissioner? Who is he?"

"Oh, I'm sorry, gentlemen. Pardon the expression. Back in England, it's an idiom we use for an informer."

"One of your British street slangs I take it, commissioner?"

"You could say that, prime minister, but there are people like that among us."

The prime minister looked surprised; it probably never crossed his mind.

"Are you sure, commissioner?"

"Most certainly, only we don't know who. Whatever our plans regarding Harry, he's always one step ahead of us; someone is telling him our business."

"Have you anyone in mind?"

"Yes, there's one particular person. We've got our eyes on him."

"Anyone, you care to mention."

"Deputy Holmes, and we'll be having a meeting with him soon."

"What do you think about that, Dave? Have you got any notion regarding it?"

"It's like the commissioner said, there's someone passing on information, and it could be the Deputy Holmes, but it's only a suspicion."

"Well, gentlemen, what are you going to do about it? You're never going to succeed if there are spies among you."

"Commissioner, do what you have to, but find this person, and I like to know when you do."

"Prime minister, I promise you this, whoever it is, we'll find him. You have my word."

After some searching questions, the meeting drew to a close. It was a good meeting; there was a general consensus as to what needed to be done.

The commissioner and the minister didn't part company; he and the minister left for the home office. They wanted to discuss a curfew before putting it to the PM. It was a warm day; so Miss Benson brought them a cold drink before they got down to business. The minister was concerned about the inconvenience to the public, but he's not going to dwell on it.

"Commissioner, if the curfew is the only way to stop the gun men entering the city, then so be it."

"The traders won't be pleased, and they might even be abusive, but it's got to be done."

He was now fully in accord with whatever the commissioner's plan was.

"If there's a curfew, I think we should begin at 6 pm. That should be ample time for people to gather whatever they need and be off the street."

"That seems feasible, commissioner, but how do you plan to enforce it?"

"Men and guns, there's no other way; only we'll be using mostly soldiers."

"If you think that's best, commissioner, then you go right ahead."

"When are you going to speak with the PM about this matter?"

"Soon, commissioner, it shouldn't be left on the table. It should be given priority, and I suspect it has to be put to Parliament."

The commissioner began to think he's not such a bad fellow. Maybe he should cut him some slacks. After all, he was thrown in the deep end, on account of disgraced Commissioner Burns. He was feeling somewhat upbeat; their bad relationship now seems to be a thing of the past. Now, he believes he can tolerate the minister regardless of his shortcomings. The meeting concluded, he must dash off for his meeting with the lieutenant and Deputy Holmes.

At the Office

The men were waiting. "Gentlemen, I'm sorry, we'll have to do this another time. The delay was beyond my control."

"When do you suggest, commissioner?" the deputy asked.

"How about the day after tomorrow. Can you make it?"

"I don't see why not."

"Then Friday it is; we'll meet here at 2 pm, prompt."

He was laying it on thick for the benefit of the deputy; the meeting was about him, but he mustn't suspect anything untoward.

"Gentlemen, we all have a home to go to; I suggest we call it a day."

The lieutenant smiled while brushing his pants legs, but said nothing.

"Lieutenant, I would like a word. Would you walk with me?"

"Sure thing, commissioner." They walked to his car.

"Tell me, Dick, back in there, did I say something funny?"

"Why do you ask?"

"I saw your smile. Why did you?"

"Oh that, well, you did say something funny."

"Like what?"

"We have homes to go to, but you're going to a hotel. When are you going to find a proper place to live, man?"

"Let's not talk about now. I want to talk about something the minister and I discussed earlier. Things are going to be shaken up around here if Parliament agrees."

"What do you mean shaken up around here? Have you been drinking?"

"No, I wasn't; later on, perhaps."

"Ok, man, go ahead. I'm all ears."

"The minister and I have agreed that there should be a curfew here in the capital, and soon."

"That's a brilliant idea. Whose thinking was it?"

"Who do you think, the home secretary? I'll tell you something else. I don't think he's up to the job. I hate to say, but it's true."

"He's got no idea about anything, but hey, who am I to criticise? I'm only an outsider. I was imported here for this job, not to criticise the man who's my boss."

The lieutenant didn't like that kind of talk, and he's going to tell him so.

"Well now, if that's your attitude, you might as well call it a day, pack your bag and return home. It's a long way to come to do a job and doing it with mixed feelings. When you begin to refer to yourself as an outsider, it's difficult for me to work with you and believe in you."

He didn't respond for a while, probably thinking of the lieutenant's reprimand.

"Like I said, Dick, you never cease to surprise me. You've straightened me out in no uncertain terms, and you know what, I thank you for it."

"At times one needs to be reminded of what matters."

"All I'm saying, man, you should be doing the job because you want to, and have the conviction to do it to the best of your ability. Regarding the home secretary, if you feel there are reasons for criticism, you should feel free the right to do so."

"I take on board your comments, Dick; it makes me feel quite humbled."

There was no malice at the end of this conversation; this friendship was forged out of platinum. Nothing was going to weaken it, not even a reprimand.

"So, you have no confidence in the home secretary, right? And you clearly think he's not up to the task."

"That's what I said; however, considering he's only in the job a short time; maybe we I should cut him some slack."

"No, I don't see it that way; I think you should have a quiet word with the PM, tell him of the minister's shortcomings, but tactfully."

"What!" he exclaimed alarmingly. "Now you're talking out of your backside. How the hell could I do that? It would be like stabbing the man in the back."

"There is a lot in what you said, but moods to the prime minister, that my friend, is never going to happen." He shrugged his shoulders as though he swallowed something with a funny taste.

"Ouch, the very thought of it makes me cringe."

"OK, man, it was just a thought; don't get all righteous on me."

"I must tell you though, lately his attitude has changed; last week we shared glasses of the 'Captain'."

"Oh! So, you're friends now?"

"I wouldn't go that far, Dick, but it seems as though he wanted a friendly working relationship, and I'm all for that. Who knows? He might grow in the job."

He groans; he treats the commissioner's comment with scepticism.

"Well, I never! You sharing the captain with the minister, and all along I thought you weren't getting on."

"You're not disappointed, are you, Dick?"

"Not at all. Only now I'm not sure if I should believe all you tell me about the minister."

"Don't make it sound so dramatic, Dick. The minister's trying to mend bridges. Now, where were we? Oh yes, the curfew, but it will have to get the approval of Parliament, and I hope it won't take long."

"If Parliament refuses, what then?"

"Then we'll have to think of some alternatives, but let's not get ahead of ourselves."

It's running late. What was supposed to be an informal chat, turned out to be quite a discussion.

"If you're not going back to barracks, Dick, have dinner with me; I hate eating alone."

"Noel, are you married?"

"Yes, why do you ask?"

"Well now, you're a long way from home, and without the wife; you should get fixed up. There are lots of beautiful females around here, you can have your pick."

"But I'm a white man, and married; black girls don't go for men like me."

"Tell me, Noel, is there another type of white men?" he asked flippantly.

"You know what I mean, Dick."

"No, I don't. I thought you were a man of the world. My dear fellow, I don't know if you noticed, the women here are of many colours: black, white, brown, and the in-between. At—"

"The in-between, Dick?" he interrupted, "who the hell are they?"

"Multi-coloured women. They're a shade different, but just as beautiful. You could pull any of these beauties; probably faster than I can."

"You really think so?"

"Sure, why don't you give it a try?"

"One day, perhaps, but as of now, I'm far too busy."

"Listen, man, come Saturday evenings; there're more people in this hotel than on the street. I'll accompany you. I certainly could do with filly myself."

"OK, Dick, Saturday it is, and I'll help you find a filly."

He looked at him with a great big smile.

"You'll help me pull a broad? That'll be the day." There was laughter.

"Now listen, Dick, I didn't come here to be taught bad habits. I have a wife and a boy. I'm a family man, and I'd like to keep it that way."

"Are you saying having a bit on the side is bad habit? Listen, every married man should have one; it keeps the relationship in door from going stale."

"That maybe so, but I might start something I can't or find hard to finish. Saturday night, however, we'll have a look in; but not because you said so."

Chapter 13
Dead Man in Store

During dinner, there was a news flash, there was a fatal shooting in a store downtown. Not everyone will get this news; not everyone has a radio. However, most will be reading about it in *The Gleaner*. Dinner was cut short; they left immediately for the store. Arriving on the scene, there were two dead bodies lying by the counter, and there was blood all over the floor. Mr Hersham, the store owner, sat looking a little pensive.

"Mr Hashem, can you tell me what happened here?" asked the commissioner.

He took a deep breath before he got to his feet, but wasn't showing concern like he should. "I sure can, commissioner, those two lying there," he said pointing. "They were browsing, then three men entered shortly after, and without a word said, they shot them. They were shot over there but dragged themselves across the floor to where they lay."

"These men, have you seen them before, and did they say anything to you or the any of the store workers?"

"No, not a word to anyone. They just did what they did, and left. I never seen them before, but I saw these two; they been in here a few times."

The commissioner knew he was lying. He'd seen the dead men before, but not the shooters. Of course, dead men can't talk. He took out his note book knowing whatever he written won't be the truth.

"Now, tell me what the killers looked like. You can do that, Mr Hasham, can't you?"

"I can't, commissioner. It happened so fast; I didn't see their faces."

"Really, Mr Hasham, then what did you see?"

"Well, one was tall and big built, the other was of medium height and stocky."

The lieutenant observed keenly; he too knew this man was lying, and he didn't seem bothered.

"Mr Hasham, five men entered your store, two were shot, killed by the other three, and you, sir, you can only recognise the dead men. It's quite a story, wouldn't you say?"

"Well, Lieutenant, I can only say what I saw."

"Do you expect us to believe that, Mr Harris?"

"Well, commissioner, I could tell you something different, but that wouldn't be the truth now, would it?"

It was plain to see this man had an attitude; it's almost certain he's in with whatever crime were committed there.

The commissioner had a thought. Last week he was told of a parcel being collected from a store, and tonight, two men were killed in another store. *Is there a connection?* Could be, but there's nothing they can do about it.

Later, he was having restless thoughts. The killing was bothering him. He shouldn't be walking away from these crimes; no one should be above the law. Knowing he can't fight the cartel; he was feeling somewhat helpless. Nevertheless, tomorrow, he's going to investigate the store where the package was collected. After breakfast the next morning, he sets off to the store downtown. While talking with a member of the store, there was one of his officers he recognised, but he didn't know his name. He was in plain clothes standing at the counter talking with one of the sale personnel, a young woman. They recognised each other, but neither man spoke. Whatever their conversation was about, he wasn't looking too pleased. He left shortly after, but he didn't leave the vicinity; he waited outside for the commissioner. The investigation turned up nothing, but that wasn't a surprise. As he exited the store, the officer called.

"Commissioner, can I speak with you, sir?"

"Sure, mister, but who are you?"

"You might not recognise me, sir, but I'm one of your officers."

"Are you?" he asked in pretence.

"Yes, sir, my name's Barry; Barry Hilton."

"Okay, Barry, what do you want with me?"

"I've got some information which I think you should know, sir."

"Oh, I saw you in the store, were you buying something?"

"No, sir, I was making investigation."

"Investigating?" he asked, surprised.

He didn't expect any of his officers to be doing any such thing, but if this fellow is speaking the truth, it's good to hear.

"Yes, sir, and what I can tell you, I heard of where Harry is, but for how long I don't know."

The commissioner though about it. If he didn't run into this fellow, would he be telling him? Still, it's good to see an officer taking the interest.

"Is that what the young woman tells you?"

"No, sir, she was telling me about something else."

"Like what, or is that a secret?"

He didn't respond. He took two steps forward to peep in the store, it's as though to see if the young woman or someone else was watching.

"It's about the men who are bringing in the cocaine, sir. It's not the same person all the time."

"Did she tell you that?"

"Yes, sir, but she told me in confidence."

"Then, tell me, Barry, why did she tell you. Did you ask her about it?"

"No, sir, but the men coming in the store, two of them killed her father, but they know she's his daughter."

"Did she give you a name?"

"No, sir, and she said the men never spoke. They just collected the stuff and went."

The commissioner wasn't unduly bothered about this piece of information; he heard but couldn't do a thing about it.

"OK, Barry, tell me what you heard about Harry."

"He's hold up in Green Bay, and there're men on the lookout."

That's no surprised. The man's no fool. Wherever he holds up, he's always going to have men on guard.

"Tell me, Barry, do you believe he's there now?"

"I really don't know, sir, but he visited there before. There's a bar there he seems to like."

"A bar, Barry? What bar is that?"

"Arum's Rum Bar, sir. They always drink there, and there're quite a few people usually there whenever he visits."

They're there for the freebies, the commissioner thought.

"Have you ever been there, Barry, the Arum Bar?"

"Oh yes, sir. I am from Bridges Head. I always go back whenever I'm on leave."

"I thought you said he's held up in Green Bay?"

"So I did, sir. Green Bay is in the parish of Bridge Head."

"I see," he exclaimed.

Of course, he can be forgiven for his ignorance; he's not too knowledgeable about the geography of the country.

He's thinking of Harry and his men at the rum bar; getting liquored up; it could be a good time to attack.

"OK, Barry, whenever you get news like this, I would like to hear of it. Would you come and talk it over with me?"

"Sure thing, commissioner. I can do that."

"But whatever you hear, keep it strictly between us."

"Of course, sir. I know that." They shook hands.

He would like to keep these officers on his side, even though he can't be sure of their loyalties. He had a similar conversation with a fellow officer before, trying to gain his trust.

It was later that evening when he met up with Lieutenant Dickson for a talk, agenda: Harry Wells, public enemy number one. They settled down in one of the army barracks. "Dick, I heard news of Harry's whereabouts."

"Oh, who from? A reliable source?"

"I'm not sure, but from the way I was told, I would like to think so. I went to question the store owner, one Mr Parkinson. One of my officers was there talking to a sales girl. He left as soon as I walked in. I thought he had left, but he was waiting for me outside. Then he told me about what is likely the cartel's operation, and about Harry."

"You say this Barry is one of your officers? How well do you know him?"

"Not too well, but I remember seeing him in uniform. I would like to follow up on his story, so here's the plan."

He took a sheet of paper from his briefcase; it was the geography of the island. He laid it out on the wooden table.

"This is where Harry is held up," he said, pointing his pencil.

"Green Bay?" said the lieutenant, "that's in Bridge Head."

"You know this place, Dick?"

"Oh yes, I know it well; nice little town. I spent some time there."

"Oh good, then you can fill me in."

"It's like any other country town. It's got a few rum bars; only this one is a bit special. It's called the…" He paused; the name eluded him. He clicked his fingers. "Oh, Arum's Bar."

"So why is it so special?" asked the commissioner.

"Well, it's a little more than special; it's famous."

He paused to reach in his pocket for the spearmint; he's never been without.

"Well, a long time ago, a famous VIP from England, along with his good lady, drank there; they were the Arum, hence the name."

The commissioner seemed to be thinking; he couldn't figure out the name.

"These Arums, do you know anything about them?"

"No, all I can tell you is that they were of the nobility."

The commissioner sighed. If they're nobles, he should know something about then, even the name.

"I'm intrigued; I would like to know this rum bar. Harry drank several times there, Barry says."

"It's nothing special to look at; you see one rum bar, you see the lot, except the drinks are more expensive than the average bar. Only those flush with cash can afford to drink there. Likewise, if you're classified as down and out, you wouldn't be allowed near the place."

"So, what are you saying? Only the privilege and better off are allowed to drink there?"

"Something like that."

"You know, Dick, there's a word for that sort of behaviour, a very nasty word. It's call discrimination."

"Oh, come on, man! One has to draw the line somewhere."

"Well now, how did I know that would be your way of thinking?"

"I have no idea, but I discovered this about you. You're far too damn liberal-minded. There're those who sweep the streets, and those who sit behind desks; there's a line that's not to be crossed. That's the way of the world."

"You think so, Dick? I suppose in your book it's every man for himself, but what about compassion? Help those who can't help themselves?"

"What the hell are you trying to do, man, convert me? Well, don't bother. I like me the way I am."

"You read the Bible, don't you, Dick? It says you should be merciful to others, give bread to the needy."

"I read the Bible. I was brought up on the book, but that doesn't say I believed all that's in it."

"Then why waste time reading it; you could be reading something else? Something you'd find more to your way of thinking."

"Look around, man. The people here are churchgoers; my parents were the same. My brothers and sisters, we were church goers. We read the Bible every night before bedtime, whether we liked it or not; does that answer your question?"

"I suppose, and I take it you don't bother reading it now?"

"Get down off your soapbox, man. Don't bother to try preaching your liberal doctrine to me. I'm beyond converting; let's concentrate on catching criminals."

"You behave as though you're heartless, Dick, but I know you're not. But as you say, let's put our attention to catching criminals."

The Plan

"I think we should get there around about 9 pm," said the lieutenant. "That's the height of drinking hours. Everyone should be having a good time. With luck, we might catch them all liquored up and off guard."

"It probably won't do any good, though. Barry said the bar is always packed with freeloaders, and he's got men posted outside."

The lieutenant mumbled something while reaching for the map.

"Let me see that map." He took it and gave it some attentions.

"We could stop a little way off, about here," he said pointing. "Then send two men ahead in plain clothes to check out the guards. If they're on duty, we'll take them out using silencers."

"Sounds good, Dick, except for one thing, we've got no silencers."

"Well, there's another way: send in two men; two who are good with knives, they—"

"Stop right there," interrupted the commissioner. "I don't like where you're going with that. Soldiers with knives? Let me remind you, we're not fighting a war. Sending in men with knives? Who do you think we're, the Gurkhas?"

"You have a better idea, man? If you do, let's hear it."

"Well, let's see now. We'll send in two men as planned. If they spot the look out, they'll report back to their position."

"Then what?" asked the lieutenant.

"Well, they won't be brandishing weapons. It will be hidden close by; they won't be expecting an attack, but that's what we'll do."

The lieutenant smiled; he thinks the plan is the same as he suggested.

"Listen, man, these men are soldier, let's do this the army's way. We'll do as you said, but with knives."

"On the other hand, we could approach and ask them nicely to hand over their weapons."

"Don't be ridiculous, Dick. You know exactly what I mean. The soldiers are trained in arm-to-arm combat, aren't they?"

"Oh, yes, and they can take them alright, but there's going to be a fight, and then the game's up. Of course, if your intention is to take them prisoners; that's different, but I must remind you, taking prisoners only clogs up the operation."

The commissioner knew the lieutenant was right. This was not a mission to take prisoners, and if they're to succeed, they must kill them all.

"Okay, Dick, we'll do it your way, but only because there're no alternatives."

"That's fine with me, man, but it won't be easy to spot the gunmen with people about, unless they're brandishing weapons."

"Somehow, I don't think they will," said the commissioner. "However, I don't want the men to concentrate too much on the drones, unless they have to. We want Harry; he's priority."

"Do the men know that?" asked the lieutenant.

"Not yet. They will when I brief them."

"Now then, you knew the area well, which is the most secretive route to get to the bar?"

Using his staff, the Lieutenant pointed out the route he thought was best.

"Good then, you will take five men from Round Tree Hill; my men and I will come up the main street. We're trying to cover all angles, makes it harder for anyone to escape."

The plan was to take ten men, police and soldiers, but the Lieutenant thought it's not enough.

"I hope it's enough; we don't want it to look as though we're fighting a war, the home secretary's words, and I agree."

"I wouldn't bother about him; he's not out here risking anything."

"I don't like that kind of talk, Dick, let's hear no more of it."

"Okay, so when are we leaving?"

"We should leave in time to be there at nine. How long you think it will take to get there?"

"About 50 minutes, allowing for the bad road."

"Okay, we'll brief the men, say 30 minutes before leaving, and no one leave the premises. We won't meet again until tomorrow evening; have five of soldiers await me at the barracks, 6:30 pm sharp. I'll have five officers with me."

They were about to part company when the commissioner remembered something.

"Oh, Dick, about our boys' night out. I'm sorry, mate, we won't be going."

"I was so looking forward to it. Any reason why we're not?"

"Well, this mission, once we embark on it, no telling how long it'll take. But don't worry, there'll be another time. Good night."

He would like to talk with the minister, let him know what he's up to, but there's no time, so he called him on the phone, but in the morning.

Friday morning, he called the minister and briefed him on the operation; they're in accord.

"Good hunting, commissioner, bring back Harry, dead or alive."

"Thank you, minister, our plans are to do just that."

That's the positive response he liked to hear from the minister, and was feeling the better for it. Now regarding the minister, he began to have remorse about the things he said to the lieutenant.

As he was leaving, Deputy Holmes walked in; and was looking none too pleased.

"Is there anything I should know, commissioner?" he asked as though he believed the commissioner was holding out on him, and of course he was.

"No, I don't think so, Mr Holmes, but why do you ask?"

"I hope you're not keeping anything from me. I'm your deputy. I should know what you know."

"Mr Holmes! If something is bothering you, do share it with me," he said deviously.

"There's nothing to share, except all this nonsense about Harry Wells."

"How do you know it is all nonsense? Do you know better than the rumours?"

"No, but I know there're people going around spreading rumours, but that's all it is, rumours."

"You sound quite sure; I must remind you of your civic duty; it's to share whatever information you have regarding these gunmen with me."

"Of course, I know that, but I don't hear anything."

"Okay, Mr Holmes, I believe you, and no, you're not being kept in the dark."

He was about to leave.

"Oh, Mr Holmes, soon we'll be having that meeting; I'll let you know when."

"May I ask what this meeting is all about?"

"Recruitment; Mr Holmes, we need men to reshape the constabulary; and you're part of it."

"Okay, commissioner, whenever you say, I'm ready."

"Thank you, Mr Holmes. I'll let you know."

After this conversation, it strengthened his belief. This fellow was an informer.

Of course, there was a meeting with him pending, but it was certainly not about recruitment. It was about him, but he didn't know that.

He probably knew about the mission, and if he was the mole, the commissioner was hoping it will be too late for him to contact Harry. He went to the barracks to find Albert; he's got a job for him. He briefed him on what he must do while he's away, *don't let Holmes out of his sight.*

The lieutenant joined him, even though they weren't to meet until late that evening. He told the lieutenant about his encounter with the deputy.

"Dick, his attitude was more than suspicious. The sooner we get him in for interrogation; the better. Until then, he's to be watched."

"Then, if he's the informer, it's a good chance Harry won't be at the location when we get there."

"I thought about that, but things being what they are, we'll proceed with the mission."

Chapter 14
The Mission

They spent most of the evening at the office discussing the mission. It was nearly 7 pm when they parted company to meet again at 6 30 pm the next day.

The following day, they met as planned. He briefed the men, telling them what was expected of them.

"Look out for Harry. The moment you see him, alert the nearest man to you. Stay alert, and remember, don't get careless."

This little pep talk he hoped would keep the men on their toes. In less than half an hour, they'll be off, but no sooner Deputy Holmes showed up, he found out about the mission that he wasn't told about. He was very angry; he now realised the commissioner was keeping thing from him.

"Are you all right, Mr Holmes?" asked the commissioner, deviously.

"No, I'm not," he answered abruptly. "Why are you hiding what's going on from me? I'm your deputy, why wasn't I told of this gathering? You told me yesterday nothing is kept from me, and here you are planning a mission."

"It was a late decision, Mr Holmes, I wasn't sure it was going ahead. Anyway, I want you here to be in charge while I'm away."

"That is no excuse; I should be told, so, who are you going after now? Harry Wells?"

"If I say yes, Mr Holmes, do you think it's right? We're going after him, or you have objection?"

"I'm saying nothing of the kind. What I'm saying is that I should be told about this or any other mission."

"Okay, Mr Holmes, you've got a point; we'll talk about it when I get back."

The commissioner didn't want an argument. Time wasn't on his side, and he didn't want the deputy to have any preconceive opinion about their pending meeting. He was livid, but there won't be any more talk, they were about to set off on the mission.

"Mr Holmes, you're the man till I return, mind the shop."

He didn't respond; he's far too angry. He dashed off probably to do what he was suspected of – inform Harry. The commissioner and the lieutenant conferred; they believed the deputy already knew about their plans; in which case, he probably informed Harry, but there's nothing they can do about that now.

They set off; they should arrive in Green Bay just before 7 pm. They made good time. The little town was buzzing. The one main street was teeming with people. Two men in plain clothes went to check out the bar. Soon, one reported back, the other remained to keep watch.

"Did you see Harry Wells?"

"No, sir, but he could be there. The bar is jam packed, and there's a section I wasn't allow in."

"Did you see the men on lookout?"

"Yes, sir, two of them and they're armed."

"Okay, Lieutenant, send in your best men, and let's do it quietly."

"I'll go myself along with two men. Give us five minutes, then start come along."

"Okay, Lieutenant, but watch yourself."

"Don't worry about me, man. I had a good life."

"Yes, I'm sure you have," said the commissioner with a silly grin.

With so many people about, it wasn't good for their plan. Civilians must avoid getting hurt at all cost. It's was 8:30 pm, and the lieutenant's mission was completed; the men were on the move, coming in from two directions.

The rum bar was in sight; Harry could be among them but there's no way of telling. The hotel that was adjacent to the bar was noted for its restaurant, those who ate at the Silver Button gave it a five-star rating. That is the kind of place Harry hangs out at – the man's got style. It was 9 pm; they circled the area and stood alert. Things were looking good, except for the crowd; he dared not fire, and was hoping the lieutenant was of the same thinking. 9:20 pm, and suddenly the people at the bar started behaving as though something was up. Then suddenly, from his position, one officer opened fire, and others follow, but there was no return of fire. The commissioner was mortified; he was almost in a panic.

"Cease fire, cease fire!" he shouted frantically.

The firing ceased, but he was livid; everything had gone wrong, but why?

"Who the hell ordered you to fire? And who are you firing at?" he asked in a rage.

"No one said fire, sir, but the others started shooting, so I shot too," said one officer.

"Did you hear me give the order to fire, mister, did you?" He was so angry at that moment, there was no telling what he might do.

"I'm not sure, sir."

"You're not sure! What the hell! Don't you know my voice, mister? Did anyone hear me give the order to fire?"

"No, sir, I didn't," said another soldier.

"What about you?" he asked, pointing to one soldier. "Did you hear me give the order?"

"No, sir, I didn't."

"Then why did you start shooting?"

"Rupert, sir, he started firing, so I fired too."

"Rupert? Who the hell is Rupert," he asked furiously.

"I am, sir, but I thought I saw Harry. I was shooting at him."

"From this distant? Mister, you're a bloody liar."

His plans were in totters; he won't say anything further to this officer; he'll be held accountable. Now, he must think fast about his next move.

There was pandemonium at the rum bar, it seemed people were shot; some probably dead. The lieutenant coming in from his position couldn't understand what was happening. He knew something had gone wrong; but knows not what. Meeting up with the commissioner, he asked angrily, "What the hell happened, commissioner? Why did you start shooting?"

"Lieutenant, someone sabotaged the operation."

"What the hell?" He found it hard to explain. But one soldier was angry too.

He asked Rupert, "Why the bloody hell did you start firing?"

"I told you, I thought I saw Harry, so I was shooting at him."

Seeing the commissioner in a fit of rage, the lieutenant took charge.

"Get over here, you, and let's have your weapon."

He then had a whispered conversation with the commissioner, and the officer was placed under arrest. Now the lieutenant suggested they should sneak away without the locals becoming aware of them, but the commissioner wouldn't hear of it.

"No, Lieutenant, that's not the way. We must face up to our responsibility. We must go and see what happened, and explain why."

But who's best to confront this angry mob, the Lieutenant seems the obvious choice.

He found an angry crowd when he arrived at the bar. Those people had no idea as to why or by whom the bar was shot up. There were cries coming from one corner of the bar; outside, a lone woman, she kept repeating, 'they killed him.'

In his army uniform, all eyes were on him. He stood his ground; after all, he's a soldier.

"Folks, you don't know me, but I'm Lieutenant Dickson. What happened here shouldn't have, and I'm so sorry, but please let me explain."

If they were angry before, now they were livid. They were behaving as though they wanted to lynch him. They didn't not even care to hear anything he had to say. What they wanted was revenge. In the confusion, one man asked, "Why are you here and who were you expecting to be here when you shot up the bar?"

The lieutenant thought about it. He was not going to lie, he best come clean.

"We were after Harry Wells and his gang; we heard he was here, but the shooting shouldn't happen, one soldier—"

"You've been fooled," one man interrupted. "Harry was never here," he said angrily. He could be the bar manager. The lieutenant felt he was lying; the gang was there; they killed the guards. They could all be of the Harry Well's fan club, but he was wrong.

The weeping woman was still mourning over the dead man, and nearby was another man's body, but no one seemed bothered about him. This is bad; this is very bad, what can he tell them to calm the situation. But the unexpected was about to happen.

The commissioner decided to put in an appearance, but he had the area staked out as a precaution. When he arrived at the bar, the reception was hostile, as he anticipated. But he's not only a good talker; but a tactician too. He had been in toxic situation before. There were whispering and mumbling; some were talking out loud, but with the lieutenant looked on. He stood his ground.

"Now, listen everybody. I'm here to talk to you, kick me in the pant, spit at me, but do listen."

The there was an uneasy silence, and some turned their backs, others facing him looking mighty angry, but he'd got their attention. He began to explain, and after some tactful and clever talking, they began to pay attention. The lieutenant was now a spectator; he began to feel as though he was the outsider. Calm was restored, and with the lieutenant, he went over what happened.

"The man who did the shooting; he is under arrest, and will be dealt with," he assured them.

For what they heard, they were satisfied; they'll grieve their dead, but in a few days, it will all blow over.

Regarding the people of Green Bay, the Englishman had struck it rich. He talked his way out of another difficult situation and into their confidence. It was a failed mission, but he thought all's not lost. The question was, however, was Harry there? The barman said he wasn't, but that was before the commissioner arrived to gain their trust. One woman of about 35 spoke, and she was very angry.

"He was here all right, walking about like he was God Almighty. How is it taking you lot so long to catch the son of a bitch."

Could it be, she was against the gangs and the killings, but was afraid to speak out? The commissioner thought that could be the case. Yet, for speaking out, she probably signed her own death warrant. But the commissioner was pleased to hear, even though it might not be wise. Now, he and the lieutenant took the opportunity to spend more time talking with them.

"We want to catch him, ma'am, and we will; even though it is proving difficult, so we need the help of everyone. This is your country, don't stand by and watch these killers destroys it. Harry along with his gang; murdered many people, some of whom might be members of your family, and living big at our expense. With your help, ladies and gentlemen, we'll catch him, soon."

He turned to the woman. There were tears in her eyes; her man was just killed.

"Madam, Harry must be hanged, but only if we catch him. I know you folks want to help, but don't put yourselves in danger. I wouldn't want to hear of anyone getting killed."

They appeared to like the way he talked, and what he's saying, and seemed ready to help.

"Now listen, if anyone has news about him and his gang, talk to your local police; they'll talk to me. But be careful whom you talk to. Trust no one; it might save your life."

There was no response, but he thought he shouldn't point that out; however, he left it at that, *quit while you're ahead,* he thought.

The lieutenant thought the woman must be crazy to be shooting off her mouth, but she wasn't the only voice. There's nothing more for them to do here, it's time for them to return to base and face the music. The commissioner thanked them for their cooperation. As they were leaving, someone shouted. "I hope you catch him, commissioner!" It was a man's voice. He looked around but couldn't see who; however, he responded.

"We'll catch him, mister; you can be sure of that."

He raised his hand in acknowledgement as he went. In time, the lieutenant will tell this story about the commissioner, and how he won over a hostile crowd at arums bad.

Chapter 15
Back in the capital

The morning after the night before was a beautiful day. Rupert was in jail awaiting interrogation. At 11 am, commissioner Wade and the Lieutenant met with Home Secretary Walker to talk about the failed mission. When he was told he seemed unsure what to make of it. The talks weren't what they had expected; there was no in depth discussion, not too many questions asked, the home secretary was melancholy about it. But the commissioner wasn't surprised; the minister tried to be nice, but his notion of matters of importance was limited. The meeting ended with nothing fundamental decided. However, that's not the end of the matter, soon they'll meet with the prime minister to give account. In the late edition of *The Gleaner,* the front page carried a caption of three dead men, who attacked the constabulary for wantonly killing civilians. But it seemed they had an axe to grind, instead of supporting the government position, they're giving them a bad press. The PM was angry when he read about it, even though he admitted to the commissioner he's aware of the difficulties regarding his job.

But he and his government were taking a pounding. They were presiding over the most unpopular government ever, and the opposition was running high in the pole. This administration was on a cliff edge, and the PM seemed at a loss.

On Friday noon, the commissioner and his team went to meet the PM; he was expecting fireworks. But to explain the fiasco; he'll bring along the evidence, Officer Rupert. The lieutenant was told, as a precaution, to get two soldiers to bring him. Well, his reputation was at stake, things were not going too well; he needed to prove the cause of the fiasco.

The day had started out sunny, but suddenly became dull and overcast. The sun was trying to break through the clouds, but with the light drizzle and dark shadow, it was a miserable day.

The meeting was about to convene; the prime minister looked aghast when the commissioner and Lieutenant Dickson walked in with a man in handcuffs, shadowed by two soldiers. But the commissioner was quick to explain.

"Prime minister, I must apologise for what must seem quite unusual, but if you would bear with me, sir, I can explain."

Prime minister Young was sitting next to his secretary; he took off his glasses and begins cleaning it with the handkerchief.

"This is highly irregular, commissioner; I do hope you have a good explanation." He wasn't angry, more like curious.

"As I said, prime minister, I'm very sorry, but there's a good reason for bringing this officer along." It was a warm day, the PM was perspiring, but he shouldn't; no one else was. It could be the pressure of office. He was holding a copy of *The Gleaner;* from time to time, he glanced at it. Adviser Hunt who always sat at the far end of this huge table, now took up a seat next to the commissioner. A strange move as he had never done that before. Lieutenant Dickson sat on the commissioner's left, but sitting almost isolated some two seats away was, Home Secretary Walker; he appeared pensive.

"Okay, commissioner, let's hear your story; why there are two dead civilians and no one is arrested, and why is this man here?"

"This is the officer who sabotaged the operation. I brought him along to explain why."

The commissioner went on to explain the operation, and how the incident happened. The prime minister looked surprised; he steered at the officer with an angry glare.

"Why did you start shooting when you weren't ordered to, mister?" There was anger in his voice. But Rupert remained silent, his head hung, looking at his feet.

"Did I order you or anyone to fire?" asked the commissioner. But he was not talking; however, his silence irritated Adviser Hunt. Well, it wasn't helping the commissioner's case. Not wishing for his newly found friend to look bad in the eyes of the prime minister, he took up the chase.

"What's your name, mister?" he asked, fiddling with the ring on his finger.

"Rupert, sir," he replied in a low tone.

"Now tell me, who was it that ordered you to shoot? And you must tell us the truth."

He didn't respond, so the adviser asked again, but this time, there was venom in his voice. The officer appeared to say something but no one heard it. Adviser Hunt looked at him with an angry glare. It was as though he would like to beat the hell out of him.

"Rupert, are you going to tell us? Two people are dead, and you killed them. Tell us who told you to, and you might escape the gallows."

The prime minister didn't take too kindly to Adviser's blunt way of talking. He asked, "Jeffery, may I have a word?"

There was a moment of whisper, probably telling his adviser to watch his language. Rupert was shaking with fear; but not wanting to reveal his source, he remained tight-lipped.

The prime minister intervened but spoke calmly.

"Now, Rupert, I must know who told you to shoot, but whatever you tell us, no one besides us will ever know."

He didn't raise his head, but spoke in a low voice.

"Someone ordered me to, sir, but if I tell you, I'm a dead man."

The lieutenant whispered something to the commissioner; he nodded.

"Prime minister, I think I know who gave him the order."

"Are you sure, commissioner?"

"No, sir, call it an educated guess, but I believe the order was given by Deputy Holmes."

"But he wasn't there, commissioner, you said so."

"No, he wasn't, but I believe Rupert was following his orders."

Adviser Hunt tried again, but Rupert wouldn't relate. It seemed he'd rather suffer the wrath of the government than the one who ordered him to.

Home Secretary Walker spoke, but he was echoing the words of the commissioner.

"It has been our suspicion, prime minister, that Deputy Holmes is working with the gangs."

"Then why wasn't I told of your suspicion, home secretary?"

"I didn't get the chance to, and so far, it's only speculation."

"If there's no evidence, when will you be sure?" he asked, looking directly at him.

"We're looking into it. It won't be easy, but we'll find the evidence."

"I'm glad to hear it, but when are you going to? If these people are among you folding up operations, you're never going to get result."

At this point, Rupert lost his nerves. The mention of deputy Homes, had him rattled.

"I didn't say it was Mr Holmes; please don't say I told you so." His voice was trembling and he was near tears. Adviser Hunt saw his reaction and took the initiative.

"Yes, you did, and you should have told the commissioner, instead, you followed the order of a traitor."

"Oh my God, I'm a dead man. Please don't lock me in jail; they'll kill me." Of course, he knew how the gangs operated; if you're of no further use, they eliminate you.

"Who, Rupert, who will come for you?" the adviser asked.

Rupert didn't respond. He sat looking dejected; his life was almost certainly over. If the government didn't get him, the gang will.

"Good move, Mr Adviser," the commissioner acknowledged in a whisper.

"So, when did he give you the order to shoot?" asked the commissioner.

"Just before we left the barracks, sir. I didn't want to, but he told me what would happen if I don't."

The prime minister looked at him with squinted eyes, probably what he was hearing was hard to believe.

Now Rupert was shaking like banana leaves on a windy day, but he related what he knew.

"Do you know of anyone else he gave orders to?"

"There are others, sir, but I don't know who."

The PM beckons the adviser; for a few minutes, they confer in a whisper.

"Commissioner, it's unfortunate for the dead citizens, and I'm beginning to realise what you're up against. I trust you'll find these informers, and quickly. Home secretary, I must ask you, are you working in cooperation with the commissioner?"

"Of course, prime minister, the commissioner has my whole-hearted support."

"Then, gentlemen, I don't have to tell you, the government is taking a beating; the killing of these civilians will blow over. I trust, however, there won't be a repeat instance."

Adviser Hunt whispered something again; the PM looked sideways into Miss Green's notebook, a look that lasted for a few minutes.

"Now, commissioner, what are you going to do about this fellow Holmes? You can't have him running loose and fouling up the operations."

"I said I am fairly sure he's our man, prime minister, but I'll give you a better answer when we interrogate him."

"Well, I hope you catch that someone quickly, whoever it is. And I want to know when you do."

"That I will do, sir. This man, Holmes, is priority."

"What are your thoughts on this matter, home secretary?" asked the PM.

"I agree with the commissioner. If there're others, and we believe there are, we'll seek them out too."

"Do you think this disloyalty has gone further than the constabulary, home secretary?" A curious question; it was asked before, and he knew the answer, probably to hear the minister's take on the matter.

"I suspect it might, but until we've done some investigation, we can never be sure."

"Okay, gentlemen, do what you must, leave no stone unturned, but root out these traitors."

Secretary Green wrote the last minute and closed the ledger.

The commissioner got to his feet, followed by the lieutenant. Rupert was taken back to jail. There was no need for interrogation, he's already drawn them a picture.

As the commissioner was leaving, Adviser Hunt walked over to him and extended a hand.

"Good luck, Noel, and we must meet some time for me to buy you a drink."

"Thanks, Jeff, I would like that."

"Well, don't leave it too long, we must have social chat."

Back at his office, the commissioner was in conversation with the lieutenant.

"Dick, I think we have more than enough to bring Deputy Holmes in for questioning. I don't think we should wait any longer."

"I was thinking along the same lines; Rupert admitted he acted on his orders. We should drag him in before he does further damage."

"Right, that's what we'll do; this hanging about is getting us nowhere. We'll meet with him tomorrow at twelve."

"I think we should have a line of attack though," said the lieutenant.

"I agree, but what do you suggest?"

"Well, I think we should use Rupert as a tool. He will know Rupert is in jail, and we're talking to him."

"Yes, and could be planning to get Rupert killed too."

"That is more than likely," said the lieutenant.

"Another thing, Dick, once he's been interrogated, we'll have to arrest him. He must never be allowed to be on the outside again."

"Quite so," said the Lieutenant.

"That said, we must make sure Rupert is well-guarded; he must stay healthy for the trial," said the commissioner.

The lieutenant collected his staff; he was leaving.

"I will see you tomorrow at twelve. You should go home and get some rest; it's been a long day."

"Good advice, Dick, I'm right behind you."

The following day was to be of mixed fortunes. At about 8 am, there was a caller, he armed himself before opening the door. It was soldier boy Albert; he seemed in a hurry.

"What's up, Albert?"

"The lieutenant sent me, sir, there was a shooting at the jail, but no one is hurt." He was already dressed. He didn't ask further questions; they set off for the jail.

"Where's the lieutenant now?"

"He said he'll meet you at your office, sir, everything was taken care of."

His fear has borne out; they've tried to kill Rupert.

"Now, Albert, this is what I want you to do. Go back to the barracks, get two soldiers and bring them to my office. Come armed with handguns, but keep them under your uniform. I'll square it with the lieutenant. You'll wait with them in Miss Scott's office; I'll tell her to expect you, and be there for 12 sharps, is that clear, Albert?"

"Yes, sir, quite clear." He dropped him off at the barracks.

Chapter 16
The Unexpected Visitor

The lieutenant was at the office, waiting.

"Good morning, Dick,"

"Didn't you hear? It's not so much a good morning." he replied.

"I heard. Soldier boy told me, and he'll be coming here with two of your men; I told him to. He also said you took care of business. What happened?"

"Well, about 5 this morning, they tried to get Rupert, but the guards fought them off; no one was hurt. However, since they didn't succeed, it's likely they'll try again, so I strengthened the guards."

"Good work, Dick, but do you really think they'll try again?"

"Who knows, man; your guess is as good as mine. We're dealing with brainless people. They smoke so much of the grass; it turns them into animals and they become brain-dead."

"I was made to understand, when one is under the influence, one becomes fearless."

"Braindead more like," said the lieutenant.

"Do you know anything about that, Dick; have you ever smoked the stuff?"

"No, man, and I have no wish to."

"So, what do you know about it? Do you really believe people react to it when they smoke it?"

"For sure; I've seen normal guys turn into animals. They would murder their own mothers."

"That said, do you think we're prepared enough?"

"I don't know, man, you tell me, you're the police man."

"Come on, Dick, you know as much as I do. I would like to know what you think."

"Noel, with the resources we have, how much more could we've done."

The clock was showing 11:30 am; the commissioner summoned Deputy Holmes. After waiting some time, he asked Miss Scott to go fetch him. "You should find him in the main hall, Miss Scott."

She left hastily. In a few minutes she returned, but without the deputy.

"You couldn't find him, Miss Scott?"

"Oh yes, sir, I found him; he said he'll be along shortly." The Lieutenant smiled ruefully.

"It seems Mr Holmes is the boss of this outfit," he said.

"Thank you, Miss Scott, we'll have to wait until the big man finds time to oblige us with his presence."

He was furious, but held his anger in check.

"How do you like that, Dick? This fellow has the audacity to keep us waiting."

"Do you think he suspected what this meeting is about?"

"I don't see how he could, but it could have had something to do with the shooting at the jail."

"Quite possible, and remember Rupert's words? He's the main man on the inside."

"Rupert never said that."

"No, but he implied it," said Dick.

Some fifteen minutes later, the door pushes open, and in walks Deputy Holmes. The commissioner did his best to hide his anger.

"Oh, there you're, Mr Holmes. Do come in. If your ears were burning, I was calling your name; do take a seat."

He pulled up a chair, but his poise was that of a man brimming with confidence.

"So, what is this about, commissioner? Why do you want to see me?"

"Only to ask you a few questions, Mr Holmes."

He didn't like what the commissioner said at all. He thought he was above questioning. But he was not smart; his arrogance and probably thinking he's untouchable will be his downfall.

"You want to question me? What the hell for?" he asked angrily.

"Why are you so angry, Mr Holmes? Are you guilty of something?"

By now, he knew this meeting was about him, and not about new recruits. He got to his feet and was about to walk out; but thought better of it.

"Mr Wade, this meeting; it was never about recruitment, was it?"

"No, Mr Holmes, it's about you. We want to know what you know about the shooting at the jail, and why did you tell Rupert to sabotage the operation?"

"I know nothing of what you're talking about. But why ask me? Shouldn't you know? On reflection, I can't understand how that Rupert isn't dead," he said boastfully.

"Since you know of the shooting, would you like to tell us about it?"

"I didn't say that. I'm just wondering how they missed a sitting target."

"I take it you mean Rupert. You're sorry he isn't dead."

"Don't go and say things I didn't. All I'm suggesting is, a good gunman would have finished the job."

There was no need to ask him about the fouled-up mission. They knew he gave the order. He was now at the point where he couldn't give a damn what the commissioner or the Lieutenant thought. It was almost as though he wanted them to know his friends are out there; and not in the constabulary.

The lieutenant was fuming; this fellow's bad attitude had gotten to him, he was darn right feisty and bad-mannered, and he didn't like it.

"Norman (the deputy's Christian name), we heard from good sources you've got links with Harry Wells and the gangs. How do you answer the charge?"

"I don't have to. You haven't got the right to be questioning me; you or anyone else."

"Are you saying the rumour is true, Mr Holmes?" asked the commissioner.

"I'm not saying anything. Believe what you want."

The man was full of confidence; he was as brash as a hunting pack of wolves, but the commissioner had enough; he made it clear.

"Mr Holmes, you're here to answer charges against you, and Mr Holmes, we must get answers."

It appeared that comment drove him into a frenzy; he rose to his feet, and with his hands in his pockets, he was about to leave.

"I'm not going to sit here and be accused of double dealings. I'm out of here."

"Sit back down, Mr Holmes," said the commissioner, "you're not going anywhere."

"What the hell! You're ordering me?" he asked like a man who was holding all the aces, but what he was holding, was aces and eight.

The lieutenant got to his feet. He signalled Albert to enter, and with the soldier, they circled the office; in case the deputy want to make a break for it. But the big man was not going to, it would dent his ego.

"What's this? Soldiers to arrest me? You're making a big mistake, you'll see."

"Don't worry about it, Mr Holmes. I've made bigger ones before, but you, sir, you're going to jail, and, Mr Holmes, you'll stand trial for being an informer."

Hearing that made him even feistier; now he was in a rage.

"Damn you, commissioner, how dare you bring soldiers to arrest me? You'll be sorry."

"I regret it already, but only because we didn't arrest you sooner."

He was now in handcuffs, but his boastful attitude wasn't dented.

"Will you tell us about your links with the gangs, Norman? It could be to your benefit," said the lieutenant.

"What are you trying to do, have me incriminate myself? I have nothing to say."

The lieutenant tried another angle, something he knew he was well aware of.

"Norman, you know how the gangs operate. When they find you're in jail, and that you're of no further use to them, you know what they'll do, and that is not to keep you alive."

That seemed to knock the stuffing out of him. His face took a different countenance. He was almost at a pleading.

"Lieutenant, I have nothing to do with the gang, you must believe me."

"No, we don't," said the commissioner. "We know you're tied in with them; save your pleas for the trial."

He was now subdued, probably reflecting on what the lieutenant said.

He was taken to jail, and put in a cell where he could see Rupert; later, he'll be moved to a more secure confinement. The lawmen had done what they must; their man was behind bars pending trial. He rang the home secretary to give him the news.

"Yes, commissioner, what can I do for you?" he sounded awfully cheerful.

"Good to find you in high spirits, minister. You'll be pleased to hear, Holmes is behind bars."

"That is good news. Did he confess?"

"Not in so many words, but the man is guilty as charged, so, will you inform the PM, minister?"

"That I will do, commissioner; he'll be gratified to hear."

"Another thing, minister, a time must be set for an early trial; having him locked up is not healthy for our operation."

"That we must do. How about we meet tomorrow to seal this deal, say 2 pm?"

"That's fine with me, minister. See you tomorrow."

Chapter 17
The Interrogation

On Sunday, the Holy Sabbath for Christians; there was to be an urgent meeting with the minister, but it had to be rescheduled. The minister had gone to church with his lady wife. It's said he's not a convert, but he never missed going to church on Sunday. Monday, the commissioner arrived at the home office for their rescheduled meeting.

"Good day, Miss Benson." She returned the compliment.

"Go right in, commissioner, the home secretary awaits you."

The welcome was friendly, something he got accustomed to.

"Now, commissioner, I must apologise for yesterday; apart from me and my good lady wife going to church, there was a little matter in the family that required my attention."

"Nothing too serious I hope, minister?"

"Let's say it's a cause for concern."

"Well, whatever it is, I hope it turns out the way you wanted."

"Thank you, commissioner, I hope so."

"Now, what is the business of the day? Mr Holmes I presume?"

"Yes, he must be dealt with quickly. I am talking days, not weeks."

"I agree; however, it won't be easy."

"Why? Should there be a problem?"

"You're forgetting, commissioner, a few weeks ago my friend, the judge, along with his two associates were murdered. They were trying a member of the gang. It's going to be difficult finding a judge for the trial, since it's gang related."

"I haven't forgotten, and I see what you mean; however, someone must be found. They will be trying to get to him; the attempt on Rupert failed, but this fellow Holmes is a bigger fish, and I don't think they want to keep him alive."

It was usually humid in the tropics, but some days could be brutally hot. Today was one of those days. They sipped ice-cold lemonade to cool the temperature.

"Commissioner, nothing must stop this fellow from going to trial, and if he's guilty, he must be made an example of."

"Quite so, and we'll do whatever it takes to make sure of that. So, what time are we talking?"

The minister pulled out a drawer and reached for his ledger; he turned a few pages then paused.

"We'll set a date for the Wednesday. Will that suit your plans, commissioner?"

"I think so. We'll take good care of Holmes till then."

He called his secretary. "Take note, Miss Benson. The trial of Mr Holmes is set for Wednesday the…" He paused; the date eluded him. She told him the 9th and noted it. He thanked her and she went back to her office.

"The moment we done here, commissioner, I will inform the prime minister of our discussion."

"Very good. From now on, we've got plenty to do."

"Quite so. So, Guard Homes well, commissioner, he could hold the key to much we don't know."

"We've taken the necessary precaution, he's being move inside the prison; he's secure there."

"There's one thing more, minister. Our plan must not reach *The Gleaner*, not yet; the fewer that know of it, the better."

"Holmes himself has no need to know until he's presented at court." It was agreed.

He felt the compulsion to tell the home secretary of his encounter with the people at green Bay. Regarding that, he felt he had accomplished something, and was chuffed about it.

"It's good to hear, probably you should do more in the way of public relation, it goes hand in hand with policing, wouldn't you say so, commissioner?"

"It might not be a bad idea, and I tell you this, to get the country back up and running, we're going to need their help."

"I'm sure you're so right, and thank goodness for those who are loyal to the country."

The commissioner was about to say good evening when the minister asked, "Commissioner, we've been talking a while. I'm famished, and I'm sure you are too; would you like a little refreshment?"

It was a welcoming offer, one he didn't expect, and he wasn't going to refuse.

"Thank you, minister. Don't mind if I do."

He called his secretary and asked her to provide something. Meanwhile, they picked up where they'd left off, but now they were talking lock down.

"Is there any word regarding the curfew, minister?"

"No, but the PM probably will want to speak with you before he puts it to parliament. However, I have a strong feeling whenever he does, it will be agreed."

Miss Benson returned with refreshment, and while they were eating, the talks continued. "You know, I discovered the other day some of the stores are doing business with the cartel."

"I can't say I'm surprised, commissioner. From time to time, *The Gleaner* wrote about it, but I'm sure you're aware by now; we can't control these people."

"That I realised, but your predecessors and people in the constabulary made it easier for them to operate. Now all we can do is sit and watch."

"I'm hoping something is done about them, and soon. I hate to see scums like them ride rough shot over the law."

"And so, say all of us, commissioner."

Refreshment was over, and he was about to leave.

"Commissioner, we should convene another meeting soon; we want to stay on top of this situation. Would you be up for it?"

"I sure will. Suggest when. I'm sure I can find the time."

"How about Thursday at my home. You could meet the wife and have dinner with us."

"I would like that very much, thank you. Thursday it is."

It seemed as though the home secretary was going out of his way to extend a hand of friendship, and the commissioner was only too willing to oblige.

It was later that evening the commissioner met up with the lieutenant; he was late for their meeting.

"I thought you've given up on me, man. Was the minister giving you a hard time?"

"On the contrary, it was quite an evening; the unexpected happened."

"What do you mean? He's not home secretary anymore?" The commissioner smiled wryly.

"Oh, he's that alright, but maybe I was too quick to form an opinion on this gentleman."

With wide eyes, the lieutenant exclaimed, "Oh, so he's a gentleman now?"

"Well, I've seen a different side to him, a good side."

"In other words, peace has broken out."

"You could say that, and it is all the better for a good working relationship."

"Are we talking about the same home secretary?"

"The very same, but the trouble with you, Dick, is you don't think people can change."

"Not many do, man, and those who do, change for the worse."

"If that's your philosophy, I'm sure there aren't many who shared it."

"I'm glad you had a good evening, but don't rest too easy, you've got troubles in the ranks."

"What kind of trouble?"

"Our man Frankie is dead, shot through the head, round about 2 pm. He was off duty." The commissioner looked at his watch.

"That's about the time the minister and I were discussing Holmes."

"Of course. It couldn't have anything to do with the deputy; he's in jail."

"Yes, but it is possible he could've given the order from behind bars."

"I suppose it's possible; guys like Holmes can be bloody devious."

"Right, I must go check it out; see if anyone knows anything."

"Good luck, man, but I doubt if anyone's going to admit seeing anything."

"Nevertheless, I must talk to them. You never know, someone might decide to talk."

He rose to his feet but remained static; he appeared to be thinking.

"Dick, I suddenly have a thought. I'll have a word with Barry; he had promise to tell me if he heard anything. I'll do it now; strike while the iron is hot, but I want to talk with him alone, so make yourself scarce. I'll see you later."

"Good luck, man." He collected his stuff and went away.

He called Miss Scott on the intercom, and asked her to go and fetch Officer Hilton, that he'll be at the county hall.

She acknowledge and left. She'd be riding her bicycle, but it will take some time; travelling through the city at any time of day can be a slow process. Sometime later, there was a knock at the door, it was Officer Hilton. The commissioner didn't ask the caller to enter, instead, he went and opened the door.

"Come in, Barry," he said in a kind of friendly tone.

They had a bit of small talk before he offered him a drink; he also had one himself – The Captain. He wouldn't be drinking with the officer, but to get what he wanted, he must lower his standard and try to be sociable.

"Now, Barry, what can you tell me about Frankie; do you know who shot him? And Barry, whatever you tell me, it's strictly between us."

Barry didn't hesitate, he tells all he knew.

"He wasn't killed by any of the officers, sir; it was men from the gang, but which gang, I don't know. He was about to leave for duty when he was killed, and they shot him many times."

"Did you see the gun mem?"

"Oh yes, sir, we all saw them."

There was no need to hear more. The Commissioner knew the situation. Those killers could carry out their killing at any time, even in front of the law. He thanked Barry for his help and sent him back out on duty. Sometime later, the lieutenant returned.

"Did you talk with Barry?"

He didn't respond; he got to his feet.

"Let's get out of here, Dick; I'll tell you on the way. These walls could have ears." In the car; he tells the Lieutenant what he learned.

"The killing was done by three gunmen, in front of the officer. They couldn't or wouldn't do anything about it, and in situation like that, one cannot differentiate those who support the gangs from those who don't."

"That's the problem, Dick, we don't know who is loyal, and if there're any, they're afraid to talk." The lieutenant was about to leave.

"Have dinner with me, Dick, there're other matters I would like to discuss with you."

"Well now, since you asked so nicely, how I can refuse? Yes, sir Commissioner, I will dine with you."

The commissioner looked at him with a smile, thinking he was behaving peculiar.

"Tell me, Dick, were you smoking one of those funny cigarettes?"

"No, man; why you ask?"

"Well, I heard it can make people do funny things."

"Like what for instant?"

"Well, they begin to see things that isn't there; make you think things can fly, among other things."

"No, man, I told you before, I never touch the stuff."

"Well, you seem to be in a funny mood."

"Well, worry no more, man, I'm back down to earth."

The commissioner chuckled but said nothing.

On the way, the conversation continued; they were talking about Deputy Holmes.

"A date has been set for the trial, Wednesday the 9th."

"Oh good, he'll will be one traitor off our radar when he's hung."

"Assuming he is found guilty, of course."

"Come on, man, this trial is just a formality, it's not even necessary."

"Of course, he's not known to kill anyone," said the commissioner.

"No, but for sure his actions sent many to an early grave."

"If he's found guilty, and according to you, he will, we still have a problem, and it could be a very long one."

"What problem is that?" asked the Lieutenant.

"The Privy Council. I understand they they're never in a hurry to make a decision. They take months, sometimes years."

"That is so, and there's nothing we can do about it, and that's a bloody humbug; we could be guarding Holmes for a long time."

"Regarding the trial, apart from the prime minister, no one else knew, except us three, so now, Mr Funny man," he said sarcastically, "we must make darn sure both prisoners stay healthy for the trial."

"Don't be too worried, man, he's fairly secure where he is, but I suggest we install a night patrol just for extra precaution."

"Okay, Dick, you see to it."

"Yes, boss."

"Damn it, man, try and be serious for a while, can you?"

"Sure, I can, I'm just trying to lighten the mood."

"You know, Dick, someone should find a stage, you could be a damn good comedian."

"Come on, man, constantly being serious is bad for the face; a little laughter is good for the wrinkles."

At the hotel, dinner was ordered along with drinks, but it would be a while before they ate. "Dick, I've been thinking t—"

"Are you sure you should be doing that, man?" he interrupted.

"Funny man," said the commissioner. "I can see we're not going to get much done this evening."

"Lighten up, man, where's your sense of humour? I heard back in England; you guys laugh at everything."

"Yes, we do, but there's a time and a place."

"Okay, man, let's talk business, but I can recall an old saying, all work and no play—"

"Yeah, yeah," interrupted the commissioner, "makes Jack a dull boy, and yes, Mr Funny man, we laugh at ourselves too, but not when there are urgent matters to discuss, and I need your input."

Well, he was getting a little weary with the lieutenant's nonstop comedy.

"Okay, man, I'm all yours; let's get down to business. Let's see what we can come up with." He didn't respond; just shook his head and smiled.

Dinner had arrived, and the waiter laid it out; she was leaving when she remembered something.

"Commissioner, this is for you," she said, presenting him with an envelope and then left.

The commissioner read it and put it in his top pocket; he looked a bit thoughtful.

"Bad news I take it, man?"

"On the contrary, it's an invitation to a garden party."

"An invitation? Who from? Someone back in England?" he asked as though he was surprised.

"Very funny, but no, it's from right here, the hotel manager a Mr..." He paused and reached for the note. "Wilson, but I don't think I have ever met him. I wonder how this came about?"

"Well now, you're the commissioner of police, a VIP. It could be he would like to make your acquaintance."

"Well, however it comes about, am glad to accept. It will be nice to see how the other half lives."

Dinner was over, and the lieutenant was about to leave.

"So, what's on the agenda for tomorrow? Are you going to see the home secretary again?"

"Well, I can't just barge in on him; I don't think he would appreciate it. However, we'll have to talk about security, and it includes you, so stay handy."

"If it doesn't clash with what I have to do."

The commissioner stood to attention; he was about to stamp his authority on proceedings.

"Now listen, we're a team, this is our duty, consider it a priority; whatever else you have to do, do it another time."

"OK, man, keep your shirt on, just tell me what time."

"11 o'clock, and don't be late, we have lots to discuss."

"Right oh, boy, I'll try to be on time."

"Where the devil did you hear that kind of talk? Have you ever lived in Wales?"

"If it's a word the Welsh are using, they pinched it from us. Good evening."

Chapter 18
Talking Security

It was Tuesday. The three men met to talk security, reflecting on last month's debacle, they wouldn't want a repeat performance. It should be a show case trial, but because of the risk, there won't be anyone in court, apart from the judges. However, it was an open and shut case. Mr Holmes was a dead man walking. The trial was just to show he got a hearing. *The Gleaner* was oblivious to this trial, but by tomorrow, like everyone, they will know. That, however, could spell trouble for the government. If *The Gleaner* were of the belief that the authority is keeping them in the dark regarding something of this importance, it's not going to make good reading for them.

The minister was uncomfortable with the arrangement, but the commissioner was adamant; it must remain a secret. But as a politician, he wanted to cover his backside. He came up with a plan. He would inform the editor the morning of the trial. He won't be pleased, but he'll explain the reason for the secrecy. But later, fearing the wrath of the media, he was rethinking his previous thought.

"Commissioner, I'm thinking we should inform the editor today. I'm concerned that tomorrow when I tell him, he might take exceptions, and knowing Mr Wicket, (the editor) he could be thinking we deliberately kept the trial from him." Of course, what the minister was mindful of was getting a bad press, but the commissioner was having none of it.

"I'm sorry, minister. I understand your reasoning, but I can't allow it. The risk is too high. You can tell him no more than an hour before the trial."

"That was my original thought, commissioner."

"Then I suggest you stick to it."

"About the judge, have you engaged anyone yet?"

"I have, and he'll be in court with the appropriate personnel from early morning; all other arrangements are in your hands, gentlemen."

The meeting concluded, but before he walked away, the minister referred to the Lieutenant.

"Lieutenant, are you confident nothing will go wrong?"

"Mr Walker, it's as the commissioner stated; everything possible is being done. In other words, we're prepared for any eventuality."

The meeting concluded. On the way home, the commissioner seemed in a reflective mood.

"Dick, are you feeling confident about tomorrow?"

"The word confident isn't what I care to use."

"We've done all we can. Let's hope nothing goes wrong."

"How can you be so calm? I'm sure I won't be sleeping tonight."

"Well, good for you. You'll be having a rough tomorrow." Said the Lieutenant.

"Have a heart, Dick." They said good afternoon.

The Trial

Wednesday was a miserable day; it continued to drizzle. The sun was out and the day was bright, the rainbow stretched across the sky, displaying its seven colours. The natives have a saying for this sort of a day, "The devil and his wife are fighting." It was approaching midday; the lieutenant was first on the scene with soldiers to secure the courthouse and perimeter. The judge and his associates were already inside when the prisoners were brought in.

"Well done, Dick, good work," said the commissioner after a look around.

Seeing the place was well-fortified, he commented, "You know, Dick, I almost wish these gunmen would try something now."

"You want to be careful what you wish for," said the Lieutenant, "you shouldn't go tempting fate."

Soon the trial was commence, but the home secretary had one last task to perform, inform the editor. When it was explained to him, he wasn't too pleased, but understood the delicacy of the situation. The minister breathed a sigh of relief.

Of course, with so many soldiers about, people were bound to become curious. They soon realised something was happening. Suddenly they began to gather and wanted to know what was happening. The lawmen got what they didn't bargain for, a crowd to control.

"Lieutenant, we have to move these people on, but calmly. This crowd is not good for the operation."

However, with calm heads and good thinking, they managed to disperse the crowd.

All this time, the court was in session, but it didn't take long before Holmes was found guilty. They could just as well find him guilty while he was in jail, but such was the law. Officer Rupert was sentence to prison for a long stretch. There, his life wasn't worth the shirt on his back. As for Deputy Holmes, he was to be hanged, and if the country had its own constitution, his execution wouldn't be delayed, but they'll have to wait on the Privy Council; and it could be months if not years. The authority could do nothing except lock him away in their most secure prison and wait. His safety was now in the hands of the prison governor. He had a reputation for running a tight shift. It's been said no one escaped from his prison, and with that assurance, Deputy Holmes might live to go to have his neck stretched. The authorities will consider the day a triumph; this tricky operation went off without disturbance. In the morning edition, *The Gleaner* was reporting favourably in support of the government. They made a big deal about rooting out traitors, a line which pleased the authority. People would be reading about this story for days, and will continue until the day Holmes is hung. The identity of the trial judge and his associates will never be known, and since there was no one in court to witness the trial, they can rest easy. By now, the gangs will know the fate of their master spy, but will they attempt to do anything about it? Time will tell.

Chapter 19
The Drill

Today, it was blisteringly hot; the lieutenant was taking the soldiers out on their routine drill, deep into the terrain. After hours of walking along the mountain pass, it was getting dark, so they decided to make camp. These terrains were always inhospitable; no one ventured here without a reason. They settled down for the night, oblivious to them, gunmen were there too; this was where they hid. However, what was to happen could be classified as a stroke of luck. It's about midnight, and the soldiers bedded down. It was a moonlit night, but among the trees, it casted a dark shadow. The gunmen had no knowledge of the soldier's presence, at least not yet. It was sometime later the soldier's movement gave their position away. The gunmen realised they've got company. But their position was not good; they were hemmed in. Not wanting to give their position away, they stayed put and kept quiet; thinking, in the morning the soldiers would be gone.

These bad men however had their own rules when it came to a shootout. They'd rather fight in the city; there they can hide behind the locals, using them as shields. It was past 2 am and all was well, there was no sentry; the lieutenant didn't think it was necessary. At about 3 am, there were lights coming up the track, and there was talking. One soldier was awake, probably couldn't get himself to sleep; he became alert.

"Who goes there?" he asked, but there was no answer. The men stopped, probably thinking who the hell was that?

"Who goes there?" he asked again, but louder.

Realising it's not one of their compatriots, the gunmen opened fire. Now the soldiers were all awake; but not yet aware of the situation, but the lieutenant was. It could only be gangsters shooting at them.

They weren't visible anymore; they turned off their lamps and took cover. The soldiers, they were armed with torches attached to their rifles. They turned on their lights. Now the gunmen were fully in their sight, hiding behind trees.

"Stay where you are," said the lieutenant.

But these men, they were not going to respond to any such order; they commenced shooting. The lieutenant didn't hesitate, he gave the order, "Fire, and keep firing." Two men were killed instantly.

Now the gunmen in their hidden area were worried; they knew the two dead men were their compatriots returning to camp. Thinking the soldiers would soon be aware of them, they were thinking of making a break for it, but any movement and the soldiers were certain to see them. Tonight, however, some won't live to see the break of dawn. They check on the dead men; they were gunmen, all right. Now the lieutenant became aware that the gang could be here. These two men were returning to camp, probably after doing their dirty deed. He put his men on alert.

The gunmen became restless and unsure of their position. Instead of standing their ground and fighting, they tried to sneak away. That action would prove to be fatal for some. The soldiers spotted them, and with their high-powered rifles, they opened up; but there was return of fire, they were busy trying to get away. In this violent silos of gunfire, tender trees were chopped down. The action didn't last long. Those who weren't killed took to their heels. They fled into the woods leaving trails of blood; the lieutenant was to discover later.

They surveyed the damage; five gunmen lay dead. In total, seven gunmen were killed. Not a bad night's work for the authorities, however, this wasn't what they set out to do, but it wasn't going to bothered the Lieutenant; These killers are wanted men. The ones who got away won't be resting easy tonight or any other night. Unfortunately, two soldiers were wounded, but not by the gunmen, they were caught in crossfire; their wound wasn't life threatening. They looked amongst the dead for Harry Wells, but no such luck. Then again, he could have no connection with this lot. They piled up the bodies and cut short the operation, mostly to get the wounded to the hospital.

Back at the yard; the lieutenant made out his report. He was to meet with the home secretary to give an account of the incident. It was evening; and *The Gleaner* ran a late edition of the incident, and the lieutenant was getting a pasting. There's no war office, all internal affairs will go through the home office.

The commissioner turned up. "Dick, my man, you're all over the paper; tell me, how did you know the gunmen would be there?" he asked with delight.

"What made you think I knew?" he asked, but his response was out of character; he appeared grumpy.

"You suddenly lost your sense of humour, Dick?"

Quickly realising he lost the plot, he apologised.

"I'm sorry, man, I just thought—"

"What did you think?" interrupted the commissioner. "Did you think I was going to ridicule you for taking out seven killers? Or is there something else on your mind?"

"Oh, come on, man, I said I was sorry."

"So, you should. I was about to congratulate you, but—"

"Come on, man," he interrupted. "I said I'm sorry. If you want me to go on bending knees, I will."

"Okay, I forgive you this time, but see that it doesn't happen again."

"Listen, man, you buy me dinner this evening; and we say no more of it."

Well, he was trying to make light heart of his blunder.

"I see your sense of humour return. I'm to pay for your misunderstanding, the damn cheek of the man." They looked at each other and burst into laughter.

"So, tell me, did you get them all?"

"I don't think so. There was blood trail leading into the woods, which means some got away, but wounded."

"They will be licking their wounds though, and with seven dead, that gang could be out of business for a while," said the commissioner. "It was a good night's work, Dick, regardless of what *The Gleaner* wrote.

"They should be supporting the government's position; instead, they're undermining it. Do they really believe these killers can be talked into laying down their weapons? Or, do they want the government to look bad? It's either one or the other, or they're truly naïve."

The lieutenant picked up his stuff. "I'm off to see the home secretary. You want to come along?"

"Of course, I can support your argument, and it will be interesting to hear the home secretary's views."

Arriving at the home office, they were greeted with what they weren't expecting.

"Gentlemen, we're having our meeting; but not here, the PM summons us ASAP."

"Sounds ominous, minister, any idea why?"

"None at all, commissioner, like you, I'm in the dark."

It could be about last night, the lieutenant thought; however, he's not one to worry. They didn't tarry, they head out on the short drive across town to parliament house; the prime minister and Adviser Hunt were in waiting. The meeting convened; the atmosphere wasn't exactly hostile, but the PM wasn't giving anything away. He was holding an issue of *The Gleaner*; it carried pictures of last night's incident. He was direct and to the point.

"Lieutenant, were all the dead, gunmen?" It was an odd question to ask. It was all in the paper he's holding.

"Yes, prime minister, but I should explain, we were on our routine drill. We decided to make camp, but unknown to us, the place was the gunmen's hideout. We settled down when—"

"Are you saying it wasn't planned, Lieutenant?" the PM interrupted.

"Quite so, prime minister. We had no knowledge of them being there."

He beckoned Adviser Hunt; they whispered something. It seems he didn't want too much of an explanation. In fact, he was more than pleased, only he was not showing it.

"What about Harry, did you get him too?"

"No such luck, prime minister, and probably he's got nothing to do with this lot."

The PM seemed pleased, and he had good reason to be; these gunmen were causing his government to lose face. Outside backers withdrew their funds, and promised never to return until the lawlessness was brought under control, or preferably a change of government.

There're those who would like to return home, but decided against it; they were deterred by the killings. The country was not at war, yet bodies were turning up all over the country. The last hanging took place nearly a year ago, and it was said they hanged two innocent men. The law enforcers were doing their best, but results are slow in coming. This beautiful paradise island, there was a time when people wanted to come here. Not now, they were afraid now.

After further deliberation, the prime minister conceded. "Mr Dickson, you're not here on trial. I believe you've taken the right line of action, and more of the same is needed if we're to get rid of these murderers. I tell you, gentlemen, the sooner we do, the sooner you and I can rest easy in our beds." He was having a well-deserved moan. The home secretary commented, he too was in line with the lieutenant's action. But the PM didn't respond; he said all he intended to on the matter. They covered all angles; and the PM was satisfied; he wished there could be more of the same again, and quickly. He'd probably raise a glass or two to the lieutenant when he gets home.

The talks are now about Harry Wells. "Tell me, minister, is there anything happening regarding Harry Wells?" The question should be for the commissioner, but for whatever reason, it was to the minister.

"As of now, prime minister, nothing at all. We have no knowledge of his whereabouts. The commissioner's team and I are looking to see what we can come up with. Isn't that so, commissioner?" he asked as though he was looking for help with the question.

The commissioner, well, he wasn't going to show dissent. He'll back up the minister, even if it's only for the sake their friendship.

"Quite so, it's a while since we heard anything about him, but we're always on the lookout."

Adviser Hunt spotted a 'rat'. He realised the commissioner was helping out the home secretary. He himself was not too fond of the minister. He asked, "In your investigation, home secretary, what do you expect to find?" The home secretary was equal to the question.

"That we won't know, Mr Hunt; not until the team and I sit down to talk. We'll find what's available to us, you can be sure of that."

The commissioner nearly applauded, an unsuitable response, would probably reflect badly on him too. The PM seemed satisfied, neither he nor the adviser asked further questions regarding Harry.

"About Mr Holmes, commissioner, it could be a long wait for a decision from England; I trust he's being safely guarded?"

"As safely as can be, prime minister, we have done all we can." The minister had a thought; however, it could embarrass the prime minister, and probably cast a shadow over the commissioner too. However, he'll say his thought as humbly and tactfully as possible.

"The security of the prisoner is really up to the governor, and no one breaks out of his prison."

The commissioner went into his pocket as though he was reaching for something; probably nervous as to what the prime minister's reaction would be. Realising he almost dropped a clanger; the PM tried to make amend. "It's being known, Mr Webster runs a tight shift. Will you talk with him regarding, minister?"

"As soon as I get back, prime minister, that I'll do."

"Gentlemen, at these crucial times, it's all hands to the pump," he said, trying to hide his blush. But the commissioner was concerned about the prisoners. Deputy Holmes, even though he's behind bars, he still put a strain on their daily work.

"Prime minister, I'm sure you're aware that the long wait for a decision regarding Mr Holmes is putting an awful strain on our operations; is there any way in which you could speed up the process?"

The PM looked as though someone has brought up his favourite subject; he took off his glasses and rubbed his eyes.

"I share your concern, commissioner, even more so, and I wish I could do something. This colonial constitution is having a detrimental effect on our ruling. All I can say, the sooner we get rid of this outdated legislation the better. I know it won't be me, but I hope whoever it is will get rid, and soon. On an important matter such as this this, we should be making our own ruling; instead, we're waiting for a decision from another country, in the meantime, it's making our lives hell.

I'm sorry, commissioner, and I hate to say it, but all we can do, is wait."

He had a right old moan, and was probably feeling better for it. Adviser Hunt walked over and whispered. The PM nodded. He walked back but remained standing.

"Gentlemen, tomorrow is a bank holiday; a lot will be happening, please be alert and vigilant, we're in troubled times."

"Rest assured, prime minister, we're on the job, but you must remember, we can't be everywhere, even if we have the manpower."

"Commissioner, if you're trying to tell me the constabulary is short on men, I'm fully aware. Unfortunately, we can't do anything about it; however, I'll bear it in mind."

"Well, gentlemen, if there's nothing more for me to know, I bid you good day." The meeting ended.

Chapter 20
Harry Is at James Town

Two days later, the lieutenant was on an errand downtown. He was approached by a man who seemed to be in a hurry, and looked around as though he was being followed.

"Mr Dickson, sir," he said in a low voice. "I will tell you something, but you didn't hear it from me."

He knew this man, but noticing his behaviour, he was rather curious.

"Milton, are you alright?"

"Yes, sir. I just want to tell you something."

"Okay, Milton, go ahead. I'm listening."

"Harry Wells, sir, he's at James Town since yesterday," he said in a low voice.

"You sure about that, or you just wasting my time?"

"Oh yes, sir, I was there. I only returned this morning."

"What about his men? Did you see them too?"

"No, sir, I didn't. I must go now," he said looking around, and off he went.

It had been quite a while since they heard anything about Harry, so the lieutenant cut short his business to tell the commissioner.

"I didn't expect to see you today, Dick. What's up?"

"I shouldn't be here, but I heard news of Harry."

"I hope it's from a good source."

"Never can tell, but I know this fellow; I don't think he would stop me and lie to me."

"So, where's Harry now?"

"At James Town, a stone throw from here, which suggest to me he's up to something, and it won't be to meet the locals."

"Okay, Dick, we'll check out the info. I'll send Soldier Boy Albert."

"You don't think Harry would be so audacious to be thinking of storming the prison, do you?"

"It would be foolhardy of him; the governor runs that place like a fortress, but then again, he probably doesn't know that."

"If that's his intention, why…" He paused. "Wait a minute there now," he said frightfully.

"What is it, Dick, what're you thinking?"

"I'm thinking, Rupert. If my hunch is right; and he intends to storm the prison, it won't be for Deputy Holmes, he's on death row. He'll be going after Rupert. He's doing time, he could be thinking there're things Rupert can tell us."

"You could be right, but you know something? I wish he would try."

"What's with you, man? You said that before; let's not go tempting fate."

Not long after, the commissioner met with Soldier Boy Albert; he told him about the errand.

"If Harry was there, you not to tarry. Come right back, I should be at the office."

"I understand, sir, and it will be done."

"Good man, Albert. You'll leave at 9 am."

"Very good, sir."

He would be riding his bicycle, but it was raining before early morning, so he took the bus. It was a short journey, but on a rainy day, it could take some time. It had nearly been a day since he was gone, and the commissioner was anxious, he was supposed to have a talk with the home secretary, but he would like to hear from Albert before he sits down to talk. Round about 9 am, the morning after, there was a knock at the door; it was Albert, and he was looking awfully weary.

"Come in, Albert and sit down. Would you like something to eat?"

"Yes, thank you, sir." He noticed the poor fellow could hardly keep his eyes open.

"Did you see Harry, Albert?" he asked kind of hastily.

"Oh yes, sir, I saw him, but he's not alone, his men are there too."

Then he mumbled something, but the commissioner didn't hear.

"What was that, Albert?" There was no answer. He then noticed the poor fellow nodding off. Any further information will have to wait, Albert was snoring.

Breakfast was ordered but had not yet arrived, and the commissioner couldn't wait; he must go. But he's not going to disturb soldier boy; he wrote a note and put it where he could see it when he was awake. It reads. *Don't leave until I return.*

On his way out, he gave the order to deliver breakfast to his room; but not to disturb his guest. Halfway across town, he came across a situation, but one he was not a stranger to. Almost in front of a store, a woman was kicking seven hells out of a fellow, but the man wasn't fighting back. He was lying on the ground with his hands over his face, shielding it from the blows. He stopped to investigate.

"Come on now, lady, pack it in," he said forcefully.

But there was no let-up; she continued pounding this fellow. Her action was a copycat he had encountered back in England. A woman beating the hell out of a man who wasn't fighting back. No one interfered, they had a fleeting glance as they walk by; the man was her husband. He grabbed hold of this woman and restrained her, but to his surprise, she didn't resist. It's as though she was glad someone restrained her. She hugged the commissioner crying, exclaiming repeatedly, "I'm so sorry." She was shaking and appeared weak at the knees. The commissioner put her in the back seat of his car. She sat sobbing with her head in her lap.

He turned to the fellow on the ground; well, he wasn't exactly lying on the ground, more like sitting up and looking fairly pleased considering the kicking he was getting.

"Are you all right, mister?"

"I think so, sir," he said smiling while brushing himself down.

"Why? Are you not sure?" the commissioner asked sarcastically.

But the man didn't respond, instead, he calmly asked, "Is my wife all right, commissioner?"

The commissioner was somewhat bemused. He almost wanted to laugh.

"Are you telling me this woman is your wife?"

"Oh yes sir, commissioner, but she wasn't hurting me."

"What's your name, mister?"

"Johnson, Don Johnson."

"Why was your wife beating you up, Mr Johnson?"

Again, he didn't respond. While brushing himself down, he asked again about his wife. She was still crying, and it appeared he would like to console her, but seemed unsure. The commissioner couldn't hide his amusement. There's no case for them to answer; it was a matrimonial matter that should be dealt with indoors. He spoke with them in the form of a reprimand.

"You should be ashamed of yourselves, two adults brawling in the street. I'm not going to arrest you; not this time, but never let me catch you at it again."

She thanked him but couldn't look him in the eye. She was too ashamed.

He was sympathetic; he could see they're good people; but it could be she was angry about something.

"Okay, Mrs Johnson, take your husband and go home."

She got to her feet, but there was a bystander; he was observing from the shadows. He then emerged to talk to the couple.

"Are you all right, Don?" he asked. But it seemed Mr Johnson didn't appreciate his concern.

"What do you want?" he asked in an abrupt manner. "We don't need your concern, f*** off!"

But the man wasn't going anywhere. He asked, "Are you all right, sis?"

"I'm alright, come along, Don, let's go home." She grabbed hold of his hand, and off they went.

This man didn't follow; he wanted to talk with the commissioner. He began to tell him the reason for the street brawl.

"They are Christians, church going people, and last night there was an evangelist meeting, but Don chose not to go. My sister doesn't like it when he's not at meetings."

The commissioner was intrigued as to why this fellow chose to tell him his sister's life story.

"What's your name, mister?"

"Bushman, commissioner."

Thinking that couldn't be his real name, he asked, "Is that your real name?"

"No, sir, but that's what everyone calls me."

He came closer, and in a whisper, he spoke. "I can tell you things you don't know."

"Really? What can you tell me that I don't know?" he asked curiously.

"Things about the gang, sir."

The commissioner became curious; any information about these gangsters, he wanted to hear.

"Now look, Bushman, don't waste my time. If you have something to tell me, let's hear it."

He came closer but looking around, he whispered, "It's about the gang, sir, I know where they are."

Hearing that, the commissioner got interested, for once the news is not about Harry.

"Okay, Bushman, get in the car, let's go to my office; we'll talk there."

"Oh no, sir, no," he said frightfully. "Let's go somewhere no one will see us."

The commissioner looked at his watch; it was long past the time for his meeting with the minister, but what this fellow had to tell him take priority. They drove to a secret location.

"Now then, Bushman, tell me about the gang, where're they?"

"I will tell you, commissioner, sir, but you have to promise you won't arrest me, and you won't mention my name to anyone."

The commissioner promised, but his curiosity was running wild. He reached into his pocket and took out his cigarette.

"Would you like one?" he asked kind of a friendly.

They lit up. Bushman slumped in the back of the car so no one sees him.

"About the gang, sir. I was a member, but I never killed anyone. I decided to break lose on account of the killings, but they don't about it yet."

The commissioner was wondering if this fellow was telling the truth; he seemed sincere enough, but one never can tell.

"So where is the gang now?"

"Here in town, sir, but they're not all at the same place."

He was somewhat dumbstruck. If this fellow's story was true, they'd been outsmarted. They'd been looking all over for the gangs, and there was one right here under their noses.

"Does this gang belong to Harry Wells?"

"Oh no, sir. This is the Burns gang; they got nothing to do with Harry Wells."

"The Burns gang?" he exclaimed.

Well, the name Burns did ring a bell. could this gang have anything to do with the disgraced minister? Bushman talked, and he said plenty.

"Would you show me where they're located?"

"Oh no, sir, I can't do that. You'll have to find them yourself. After I finish here, you'll never see me again."

The commissioner didn't shake his hand, but he thanked him for the info. He asked the commissioner for another cigarette as he's about to leave; he probably had a short life. He was deep in thought about the gang, about how easy they find it to operate. They were right there, in town.

At the Home Office

When he arrived at the home office, he wasn't expecting the minister to be waiting, but he was.

"I'm so sorry, minister. I ran into something unexpectedly, something that needed my attention. I suppose we'll have to do this another time."

The minister was quite understanding.

"No apologies needed, commissioner, if your duty requires your immediate attention, then you are obliged to. However, the day isn't over, let's see what we can get through."

The commissioner was pleased to hear, but before they got down to business, he told the minister about his encounter with the odd couple.

"What you should understand, Mr Wade, in this country of ours, most people are churchgoers, but few are Christians. Even though there're those who will tell you otherwise. My wife, she fits the bill, and as for me, I go to church because I find it refreshing, and to please my dear wife. For us, going to church is a way of life; some might even tell you they're the chosen ones, and who's to say they aren't."

"You know, Mr Walker, religion at times can be a dangerous business. One has to be careful with whom it's being discussed. The stance some took, they're prepared to die for it."

"Good heavens, I wouldn't figure you for a Bible puncher, commissioner? Well, well, there's proverb; 'the longest livers see the most."

The commissioner looked at him with a smile.

"Think nothing of what I said, minister; I was only stating a point. I'm not even a church goer."

"Well, it's not so bad, commissioner; you should try going sometimes."

"I'm not an atheist, minister. One day perhaps; I might just do that."

"Then I won't say more on the subject, commissioner, let's talk business."

"Yesterday, I head Harry is at James Town, however, I haven't decided what to do about it."

"Sound like you know he's there, commissioner?"

"Oh yes, I had him checked out, but why he's there, we'll never know."

"Commissioner, you don't need to know why he's there, just go after him."

"That a sound statement, but I'll decide when I discuss it with the lieutenant."

"I trust you'll make the right decision, commissioner."

Time had beaten them; they'll have to meet again for unfinished business.

It was a short talk that shouldn't have happened, but it shows they have the appetite for a good working relationship. The commissioner went to his hotel, but when he got there, Albert was gone, and the note was exactly where he left it.

Chapter 21
The Day After

It was the middle of July, and the days were awfully hot. Even though one is accustomed to the climate, it's wise not to be in the sun too long. Today the commissioner met with the minister for unfinished business. It was eleven o'clock when he arrived. Miss Benson alerted the minister.

"Good morning, commissioner; come in and pull up a chair." He was quite exuberant, the commissioner noticed.

"Good morning, minister; it's good to see you're cheerful and raring to go."

"Commissioner, at times one should try and display a happy outlook, even if he's not."

A strange thing to say, the commissioner thought, *why pretend to be happy if you aren't?*

"Are you pretending now, minister?" he asked with a smile.

"Oh no, today is one of those days I got out of bed and everything seemed right; that is good, isn't it, commissioner?"

"Quite so, minister, only everything isn't right, and it will never be right until we achieve our aim."

"Point taken, commissioner, but I was only expressing my feelings. Now then, what's on the agenda?"

"Well, yesterday I told you about Harry at James Town, but I haven't got the chance to talk it over with the lieutenant; until such time we can give that discussion a miss. However, I would like to know about the curfew, where are we regarding it?"

"Commissioner, I am as concerned as you are, but we have to wait until Parliament decides."

"But tell me, how difficult it will be to operate a curfew?"

"With good planning, it shouldn't be difficult, and if we put our heads together, I'm sure we can make a job of it."

"I'm sure we can, and apart from an all-out war, this could be the only way of stopping these gum men coming into town."

"In deed, minister. I'm aware the capital will be closed down during the night, but for how long, and from when?"

"There is really no time set. The capital has to go on functioning as normal; then again, it depends on the situation."

"However, before we get the ball rolling, there're a few criteria to be met, and—"

"Oh, like what, commissioner?" he interrupted.

"Well, if Parliament agrees, we—"

"Mr Wade," he interrupted, "on an issue like this, Parliament will agree."

"That's good to hear, but if and when we get the go ahead, the PM will have to do a ministerial broadcast. This kind of operation is new to the nation, so it should be made clear to them why such action is necessary."

"They're not going to like it. The storekeepers, and those who make their living from the street, they're going to feel hard done. Bear in mind, they trade late into the night."

"I know they won't, and who can blame them? But the curfew has to be done," said the minister.

The day was quite warm. From time to time the minister mopped his brow. He constantly sipped from the glass of cold lemonade. The commissioner, he was hot too, but he was not sweating. He didn't seem too bothered about the heath.

"Then what about the work on the ground? How do you fix that, commissioner?"

"Well, for what we got in mind, we've got the manpower; of course, we're talking soldiers and…" He paused and took a drink from his ice-cold glass of lemonade, probably giving himself time to think.

"Minister, this won't be an easy operation, but it is workable, and we must see it through."

"Commissioner, I'll play my part; whatever you think needs beyond what I know, go right ahead."

"Of course, minister, whatever we decide, you'll be the first to know."

The comment sounded somewhat condescending, but the minister smiled.

"Well, thank you kindly, commissioner, that's very gracious of you."

Both men saw the funny side; they laughed. Was the quote deliberate or was the commissioner testing the minister's resolve? The meeting concluded.

That Evening

He met with the lieutenant later that evening. He was at the Orange Tree; the lieutenant's favourite restaurant. It was supposed to be a business dinner – agenda, Harry Wells.

"We should go after him," said the lieutenant, who sat waiting for him to make his move.

"It's not a good idea. We should be on the offensive, do what he least expects."

"Only we've been doing that for some time, and so far without success," said the commissioner.

"We heard news of him, but we never saw him – correction, I never saw him."

"You're forgetting one thing," said the lieutenant, "he's always one step ahead of us; but with Holmes behind bars, things might change."

"Let's hope so, Dick. We could do with a change of fortune. Harry has played us long enough."

"But there're others; Rupert said so, and we have no idea who, not even suspicion."

"We'll have to be more vigilant, and be careful of what we say and to whom."

"Do you think he's the head of the gangs, 'the don', so to speak?" asked the lieutenant.

"He's not, and I'll tell you why; but hold on to your hat, what I'm going to tell you I didn't tell it to the home secretary; I didn't think it would serve any purpose. Yesterday, I had an encounter with the Johnsons. I—"

"The Johnsons? Who were they?"

"A Christian couple, they were brawling in the street."

"So, did you arrest them?" he asked with a huge grin.

"Do you want to hear, or should I not bother?" he asked with a stern face.

"I'm sorry, man, carry on. Only a Christian couple brawling in the street, doesn't seem right."

"Well, that's what they were, and don't interrupt. Bushman, the brother of Mrs Johnson, approached me with some stalking information, and I must tell you, I was aghast."

"Listen, man, I don't know what the hell you're talking about. So far you've not told me a damn thing."

"Patience, Dick, patience; I'm just preparing you for the surprise."

"Well, I'm ready and waiting, so go ahead; talk."

The commissioner however was just playing the lieutenant; let him stew a little.

"Now this Bushman was jumpy as a cat on burning ember. Firstly, he asked if his sister was okay, and then he explained who he was even without me asking."

The lieutenant looked at his watch. *He's impatient; his patience is running thin.*

"Noel, why are you going around the houses, man? I'm beginning to lose interest."

"You want to hear all the details, don't you?"

"Yes, but don't take all day, come on now."

"Now this fellow Bushman was one of the gangs. Said he decided to break free on account of the senseless killings."

"He actually said that?"

"He did so, and he made it clear he has never killed anyone."

"You arrested him anyway, didn't you?"

"No. If I had, he wouldn't have told me the rest. He said he'll tell me what I need to know if I promise not to arrest him. So, I promised."

"I hope it was a false promise, a little white lie, and you arrested him later?"

"No! How could I? I gave my word, and I wasn't going to renege, so, he relates, and he related plenty. This gang is here in town; right under our noses, and they've got nothing to do with Harry. It goes by the name of Burn's Gang."

"The Burn's Gang!" exclaimed the lieutenant. "You're not making it up, are you, man?"

"Why would I? I was just as surprised as you."

The lieutenant appeared to be thinking. He brushed back his curly black hair, then reached in his pocket for a spearmint.

"I can see you're thinking the same thing as I was, Dick. Now the question is, could it be Home Secretary Burns was part of this gang, or even the head of it?"

"I'm thinking along the same line. Then why did they kill him?"

"That's the 6400$ question, and I don't suppose we'll find the answer."

"You should arrest this Bushman regardless; as a part of a gang, and a marijuana smoker, I can't believe he never killed anyone."

"I suppose I should, but it wouldn't feel right; after all, he told me what I didn't know. Moreover, I do believe him; he didn't have to tell me, and if his information turns out to be true, we should be thanking him."

The lieutenant wasn't convinced. This Bushman was a criminal, and regardless of what he said, he should be arrested.

"He could be a reformed gang member; seen the light, you might say."

"Well, I don't believe that; once a murderer, always a murderer."

"Anyway, we'll never see him again. He's leaving town, his words."

"Running away more like, probably feeling guilty for his crimes."

"We should now concentrate on finding this gang; we have the edge. They don't know we know of them."

"But where to start looking? In this crowded city one could hide an elephant."

"Yes, and these people are so devious; they could operate freely, moving among the crowd, and not knowing what they look like. How the hell are we going to find them?"

"Well, we know they operated moving among the crowd. We'll try catching them red handed."

"Now there's a problem," said the lieutenant, "but let's not think about it now. Let's eat. I don't think too good on an empty stomach."

They had a three-course meal. The commissioner had become quite fond of the curry goat and rice, and the pepper didn't bother him anymore.

"Dick, I could have seconds, but I don't want to appear greedy."

"Appear greedy to whom? Me? Listen, man, if I feel for seconds, I couldn't give a monkey's backside what you or anyone thinks."

He ordered seconds, but only dessert.

"Listen, Dick, I've been thinking; we won't go chasing after the Burn's Gang; we know they're here; they can keep."

"You think that's wise, man?"

"Well, they're going nowhere. They can keep, we'll leave them alone, for a while. As for Harry, we're not sure what he's up to. I think we should make him priority." It was agreed.

"Listened, Dick, I was thinking about Janet. I wondered if she and Harry are still an item. Even that we don't know; some policemen we are."

"Don't beat yourself up, man, we're doing what we can. Come to think of it, he could be coming and going at the estate."

"Could well be. I we'll put an around-the-clock watch on the manor. If he's playing with the big boys, it's best we know."

He suddenly remembered something.

"Good heavens, Soldier Boy Albert," he exclaimed frightfully.

"What about him?" asked the lieutenant.

"I have to go find him; we have unfinished business."

"Oh! What business is that?"

"Well, he didn't finish telling me about this errand. He was too sleepy, and I was running late. Come along, Dick, pay up and let's go find him."

They headed for the barracks; Albert was cleaning rifles.

"Albert, I am so sorry, lad. Didn't you see the note I left you?"

"No, sir. I only saw the breakfast, and thank you, sir."

"Wasn't it gone cold when you awoke?"

"Yes, sir, but it was okay."

"We need you to come back to the hotel with us; we need to hear the rest of your story."

At the hotel, dinner was ordered for Albert, and drinks for themselves. Albert began to tell his story.

"He was at the bar, sir, and that woman, Mrs Nelson, was with him. She was listening to the duke box."

"What!" exclaimed the lieutenant. "Janet Nelson? Are you sure?"

"Quite sure, sir."

"Our presumption has borne out, Lieutenant, and if that be the case, we'll have to re-think our plans. Albert, can you be sure that the woman was Janet?"

"Oh yes, sir, Lieutenant, it was Janet Nelson, alright. Everyone knows her."

"Lieutenant, I think we been had. Harry's probably been coming and going at the manor all along, probably even laughing at us."

"Could be, but there's a saying about he who has the last laugh."

Dinner had arrived, and while Albert ate, they continued their discussion over drinks. The commissioner was quite generous; the men who served him well, he liked to treat them well. The plan about Harry had change, they won't be going after him. This fellow is no fool; he has his informant, and he'll know they're aware of his whereabouts. He's not going to hang around. But to make sure, they'll send back Albert to check if he's still there.

"Albert, I would like you to run another errand to James Town in the morning. Are you up for it?"

"Oh yes, sir, when do I leave?"

"At first light, say 8 am. They should be having breakfast."

"Good enough, sir. Do you want to see me before I leave?"

"No, Albert, you go right ahead, and you know the drill: if he's there, come directly back."

"Very good, sir."

He finished his dinner and was about to leave, but the lieutenant told him to wait up.

"I'll say good night, commissioner; I'll see you tomorrow."

"Good night, Lieutenant, and remember, we have to plan the curfew. I haven't got the word yet, but I think we should plan ahead, and tomorrow I'm meeting with the home secretary. I would like you along."

"What time would that be?"

"Say eleven?"

"Is there a reason why it always has to be in the morning?"

"The minister said he thinks it's better early in the morning."

"Is that supposed to be a joke, man?"

"If it is, it's not on me."

"Okay. 11 am it is. Goodnight."

Chapter 22
Fighting in the City

The following day, it was raining quite heavily; but since most people don't used parasols, not many people were out and about. But it was a quiet sort of day that was about to erupt violently. Be careful what you wish for. In conversation with the lieutenant, Commissioner Wade wished Harry would attack the prison. He was about to get his wish, even though it wasn't Harry. The lieutenant was on an errand when the news broke; there was gun fight outside the prison. In a hurry, he gathered some soldiers and raced to the scene. The gunmen couldn't get inside so they clashed with the guards outside. The lieutenant joined the fight, hence a running gun battle. The fighting spilled over in the city and continued. Soon, the commissioner joined the fray with officers. Gunmen were taking shelter in homes, using people as shields. On the streets, people were running for cover; of course, the law men had the responsibility to avoid killing civilians. They were winning the fight, but there were dead civilians too, but they were killed by gunmen.

Determined not to allow anyone to get away, the lawmen kept up the pressure. About 4 pm, there was a loud scream; it was coming from a store owned by one Mr Ahriman, a

Persian. Angry and grieving, he came to the front of the store holding his eighteen-month-old baby.

"They killed him," he repeated, along with his wife; they were distraught. The rain continued and the lawmen were still on the hunt. They had no idea how many there were, but there was no let-up in their search. In this busy city, a gunman could lay low, waiting for his chance to mingle with the crowd to get away. One gunman did just that; he lay low waiting till the fighting ceased. It was nearly 11 pm, and even though the city was well lit, some places were quite dark. But the law men left nothing to chance. They search everywhere. At about 1 am, the search was called off. They counted up the casualties: eight gunmen killed, along with two civilians and a baby.

Early morning, the sun was up and the day was bright. It didn't take long for the city to be buzzing again. The lone gunman seized his chance to get away. Without a weapon, he tried to mingle with the crowd, but his luck had run out. Of all the people for him to run into, it had to be his old foe, one Mr James, probably the only man who could recognise him. A former detective, he had been chasing the gang. As leader of the gang, this fellow was one of his main targets. A highly respected man was Mr James, but due to irregularities and deceptions in the constabulary, he resigned. Spotting this lone gangster without a gun, he couldn't believe his eyes. He didn't hesitate; moving quickly through the crowd, he grabbed hold of him and wrestled him to the ground. But he didn't put up much of a fight. As he held him on the ground, he exclaimed. "Well, I'll be damned if it isn't Pinkie. What the hell happened? You lost your way?" he mocked. But Pinkie didn't struggle, probably realising the game was up. One soldier was nearby. He was no stranger to the ex-detective. He moved in and help.

He asked, "Do you know this man, Mr James?"

"Oh yes, do we know each other, Pinkie?" he asked mockingly.

But Pinkie didn't respond. He looked like a broken man.

"I've been chasing this S.O.B. and his gang for a long time; I nearly had him a couple of times, but he had help from inside."

"From where, sir?" asked the soldier.

He didn't say; but commented, "Today of all days, he walks right into my arms. We're in luck, soldier; this man is a brute. Aren't you, Pinkie?"

Pinkie didn't response. He was still on the ground, and made no attempt to move. The detective was no doubt feeling mighty chuffed, catching his man at last, even though he was off the force.

"It's just not your day, Pinkie, but you won't be having another." All through his ordeal, Pinkie never said a word. He took him to jail with the help of the soldier, but old habits die hard; he behaved as though he was back on the force.

"You know, soldier, at times one never knows what's going to happen the next hour. I was only out for my early morning walk when I ran into Pinkie, and seeing him without a gun, I couldn't believe it."

"It's a good thing you did, Mr James."

"That's all right, soldier. I'm glad this man is behind bars. Tell the commissioner to take good care of this man; he's dangerous."

With his hands tied, they took him to jail. Later, the detective was to reflect on how easy it was, wondering why.

It was about 9 am and after the pounding the city had taken, it quickly got back to normal. However, neither the commissioner nor the lieutenant were aware of what took place that morning; they thought it was all over. The soldier found the lieutenant; he told him of the man in jail. The lieutenant was more than curious, he was intrigued.

"Are you sure?"

"Oh yes, sir. Mr James told me."

He's a good friend of the ex-detective, but he was amazed of what he was hearing.

"Ex-detective James told you?" he asked surprisingly.

"Yes, sir. He wrestled Pinkie to the ground while I tied his hands, then we then took him to jail."

"Okay, soldier; I'll take it from here."

He left to find the commissioner; he was at his office. He relayed what was told to him. They left immediately for the jail, eager to see the man they called Pinkie. Looking at the prisoner, they didn't talk to him; satisfied he was safely locked away, they placed two soldiers on duty. After the lieutenant's story about this Mr James, the commissioner was intrigued; he wanted to meet him. But first, he had some explaining to do; to talk to the relatives of the civilians who got kill. He then went to see Mr Ahriman. He apologised for his loss. It was of no comfort to the Ahriman's, but that was all the commissioner could do. *The Gleaner's* report was damning for the authorities. On page two, they ran a caption of eight dead gunmen, but on the front page, they depict the 18-month-old baby. They castigated the authority, even though they knew what had happened was unavoidable. On air, the prime minister apologised and tried to explain the situation; his words probably fell on deaf ears. Yet, whatever they thought of the authority, they were doing what they needed to, trying to clean up the country. The media and citizens should realise that, but because there was an anti-government feeling; they neither cared nor believed anything they said.

Two days after the fight; they went to interrogate Pinkie. They were thinking this hard man would be difficult, but they were wrong.

"Were you the gang leader?"

"Yes, but only after Percy was killed."

"Was Home Secretary Burns a member of your gang?"

"Oh sure, and other gangs too, but he got greedy." Pinkie talked and told them plenty.

They were surprised at how easy it was for him to talk, but they couldn't get any information from him regarding Harry Wells. He probably didn't know anything; then again, it could be the old rule, honour amongst thieves. They were feeling rather pleased with the operation, despite the killing of two civilians and a baby.

Sometime later, they'll have to give a full account to the PM, and they were hoping they'll be exonerated. It was almost a week, and the killing was all but forgotten. These people don't dwell on incidents like this; they've being through it only too often. The commissioner was at the office when the lieutenant visited. "Dick, the next time you see Mr James, would you tell him I would like to speak with him, at his convenience, of course."

"Sure thing, man, but may I ask why?"

"To thank him for his assistance in catching Pinkie; it's the decent thing to do, don't you think?"

"I guess; I'll convey your message."

The day after, the ex-detective turned up at the office. He was welcomed by Secretary Scott; they were no strangers.

"Good day, Mr James, long time no see. Are you coming back to work, sir?" she asked with a broad smile.

"Good day Julie. No, I'm not coming back. I only come to see the commissioner."

"Take a seat, sir, I'll go tell him you're here."

She didn't return alone; the commissioner came along too.

"Mr James, I presume?" he said with his hand outstretched.

"The very same," he responded as they greet each other.

"Good of you, Mr James. Do come in."

They returned inside and the ex-detective was offered a seat, but he stood looking around. "I take you're accustomed to this office, Mr James?"

"I've spent some time here, most of which quite unpleasant."

"I'm sorry to hear that. If you care to talk about it, I'm a good listener."

He didn't respond. He wanted to know why he was summoned here. But if he was thinking it was to thank him for apprehended Pinkie, he couldn't be more wrong; the commissioner had ulterior motives.

"I've been hearing much about you, Mr James."

"All good things, I hope. Mr Wade."

"All good. You're the man who apprehended Pinkie. Tell me, Mr James, how you came to know this man?"

"Oh, we've got history. Of the gunmen who were on my radar, he was one of the most wanted. A brutal induvial. I can't understand why he didn't put up a fight."

"He was the deputy, but after Percy was shot, he became the boss. A few times I could have had him, but he was getting help from inside."

"Inside, Mr James? What do you mean?"

"Your predecessor, Commissioner Michael, those two were thick as thieves."

The ex-detective was spilling more than what was asked of him; it could be he was proud to catch his man at last.

"I'm sure you're feeling all the better for arresting him, Mr James, don't you?"

"I suppose I am; call it a citizen's arrest."

"You know what I think, Mr James? You care about your country and law and order, and that was your thinking when you saw this man."

"Don't made more if than it worth, Mr Wade, I only did what a good citizen should. So, what are you going to do about this man? If other gangs discover he's alive and, in your jail, they'll come for him. Not to kill him; perhaps they look out for their kind."

"I would like to ask you about that, Mr James. I spoke to someone a few days ago who told me about a gang. He said he was a member but was quitting on account of the senseless killings. It goes by the name of the Burn's Gang. Did you or anyone in government even suspect the home secretary to have links with this or any other gangs?"

"Sure, myself and others, but dared not speak out speak against it; speak and you're dead."

Mr James went on to talk about Home Secretary Burns, and his sudden increase in wealth.

"He didn't win the POW (a form of lottery), so where did his wealth come from? Cocaine and marijuana. Where else?"

"I didn't have long dealings with him," said the commissioner, "but from what I heard, thank God I didn't."

"Mr Wade, they say one shouldn't speak ill of the dead, but he being alive wasn't good for the country."

With the passion with which he spoke, the commissioner felt it wouldn't take much in the way of persuasion for him to return to the force. He needed a deputy, and he seemed to think the ex-detective could fit the bill.

"So, you still didn't tell me why I'm here, Mr Wade. If it's for catching Pinkie, I considered it my duty."

"That may be so, but it takes a brave man to tackle a gun man single handed."

"Well, there's a surprise for you, Mr Wade, and so you know, I don't carry a gun, not anymore; then again, it could be Pinkie wanted to get caught."

"You don't believe that, do you, Mr James?"

"Not really, just an off-the-cuff comment you might say."

"Mr James, there's an old saying, 'once a policeman, always a policeman'. I might be presumptuous, but tell me, why did you leave the force?"

"A feasible question, and I'll tell you. There're times when a man gets tired of doing the same thing daily, and would like a change."

The commissioner wasn't buying that, he talked with so much passion, like a man wanting to return to the force.

"I must tell you, Mr James, from the way you talked, it sounds like a man missing the action."

The ex-detective seemed stumped for a reply. He reached into his pocket and took out a pack of Woodbine. He offered one to the commissioner. The commissioner was not a smoker, even though he always carried a pack; but not to appear unsociable, he'll smoke with the ex-detective.

"I'm not so sure about missing the action, Mr Wade, but it sure felt good when I grabbed hold of Pinkie."

The commissioner decided not to beat about the bush. He asked directly.

"Have you ever felt the desire to return to the force, Mr James?"

"Now there's a question; and a loaded one too, but tell me Mr Wade, is that the reason you asked me here?"

"No, not particularly; call it curiosity."

"You know what curiosity did to the cat, don't you, Mr Wade?"

"Yes, Mr James, but I still would like to know."

"Well, I'm not saying I wouldn't, I've just never given it much thought."

The commissioner wasn't buying that either; probably, he just wanted someone to ask him. His intention almost got the better of him; he would like to offer him the position here and now, but he was not going to, he'll bide his time. Mr James was about to leave, but the commissioner wasn't finished; his interest in the ex-detective grew even stronger.

"Would you like to have a drink with me at the hotel some time, Mr James? We could pick up where we left off."

"I wouldn't mind at all, Mr Wade, but it depends on when."

"Oh good, then how about tomorrow at about 5 pm?"

He didn't response immediately. He appeared to be thinking of the time.

"5 o'clock will be fine."

"Good, I'll see you then." They said goodbye.

The commissioner called Miss Scott; he wanted to know how if she was the secretary during the time of the ex-detective, and if she was, she probably can tell him something about him.

"Oh yes, sir, |I was here, and I've seen off two commissioners before him."

"You probably seen me off too, miss Scott, but who were these commissioners?"

"Mr Harvey, Mr Jordon and Mr Mitchel. Mr Harvey, he was a very bad man; he was always making deals; he eventually wound up in a well with his throat cut."

"Tell me about Mr James. Was he a good detective?"

"The best, sir, but he couldn't get any work done. He and Commissioner Mitchel couldn't get along; they argued all the time."

"I was told Commissioner Mitchel was on the take. You think he was?"

"That's what everyone thinks, but no one talked about it."

"He was eventually shot, wasn't he?"

"Yes, sir, they assassinated him at his home. Whatever he was in, the home secretary was too, those two were as thick as thieves. They blocked everything Mr James wanted done. One afternoon, Commissioner Mitchel and Mr James came to blows. Mr James broke his nose; it was shortly before, he was assonated."

"Home Secretary Burns, you knew about him, he suffered the same fate."

"Oh yes, he resigned from the government because of ill health; shortly before he was assassinated."

But the commissioner wasn't speaking the truth; he resigned from government but not because of bad health. As she was going through the door, she turned and asked, "Is Mr James coming back to work, sir?"

"I don't think so, Miss Scott. Whatever gives you that idea?"

"Nothing at all, sir. I just thought he was."

Chapter 23
The Visit

On his way to the hotel the following day, the ex-detective was concerned as to why the commissioner took so much interest in him. He arrived at the hotel and was greeted at the front desk by some old acquaintances. The receptionist alerted the commissioner of his arrival. The commissioner asked to send him up, while he awaited at the door for him.

"Come on in, Mr James, and do make yourself comfortable."

He was doing all he can to let the ex-detective feel at ease. His intention was good, but later will appear a little devious. He didn't sit but remained standing, looking around.

"I take it you've been in this suite before, Mr James?"

"No, but I've had reasons to visit the hotel quite a few times, and it wasn't always pleasant."

"I'm sorry, where are my manners? What would you like to drink?" he asked. But it was all a pretence. Everything he did or said, it was for the benefit of the ex-detective.

"I could do with a cold beer, thank you."

"I'll have to disappoint you there; I've only got Captain Morgan and scotch, but I could ring for a cold beer."

"No need to; I'll have a scotch, thank you."

He served up the scotch, but not for himself. He was having The Captain, as he chose to call it.

"How would you like it, neat or on the rocks?"

"I'll have it neat, thank you."

"Good man, just the way I take mine, but I'm having The Captain. Have you ever taken The Captain, Mr James?"

"Oh sure, but I'm really a rum man; however, a drop of scotch is always welcome."

"Each to his own, Mr James."

There was a call put through to the commissioner from the front desk. It was the home secretary, to tell him the Privy Council came through, they've given the okay for the execution. After a short conversation, he was still holding the phone looking pensive. Observing he was a little sad, Mr James asked. "Bad news, Mr Wade?"

"Oh no, that was the home secretary. The Privy Council gave the go-ahead for the execution."

"They are quick with the decision; I wonder why. From what I've been told, it usually takes months, sometime years."

"They usually do, and it's so wrong; we should be making our own decisions," said Mr James.

"Quite so. We shouldn't be waiting on a foreign country to tell us who we can or can't execute. It's is not only undemocratic, it's darn right backward."

"Then what do you think of the court's decision? Is it a correct one?"

"Mr Wade, the man is a traitor; he and the commissioner, whatever they were in, they were in it together. They caused the death of many innocent people. He got what he deserved. Hang him but hang him high."

The smiling commissioner replied. "I saw the movie too."

Mr James took a sip from his glass; seems he just realised his comment.

"Well spotted, Mr Wade; I too have seen the movie, so, when is the hanging?"

"I don't know yet, I will know when I meet with the home secretary, but it won't be long in waiting."

"What are these hangings like, Mr James? Apart from the movie, I never witnessed one."

"Nor have I. I'm not going to join a crowd to revel in someone's demise, even if it's someone like Holmes."

"You know, Mr James, whatever way one looks at it, it doesn't seem right; some might even think it's barbaric."

"For these people, Mr Wade, it's a way of life. They don't see it the way others do."

"I have nothing but contempt for people like Holmes, but such behaviour is nothing short of immoral."

"Mr James, I'm thinking, your citizen arrest of Pinkie could start a trend, after what *The Gleaner* wrote about it; it could inspire others."

"Mr Wade, you have heaps enough praised on me. I will begin to blush. Is there an ulterior motive?"

"Whatever gives you that idea? I'm simply paying you a well-deserved compliment."

The ex-detective didn't respond; he helped himself to another drink from the bottle. He reached for his cigarette and gave one to the commissioner, but remain tight lipped. The commissioner however, wanted to talk, all the while thinking when to ask the question he's got in mind.

"Mr James, I would like to know about Commissioner Mitchel. What kind of a man was he?"

The question was fill with deception; his secretary already told him about the man.

"His, Mr Wade, is not a very nice story. Like Holmes, the man was a traitor; the least said of him the better."

"I understand he did nothing in regards to stopping the gangs."

"Well now, there was always the pretence, but that was all it was. He blocked any attempt to apprehend certain gang members. The man, Mr Wade, was as shifty as he was evil. My team and I brought in Ralph Murry, alias Happy, a lone wolf you might say, but the man was a brute. There shouldn't be the need to prove his guilt; everyone knew he was a killer; God only knows how many people he killed. He raped two young girls; one was as young as twelve; the sixteen-year-old committed suicide. Commissioner Mitchel knew all this, yet he defended him."

"So, what happened to this Happy fellow?"

"He was killed, but not the way he should; even though it wouldn't be enough to pay for his crime, he should've been be hanged."

"So how was he killed?" the commissioner asked again.

"Commissioner Mitchel had him shot; they probably were planning something big, but it seemed they couldn't agree. Happy probably decided he didn't need the commissioner and probably was going to kill him, but the commissioner being the devious bastard he was, acted first; he had Happy shot."

"What was Home Secretary Burns doing all this time? Had he any knowledge about the commissioner's dealings?"

"Of course, the man was an accomplice, I'm sure of it. He backed the commissioner all the way. Of course, he was your boss, Mr Wade; you know his fate."

"It was only for a short time, thank God, and in that time, I realised the man was devious. It wasn't a surprise when the news broke that he was assassinated. The evils that men do shall follow them, Mr James."

"A bit of Shakespeare I hear, Mr Wade."

"Just a line I remember; I couldn't quote another."

The time was approaching four, and the conversation continued. The commissioner was expecting the lieutenant; and hoping he'll arrive before the ex-detective left.

"Mr James, I'm about to ring for dinner. Would you like to eat?"

"You know Mr Wade, I've got this feeling you're being nice to me for a reason; however, dinner would be nice."

"Probably, I know a good man when I see one, Mr James. Tell me, you know Lieutenant Dickson? I am expecting him soon."

"Oh yes, I know him; a damn good man is Dick, he had his troubles with commissioner Mitchel too; they nearly came to blows."

"Why was that? Dick is an army man?"

"Well, put it this way, if he could, he would have had the lieutenant removed."

"He kept that quiet," said the commissioner.

"I don't suppose he wanted to talk about it, Mr Wade, somethings are better forgotten."

Dinner arrived. They had been drinking for some time; however, to Mr James the scotch is more appetising than dinner. He poured himself another. "I'll join you," said the commissioner. He poured from the bottle of Captain Morgan. Mr James, however, was a man who likes to talk. He wanted to know about policing back in England.

"Mr Wade, what policing is like in England; is it as tough as it is here?"

"It appears to be tough here, Mr James, but only because we're fighting on two fronts: the citizen as well as the criminals. Back in England, with co-operation from the public, at times, we succeeded where we shouldn't."

"You're not going to get such co-operation here; not while this government is in office. The people despise everything about this administration, and for good reason; they're of no help to them."

"What do you mean, Mr James?"

"Well, you might not notice, but it's not easy earning a living, and thee people moan about it, that's the way they are. This government, couldn't give a damn about them, yet they're the ones who put them in office. With nothing to gain, they turned to the men with guns, probably out of fear. Sometimes I wonder why the hell we bother to elect members for Parliament."

He sounded as though he was lamenting, but not for himself, but for his countryman.

"Strong words, Mr James. It seems to care very much for your country."

"I go without saying, Mr Wade, I've got only one country, and I love it dearly. What it has become, is the result of government."

"Are you saying they allow the situation to get out of control?"

"Certainly, if they started from the off set to rid the country of the gangs and the crooked people, they would be on top of things today. This situation builds and builds until it became septic. Now, it's a monumental task to rid the country of these criminals."

The commissioner observed the passion with which he spoke; he sounded more a politician than an ex-law man.

"Tell me, Mr James, have you ever considered going into politics? I think you would do well there."

He picked up his fork but didn't use it. He was looking at it as though something was wrong with it.

"I'm sorry if I sound like a politician, Mr Wade, but this is the party I voted for; the party I always voted for, but not this time. To solve this country's problems, it's going to takes men with guts, integrity and imagination; qualities this government hasn't got."

"Then where have all the good men gone; men who feel honoured to serve their country?"

"You won't find them among this lot, Mr Wade, these're men with criminal intent, wanting to get rich quick."

"The world over, Mr James, there's always people who're like that. All we can do is try to see they don't. As things stand now, we're doing our best, and we'll continue to, but we could do with a few good men."

"I'm sure you could, and I hope you'll succeed in all your undertakings. You've made a good start, but don't underestimate what lies ahead. Harry Wells is still out there, and as long as he's at large, there's sure lawlessness."

Hearing all that, the commissioner decided the time was right to pop the question, but tactfully.

"Tell me, Mr James, do you ever consider returning to the force? The constabulary needs a deputy; I think you're just the man."

"I remember being asked that question before."

"I remember too; I asked it. Well? Would you, Mr James?"

"I didn't burn my bridges, so if the opportunity presented itself and my country needs me, I'm not saying I would gladly comply, but I would have to give it some thought."

"Would you care to elaborate on that, Mr James?" He then went on to talked about the country he loves, and what should be done that's not being done.

Hearing that, the commissioner thought he was ready to return, but in what capacity? He would dearly like him to be his deputy.

"If there are people who are sincere and willing to work for the good of the country, regardless of the benefits, then yes, Mr Wade, I think I would."

"Then how would you feel if I was asked you to be my deputy. Would it appeal to you?"

He didn't respond immediately. It was quite a warm day, so he took a drink of ice-cold water, and all this time, the dinner was hardly touched.

"You know, Mr Wade, I had my suspicions all along. You were buttering me up for something; there's word for that – deception."

"I take exception to that, Mr James. Deception is an ugly word, all I did was ask a question. I'm not going to deny my intent, but deception, sir? I resent it."

Their eyes made contact, and there was laughter. "Mr Wade, I learnt a long time ago, one must be true to one self."

"I can assure you, Mr James, I'm very much that."

The commissioner took a piece of mutton on his fork, but he didn't eat it; in fact, up till now neither man ate much; the food had probably gone cold. For the commissioner, there was one thing on his mind.

"So, how about it, Mr James? Would you come back to the force as my deputy?"

"I say this for you, Mr Wade. You're persistent; it seems once you get your teeth into something, you never let go."

"Well now, it all depends on what I'm biting into."

"I have a question for you. When you invited me, was it your intention to offer me a job? And if the answer is yes, then you didn't have to try and get me liquored up for an answer. So, you see, Mr Wade, there's no other word for your action than deception."

"Come, come, Mr James, a man like you resigned from the force not because you wanted to, but on principles. You hold your country dear; you're a patriot, so, I will tell you now, you're going to accept the post, but not because I asked you, but because you wanted to."

The ex-detective took a deep breath; he gazed into his glass of scotch; it seemed the commissioner's comment hit a spot.

"Mr Wade, I have no knowledge of that side of the constabulary; I'm the guy who goes chasing criminals; that post should go to someone knowledgeable with the position."

"Regarding the differences, there aren't any. A man with your knowledge and experience, you will master the job in no time."

"There you go again, trying to butter me up. You know, Mr Wade, I might not be the man you think I am, and I would hate to disappoint you."

"Mr James, I think you're that man. I knew from the first time I set eyes on you. You're going to make one hell of a good deputy."

"Mr Wade, I haven't accepted your offer yet. I will sleep on it and give it some thought."

"However, the job isn't mind to offer, I can only make recommendation, that rest with the home secretary."

"Yes, Mr Wade, that I know; and I also know you can influence the decision, and in this case, that's what you'll be doing."

"You credit me with far too much clout, Mr James."

"Don't worry, Mr Wade, I fully understand."

The lieutenant arrived; he rapped on the door in his usual fashion.

"Come in, Dick, the door is open."

Mr James looked at the commissioner kind of curiously.

"How the devil did you know it was Dick?"

"Only the lieutenant raps on the door like that; he's heavy-handed."

The lieutenant walked in with his usual zest.

"Good evening, gentlemen. It seems I've got long legs."

"Long legs, Dick, what do you mean?"

"It's an old wives' tale, Mr Wade," Mr James interjects. "He arrived just in time for dinner."

The commissioner groaned as though he was in pain, but didn't comment.

"Good to see you, Jamie. I didn't expect to find you here. What gives?"

"Don't tell me you're disappointed, Dick."

"Disappointed perhaps, but not for the reason you might be thinking."

"Well, what's your thinking?"

"After hearing your heroics with Pinkie, I'm wondering, why you're not back on the force where you can do some good. I hope the commissioner was trying to reel you back in."

"I would never do that," said the commissioner, "but we talked about it."

He looked at the commissioner with squinted eyes as if to say, *you bloody liar*, instead, he turned his comment to the lieutenant.

"So, I take it you both are in cahoots regarding getting me back on the force?"

"I don't know what you mean, Jamie. I said my piece, I have no part in what Noel's doing."

"Of course, you aren't," said the ex-detective sarcastically.

"Dick, we've been friends for many years, but I didn't think you would have joined the commissioner in his deception."

The commissioner didn't respond. Instead of pleaded his innocent, he's got a story to tell.

"Mr James, I'll tell you about my Uncle Bernard. I come from a long line of policemen; before me, Uncle Bernard was the last. He retired early but soon realised he made a mistake."

However, he continued with the story but in fine details, going back to his great granddad.

"Is this going to take long, Mr Wade?" the ex-detective asked impatiently.

"He's like that, Jamie, you have to have plenty a time to listen to his story,"

said the lieutenant.

"Okay, I'll cut to the chase. One day, he walked in Headquarters and asked for his job back."

He paused for a while, fiddling with the fork for no apparent reason, while the others sat looking at him as though he had done something wrong.

"You know, Noel, you've got a damn bad habit. You begin telling a story then you stop. Tell us what the hell happened?" said the lieutenant.

"Simple, he was given back the job."

There was a loud groan from the lieutenant. "I think you made that up."

"No, I didn't."

"What position was that, Mr Wade?"

"Pounding the beat, Mr James; he was a tender foot."

"Then, I take it there's a moral to this story?"

"Only this; at times one does things on impulse and later regrets it."

"Are you regretting your action, Jamie?" asked the lieutenant flippantly.

"Gentlemen, I can see you got my interest at heart, but if you don't mind, leave me to decide."

The talk continued through the evening. The others were having the hard stuff, the commissioner ordered a cold beer for the lieutenant. However, the ex-detective was still thinking he was set up.

"The truth, Dick, when you told me Mr Wade would like to see me, you knew his intention."

"No, I thought he wanted to thank you for arresting Pinkie, however, from what you said he did, I'm not surprised; at times, he can be quite a devious fellow."

"I resent that. I never at any time acted underhandedly," he said with a cheeky smile.

It was all a comedy between friends. Mr James really wanted to re-join the force, but was not showing it.

"Dick, the Privy Council has approved the hanging; news came through earlier."

"Really? That was quick. I wonder why."

"I said the same," said the commissioner.

The Attempted Assassination

There was a knock at the door. It was an officer; he was looking quite anxious and blowing quite heavily.

"Commissioner, there's a shooting at Home Secretary Walker's home, sir."

"Is the home secretary hurt?"

"I don't know, sir. I haven't been there; the message was given to me to give to you."

They wasted no time; they set off to the minister's residence. Two policemen were there; they weren't doing much, just standing there. Also on hand was a reporter, they're certain to make a big story out of it.

The minister wasn't hurt, neither was his wife, but they were badly shaken.

"Thank God, you're all right. We got here as soon as we heard."

"It was a close call, commissioner, and a frightening experience."

"I'm glad to see you're not hurt, Mr Walker. How is Mrs Walker? Is she alright?"

"Good to see you, Mr James; yes, she's all right, but as you can imagine, she's badly shaken."

The commissioner turned to the officers for his report, but there wasn't much to tell.

"When I got here, there were no gunmen about, sir."

Of course, that's the usual story. Never anyone has anything to tell. If they do, they could be lying. If they find out the job was done, they'll no doubt try again. The ex-detective had a thought, he's knowledgeable how these gun men operate.

"Mr Wade, it could be they're trying to force the minister's hand, wanting him to let Pinkie go."

"If that be the case, Mr James, why didn't they send him a note? No, I don't think so; this looks like a genuine attempt on his life."

They conversed.

"Dick, get three soldiers here pronto; I want a round the clock guard on the home secretary."

"Mr Wade, what you should be mindful of is, one of their kind is behind bars; they're going to try to get him, one way or another."

"That I'm aware of Mr James, but we can't be everywhere."

The lieutenant returned and placed the soldiers and secured the perimeter. The commissioner conversed with the minister.

"Will you be all right for our talk tomorrow, minister?"

There was a pause; he appeared hesitant. The commissioner had a re-think, due to his ordeal; he probably shouldn't ask.

"Sorry I asked, minister, you've been through a terrible ordeal. If you feel you can't make it tomorrow, and you might want to stop at home with your good lady, don't worry, we can do it another time."

"Commissioner, thanks for your concern, but it's my duty to be there. I'll see you tomorrow."

"If you're sure, minister?"

"Yes, commissioner, I'm quite sure."

"Then tomorrow it is. I've posted three guards outside; they'll be here around the clock."

"Thanks, commissioner, you've been most considerate."

At his office the following morning, he was thinking; the minister said he'll be all right for their meeting later today, but he was never going to say he can't. After such an ordeal, his time will be better spent staying at home with his wife. This matter regarding the date for the execution can be done over the phone. He asked Miss Scott to get him a line to the minister's resident. It's not unusual for them to talk business on the phone if there's a situation.

"Good morning, minister. I trust you and Mrs Walker had a comfortable night."

"Not really, commissioner, but we're trying to get over it."

"I suppose what happened should be expected; when one took a stand against criminals, one's life will always be at risk."

"Quite so, commissioner, but I feel there's another reason for calling me."

"There is, it's about the date for the execution. This is an urgent matter, but one I feel we don't have to meet to decide."

"I agree, if I said in two days, would that be all right for you to make arrangements?"

"I don't see why not. We'll start today."

"Good, then Tuesday the 20th it is. I'll call my secretary to note it, and inform the PM."

"Thank, minister, you have a good day now, and we'll talk again soon. My regards to Mrs Walker."

Chapter 24
Hanging the Deputy

After last night's heavy rain, the day was warming up nicely. By the time the sun was overhead; it was blisteringly hot. The people had camped out in the baking sun, waiting for the hanging. The commissioner turned up for his early morning meeting with the home secretary, but he still seems out of sort. The commissioner detected he was somewhat hesitant in his approach, and not wanting to overtax him with the situation, he was treading carefully. But he was aware of the commissioner's action so he picked him upon it.

"Commissioner, I'm fully aware of your concern for my sanity; thank you, but there's no need. I can assure you I'm fully compos-mentis. Now then, the moment we finished here I will assure the PM we're ready to go, and there won't be any slip-ups. Would that be a fair assessment, commissioner?"

"A fair assessment, minister, we're prepared and ready for any eventualities."

"That's good to hear, so, will you be at the hanging, commissioner?"

"Oh no, my presence is not required. What about you? Will you be there?"

"Like you, commissioner, I'm not needed; the governor is in charge of matters there."

"Is there any news regarding the curfew, minister? I just got the feeling that after today, the gangs will ramp up their activities."

"In truth, commissioner, I missed the last sitting of Parliament, so I'm not up to speed with matters there. However, I will raise the matter again with the PM when we talk later."

It was approaching 1 pm. The meeting ended, in two hours. Mr Holmes will face the gallows. He was about to exit the door when he remembered. "There's a matter I forgot to bring to your attention, minister."

"Does it have to be now, commissioner?" It seemed he was feeling the pressure of yesterday's happening.

"Oh, I'm sorry, minister, how insensitive of me; it can keep."

But he wasn't going to put on hold what could be done today for tomorrow.

"Mr Wade, now I know, I could never rest easy knowing there's a matter pending my attention; go ahead, let's hear it."

"About the position for deputy commissioner, is there anyone lined up for it yet?"

"I have, but I haven't gotten around to interview the candidate. Why do you ask?"

"I would like to suggest a possible candidate. One I think you know quite well."

"Oh, and where did you find this person you think I know well?"

"A coincidental meeting you might say, but I think this man is the real deal; he's Mr James."

"Ex-detective James?" he asked somewhat surprisingly. He knew much about this man, and held him in high esteem.

"Yes, the very same. I would like you to talk with him."

"Was that the reason he was at my home the other day?"

"Oh no, we were together when the news broke. I asked him along."

"I know Mr James quite well; he was a good detective, dedicated to the job; a shame he resigned when he did. But what made you think he would be right for the job? Or more to the point, what made you think he would accept it?"

"Call it a policeman's hunch, and I like this man's attitude regarding policing."

"I can see you want this man, commissioner."

"In a word, yes, minister. I need someone responsible and loyal to his country, someone I can trust."

"Okay, commissioner, ask Mr James to come see me."

He called in his secretary to make a note. "Mr James is due here for an interview on Thursday the 19th at 11 o'clock."

"Would you pass on this appointment to him, commissioner?"

"Sure will, as soon as I can speak with him."

"Thank you, commissioner. I'll say good day, and I hope everything go well as planned."

On returning, he drove by the prison. Outside there were the kind of activities one sees at a fanfare. Later at his office, he had a visitor, ex-detective James. He heard news about Harry Wells, but the commissioner won't be following it up; the hanging takes priority. He told him of the appointment with the home secretary. He wasn't surprised. He knew it was commissioner's doing.

"Will you be able to make it, Mr James?"

"I think I can, but will you be there too?"

Before he could respond, the bell began to toll, signalling the execution was over. They both sat in eerie silence while the bells continued; it lasted one minute. The phone rang; it was Mr Webster, (the prison governor) he called to inform the commissioner the job was done. Deputy Holmes was hung.

"You've gotten rid of one traitor, Mr Wade, but the job is only half done. It is going to take some concerted effort to rid the force of these vermin."

"Don't I know it, but it's easier said than done; however, I'm hoping with you, me and the lieutenant, we can clean up the constabulary."

Anxious to get the ex-detective in the job, the commissioner was getting ahead of himself. Mr James smiled wryly. He knew what the commissioner was doing, but he didn't mind one bit.

The phone rang again, and this time it was Home Secretary Walker. He asked about the hanging.

"Yes, minister, I've gotten the news along with Mr James. The prison governor rang to inform me."

The home secretary was wise to the move. The commissioner's point couldn't be clearer; Mr James was the man he wanted as his deputy.

"Oh, about the meeting on Thursday, I take it Mr James won't be alone?"

"No, minister, the lieutenant and I will be along too."

"Okay, commissioner, I take your point, good day."

"That, Mr James, was the home secretary. He asked to remind you of the appointment."

"I suppose that is when I sign up for the job, right, Mr Wade?" he asked sarcastically.

"I can't answer that, Mr James; you'll have to wait to find out."

The ex-detective had a little smile; he knew the job was waiting for him.

"Mr James, I would like to have you on board. This fellow Harry Wells is proving a tough nut to crack; tell me what you know of him."

"Well now, are you asking me as a citizen, or a policeman?"

"I'm asking as a man who had troubles with him in the past, or didn't you?"

"No, I never met the man; in my time, he wasn't a big fish. If I tell you anything about him, it's not what I know; it's what I heard."

"I heard news of him earlier, that's the reason I'm here. He's at Green Bay, but I've got no idea why this fellow chose to tell me."

"Green Bay in Pen Hill?"

"That's what the fellow said. You been there before, Mr Wade?"

"Don't you read *The Gleaner*? That was where the fiasco took place that led to the conviction of Holmes."

"Oh yes, I remember, but that being so, why is he going back there?"

"No idea, but in conversation with the people there, I was to learn they're not too fond of him."

"Mr Wade, are you saying you actually had such a conversation with the people there?"

"So, I did, they were at the arum bar, and it was good to know not everyone thinks of Harry Wells as a hero. It could be out of fear they gravitated to him."

"I'm sure there is some truth in that, but the government is doing nothing to help; they been abandoned. However, opinions could be changing; they've probably begun to see these killers for what they are."

"I hope so. It would make a whole lot of difference, so, what you aiming to do about Harry? Go after him?"

"No, not this time. We'll leave Mr Wells be, for now."

"Mr Wade, you're not going to catch him this way. You'll have to go chasing him, even if you think the information isn't reliable."

"I'm mindful of that, Mr James, but right now, I would like to concentrate on the curfew. We haven't got the word as yet, but I would like to plan ahead."

"Have you got any advice on the matter, Mr James?"

"I can think of something, like a ministerial broadcast, and putting up posters all over the city. The people need to be reminded every day leading up to the appointed time."

"I like that way of thinking; I will put it to the home secretary."

He was doing all he could to let the ex-detective feel as though he was back on the force.

"We should be mindful of those gunmen wanting to coming in during the curfew; the people they do business with are here in town, and they won't want to lose trade."

"If they do, Mr James, we'll be prepared for them, that's the purpose of the curfew."

The commissioner smiled broadly but said nothing. He just realised something the ex-detective said.

"Did I say something amusing, Mr Wade?"

"Well, it just something you said, 'we'; you did say we, didn't you, Mr James?"

"Yes, but I was making it for you, Mr Wade; think nothing of it. I'm still a civilian."

"Tell me, what do you think of arming the police? Have you any notion regarding it?"

"For sure. I argued the point, but Home Secretary Burns and Commissioner Mitchel wouldn't hear of it. Law men should be armed, even though I'm not too sure about brandishing weapons on the street in broad day light."

"Then what about small arms? I usually carry a piece under my coat."

"That could be the answer, but I feel the government won't agree to it."

The lieutenant arrived just in time to hear the commissioner's last comment. He himself argued to arm the police.

"They should be doing that from the offset," he commented. "One can't be keeping the peace bare-handed while these lunatics run around carrying high-powered rifles; it's madness."

"Dick, I must tell you, it's not a good habit to eavesdrop on people's conversation."

"Just giving you my opinion, man; in your police force, there're too many loopholes, this is one of it."

"Hear, hear to that," said the ex-detective.

"Hi, Jamie, were you at the hanging?"

"Oh no, we were right here, but I'm gratified that the country rid itself of a traitor."

"And so said all of us."

Discussing Pinkie.

The two men were about to leave, but the commissioner would like to talk something over with Mr James.

"Go ahead, Dick, I'll see you when I see you. I want to talk some more with Mr James, if he doesn't mind."

He turned to face him. "Mr Wade, haven't you got enough of me for one day?"

"Yes, but there's a matter of importance I would like your opinion on, but only if you can spare the time. It's about Pinkie, I would—"

"Have you decided what to do about him?" he interrupted.

"No, not really; that's what I want to talk to you about."

"You know, Mr Wade, having him locked up like this, you could be inviting trouble."

"Yes, I know it's a threatening situation, but he has to face trial, and we're going to make damn sure he does."

"I'll talk to the home secretary to try and speed up proceedings."

Mr James took a deep breath; he was thinking further ahead, and he was not thinking of a trial.

"I suppose when the time comes, he'll be found guilty and sentenced to be hanged, but only if the Privy Council agrees, and it could take a long time. In the meantime, we're left with a problem."

"Yes, but such is the law, Mr James."

The commissioner talked about the problem, and how difficult it's going to be. Mr James, he didn't say anything for a while, he had an idea regarding the problem, but was coy to put it the commissioner.

"Are you still with me, Mr James?"

"Yes, and I would like to make a suggestion regarding the situation, but you might consider it too extreme."

"Let me be the judge of that, Mr James, please make your point."

He made a sound as though he was going to break out into songs, he then reached into his pocket as though he was feeling for something. Observing his action, the commissioner asked. "Is there something bothering you, Mr James?"

"No, nothing at all, but I would like to ask you a question. Do you think the life of one's worth more than the lives of the many?"

"Is that a trick question?"

"Not at all, it's just a yes or no question. One which I think doesn't need much consideration."

"That may be so, but on the grounds that I might incriminate myself, I would like to know the reason for the question."

"Okay, Mr Wade, this is my thinking. Why lumber ourselves with an unnecessary problem." He paused. It was as though he was coying to talk about what he was thinking.

"Mr James, I'm most intrigued, please go on."

"Okay, this might sound callous or brutal even. Pre-amp the outcome of Pinkie's trial; the man is going to the gallows. So, why wait? Get rid of him now, at a stroke."

The commissioner was wide-eyed, looking amazed.

"What do you mean? No, don't tell me, I can fill in the blanks."

He got up and moved to another chair; he sat down somewhat uncomfortably. There was a long pause.

"By God, man, I never thought you were so damn devious, or should I say callous. How the hell you thought about that, did you find it difficult?"

"No at all. It would be a logical outcome to an unnecessary problem. However, it was only my thinking, if you find it too extreme, I'll say no more about it."

"It's a solution to the problem, alright, but I'll have to give it some thought."

"What's there to be considered? You would be relieving yourself of this burden, and from the threat of a shootout."

"I will run it by the lieutenant; I would like to hear his take on it."

"That will be interesting," said the ex-detective.

"Why is that? Do you have some kind of a notion as to what the lieutenant might say?"

"Only this. Knowing Dick, I would be surprised if he didn't laud the idea."

The commissioner had second thoughts regarding Harry Wells. After deciding to let him be, now he thinks he should be checked out; just to see if the information was true. After discussing it with Mr James, he sent for soldier boy Albert. It was around 2 pm when he arrived, "Good evening, sir. You sent for me?"

"Oh yes. Have a seat, Albert."

"Good evening, Mr James. Are you back at work, sir?"

"Good to see you, Albert. No, I'm not back at work. What made you think that?"

"No reason, sir. I just thought."

The time was approaching 4 30; there were plenty of hours before dark.

"Can you run an errand before night fall, Albert?"

"Yes, sir, I suppose I can."

"Good man, I want you to check on Harry. I heard he's back at Green Bay."

"Green Bay, sir? But that's where he was last time."

"Maybe he likes it there, Albert, or maybe he thinks he's untouchable, or probable thinking he's invincible."

He turned a couple of pages of his ledger, and didn't speak for a while.

"Now then, Albert, I want you to leave now; you should get there before dark. You know the drill; whether he's there or not, you're not to tarry."

"You've been there before, Albert?" asked Mr James.

"Oh yes, sir. I know the town quite well. How long will I be going for, sir?"

"If he's not there when you get there, come right back."

"Very good, sir."

The talk ended, and Mr James said good evening. The commissioner had one last word with the soldier.

"Report to me the moment you get back, no matter how late."

"Very good, sir." And off he went.

It was about 4 am when Albert returned; he didn't call the commissioner, he thought it was too early; he waited until daybreak. It was 8 am that morning when he went to the hotel.

"Take a seat, Albert; would you like breakfast?"

An army guy like Albert was never going to say no to a free meal, but it would be sometime before it will arrive. In the meantime, he would relate to the commissioner the errand.

"He's there, sir. I've seen him, but I don't think he'll be there for long. I heard him talking. He's pulling out."

"Were you that close to him talking?"

"Yes, sir. He must be gone by now, and Mrs Nelson was with him."

The commissioner didn't respond; he seemed to be in deep thoughts.

"He doesn't go anywhere without her, it seems. What about the men? Did you see any of them?"

"It's hard to tell, sir, but I had a feeling they were there."

"So, he's pulling out. I've said it before, and I'll say it again, either this fellow has ESP, or his informer is on the job."

Breakfast had arrived. While Albert ate, the commissioner was taking his shower. It was a long shower. By the time he did, the soldier had finished eating. It could have been a ploy; he didn't want to share a table with the soldier; like the lieutenant said, line had to be drawn.

"OK, Albert, you can go, and tell the lieutenant to meet me at the office."

"Will do, sir, and thank you for breakfast."

Shortly after breakfast, he set off to his office. Now that Harry Wells was off the agenda, he'll be thinking about the curfew. Soon after he settled down, Miss Scott buzzed. The home secretary was on the line. He called to tell the commissioner, parliament had given its approval for the curfew.

"I am pleased, minister. We're halfway through making plans, it in anticipation of the outcome."

"Commissioner, we're not going to discuss this matter over the phone; let's do it tomorrow. Mr James can come along, if you don't mind."

"Not at all, and I think he would like that."

He called Miss Scott; he wanted her to go fetch an officer.

"Any special officer, sir?"

"Yes, Miss Scott. Ben Murry, you'll find him at the market."

She set off on her bicycle, but it'll take a while, travelling through the city was a slow process. She returned sometime later, along with the officer.

"You sent for me, commissioner?"

"Yes, Ben, I want you to go find the lieutenant. Start at the barracks, and if he's not there, ask for him."

"Very good, sir." And off he went.

He too will be riding his bicycle; every policeman had one. That was the main means of transport.

Sometime later, the lieutenant arrived.

"What kept you, Dick? Couldn't find your way?"

"I was seeing to your prisoner, among other things, but why the urgency?"

"No urgency. You remember yesterday we were thinking of going after Harry if the information was good? Well, not anymore."

"What happened; he found dead?"

"No such luck. Albert overheard him talking. He's pulling out, and that was late last night, and that woman was with him."

"It seems he goes everywhere with her these days."

"That's what I said."

"That raises the question though, where the hell is she sleeping? I don't think she's the type to be sleeping rough."

"I don't think so either, and since they haven't been seen at the estate, where the hell are they staying?"

"I'm telling you, Dick, I'm beginning to admire the guy; he's not only got style, he's smart too."

"I don't like that kind of talk. He's not some kind a genius. He's just a cold-blooded killer, who up until now got lucky."

"Okay, so Harry is off the agenda. A suggestion was put to me yesterday. I want to hear what you make of it."

"Oh, from whom? Anyone I know?"

The commissioner hesitated; he appeared somewhat apprehensive to talk about it. He reached for the cigarette that he was not going to light.

"Well, go ahead, man, I'm listening."

"It's about Pinkie. Mr James suggested we should get rid of him."

"What's that supposed to mean? Explain yourself, man."

"Well, as long as we hold him in jail, there will always be the threats of a shootout. Pinkie is a dead man walking. It's just a matter of time. Not my words." He went on talking about it, but without the details.

"So, let see if I understand what Jamie is saying: turn Pinkie loose, tell him he's free to go then shoot him trying to escape?"

"Well, he didn't say it that way exactly, but that's the general idea."

The lieutenant's face lit up; he slapped his thigh.

"God damn! Why didn't I think of that? Three cheers to the man, Noel, you've got a good man there."

"You know, Dick, at times you worry me; that certainly wasn't the reaction I expected."

"Don't you see, man. It's perfect; a simple solution to a big problem. By gully, that Jamie is thinking. I hope you agreed."

"Well, I'm not averse to the idea, only you shouldn't be so gleeful about it, even if it's someone like Pinkie."

"Listen, man, don't give me all that righteous liberal nonsense. You've killed more criminals in the time you've been here than all your predecessors put together. You get nothing for being nice; not with these killers. You have to be like them, brutal."

But the commissioner knew it was a solution to their problem, even though he's less enthusiastic about it.

"About the curfew, we've got the go-ahead, the—"

"Then why didn't you say?" the lieutenant interrupted.

"I only heard today; the home secretary rang to tell me. We're going to see him tomorrow, along with Mr James. We'll put the final touch to it."

"You said we, does that include Jamie?"

"Yes, and he's another matter to be dealt with on the same card."

"Does that mean he'll be made up?"

"I don't know, why don't you wait and see."

It was approaching 4 pm; the evening would be long, he felt they should be working on the idea.

"We could be discussing Pinkie, but since it's Mr James' idea, we'll wait until he's available."

"No time like the present. I can go fetch him; he's likely to be home."

"Okay, Dick, you do that."

About 45 minutes and he was back; along with the ex-detective.

"Mr Wade, I wasn't planning on leaving home today; it seems you can't get enough of me," he said facetiously.

"It seems that way, doesn't it? But since this thing about Pinkie was your idea, we think you should be in on the discussion."

"What suggestion was that, Mr Wade? Refresh my memory," he asked with a smile.

"Damn it, man, we haven't the time to be flippant; we have to see the home secretary tomorrow, remember? We need a plan to deal with the Pinkie situation."

Mr James didn't respond, the lieutenant smiled cagily, but didn't utter a word either.

"What are you smiling about, Dick? Get your thinking hat on."

"Oh nothing, just that the last time I looked, Jamie was a civilian."

"Well, that won't be for long; tomorrow he will be a law man."

"Are you sure about that? You're the only one who seems to know."

"Don't bother about it, Mr James isn't."

"Only because he knew his future has already been decided."

Chapter 25
The Pinkie's Project

"Gentlemen, this matters is strictly between us three, and one other person, Mr Webster; without him this project is a non-starter. So, gentlemen, focus; this is top secret."

He outlined how he thinks they should proceed. Mr James agreed, but the lieutenant had doubts about the governor. Well, like the others, he knew, even the ones thought to be loyal, could be a traitor.

"Sounds like a good enough plan, but do you know the governor well to trust him with what is a plan that holds the secret of our future?"

"I do," said Mr James, "and you can put your mind at rest, Dick, he's a trooper, in the circle, he's known as smiley, and—"

"Yes, I know he never smiles," interrupted the lieutenant.

"Quite so, but what makes you thinks he can't be trusted?"

"Oh, come on, Dick. We're talking about Bob here. Do you think he would double-cross us. This situation is a problem for him too."

"Well, let's say I don't know the man as well as you, Jamie."

"Dick, that question shouldn't even arise. Do you think Bob wants to have scum like Pinkie in his prison? I don't think so," asked the ex-detective.

"Listen, Jamie, we're living in troubled times, everyone's a suspect – not my word. However, if you say the man is trustworthy, it's good enough for me."

"Okay, can I proceed now, Mr Thomas?" asked the commissioner sarcastically.

"Sure, man, go ahead."

"The governor goes to see Pinkie; they have a little chat, then—"

"What about?" the lieutenant interrupted flippantly.

"The birds and the bees, what the hell do you think?" replied the commissioner harshly. Well, at times, the lieutenant couldn't help himself with his wisecracks. James couldn't hide his amusement; he laughs out loud.

"OK, man, carry on. I was just fooling."

"I've said it before, Dick, and I'm going to say nit now. You're in the wrong business. Now, where was I? Yes, Bob closes the cell door, rattles the key as though he's locked it, but the door is slightly ajar, enough for Pinkie to notice."

"But, is there any assurance Pinkie will walk?" asked the lieutenant.

"He will walk," said the ex-detective, "he's not going to pass up the chance to get away."

"What happens if he doesn't?"

"Then the operation is off, and no one's the wiser, except us," said the commissioner.

"Are you having doubts, Dick? Because if you are, say it now."

"No, man, just trying to cover all angles."

"It's one way to high street; that's where he'll be heading. You two will lie in wait."

But the lieutenant still had doubts. He seemed uncomfortable even after all that had been said.

"Relax, Dick, once Pinkie is out in the clear, he's not going to hang about," said Mr James.

"Then what next?" he asked.

"You wait until he reaches the entrance to the high road, then open up on him."

"Okay, then, let's recap," said the commissioner, and they did.

"Are we at one with the plan?"

"We are," replied Mr James.

"How about you, Dick, still doubtful?"

"No, man, as long as we stick to the script, but what time we doing this thing?"

The commissioner seemed to be thinking on it; he looked at his watch and kept looking at it while talking.

"How about 2 am? Few people will be out and about."

But the ex-detective disagreed. He thinks there'll be snag there.

"Too late. I think it should be early morning, say about five, and here's why. People will be returning to work, and the street getting packed up, Pinkie will see it as his chance, mingling with the crowd."

The Pinkie plan

"So, this is how we proceed, 4 40 am, the governor go to see Pinkie and does as plan. Pinkie would be thinking he forgot to shut the cell door. He then make a break for it; the rest is up to you, gentlemen."

"I suggest we do it on Friday; the day after our meeting with the home secretary. And remember, gentlemen, it's strictly between us three; the governor will know the plan when I go to see him. After the job is done, we'll go to our homes and meet back at the office around midday. The news should break long before. How does that sound?"

"Sounds alright to me, how about you, Dick?" asked Mr James.

"Sounds good to me, too. When *The Gleaner* reports the killing, let's hope they point the finger at the gangs."

"I have a good feeling they will. Who else could they blame?" he asked.

"Okay, gentlemen, we'll meet at the home office tomorrow." The lieutenant was about to leave when he remembered.

"Oh, what about the invitation to the garden party on Saturday? Have you forgotten?" asked the lieutenant.

"Well, I did, but now you mention it, I won't be going. There's too much to do."

"Noel, the job isn't going anywhere. Get out there and meet your public."

"The hotel manager thinks of you enough to send you an invite. Pay him the compliment by attending; use it as a public relation exercise."

"Who the hell do you think you're, my guru?"

"No, man, just looking out for you. Gatherings like these, you can learn a lot about the people, and who knows? You might even pull a pretty lady."

"Tell me, Dick, are you up to something you don't want me around?"

"Not at all, man. If I'm up to anything, the only person I wouldn't want to know would be her indoors. Seriously though, man, you should go, let your hair down, hang loose, as the Yanks say."

"The trouble with you, Dick, you just want me to pick up bad habits."

"Not at all, but I'm concerned about your well-being. I just want to see you live like a man. As a married man away from home, you should have a woman; it's not only proper but healthy too."

The commissioner conceded. He was not going to talk his friend out of his idea.

"Okay, I'm going; but not because you told me to."

"Oh good, and there'll be lots of pretty women there; women of all shapes, sizes and colours. You, my friend, you can have your pick. Then early morning, I'll pop in to see you; to see what kind of a lady you spent the night with."

"You'll do nothing of the sort," the commissioner snapped. "Who the hell do you think you are? Mr James, did you hear that? The audacity of the man."

"I heard, and I think Dick is right."

"Ganging up on me now, I see." Then they laugh.

Then he remembered he had an urgent matter to deal with on that very day; a matter that could last till the early hours. "Dick, my friend, I just remember, I can't go."

"What's wrong with you, man? The work is going nowhere. Get out there and enjoys yourself."

"I see you forgot the task in hand. We start the curfew on Saturday."

The lieutenant looked a little subdued. He'd completely forgotten and now he felt a little silly.

"Business before pleasure, right man, but why didn't you say?"

"I'm sorry, Dick; I thought I did."

"Okay, but as a matter of principle, you should send an apology. Show you didn't ignore his invitation."

"You think of everything, don't you, Dick?"

"Just looking out for you, man."

"Well, thank you, most kindly. I don't know what I'd do without you," he said sarcastically.

Mr James smiled wryly; these two were like a pair of comedians. It was late in the evening; the sun was getting low and about to disappear; they bid good evening.

The following morning, the commissioner had a brainwave; he would like to bring the Pinkie Project forward, but his meeting with the minister would have to be cancelled. He got to his office in haste; he asked Miss Scott to get him a line to the minister's home.

"Good morning, minister, I'm sorry for the early intrusion, but it's important I speak with you. Regarding the meeting later, I'm not going to make it. There's an urgent matter that needs my attention."

The minister didn't ask what. He was content with the commissioner to carry out his duty, whatever it was.

"Commissioner, I won't ask you what, I suppose you'll tell me at some point. You do what you have to do."

"I'll tell you now, minister, it's about Harry. I heard an info about him; we might go after him, but only if we think the info is reliable."

Of course, it was a lie, but the minister bought it, and was satisfied.

"Okay, commissioner; we'll set another date, but we won't do it now."

"Good enough, minister. We'll talk soon; have a good day."

The commissioner thought he would have to argue the point; but lately, the minister doesn't seem to have the zest for the job. It's noticeable, the job's becoming more difficult for him to handle. It could because of the attempt on his life. The commissioner finds the lieutenant.

"You can't stay away, can you? Man, I must be quite important, but I don't mind your company."

"Don't flatter yourself, important man. There's a change of plan. Come along, we're going for a drive."

"To where? Or you're not telling."

"We're going to find Mr James, and I don't know where he lives, but you do, so guide me."

"How the hell you know that, did I say I do?"

"Well, do you?" he asked, knowing the lieutenant did know.

"I do as it happens. Keep going, I'll tell you when to turn."

The commissioner glanced at him warily. He shook his head and commented,

"God help us."

"No, man, I'm the one helping you," he replied.

When they arrived, Mr James was having breakfast. He was surprised to see them, but he suspected it wasn't a social call. At the door, the commissioner apologised for the intrusion.

"Oh, never mind that, gentlemen, come on in."

He took them to the dining room; his wife was at the dining table, eating.

"Dear, this is Commissioner Wade. ay hello to him."

"Good to meet you, Mrs James. I'm so sorry to interrupt your breakfast, but—"

"Good to meet you, commissioner, and no apology necessary. I trust my husband done nothing wrong that brings you here?" she interrupted as she stood to greet him.

"No, ma'am, not yet, but I keep an eye out for when he does." They smiled warmly.

"I can't shake your hands, commissioner, as you can see, we were having breakfast, and my hands—"

"Oh, that's alright, Mrs James," he interrupted. "If you don't mind shaking mine, I would like to shake yours."

"Oh my, a sweet-talking commissioner. If you would like, I could set you a plate, sweet-talking commissioner."

"Well, thank you most kindly, ma'am. I would like that very much."

There were four people at the table, but the lieutenant was no stranger; he'd dined there often. Sometime later, breakfast was over. Mrs James got to her feet. She knew this wasn't a social call; they wanted to talk business.

"Gentlemen, I know you're here for a reason, so I'll take my leave of you."

The commissioner stood.

"Thanks, you, ma'am. It was gracious of you to offer us breakfast; thank you, kindly."

"Don't mention it, commissioner; and you're welcome anytime," she said as she withdrew.

Seeing the commissioner come to see her husband, she began to think, he hasn't done anything wrong, the commissioner's words, then why? Her gut feeling had to do with him returning to the force. In these parts, it's not a custom for husbands to discuss matters of such importance with the wife. Women tended to the chores in the home; matters of importance were left to the men. However, she'll be finding out soon.

The Ambush

At the dining table, the commissioner outlined the reason for the unexpected visit.

"Gentlemen, I'm bringing the Pinkie Project forward, but Firstly, I must come clean, the—"

"What' in God's name have you done, man?" the lieutenant interrupted sarcastically.

"I turned Pinkie loose, what do you think?" They laughed.

The commissioner reached for his cigarette, but he was not going to light up; he never did. It's just the lieutenant's Banta could becoming a little tedious.

"Dick, try and hold yourself together, and don't interrupt. In a telephone call from Mr Webster, he asked me to bring the operation forward. Word's got to him; there's to be an assault on the prison; they want Pinkie out. Now then, gentlemen, that must never happen, so, we stick with the plan, only we do it tonight, and that's the size of it."

Mr James needed no convincing. He said it would happen, he's ready to move now, but the lieutenant had doubts, he always had.

"Listen, man, I know what you said about the governor, that he's trustworthy. I'm sorry, I can't feel the same as you, and I bet he didn't say the source of information."

"I didn't expect him to, why would he?" asked the commissioner.

"Dick, you're right to have doubt, but let me worry about the governor."

"Gentlemen, the talking is over. I think we should go now and check out vantage points," said Mr James. They agreed.

Mr James went to see his wife; she was in the living room. They emerged together.

"It was good to meet you, Mrs James, but duty calls. we must dash."

"Likewise, commissioner; and whatever you have in mind for my husband, I want him back home, alive."

"Ma'am, you can rely on me, I'll make sure of that."

"Thank you, commissioner. Dick, come to dinner on Sunday, and don't be late," her last words.

"Thank you, Joan, I'll be here," said the lieutenant, kind of coy.

It sounded like an order, not an invitation. There was certain to be banters at some point regarding it.

They went back to the office. There, they put the finishing touches to their plans.

"Gentlemen, immediately after this operation, we turn our attention to the curfew, so there mustn't be any slips up, and in the morning when the news breaks, our investigation must look authentic."

"That goes without saying, Mr Wade," said Mr James.

The commissioner got to his feet. For the first time, he picks up his stuff, but he won't be carrying it.

"Gentlemen, there isn't anything more to discuss; we'll go home and sit tight. In the morning, we'll rendezvous outside the prison at 4 30 am, prompt."

He pulled out his desk draw and took out a bottle of Scotch and a bottle of Captain Morgan, then, went to the fridge for a bottle of red stripe for the lieutenant.

"Gentlemen, let's drink to success."

They raised their glasses and the lieutenant his bottle, and drank to a successful operation. Then they said good night.

Later that night, something was to happen that would increase their chances of success. About 10 pm, it began to rain, and continued through the night. It was nearly 4 30 am when they met as planned. The commissioner went ahead to see Governor Webster. From then on, nothing must go wrong. It was nearly 5 am when the governor went to see Pinkie; after a short chat, he walked away leaving the cell door ajar. Now, there was one way Pinkie could be looking at this situation. He could be thinking his friends got on to the governor, and forced his hands, or, the governor thinks he locked the cell, whereas he didn't. But, to him, it didn't matter. This was his chance to break free, and he was going to take it. But these marijuana-smoking gunmen hadn't got the brains to think. There's a saying, 'if one smoked the stuff long enough, it made them go loony'.

He didn't tarry; he walked out, and tried to make good on his getaway. It was dark and still raining, and the streets were empty. In a hurry, he made his way up the narrow road leading to the high way. He'd be soaking wet soon, but that's not going to bother him. He was thinking he was away and gone. The men lie in ambush waiting for him to enter the main road; that's where he should fall when they shoot him. They waited and waited, watching him as he went. It was nearly 5 45 am. The street was quiet, but only because of the rain. He was in the centre of the high way, and must have been thinking he's got away; that's when the men opened up on him. They turned on their torches attached to their weapons, making sure of the target. Pinkie was a sitting duck, and in coordination, they opened fire; a silo of bullets rang out, then there was a cowardly scream. They hurriedly checked out their night's work – Pinkie lay dead. They disappeared quickly into the dark, early morning, leaving Pinkie where he lay.

The morning was still dark; it'll be couple of hours before sunrise. The wet asphalt glistens against the streetlights. To the assassins, it felt as though a weight had been lifted. As the rain gradually ceased, it's became clearer by the hour. Where Pinkie lay, the place was visible from quite a distant. It won't be long before the body was discovered.

Quietly and secretly, they went back to their homes. They won't be going to bed, they'll be waiting to hear the news. It was morning, but the commissioner was in no in a hurry to get to the office; like the others, he' wait in anticipation. About 6 30 am, there was a knock on his door. He put on his gown before he attended the door. It was Officer Jones.

"Good morning, commissioner."

"Good morning, Jonesy, what's happening?" he pretended.

"It's about Pinkie, sir. He's dead. He was found on Harvest Street not too long ago." He didn't hide his glee; no reason to.

"Okay, Jonesy, come on in, I'll put some clothes on; we'll go back together."

He took his time, no need to rush. The dead man was a criminal; any investigation will only be a pretence.

Arriving on the scene, a reporter rushed to his car.

"Do you think the gang did this, commissioner?"

"I have no idea, Jerry. I only just got here."

He inspected the body; of course, it was for the benefit of the press. No one was expecting anything to be done, other than remove the body to the mortuary.

After talking to the paper, his work here was done. He went directly to his office. Now he would like to talk with his partners in crime, but he's got a few hours to wait. It was nearly 12 noon, and as planned, his colleagues arrived; they're feeling awfully pleased with themselves.

"Gentlemen, we should congratulate ourselves for a job well done; let's break out the drinks," he said with delight.

"Yes, but did you speak with *The Gleaner*?" asked Mr James.

"Yes, and Jerry asked me the question but answered it himself."

"What was the question?" the lieutenant asked.

"Do I think the killing was done by some other gangs. I have no idea, I replied."

"I'll drink to that when I get a beer," said the lieutenant.

"Hold that thought, Dick, while I get you a bottle."

He looked at his watch; he was feeling great with himself.

"Gentlemen, you know it's not a good habit to be drinking this early?"

"Maybe so, Mr Wade, but on this occasion, we can make an exception, don't you think?"

He poured the ex-detective a scotch, and The Captain Morgan for himself. Miss Scott buzzed the Governor Webster on the line. They talked for a while, then he hung up.

"Gentlemen, that was the governor; I assured him the job is done, and done well."

Miss Scott buzzed again. This time it was the home secretary; anticipating what the call was about, the commissioner puts him on speaker for the benefit of his colleagues. "Good morning, minister; isn't it a glorious morning?" he said exuberantly.

"Mr Wade, are you drinking this early?" Hearing that, the others smiled.

"I only had one of The Captain, minister; I was drinking to the demise of Pinkie, I suppose you've heard."

"Yes, commissioner, I heard. They're saying he was killed by some other gang."

"That's the story I heard too, and I hope they're right."

"Commissioner, do you realise what this could mean? We could have a gang war on our hands."

"I hope so, minister. They could destroy each other while we stand and watch."

"I hear your delight, commissioner, but I'm not sure if I share it. I'll say good day to you."

"Did you hear that, gentlemen. The report we're hoping is the story the paper reported."

"Mr James, I should pat you on the back; in fact, I'll drink a toast to you." He raised his glass along with the lieutenant. "To the future deputy commissioner, the man who solved one of our problems at a stroke."

"Hear, hear," said the lieutenant. But now he was curious about the commissioner's comment.

"You said it before and you said it again, is Jamie the new deputy?"

"I would like to know too," said Mr James. "What's the score here, Mr Wade?"

"Well, gentlemen, I'm not going to say sorry for pre-amped the situation, so I jumped ahead of myself. Is there anything wrong with that?"

"Well, yes," said the lieutenant, "are you sure the home secretary is in agreement?"

"Relax, gentlemen; on Wednesday, it will all become clear. It's a little anxiety on my path, and I won't apologise"

But he wasn't totally honest. He knew the home secretary was awaiting Mr James's signature. Mr James was leaving.

"Gentlemen, I'm going to get my head down. I'll say good morning."

"You know, Dick, I like that Mr James, and I like his way of thinking; I think we're going to make a darn good team."

"I hear you, man; I'm going to get some sleep too, and you should do the same, even for a few hours."

"I can't sleep now, Dick; I'm too hyped. You go ahead; I'll see you later."

Chapter 26
Mr James Is Made Up

It had been two days since Pinkie was assassinated, and still there was an uneasy calm in the city. *The Gleaner* alleged the gangs were fighting amongst themselves, and although it made for pleasant reading for the authorities, it was only speculation. Today, they'll meet with the home secretary, the agenda, Mr James, he'll signed up to be the new deputy commissioner.

Miss Benson alerted the home secretary of their arrival; he met them at the door.

"Come in, gentlemen, and take a chair. Mr James, how are you today?" he asked thoughtfully.

"Oh, I am feeling fine, Mr Walker, thanks for asking. Are you well yourself, Mr Walker? And how is Mrs Walker? Is she well?"

"We are doing just fine, Mr James, thank you."

He began to tidy up a number of sheets of paper lying on the table, looking like documents. There was a shiny tray at the end of the table with glasses and drinks. It seemed prepared for the occasion. The home secretary walked over and handed the ex-detective sheets of documents, saying,

"Take a look at these, Mr James, they require your signature." The others looked on as this transaction took place.

The lieutenant whispered, "Noel, this must be the worst-kept secret ever."

It didn't take the ex-detective long to look over the papers; he probably knew what they entailed already. The home secretary collected the documents; he looked them over before putting them away. Then, with his arm outstretched, he welcomed the ex-detective.

"Congratulations, Deputy Commissioner James; welcome back to the force."

The others followed after with their congratulations, now the talks that followed was about the new deputy commissioner.

"Tell me, how it feels to be back on the force, deputy commissioner?" the minister asked.

"Feels rather good, Mr Walker, even though there was an air of deception about it."

"Deception you said, Deputy James? Why do you say that?"

"Should I relate, Mr Wade?" he asked looking at him rather sternly.

"I resent your insinuation, Mr James; all I did was give you a little nudge."

"A big nudge more like," said the deputy.

"Now let's see if I understand," said the home secretary. "Are you saying you were conned?"

"I couldn't put it any other way, Mr Walker."

"Lieutenant, say something," said the commissioner. "Did we do anything dishonourable or deceptive?"

"No, man, I didn't." The commissioner made forty-five degrees turn to look at him.

"You double-crossing son of a—"

"Now, now, Mr Wade," the deputy interrupted. Then there was laughter.

"Gentlemen, jokes aside, I must thank Mr Wade for that little nudge, but it was more than that, he was insistent. I wanted to ask for my job back, but my pride wouldn't let me. But you know gentlemen, I came to realise that pride is like an asset, but it can be a hindrance, depending on one's way of thinking. I was allowing my pride to cloud my thinking, but thank you for being so persistent, Mr Wade, I am back where I like to be."

"Gentlemen, I have a little something prepared for the occasion," said the minister. He brings out the drinks; and everyone's glass is charged.

"Gentlemen, let's drink to the new deputy commissioner; we're pleased to have him back."

"Hear, hear," said the others.

"Now let's drink another toast, to the commissioner." And they did.

The niceties went on for a while, but this little jolly must come to an end.

"Now then, gentlemen, about Pinkie breaking out of prison block. How do you suppose he managed to do that, bearing in mind the kind of prison Mr Webster runs?" he asked as though he suspected foul play.

"I've had no idea, minister, maybe you should ask the governor. But I'll say this, whichever gang did the killing, has done us a favour, don't you think so, minister?"

"That may be so, commissioner, but the question remains, could the gang have someone on the inside? And if that be the case, we need to find who, and fast."

The commissioner picked up his glass but didn't sip from it. He turned it around looking through it as though something was in his drink.

"I'm sure the governor will be taking stock, and if he needs our assistance on the outside, we're be ready to comply."

"Gentlemen, if the gang's infiltrated the prison service, we need to know, and the PM wouldn't take too kindly to it. I'll talk with Mr Webster."

"We shouldn't be beating up ourselves over Pinkie's demise. He was just another killer off the street. He was one problem we need not bother about," said the commissioner. The lieutenant looked up to the heavens – in this case, the ceiling, as to say, *this man is one hell of a story teller, how can one not believe him?*

"All I will say is good riddance to a murderous scum; he got what was coming to him."

"And so, say all of us, Lieutenant," said the new deputy.

"Mr James, you must take some comfort from this man's demise. You arrested him, I was made to understand."

"Quite so, but I've chased him for some time, and could have had him, but for Commissioner Burns."

"Isn't it ironic though; you couldn't bring him then, but you did when you were no longer on the force?"

"Quite so, and I must tell you, it gives me great satisfaction. As for him being killed, it didn't happen a day too soon."

There was a tap on the door. Miss Benson walked in; she presented the minister with the latest edition of *The Gleaner*. He glanced at the headline but didn't comment.

"Gentlemen, Pinkie is no longer an issue. We can deal with the other matter, the curfew. Are we ready to go, commissioner?"

"Yes sir. All plans are in place. Saturday, we're off and running."

"Very good. I'll inform the prime minister." The meeting concluded.

Chapter 27
The Curfew

It was Saturday and the city was buzzing, but the talks on the streets were about the curfew. Of course, it's been broadcasted nonstop for days and was supported by posters all over the country. *The Gleaners* was not totally supportive; they were half-hearted about it. The locals weren't happy about it, they weren't expected to be, and the business people, even more so. There was no set time for trading. Street dealers would be doing business all through the night, and shops would be open all hours. So, it was no surprise that they were angry about the ruling. However, whatever they though or however hard done they thought they are, the curfew went ahead. They were expecting trouble, but it might not happen, but they'll be on high alert in anticipation.

It was 5 PM. The commissioner was present along with his team brief the men, officers and soldiers. "Men, this operation is the first time for all of us. Prepare yourselves for the unexpected. Shoot if you must, but be sure of who you're shooting at. It mustn't be civilians. You must make sure of that. Be alert at all times, and never let your guards down; don't be taken by surprise."

That chat went on for a while. He then asked the deputy if he would like to say something. "Only this, you probably have to shoot someone, some of these people are stubborn, others couldn't give a damn, and there're those who want to test the system. It's up to you to read the situation, and act accordingly."

"Thank you, Deputy James, so, that's our dilemma gentlemen, take nothing for granted. I want to see you all back here in the morning."

One officer had a question; he'd heard something he wasn't sure of.

"Excuse me, commissioner, did you say Deputy James?"

"So, I did, officer, but I was waiting for the right time to tell you all. However, now is as good a time as any."

"What's your name, officer?"

"Harold, sir."

"Men, this is your new deputy commissioner. I suppose you all know him."

"Yes, sir, we sure do." some shouted. One officer, Vinny Murry wanted to shake his hand, and he did.

"Welcome back, Mr James, and I speak on behalf us all, sir."

"Thank you, Vinny, and thank you, men. It's good to be back." The talks were over, and the men were divided into units: there were three sectors, each controlled by one of the principles. It was one of those long summer days. The evening was bright and will be so for some time. For those looking through their windows, the streets must seem like a ghost town; this busy city came to a standstill. The commissioner was concerned about the men brandishing weapons in broad day light; he wished if there was any other way.

"We're just as concerned as you, commissioner, but these weapons are their tools, and the people won't be concerned, they see it almost daily."

He didn't like the deputy's turn of phrase, but he didn't argue the point.

As they were about to leave, there was a call for the commissioner, it was Home Secretary Walker.

"Commissioner, are we all set to go?"

"Yes, minister, we are. Are you coming too?"

"Very good, commissioner, I see you detected my turn of phrase."

"Well, good luck for tonight, and hope there won't be trouble."

"Thank you, minister, I have a feeling we're going to need it."

The sun was about to disappear and it casted a long shadow. It was quite warm, and with the density of the city, it was even more humid. It was an eerie feeling. This busy city grinded to a halt. Apart from dogs roaming the streets searching for food, it was as quiet as a sleeping baby.

They take up their positions; it was going to be a long night. It was 2 am, and all was well. The lieutenant met with Deputy James, they conferred.

"Jamie, the city is so quiet, it's creepy."

"Yes, but so far so good, let's hope…" He paused. There was a burst of gunfire, but it didn't continue. It was coming from the south side, his sector. They dashed to the area. It didn't take long; the streets were empty. But it wasn't much to be alarmed about, the culprit was a hobo.

"What happened here, soldier?" he enquired.

"He walked out from the shadow, sir. I ordered him to stop, but he kept coming. I fired over his head; he stopped but said nothing. I kept him covered while Jerry checked him out. We discovered he was a tramp."

They took him back to his bed on the far corner of the street, and ordered him to stay put. This tramp could be disturbed from his sleep, and decide to go walkabout, unaware of the situation. The soldiers were lauded by their superiors. Nothing further happened; the night passed off peacefully. It was 6 am, and the men were about to withdraw, but they won't be walking home brandishing their weapons. They're being picked up by the paddy whack wagon. It was 7 am, and the sun rose. The city was handed back to the people. It won't be long before the place is buzzing again.

4 p, that evening, the commissioner returned to his office. Immediately, there was a call. It was the home secretary.

"Good evening, commissioner. I trust the night went well?"

"Quite well, minister. Nothing untoward happened."

"That is good. Let's hope tonight will be the same."

"I certainly hope so too, minister."

Night two went even better than the night before, but there was an uneasy calm; one that won't last, it felt. In the evening the following day, the commissioner met with the lieutenant; he was in good spirit and looking fresh as a daisy.

"Were you on duty last night, Dick?"

"Is that a trick question, man?"

"No, not really."

"Then why do you ask?"

"Well, you look as though you were in bed all night. How the hell do you do it?"

"Listen, man, I don't think you've come to congratulate me on my appearance; what's up?"

"Dick, I've been thinking, it's over a month since the last sighting of Harry, it's as though he doesn't exist."

"Well, I suppose, like everyone, he knows there's a curfew; I don't think he would venture into town. That said, I don't think we should concern ourselves with him. He exists alright, probably lying low for a while. But, whatever the reason, he'll make himself known in some time, you can be sure of that."

"I hear you, Dick, but I'm concerned. You must remember that here in the city is where he and the others do most, if not all their dealings. they might want to try their luck and venture in."

"A possibility, but one we have no control over. We can only be extra alert. If they do, we'll be ready for them. But I'm sure Harry would never venture in while the city is under curfew, he's too smart for that."

"That's my thinking, Dick; it just doesn't feel right not knowing where he is or what he's up to."

Night four passed off trouble-free, but now, there was unrest coming from some quarters of the community, especially the storeowners; they were not happy. They were losing trade. Nevertheless, with the support of *The Gleaner*, the authorities remained steadfast in their undertaking. On the fifth night, the operation continued, but sometime during the morning, there'll be trouble. Just as the ex-detective had suggested, if the dealers were going to come in to trade, they won't be doing so during the curfew. They'll come in during the busy hours, mingling with the crowd. These dealers were doing just that, mingling with the crown, knowing that apart from the law, no one was going to bother them. This dealer, one of the big men in the trade, wasn't expect to be recognised, and if he did, no one would point the finger. But he was wrong; someone was a loyalist who despised these drug dealers. He didn't approach him; instead, he seeked out a lawman, Deputy James. He told him about the dealer he saw. This man was Bannon. The deputy knew him well, he had run-ins with him. But he doubted the citizen's story, Bannon wouldn't be doing his own dealing, he's got men for that.

"Are you sure about this man, mister?"

"Yes, sir, Mr James; I'd never forget his face. He's Bannon alright. His face was all over the paper not so long ago."

"Okay…" He paused. "What's your name mister?"

"Ben Williams, sir."

"Thank, Ben; I'll check it out."

Mr James was a smart lawman. He was not going to look for him; if Bannon was there, then so were the other dealers. He went to find his colleagues and told them what he had been told. They wasted no time; they went looking. In this busy city, one could easily become inconspicuous, but not knowing he has already been recognised, he continued to trade. The lawmen spotted him, but not wanting a shootout, they moved cautiously. They circled his position and cornered him; they grabbed him before he could put up a fight. Soon they apprehended other dealers without a shot fired. However, not knowing how many there were, what they were trying to avoid was about to happen. Others realising they'd been spotted, tried to getaway; hence a running street battle pursued. Of course, the lawmen had no choice, they had to take on these killers. It was now approaching 10 am, and people were returning, but now had to run for cover. One thing was for sure. The lawmen will play these killers at their own game; they'll be show no mercy.

The street fight raged on for some time, gunmen taking shelter amongst civilians. Gradually with the help of some law-abiding civilians, four gunmen were killed. It was 3 pm, and the city was still on edge; people going about, but cautiously. The shooting ceased but the lawmen knew it wasn't over. It was approaching midnight; and the commissioner was about to call a halt to the action, when suddenly, there was a shout coming from a store nearby.

"There's one in here," the voice repeated. It was the voice of a woman.

They rushed to the store.

"He's in here. We got him," said the woman with a stern look.

In a way, the commissioner was pleased; members of the public were backing up the law. Not so long ago, such action was unheard of. He recalled back in Green Bay; the people were surprisingly cooperative.

This lone gunman, he probably would have killed someone, but his pistol was empty. The fight was over; and it was time to count up the dead.

"Mr James, you think we've got them all?"

"Unlikely, Mr Wade, and we'll never know, and not knowing how many there're, it's a guessing game."

"Jamie, how did you recognise Bannon?" the lieutenant asked.

"I didn't; it was Ben; he came and told me."

"I take it you knew this, Ben?"

"I don't think so, but he seems to know me. But I know it was Bannon the moment I saw him."

"Who is this Bannon, someone of interest?" asked the commissioner.

"Mr Wade, we must lock him up tight. He's the boss, a nasty piece of work and a murderous brute. What I can't understand is, why is he doing his own dealing; it's usually done by the drones."

"You speak of him fondly, Mr James, why?"

"You think so? Let me tell you. I chased that son of a bitch many a times, like Pinkie, he was there to be had, or even killed, but he had friends in high places, he might even laugh at me. I don't know why he didn't kill me; he could have many of times."

"Perhaps he had words from above, don't harm the detective," said the commissioner.

"That, Mr Wade, is more than likely. I've had him in my hands and have to let him go, Commissioner Mitchel's orders."

"Then you could say the commissioner kept you alive."

"You said it as though I should be grateful. The man was evil. Many a good people died because of him."

They count up the dead: seven-gun men, two civilians hurt, but not life threatening. Bannon was locked up; his future will be decided soon. The gun man who was hiding in the store, died of his wounds on his way to jail.

"You know Mr James, it seems the people's opinions are changing; they're turning against these gunmen. Isn't it wonderful?"

"It certainly looks that way, and long may it continue."

The home secretary requested a meeting with the commissioner before tonight's action. It was late evening when they convened.

"Commissioner, I must congratulate you on a job well done; you think you've got all?"

"No way of knowing, minister, and I don't think we'll ever know; however, Harry isn't among the dead, so we can assume he's still at large."

"Commissioner, that man must be caught. The country will always be on edge as long as that killer is out there."

"We shared the same sentiment, minister, but we can't do a thing about it; not until we find him, and as of now, we have no idea."

"You think he might be dead, commissioner? And yes, I am clutching at straws."

"I doubt it. Men like Harry don't die from natural causes, and we would have heard if he was killed by a bullet."

"One thing's for sure. After tonight's action, the dealers will think twice before entering the city. The recipients won't be getting their usual supplies; they'll have to go looking for it."

"But these gunmen were here all along, you said so yourself, commissioner."

"Not this lot. They come from outside, mingling with the crowd. The Burn's Gang, they're here, they're always here, only, they don't know we know they're here."

The minister took off his glasses and cleaned them with his handkerchief; he appeared to be thinking.

"Tomorrow will be five days since the curfew, how much longer you intend to continue?"

"All I will tell you, minister, the curfew continues, indefinitely. We're making sure the gun men don't return."

The minister asked awkward questions; it seemed the limit of his vocabulary, but his heart was in the right place.

Miss Benson buzzed, the prime minister was on the line. They talked for a while, but hearing the commissioner was there, the PM would like a word. They talked for a while; the PM congratulates him on a good night's work.

"Thank you, prime minister, but you must understand, the operation was team work, and may I say, it shows what can be done with a few good men."

He was trying to tell the PM what he told him before; the force needed men, but indirectly.

"Commissioner, if you're telling me force needs men, I know. You told me before, and the answer is the same as before, no money in the kitty." He hung up.

"I take it that the PM is quite pleased, commissioner?"

"It would seem that way, but I would also like him to realise we have no idea when we'll have total control, that time is some way off to use a layman's phrase, minister, we just have to keep plugging away."

"If there's nothing further to discuss, commissioner, I'll say good evening, and good luck on tonight's operation."

"Thank you, minister."

Chapter 28
Holding Bannon

The curfew was going as they hoped, but Deputy James was concern about Bannon. He thought he should move to more secure confinement, inside the prison. The commissioner was with the lieutenant when he found him. They were dining at the Orange Tree, the lieutenant's favourite restaurant. The commissioner spotted him entering.

"Mr James, do come and join us," he exclaimed.

"As it so happens, Mr Wade, I was looking for you."

"Is there anything wrong?"

"No, not yet, but I think we should do something about Bannon. It's not wise having him in jail."

The lieutenant stopped eating to look at him. He was thinking the deputy was thinking of a repeat of the Pinkie's project.

"Jamie, you don't mean—"

"No, Dick," he interrupts; pre-amping what the Lieutenant was thinking.

"What were you thinking, Dick?" asked the commissioner as if he didn't know.

"Come on, man, don't you remember Pinkie?"

He didn't respond; he seemed to be mulling over what the lieutenant implying.

"Have a seat, Jamie; I'll order for you," said the lieutenant.

"Now then, tell us what you're thinking; I'm eager to hear."

"This man Bannon, he's of no threat to us, but as long as he's in jail, there's always the chance some other gang might want to break him out; they do look out for their own."

"So, what are we going to do about it? And no, we're not going to have another Pinkie's type project, that wouldn't be wise."

There's no need to debate the point; it was a logical suggestion, only the deputy thought about it first.

"Mr James, you're right, we should have thought about it from the off set. We'll move him to secure confinement."

"Of course, you'll have to talk with the governor. He'll have to be briefed on the man we're asking him to keep," said the deputy.

The commissioner didn't respond. He perhaps thought he'd been outwitted by his deputy. He should be thinking along the same line, and like the lieutenant, he didn't.

"Gentlemen, we have work to do, and it must be done before the nightfall, and, Mr James, thanks for thinking for all of us."

The deputy was quite modest in his response.

"Mr Wade, we can't always think of everything. There's an old saying, two heads are better than one, moreover, we're a team."

The lieutenant looked at him sternly. He was not satisfied with that sort of response; they were a team of three.

"Don't you mean three heads, Jamie?" he asked, looking directly at him.

"No, the adage didn't say that." The commissioner smiled wryly while putting his cutleries together.

"Why are you smiling, man, did I say something funny?"

"Well, yes, just how eager you're not to be left out."

"So, what are we going to do now?" he asked.

"I'm going to the prison; I must talk with Bob."

"Don't you have to ring him first, man?" asked the lieutenant.

"Sure, but back at the office."

It was about 5 pm. The deputy commissioner was still eating. It won't be long before they're out on duty. The lieutenant was concerned they haven't got time to spare, and the deputy was long way from finish eating. He commented, "Jamie, you really are a slow eater."

"Don't rush me. You want to give me a bad stomach?"

But the deputy was thinking.

"Mr Wade, why don't you go and make the call? If Bob will see you, come back and pick me up here."

They agreed, but not the lieutenant. "What about me? Don't I come along too?"

"No, you'll be in charge to get the men. I don't know how long we'll be away."

He took a sip of his lemonade. "I'll be back shortly." And off he went. In about half an hour, he returned.

"Hold the fort till we return, Dick, we'll join you as soon as."

It was nearly 6 pm when they sat down to talk with Governor Webster.

"The situation isn't grave as yet, Bob, but we're taking no chance," said the commissioner. "Not knowing how many gangs are left out there, Bannon should be in a secure confinement, pending trial."

The governor didn't need too much details. He agreed.

"Okay, gentlemen, this matter need not be discussed any further. Bring him in. We'll put him in the north wing. There he's going to be awfully lonesome."

"That's music to my ears, Bob," said the deputy. "Yet solitary confinement is far too good for Bannon; he should be made to suffer the way he let some innocent people suffered."

"Does that mean he won't be seeing anyone, Bob?"

"No one at all, commissioner, only when he's being fed."

"Then what about exercise? Don't the prisoners get to exercise?"

He was quick to respond.

"The prisoners, yes, but for Bannon, where he'll be, he can do what the hell he likes, but from inside his cell. But as a matter of interest, how long how long will I be holding him for?"

"No idea, that's for the home secretary to decide."

"OK, gentlemen, go fetch the prisoner."

By 8 pm, Bannon was in secure confinement; his future will be discussed sometime soon.

11 am Friday morning, the commissioner and his deputy went off to see the home secretary. The situation in the city since the curfew was looking good; however, there were violent disturbances elsewhere in the country.

"This is what I think," voiced Mr James, "here in the city, things are looking better by the day; the gunmen have stopped coming in. Whether we've got them all, it's a matter of conjecture, but if we haven't, we have weakened them considerably. However, the killing isn't going to stop as long the marijuana is being cultivated. Another thing, and it is only an observation, Bannon, for him to be doing his own dealings, it could only mean one thing, he's alone."

"That makes an awful lot of sense. Why else would he be risking his life?"

"I see what you mean, gentlemen," said the minister, "but we still can't be sure."

"No, and we're never going to, not for a long time," said the commissioner.

"Now, about Bannan's trial, how soon can it be?"

"I'll work on it, commissioner. I'm sure we can push through an early date. I'll raise the matter with the PM no later than tomorrow." The meeting ended.

Chapter 29
A Church Minister Murdered

It was nearly a month since the curfew, and the city was enjoying a peaceful existence. Things were looking up for the government in that regard. However, within the calm there was a storm brewing; the cocaine barons were stepping up their activities. They were shipping their stuff from South America to the island, and then to Europe. Their operation was humongous, but the local police made no move against them, they couldn't; their organisation was far too powerful. Parliament debated the matter; the government were urged to ask the British for help, but they ruled against it. In the meantime, the constabulary will stick to what they can handle, the killers in the marijuana business. Today was the first day of spring, and as usual the country was bathing in the sunshine. The news coming out of Hanover Bay, the second-largest city, wasn't good. At night, men shooting off their guns in the air with no concern about the local safety. That's what happens when they smoked the weed. It blows their mind, they have no regard for anyone. In the past, these disturbances went un-noticed. No one bothers, or cared. But not anymore; the law men will take the fight to them, their free for all has to stop. A few days later came a report, a man was murdered, but he was no ordinary man, he was a man of the cloth. *The Gleaner* got hold of the story; the dead man was Mr Wilson, an Anglican minister. The country was outraged; this atrocity cannot and will not be tolerated. *The Gleaner* didn't hold back; they were blaming the government, but wanting reprisal. The country was grieving; you don't kill a man no God. The authority must make a concerted effort to find the killer or killers, and bring them to justice. For this, the government was under attack, not only from the media but from the opposition too, who're having a productive time in the pole. The locals knew the killer, but he was not around, he'd gone to hills. That's the usual pattern, when they committed their crime, they head for the hills; these are some of the most inhospitable places in the country, no law men will follow them there.

The home secretary summoned the commissioner; the prime minister was on his back; he wanted something done, pronto. It was about 11 30 am when he arrived at the home office. Miss Benson buzzed the minister, but there was no reply. She went and check, he wasn't there; however, she showed the commissioner in and asked him to wait. As a church going person himself; the minister was dumfounded by the killing. He went to a secret corner in the building to pray for the dead minister. Before long, he returned, but looked sombre; he even shed a few tears.

"Morning, commissioner. A sad state of affairs, isn't it? A man of God is brutally murdered. What the world is coming to? Is there no end to their evil doings?"

"A crying shame in deed, minister, but it shows the kind of people we're dealing with, people with no regard for life."

"One shouldn't live in fear on account of one preaching the words of God, it's what gives us hope."

"But we don't know why he was killed, minister. It could even be a robbery gone wrong, we don't know."

"Whatever the reason, it shouldn't have happened. He was a servant of God."

"I agree, and it's a bloody outrage; these people are just plain brutes, and they must be stopped."

"Mr Wade, the prime minister wants you to go to Hanover Bay ASAP; do whatever you think is necessary, but find the killer or killers."

"I understand. I'll make plans to leave first thing in the morning, but you can't say we weren't aware of the situation there, and for some time too, but nothing was done."

"Yes, commissioner, but there was little we could do. You said it yourself, we're thin on the ground in regards to manpower."

It sounded as though he thought the commissioner was passing the buck, but when the matter was raised, the minister showed little interest.

"Mr Walker, I wasn't pointing fingers. I was merely stating the fact. We knew of the situation there, but did nothing."

"Okay, commissioner, let see what we can do about it now. Find these killer, and commissioner, this is priority." Well, he was feeling strong about the killing of the minister. There was a time when the killing of church people was common; he was probably reflecting on those days.

"So, commissioner, do you think the gunmen have taken their business to the country? Hanover Bay for instance?"

"I couldn't really say. We don't know the fact, and we won't until we get there and investigate, and if the situation there proved detrimental, we'll have to scale down operation here, and move some of the men there."

The minister seemed bemused; he didn't like the idea; to weaken the position there, might bring the gunmen back.

"Commissioner, I must tell you, I don't like it, and I'm sure the PM won't either. Taking the men away, you'll be leaving the city open for the gunmen to return; there must be another way."

The commissioner reached for his cigarette, but he didn't take one out. He gazed at the pack as though he was reading from it. Maybe it was an instinctive reaction whenever he thought one was talking out of one's backside.

"Minister, the capital is fairly secure; we're not considering taking away all the men. However, in Hanover Bay, there are only ten policemen serving the city and districts. Would you like us to take them away?"

"Commissioner, you shouldn't be asking me. You're the chief of police, you do what's necessary."

"That is so, but I cannot make blood out of stone, and, may I add, these cities or open to abuse. There aren't enough law men there."

He was getting more than a little tedious with the minister. He was not entirely out of touch; he knew what was required, but appeared nervous to put it to the PM.

"Mr Wade, there's no need to be sarcastic. My opinion is mine, and I think I'm entitled to voice it. You been using the soldiers, continue using them, so long as the job gets done continue using them, can't you?"

"I don't wish to be contrary, minister, but the soldiers made up the numbers we're using, but if you're telling me to strip the armed force to make up the constabulary, then, sir, you'll have to take it up with the lieutenant, and ultimately the prime minister."

The minister was somewhat unsettled; these were matters he should be dealing with, and to put them to the PM, it would appear he was not doing his job.

"Commissioner, I'm not averse to your comment, and I know you're working under difficult circumstances, but rest assured, this matter about recruitment has to be addressed, and soon. However, as of now, you'll have to work with what you got. I believe those were the PM's words."

It was an obvious climb down; and not wanting this matter go any further, he was treading softly.

"Minister, I don't want to sound condescending, but have you any idea at all what is happening out there? Maybe, occasionally you should take a walk and have a look around, get a feel of what goes on."

"Commissioner, if you're trying to tell me I know nothing of what goes on out there, then you're wrong. I keep abreast of events."

But whatever he said, the commissioner wasn't impressed. He already knew of the minister's short comings. In all their undertaking, he was of no help.

"Minister, as I stated before, in some cities there're less than ten police officers, that's no way to police a city. What we're doing, is, protecting one section of the country and leaving the rest to the mercy of gunmen."

"A logical point, commissioner, but it should be addressed to the prime minister, but I can tell you what he's likely to say, 'there's no money in the coffer to pay for anything; the country is broke'."

"In that case, minister, the dealers and gunmen will always have the freedom of movements. We'll be playing catch up."

"Don't be too dismayed, commissioner, I'll put the matter to the PM, and express the seriousness of the situation." The meeting ended.

Chapter 30
Hanover Bay Project

The commissioner discussed the situation at Hanover Bay with the deputy. They'd be going there in the morning. They were not only going to investigate the killing of Church Minister Wilson, but they'd be assessing the situation, to see if it's necessary to set up a curfew there.

"I think you're acquainted with the area, Mr James, so I'll be following your lead."

"You don't have to, Mr Wade, it's no different from any other city. Cities are made up of people, and they're all the same."

"The only time I was there, I think I made a good impression; I hope I can do the same again."

"Yes, I heard. Dick said they wouldn't respond to him, but they did to you. So, tell me, what did you do?"

"Nothing you might refer to as extraordinary or amazing. They probably liked what I was saying, or it could be they took sympathy on a white foreigner."

Deputy James was not only disappointed with the commissioner's comment, but was disgusted too. To use the racial argument to justify a point, he thought the commissioner was bigger than that.

"Mr Wade, I don't know if you've noticed, but the people of this country are of many colours, or should I say many races. I would say the whites made up more than a third of the population, so, if that is your thinking, you're way out of line. You're away from home, but there's no reason you shouldn't feel at home here. Of course, if you chose to feel you don't belong, then that would be your choice."

The commissioner was feeling as though he was castigated. The deputy's comment had struck a chord. He probably used the white word for a laugh, but the deputy didn't see it that way.

"Mr James, when I made the point, I wasn't expecting a lesson in mannerism; however, I appreciate it. At times, one can be misled by one's own thoughts."

"That's all right, Mr Wade. At times, one can be looking at a situation from a different point of view."

They said good evening; they'd meet again in the morning. On his way home, the commissioner called on the lieutenant. They talk for some time regarding his trip to Hanover Bay.

"Now, Dick, you'll be in charge while I'm gone, but I can't say when I'll be back."

"What the hell are you saying, man? Are you making me out to be a policeman?"

"You could say that. You'll be managing the operation while I'm gone. Make sure everything runs smoothly."

"Yes, boss man, I hear and understand, boss," he said flippantly.

"Damn you, Dick, can't you be serious?"

"'Course I can, but don't worry, I'll see to your job while you're gone."

"Make damn sure you do," he said sternly. Then there was laughter.

At the office the morning after, he was joined by the deputy. They talked about the possibility of a curfew at Hanover Bay; an idea voiced by the deputy some time ago in his previous position.

It was about mid-day when they set off. It was over forty miles but they made good time. They were greeted by Sergeant Maxwell, one of the ten police officers in the town, and there was a special greeting for Deputy James; they were old acquaintances. They conversed for a short while, and the sergeant congratulated him on his new appointment. After some light refreshment, they got down to business. Sergeant Maxwell briefed them in regard to the situation there.

However, the first line of business was to pay Mrs Wilson a visit, the wife of the murdered minister. She'd be a bit surprised; previous commissioners wouldn't leave the capital, they never bothered to. It was late in the evening, but it will be a long time before sun set; the commissioner seemed eager to meet the lady.

"Okay, Sergeant, lead the way. Let's go see what we can find."

He took them to the scene of the crime, the vicarage, the home of the murdered minister.

The sergeant rang the bell, and Mrs Wilson emerged, wearing black, but not looking too gloomy.

"Good evening, Mrs Wilson. This is the commissioner of police, Mr Wade, and—"

"Good evening, commissioner," she interrupted, "it's good of you to come."

Of course, she knew why they're there, but she didn't expect a visit from chief of police.

"Come in, gentlemen; it's good to meet you, Mr James," she said, making a point of it.

As the sergeant didn't say, the commissioner was thinking, why did she singled out the deputy, and how she came to know of him? But the deputy was thinking the same thing; like the commissioner, he was a stranger too.

"I know why you're here, gentlemen, and I'll tell you all I know," she said before she asked them to be seated.

Before the deputy took a chair, he asked, "Tell me, Mrs Wilson, have we met?"

"Oh no, Mr James, but I never forget a face."

That's rather odd, he thought. They'd never met, yet she never forgot his face?

"How is that, Mrs Wilson?" he asked curiously.

"My husband and I, we're avid readers of *The Gleaner*. Your picture was often in it. I recognised you instantly. Correct me if I'm wrong, but you had a few busts up with that Commissioner Mitchel, which led to your resignation. Am I right?"

"Absolutely, ma'am, that is exactly so."

"A beastly man he was, even though I never met him."

"I can see you kept abreast of occurrences, Mrs Wilson."

"Well, Mr James, one should keep up to date with matters in one's country. So, tell me, have you returned to the force?"

"Yes, ma'am, he's now the deputy commissioner," the commissioner replied.

Mr James looked at him with raised brows; the question was addressed to him yet he responded to it; however, he said nothing.

"Well done to you. It's good that you returned to the force. The country needs all the good men. My husband used to comment on that Commissioner Burns. He was a dishonest man. He used to say, he was assassinated in his home, wasn't he, Mr James?"

"Yes, ma'am, that's the general belief."

It's good to talk, but they must get on with the business in hand; try to find her husband's killer.

"Now, Mrs Wilson, what can you tell us about your husband's death?"

"He was murdered, commissioner, killed by a mindless brute."

"I'm so sorry, ma'am, and—"

"Don't be, commissioner," she interrupted, "just find him and show him no mercy. He didn't show my Tom any."

Well, she was only human, and even though she was a minister's wife, she was not thinking of forgiveness; she wanted revenge.

"How did it happen; did you see the killer?"

"Oh yes, I saw him alright; he murdered Tom right in front of me. I thought he was going to kill me too. He shot Tom at point blank, took his watch and the money on the table," she said with tears in her eyes.

The commissioner hung his head; he too was filled with emotion. He didn't ask any question for a minute or two, giving her time to compose herself.

"So, it wasn't a gang that killed your husband, ma'am?"

"A gang, commissioner? There're no gangs operating here, didn't the sergeant tell you? It's just mindless people wreaking havoc, shooting up the town at night. They couldn't care less for people's lives."

"Ma'am, I'm aware of it, and will be doing something about it."

"Sounds good, commissioner, but how soon will that be? What they're doing hasn't just started, but the government does nothing."

"Ma'am, it's got to stop, that's one of the reasons we're here."

"So, could you give us a description of the killer, ma'am?"

"Sure, I can. As I've told the sergeant, I've seen him before, and he could be living in the neighbourhood. He's short and stocky, very red, and—"

"Red, ma'am?" interrupted the commissioner.

The sergeant explained.

"He's who we call 'dundos'; when he's exposed to the hot sun for long, he goes red, like a sun burnt mongo."

The commissioner took notes, probably thinking of the kind of person described to him.

"Once you see the brute, you'll never forget him. Part of his left ear is missing."

"Missing, ma'am? How do you mean?"

"Part of his left ear is missing; probably chopped off or shot off."

She told them all she could. Satisfied with what they heard, the commissioner stood, followed by his colleagues.

"Mrs Wilson, we're sorry for your loss, and you have our condolences."

"Thanks, you, gentlemen, but I will be feeling much better when you catch my husband's killer."

"We'll do all we can, ma'am; you have given us plenty to go on," said the ex-detective.

"Ma'am, we might need to talk to you again. Can we call on you?"

"Anytime, commissioner, I'm going nowhere."

At the Station

Back at the station, they discussed the situation further. Of what they learned; they were going to make enquiries. Around 7 pm, they decided to take a look around the city. They were astounded by what was happening. Men were roaming the streets and shooting off their weapons for no particular reason. It was obvious they were under the influence. That was how they got their fun. People running for cover, trying to avoid being shot.

"This is an outrage! Is it always like this, Sergeant?"

"Every night, commissioner. They know there's no one to stop them. Ten police officers policing the entire city, they probably laugh at us. Out in the districts, it's a free for all; killings go un-investigated."

"Sergeant, I was made to understand it was bad, but I couldn't envisage it was this bad. How they haven't killed anyone, I will never know."

"Oh, but people do get shot. Luckily no one dies. Should it allow to continues, they'll probably turn their weapons on the people."

The commissioner needed no further proof. There had to be a curfew, and will follow the same pattern as that in the capital. It will start on Sunday, allowing two days to broadcast it to the nation. It was nearly midnight, they decided to book into a hotel.

"Sergeant, we don't want to sleep in your jail, so we're going to phone a hotel to make a reservation. Which would you recommend?"

"No need for that, gentlemen. I'll take you there directly."

It was only a short drive to the hotel. They booked in, and there was a short discussion. They were about to part company, when the commissioner said, "Sergeant, we won't be seeing you again until Sunday. Make whatever enquires you can till then."

"I never stop, commissioner, but as you'll see, the people won't talk." "I understand, sergeant."

They were about to say good night, but Mr James has a question for the sergeant, one that's been bothering him ever since he got here.

"Tell me, Sergeant, have you ever crossed swords with Harry Wells?"

The sergeant thought long and hard before he responded; he could be thinking the question had implications.

"I've never shook hands with him, Jamie, but our paths crossed when he and his woman stopped in this very hotel. Along with four men, they behaved as though they owned the place. I made no attempt to arrest. So, if you're thinking I didn't do what a police man should, then, Jamie, you go right ahead."

His reply was somewhat evasive, but his thinking was wrong; there was no implication within the question.

"Victor (the sergeant), there's no hidden agenda in the question, I can assure you. I merely wanted to know if he ventured in these parts. So, do you know what he got up to while he was staying here?" asked the commissioner.

"No, but I stood next to him; I even spoke with him, and before you ask, yes, I was in uniform. Don't you see? He knew we couldn't touch him; he could do whatever he wanted."

"There's nothing to feel bad about, Sergeant. What we learned here, we didn't know, and we don't hold you in any way complacent." They said good night.

It was early night, with gentle breeze blowing. It was a special feeling out there, away from the big city. It was 9 pm when they decided to have one last look around the Metropolis; they were in for a surprise. Whether it was in the big city or any other cities, the malted milk was a special treat, but the commissioner never had it, but that was about to change.

"Mr Wade, would you like malted milk? I'm having one myself."

"A malted milk, Mr James? What is that?"

"It's a delicacy, and I…" He paused. "You should taste it; I think you'll like it."

They walked up to the stall. The peddler was quite talkative. Well, that's how they do business, telling you about their product. However, this peddler knew who they were, and probably anticipated a good sale.

"Can I have two malted milks, please?" asked Mr James.

"Yes, sir. Large or medium?"

"Make it medium, and I hope it's cold."

"Oh yes, sir, it's not only cold, but the best anywhere."

He made up two concoctions and presented it to the deputy. He presents it to the commissioner.

"Here you are, Mr Wade. Enjoy."

He looked at it strangely as though he didn't like the look of it.

"What is it?" he asked.

"Go ahead, taste it," said the deputy.

"I think you'll like it, sir," said the peddler.

He was eager to please and make himself another sale. His effort wasn't wasted; the commissioner liked it. After a few minutes, Deputy James was going to have another, but he's waiting to see if the commissioner would like another one too, and he did, they placed an order for two again.

"I knew you would like it, sir, everyone does," said the peddler.

While they were enjoying this little pleasure; Mr James had a thought; his detective instinct gets the better of him. He thought this fellow might be the right person to ask about the man with a part of one ear missing.

"What's your name, mister?"

"Sweetie, sir," replied the peddler.

"Sweetie? What kind of a name is that?"

"That's what everyone calls me, sir," he said, looking pleased with himself. The commissioner found it amusing; he smiled.

"Tell me, Sweetie, have you ever seen a fellow around here, who's got half of one ear missing?"

Their evening was about to get better. They'd struck it rich.

"I know who you're looking for, Mr James; the man who killed Mr Wilson."

"You know who I am?" he asked.

"Oh yes, sir. I recognised you from your picture in *The Gleaner*."

"It's nice to be recognised," he said. "So, what can you tell us about this fellow?"

"You won't find him around here. The people don't like him; he lives at Yellow Mountain."

"Yellow Mountain? Where's that?" asked the commissioner.

"Where no one goes, sir. It's too dangerous."

"You saying the people would kill him if they got a hold of him. Did they try to?"

"They probably wouldn't kill him, but they sure would beat him badly. We know he robbed and killed the minister, and we're angry about it."

"You think you could show us to where he's hiding out, Sweetie?" the commissioner asked.

"Oh sure, I know the place quite well; just say when, sir."

But this fellow was no fool. By helping the law men, he'll be helping himself too, knowing he'll be paid.

"Good man, Sweetie. Now listen, say nothing to anyone about this conversation; we'll talk again on Sunday, and Sweetie, do you mind working with us?"

"Oh no, sir, I don't mind at all."

The commissioner gave him a ten-pound note; he was looking to make a change, but slowly. That's the usual ploy when he's been given a big note, it's a chance he'll be told to keep the change, and in this case he did. He looked a little surprised; ten pounds was over a week's earnings. He thanked the commissioner and told them to have another malted milk on the house, but they declined.

They left feeling they'd made a friend, Sweetie; they'll be counting on his assistance when they'd return. They set off back to the capital; they'll have plenty to talk about.

"You're a famous man, Mr James. It seems everyone knows you."

"Well, I'm not entirely surprised. Most people are avid reader of *The Gleaner*, and I made the front page a few times."

"You should be chuffed; they talk of you in high esteem. You obviously were doing something good."

"Oh, but I am chuff, Mr Wade, how could I not be?"

Chapter 31
Back in the Capital

It was midday when they arrived back in the capital. The commissioner summoned the lieutenant; he arrived looking jubilant, and as usual, he had to make a wise crack.

"Good heavens, they didn't string you up then?"

"What are you talking about? Come and sit down; we've got business."

There were no further immediate comments from the commissioner; he was taking his time looking through his diary. The lieutenant got impatient.

"Are you going to have me sitting here like a lemon, man, or are you going to tell me why you summoned me?"

"Don't be so impatient, Dick, you just got here."

He took time to close his diary, but his action was deliberate, letting the lieutenant stew for a while.

"Well, I'll tell you, I've got a few surprises; but pleasant."

"Oh, what happened, did you run into Harry?"

"That wouldn't be pleasant now, would it?"

"No, I suppose not, so what happened? And don't take all day telling me."

"We stayed at the Beach Hotel last night. We were told Harry and Janet stayed there a few times."

That news didn't surprise the lieutenant. Harry stayed wherever he wanted. He wanted to hear about the investigation regarding the church minister.

"So, what else? What about the investigation, how did that go? You arrest anyone?"

"Give me a chance. I have to make investigation first, but we talked with Mrs Wilson, and she gave us a good description of the killer. When we return on Saturday, we'll be going after him."

"So, I take it you know where he is?"

"Well, I don't, but I know a man who does. He'll be taking me to One Ear."

"What the hell you talking about, man? This Sweetie, who the hell is she, and One Ear, where's that?" he sounded somewhat annoyed.

"If you were listening carefully, you would've heard me say, a man who knows, Sweetie, he's a fellow, and he'll be our guide to One Ear."

"Listen man, if you're going to talk in riddles, don't bother. Sweetie is a man? And where the hell is One Ear?"

He didn't respond to the lieutenant's question, instead, he began to talk about the treat he had – malted milk.

"Sweetie is a street trader; he sells malted milk. Have you ever had malted milk, Dick?"

"Of course, what do you think?"

"Then how is it you never treated me. We're friends, aren't we, Dick?"

"It didn't cross my mind, and I doubt if you would've like it."

"You should let me be the judge of that, and for your information, I did like it."

"Okay, man, so you had malted milk and liked it, big deal! Come on, tell me what else happened?"

"Well, One Ear is not a place, he's a fellow; he's the killer. He lost a piece of his left ear, hence the name."

"Then I suppose this Sweetie fellow, he just approached you and told you about what's name…" He paused.

"One Ear," said the commissioner.

"Well, not exactly. We had a couple of malted milk, then Mr James asked him about One Ear. He told us everything; a stroke of luck, wouldn't you say?"

The lieutenant scratched his head; he seemed a little confused. The commissioner's story probably seemed like a tall tale.

"Are you sure you're not making up stories, man?"

"No stories, and why would I? There's something else. Our deputy commissioner, he's a well-known copper, even out there in the country."

"No surprise there, man; he did make a few headlines."

"We'll be going back tomorrow. Have six soldiers ready to travel. I'll be taking four officers too, the time I'm not sure, yet. We mustn't weaken our position here; I'm hoping the ten men strong will be enough. You'll continue to mind the shop, Dick. I can't say how long we'll be gone for."

"That's all right, man, I know where I'm not wanted."

"Well, someone has to do the dirty work," replied the commissioner.

Miss Scott buzzed; the home secretary was on the line. She put him through, and for the benefit of the lieutenant, the commissioner put him on speaker.

"Commissioner, when are you going to bring me up to speed with events in Hanover Bay?"

"I was going to call you, minister; I would like us to talk sometime today. Tomorrow, we're up and away."

"What time were you thinking of, commissioner?"

"Say about 3 pm?"

"That'll be fine; I'll see you then."

"You know, Dick, the home secretary is a nice man with good intent. He goes through the motion of wanting to know, but nothing to contribute."

"Oh, come on, man, you've known that from the offset."

"Yes, but he's not such a bad fellow after all, and I think his intentions are honourable."

"What!" exclaimed the lieutenant. "The man is in the wrong job; your words, remember?"

"Yes, and I stand by it, but at least, he's loyal."

"I don't know what he's done to you, man, but he's done something."

"Well, let say he's grown on me. I've learnt to tolerate him."

"Listen, I'm going before you come up with another tall tale; a nice man indeed," he mumbled.

"Give the man a break, Dick, he's trying his best."

"Oh, Janet Nelson is back in town. She's been seen on the estate, but there's no sighting of Harry. It could be they parted company."

"What? How long have you known that, and you're just telling me?" he asked anxiously.

"Keep your shirt on, man, you only just got back; it was told to me only yesterday. Are you forgetting we have a round the clock watch on the property?"

"So, what do you suppose happened? You think he dumped her?" asked the commissioner.

"She probably had enough of him and his gunmen. A woman like her is not accustomed to rough living, and I don't think she's going to walk away from her estate, not even for Harry Wells."

"You know, Dick, if he shows up at her home, we—"

"He's not going to," the lieutenant interrupted, "he's much smarter than that."

The talk was over, and the lieutenant was going through the door.

"Are you in a hurry to get away, Dick?"

"Not especially; why do you ask?"

"Then sit your ass back down, man, and let's talk," he said abruptly.

He sat and reached for his for spearmint, but didn't unwrap it. The commissioner looked at him curiously.

"Are you comfortable, Dick?"

"Quite comfortable, man, what gives?" He laughed out loud.

"You know, Dick, you're getting more peculiar by the day."

"I'm not surprised, look at who I'm working with."

"Oh no, we're not the cause for your peculiarity, you're a funny man, Dick," he said facetiously.

"See what you think of this, have an all-out search for Harry, now Janet is home; but after the operation in Hanover."

"I can see you didn't give it enough thought. Where are you going to start looking? Without information; that suggestion is a non-starter."

"Play the waiting game, he's not going anywhere. We'll get news about him."

"That is what we've been doing, Dick, and without success I might add. I don't think we should sit back and wait."

"So, you think we should go chasing shadows? Listen, man, you seem to have that defeatist feeling, but let's not go overboard and do what we shouldn't do."

The idea was shelved; the commissioner was clutching at straws because of pressure from above. "Another thing. Because of Janet, he might be in cocaine. Mr James seems to think so."

"It's quite possible, she could drag him into it, but let's hope he's isn't. We don't need to tangle with the cartel."

"I'm off to have dinner at Jamie's, I'll see you tomorrow."

"Don't you think it's about time you get yourself a woman, someone to cook for you?"

"Not yet, man, I'll enjoy my freedom from Beryl a while longer. In the meantime, my friends will see to it I don't go hungry."

"The man is a scrounger," remarked the commissioner.

"Well now, I remember a saying about the best things in life."

"Yes, and there's another word for, free loading, you ever think of that?"

"No, man, we're friends, remember? We share what we get. Good evening." And off he went.

It was beginning to rain, but people went about their business; they were not bothered about the rain. The gunfire that usually disturbed the peace was no more; the respite was a welcome relief. The authorities were beginning to think they were getting on top of the situation, but only there in the capital. Now they were hoping to create a similar condition in Hanover Bay and other cities.

The time was 3 pm. The commissioner called for his deputy; they were off for their meeting with the home secretary. Miss Green greeted them with her usual exuberant fashion. Inside, the minister seemed a little anxious; it appeared something was bothering him. He was holding a glass of cold lemonade, and looking somewhat disturbed. On observation, the commissioner made a friendly enquiry.

"Is everything alright, minister?"

There was no immediate response; he sipped from his glass and refilled from the decanter but didn't drink from it. He didn't want to appear intrusive, the commissioner didn't ask again. Deputy James looked on; he too thought the minister looked troubled. But the commissioner not wanting to be there long, he thought he should get the meeting started. He opened his briefcase and took out his ledger, but before he could say anything, the minister spoke.

"Gentlemen, I must apologise for my un-gentlemanly behaviour, but you see, my family is being threatened."

"By whom may I ask, Mr Walker?"

"I have no idea, Mr James. The letter was given to me by the maid. She said it was given to her by person unknown."

"How did that person manage to get past the guards?"

"That is the question, Mr Wade. It left me thinking all sorts of things."

The ex-detective waded in; he knew how these gunmen operated. They'll get to you if they choose; not bothering who sees them. Of course, at times the men on duty can't be trusted, but the men on duty there, were soldiers. They're whom the commissioner had much confidence in.

"May I have a look at the letter, Mr Walker?" he asked.

He pulled out the drawer and handed him the envelope; there wasn't much to read, but the ex-detective was looking for clues.

"Anything stirred your memory, Mr James?" asked the commissioner.

"Nothing, except this person has a good fist, and he's quite clear as to his demand."

The commissioner would like to see for himself, after all, the ex-detective could be missing something.

"I see what you mean. Beautiful writing. Could it be Harry?" he asked.

But no one responded. He read out loud.

"You won't be told again, keep the commissioner off my back."

He paused to look at the minister.

"Yes, commissioner, he warned me of you."

"Then this, minister, could only come from one man; Harry Wells." Deputy James agreed.

He didn't say anything for a while, neither did the others. He then placed the open letter on the table.

"Gentlemen, this is how I see it. The gangs, we don't make them priority, mostly because they present themselves to us. Mr James, you know this more than most; some of the bosses for these gangs, if not all, are dead, and Bannon is behind bars. But Harry, he's a priority. He knows we're chasing him. We wrote an article in *The Gleaner* about him. So, you see, gentlemen, this letter could only come from him." Again, the deputy agreed.

"So, what are you going to do, commissioner? Are you going to sit back and do nothing?"

Another of the minister's unthinkable responds, but the commissioner knew the question was that of a frightened man, and all being considered, he could be forgiven.

"As of now, minister, we're not in a position to do anything; we can't. We don't know where he is."

He glanced up at the clock on the wall; it was nearly 5 pm. He can't be here much longer.

"If it's all right with you, minister, I would like to run by you the situation in Hanover Bay," he said calmly, trying not to distress him further.

"Commissioner, I realise you're being considerate, but I'm alright, let's hear what you've got to say."

He turned a couple of pages in his ledger and wrote something; then calmly explained the situation. Deputy James however was more direct. He asked, "Mr Walker, are you alright to discuss the agenda? If not, we can give it a miss."

"Yes, Mr James, I'm not only alright as you put it, but I'm fully compos-mentis." He paused for a while.

"Now, sir," he said with a bit of assertiveness, "about the curfew tomorrow, have you got everything you need?"

"We have," the commissioner responded.

"We're hoping it won't be a long operation; we don't think the situation there is half as bad as we thought."

"Would you explain that, Mr Wade?"

"From what we saw and what we've been told, they're just mindless thugs shooting up the town at night, but they're not shooting at anyone. But, it's a dangerous situation, people got shot; luckily, no one got kill."

"So, the disturbance is not caused by gangs, is that what you're saying, commissioner?"

"Yes, more like vandalism, caused by the lack of police presence."

The minister wanted assurances, something he can tell the PM when asked.

"From what we've seen of the city, that is our conclusion. In the words of Mrs Wilson, the dead minister's wife, there're no gangs operating around here."

"Yes, and that was confirmed by Sergeant Maxwell," says Deputy James.

"Well, let's hope that be the case, gentlemen, and regarding Mr Wilson, is there any news of the killing?"

"We were given what seems good information; we'll follow it up when we return."

"Okay, gentlemen, do what you must; and I pray to God you find that killer."

"You know, Mr Walker, if we were hard pushed by the gangs, we certainly would find it difficult to function; a recruitment programme is desperately needed."

"Commissioner, we talked about this before, it's never going to happen. I spoke with the PM regarding. The government is short on funds; we'll have to manage the best we can. Not my words, gentlemen."

Deputy James looked on as the commissioner wrote in his ledger; they were both rather dismayed and disappointed. They realised that were the final words of what they thought was possible. The commissioner felt the minister was feeble in his efforts. However, one can't get out of a man what's not within him. Even so, he's concerned about the threat upon his life; it must be an awful feeling having a death threat hanging over one's head. He placed both hands on the table, he thought he should do more in regard to security.

"Mr Walker, I'm going to change the guards. I'll tell the lieutenant to send in four fresh soldiers to take over."

"Thank you, commissioner, I know that's the best you can do; it's appreciated."

"I wish you a good day, minister, and remember, your troubles are our troubles too."

He was trying to let the minister feel a little more at eased, but there was not much more he could do.

"Mr James, that man is under severe pressure; he has my sympathy. I wish I could do more to protect him."

"I recognised the signs, Mr Wade, and it let my blood boil; an honest man and his family shouldn't have to live in fear."

He then had a thought.

"Mr Wade, I've been thinking about this for some time, see what you make of it. Since the government is short of funds for recruitment, they could turn their attention to Specials. They don't cost half as much, and don't need much training. They could be out on the street in no time; a kind of stop-gap policing, what do you think?"

"Sounds like a great idea; I'll put it to the home secretary. I'll get him on the phone now – strike while the iron is hot." Then he paused to reconsider.

"No, I don't think I will, not now."

"Why not?" asked the deputy.

"Have a heart, man, the poor man is under enough pressure as it is. No, I'll talk with him when we gets back."

The deputy was a hard man; he seemed to lack compassion. He was not thinking of the home secretary's sanity. He wanted what he wanted.

"You know, Mr Wade, there's an adage: if you can't stand the heat—"

"Yes, I know. Get out of the kitchen," the commissioner interrupted. "But there's also another saying, have compassion on those who're less capable."

The deputy smiled; he was sceptical of the quote.

"There's no such saying, is there, Mr Wade?"

"No, Mr James, I just made it up. All I'm saying, there's no need to put further pressure on the minister. This matter can wait."

Saturday, and it's another beautiful day; if one is a city slicker, this is the kind of day for a walkabout. It's also the morning the commissioner and his troops will be leaving for Hanover Bay. It was 10 am and the commissioner met with the lieutenant; he told him about the home secretary's predicament.

"When did this happen?" he asked.

"Sometime yesterday. The letter was delivered by the maid. We don't know who it's from, but I want you to change the guards at his home; send in four fresh men with orders to be extra vigilant."

"Okay, man, I'll see to it. What did the letter say?"

"No more warning, keep the commissioner off my back."

"So, the threat includes you?"

"Quite so, and we're an open target, but hey! We knew what the job entailed when we took it on, didn't we?"

"We sure did. Okay, man, I'll get the men there, pronto."

"Dick, you don't seem surprised."

"Come on, man, we're dealing with mindless nasty people; whoever the letter is from, we're probably getting close, which is making him nervous. Threats to the home secretary's life is something we should be expecting; they took out previous home secretaries, remember? And they were playing ball."

"Quite right, but I feel for the home secretary. This honest man shouldn't be tormented."

"Okay, I'm off; wish me luck."

"You got it man, and remember, if you need further help, I'm a phone call away, but hell, you won't need it."

"Thanks, Dick; mind the shop."

Chapter 32
Hanover Bay Curfew

They arrived in Hanover Bay in good time. For some of these men, it was their first time in this part of the country. It was quite a few hours before they went on duty, and wanting to maintain a good rapport, the commissioner offered them a few hours leave.

"Men, if you so wish, you can go have a look around, but be back here at 5 sharp."

It was a welcoming gesture; the men headed out in the city. While they were gone, he and his colleagues discussed the situation. Sometime later, the men returned; he reminded them of their duty. However, they didn't need too much of a briefing; they were experienced in this sort of operation, but Mr James felt they should be reminded.

"Remember, men, this sort of operation is new to these people, and some won't like it, and some might be playing silly buggers. Shoot them because of their obstinacy, encourage them to go, but be on your guard."

"Thank you, Mr James."

"Men, that is sound advice, see that you remember it, I want to see you all back here in the morning."

They went and took up their allocated positions; they'll be hoping that the night be trouble-free. The evening was long, and even though the sun was gone behind the horizon, it would be sometime before dark.

The commissioner patrolled his sector, and Deputy James his; whatever they hoped for, an operation such as this was not expected to be trouble-free. 3 am and all was well; the silence was deafening, the city had gone to sleep. It was nearly day break, and the silence broke with gunfire. The commissioner rushed to the scene expecting the worst. But the intruder was a drunkard, and probably under the influence of marijuana, shooting of his weapon in the air. It seemed that's how they got their kicks. But the soldier had no problem apprehending him; they took him to the station and locked him up. Other than that, the night passed off peacefully. The trouble makers who usually shot up the town at night, stayed away. It was daybreak, and the people were returning; but the traders are moaning, they're losing trade.

It was morning, and the commissioner was up early. Immediately after breakfast, he went to see Sergeant Maxwell.

"Sergeant, when we were here, Mr James and I ran into Sweetie, a malted milk seller. I would like to take me to him, if you know where to find him."

"Oh, I know where to find him; these traders work every day; seven days a week. He'll be at his stall, but what do you want with him, if you don't mind me asking?"

"I was going to tell you, Sergeant, you are part of what I'm going to see him about." "I'm thinking of going after One Ear, but only if Sweetie can guide us."

"Did you ask him to?"

"Not in so many words, but he's got no objection working with the police."

"Did he say that?"

"Yes, Sergeant, and I take him at his words."

"Of course, he'll be expecting payment. These traders don't anything without expecting to be paid."

"If he can help us find this killer, I'll certainly pass a few bobs in his direction."

The man they arrested earlier came walking towards them; the commissioner was somewhat surprised.

"Sergeant, isn't this the fellow we arrested last night? Why is he not locked up?"

"He was. His name is Jack, but I gave the order to let him go."

"But why? This man broke the curfew, he was carrying a weapon and shooting it off."

"Well, it's like this, whenever Jack is hungry, he disturbs the peace to get arrested. Well, we can't afford to feed him every time he's hungry; the government doesn't allocate us money for that. Anyway, Jack is harmless; I can't think where he's got the gun."

"Be that as it may, Sergeant, he breaks the curfew when he begins shooting off his weapon."

"I was made aware, commissioner; I confiscated his weapon, and he won't be getting it back."

It wasn't to the commissioner's taste, but he was not going to make an issue of it; they set off to see Sweetie.

He was pleased to see the commissioner, and why wouldn't he be? Last time he was treated to a ten-pound note.

"Hello, Sweetie," he said out loud, but immediately slapped himself on the wrist. Addressing a man as Sweetie is something he never thought he would hear himself saying.

"Good afternoon, sir, would you like a malted milk?"

He probably didn't, but for the sake of his intention, he was obliged to accept.

"I'll have one if the sergeant is having one too."

"Oh, I never say no to a malted milk; make mine a large one."

"Sweetie, I would like you to guide me to this fellow, One Ear, can you do that?"

"Yes, sir, I can take you, but not us two only."

Like the population, he was afraid going to where no police went, or wanted to go.

"We're not alone, Sweetie, there'll be soldiers too."

Hearing that, the fear disappeared, and with the expectation of being paid, he would take them to wherever they wanted to go.

"Then when are we going, sir?"

He looked at his watch. It was approaching 4 pm. There were still some hours left in the day; they could do it before dark.

"Could you go within the next hour?"

"Yes, sir, I can go at any time. You just say when."

"Good man, Sweetie, then come to the station in half an hour. Can you do that?"

"Oh, yes, sir, I'll be there."

Back at the canteen, the three principles met to dine. The commissioner outlined the order for the night.

"Mr James, you'll be in charge tonight; we won't be here."

"I take it you'll be going after One Ear."

"Yes, as soon as Sweetie gets here."

"I take it you already spoke to him?"

"That I did, Mr James, and you'll be short of three men. I'm taking them away along with the sergeant."

The sergeant looked at him but couldn't speak; his mouth was full. It seemed he wasn't expecting to be going on the manhunt, or knowing what he knew of those who went there, he rather not go.

"I wasn't aware you required my service, commissioner?" he asked, looking somewhat concerned.

"I did say you're part of what I'm going to do, Sergeant. Did you not hear? And I take it you know something about the terrain; if Sweetie misses out on direction, then you can fill in."

The sergeant didn't respond; probably didn't want his fear of the place to be suspected.

"You do know about the mountain, don't you, Sergeant?"

"Well, it's been quite a while since I last went there, but I still remember. I won't let you get lost, commissioner."

"I'll be counting on that, Sergeant, even with Sweetie's knowledge of the terrain."

Sweetie arrived. He was no stranger; the soldiers treated themselves to malted milk at his stall, but they didn't know why he was there.

"Come and sit here, Sweetie, would you like something to eat?"

It was a welcoming offer, to be treated to dinner by the commissioner of police, a trader was never going to refuse.

"Yes, thank you, sir."

The commissioner didn't ask him what he would like. He ordered the same as he had. He began to eat but didn't dolly over the meal. He knew the commissioner wanted to go. The commissioner had a quiet word with Deputy James about the four men he was taking; he didn't want to leave him short. The deputy conceded, he'll have to manage, as he needed them. He was about to leave, but before he did, he'd talk to the men; they were in the little mess hall. Standing next to Deputy James, he picked four soldiers from among them.

"Men, I'm going on an errand. Mr James will be in charge; don't make his job any harder, and I'll see you all in the morning."

The men were accustomed to his pep talk; he thought it boosted morale, and as usual, the men responded to it.

The talking was over, but he was in for a surprise. The men wanted to show their gratitude; they stood and cheered. He was amazed. He stopped dead in his tracks; strapped for words, he said the first thing came to his mind, "Men, whatever you do, please be careful out there. We came here together, and I would like us all to return together."

He was overcome with emotion, but he was not going to show it, it's a sign of weakness.

Mr James was most impressed; the men's reaction he had never seen before, the commissioner was setting a new standard to policing.

"Mr Wade, I don't know what you've done, but you've made one hell of an impression on these men, I must tell you, I'm impressed," he said.

"Mr James, I can assure you, if I done anything, I not aware of it."

But the commissioner was modest, but showing the qualities his predecessors never showed.

The Man Hunts

The hunting party set off at 6 pm. Following Sweetie's direction they drove out of town to Lavender Hill district, and parked out in front the district's only church, and set off on the safari. They travelled along the narrow meandering track leading through the terrane. It was quite a distance, and the evening closed in. The commissioner was getting concerned; the terrane was what they say, but it will be dark soon. Sweetie kept up a good pace, it was hard to keep up with him.

"How much further, Sweetie?"

"Not much further, sir, we're almost there," he said confidently.

After another half an hour, the cabin was in sight.

"There it is, sir, and I think he's there; smoke's coming from the chimney."

Before they left base, the commissioner told them, he would like to take this fellow alive, but only if possible. They moved in quietly, circling the cabin. If the target was at home, his life doesn't worth the smoke coming from the chimney. Visibility wasn't good as dark clouds started gathering, and it looked like it was going to rain. The commissioner rose from his hide to talk to the resident, but not having a loudhailer, he had to shout.

"You, in the cabin, come on out with your hands up, and you won't get hurt."

There was no response. It could be that he wanted them to think no one's at home. The commissioner called again, but louder. This time, the response was instantaneous, but with gunfire. He made no attempt to leave the cabin; he just fired in all directions. Realising they were not going to taking him alive, the commissioner gave the order to fire. Bullets rain down on the cabin and continued to for a good twenty seconds. When the shooting ceased, there wasn't much of the cabin left standing. No need to move in cautiously, no one could have withstood the onslaught. They moved in; one lone gunman lay dead. There was no doubt about his identity, he was One Ear, alright. Looking around, they were surprised at what they found, an arsenal of weapons: two MK 47 rifles, a couple of machetes and two daggers.

"Tell me, Sergeant, could this fellow be part of a gang?"

"I have no idea, until he killed the minister; I understand he was always seen around town, he could a lone operator."

"Sergeant, I don't think that was his first murder; the way he opened fire leads me to believe he has killed before."

"I think he has killed before, sir," said Sweetie. "I believe he killed old Mr Moody; and many others think so too."

"Who is this Mr Moody?" asked the commissioner.

"He was a nice old man; he lived on the edge of town, very independent, wouldn't let anyone do anything for him. He raised a few goats and chickens, and—"

"Which means he's got a few bobs," interrupted the commissioner. "Probably hidden under his mattress or tied on his person."

"I think that's why he killed Mr Moody," said Sweetie.

"Tell me, Sergeant, did you suspect him or anyone of the killing?"

"Yes, I suspected a few, but came up empty. Of course, you're aware of the situation here; with ten policemen, it's impossible to carry out any inept investigation. I couldn't even chase anyone suspected, there wasn't the man power. Does that answer your question, commissioner?"

"It does, and I'm aware of it elsewhere too, but let's be clear, you weren't being accused of lacking in your duty. On the contrary, I think you've done well, considering."

"So, I expect you'll be doing something about it?"

"Sergeant, the supply of manpower doesn't rest with me, but you'll be pleased to hear I've raised the matter with the home secretary, but don't expect anything to happen anytime soon in that regard."

"I'm not, commissioner. This situation's been around a long time. I was only reiterating what you already knew."

The commissioner pointed out to him that if there were to be more boots on the ground, it could be Specials. The sergeant never worked with them, but he's not bothered, so long as he has more men. These Specials work elsewhere in the country, but they're only a few.

They were about to move out, but One Ear was staying; they'll set fire to the cabin – cremate the body. It was past midnight when the hunting party returned; the commissioner sent the soldiers to rejoin the curfew. He will stop at the station along with the sergeant, they needed to corroborate their story for the benefit of the media. The following morning, the commissioner and his deputy conferred; he brought the deputy up to speed regarding last night's mission. Later that day, they'll pay Mrs Wilson another visit.

Visiting Mrs Wilson

It was past 3 pm when they called on Mrs Wilson; she was still in mourning. She welcomed them; it was awfully hot, so, she was quick to offer them glasses of cold lemonade. After a light conversation, while sipping the cold drink, the commissioner began with the matter in hand.

"Mrs Wilson, we're here to tell you, we caught your husband's killer, but we couldn't take him alive."

Standing by her portable trolley, and dressed in black, she asked politely, "Remind me your name, commissioner?"

"Wade, ma'am, Noel Wade."

"Mr Wade, last week I was angry. I allowed my rage for revenge to get in the way of my better thinking. I said thing I shouldn't have. Now, I've gathered my thoughts and prayed to the good Lord, and begged him for forgiveness. I also prayed for my husband's killer. In a word, gentlemen, I'm not bitter anymore, and I wish you hadn't killed him."

"There was no alternative, ma'am; if we hadn't killed him, he would have killed us."

But Mr James, a man with little or no compassion, believed in 'an eye for an eye' and murderers were given no quarters.

"Mrs Wilson, I respect your belief, ma'am, and it should be admired. Nevertheless, but righteous dogmas only worsen the situation. In my opinion, it is not always best to be too forgiving; this man killed your husband, and it's a certainty he killed others too. If he wasn't stopped, he would kill again. To kill a man of God, it shows the mind set of this brute; he had to be removed from society."

Sounded as though the deputy was on his soap box, but his words would be applauded by most. But the commissioner wasn't impressed. He didn't take too kindly to the blunt speaking deputy; he glared at him but said nothing; perhaps thinking this grieving lady should be left to her thoughts.

"Ma'am, we're sorry; and you have our condolences. I wish there was more we could do."

"You have done your duty, Mr Wade, even though it ended in the way my husband wouldn't have approved."

They wished her well, and said goodbyes.

In regard to her husband's killer, she had made a complete U-turn. If they'd brought him back alive, she probably would have fed him.

"Mr James, I've came across people like Mrs Wilson before. Are they as sincere as they appear?"

"They probably are, but I think their belief is misguided; however, I won't criticise her."

"Nor will I, Mr James, they're better left to their own dogmas."

Thursday, another of those beautiful day, after lunch, the commissioner sat with his two colleagues to assess the situation. The curfew was going well; the local rag and *The Gleaner* were favourable, and the locals were beginning to appreciate it. The killing of One Ear didn't cause any controversy; perhaps it's because the victim was a man of the cloth.

Sunday, and things continued to looked good. Now, a decision had to be made in regards to the men there. Should they withdraw and return to the capital? The sergeant voiced his opinion on the situation.

"Commissioner, I must tell you, I didn't think it would have gone as well. It shows, if we have a police force, we could control the situation ourselves."

"I dare say it looks that way, Sergeant, but things being what they are, we have to work with what we've got. Now it's up to you. We are pulling out in the morning."

Sergeant Maxwell appeared perplexed. Things were looking good, but the commissioner was taking away the men; the city could be back to square one.

"Don't look so worried, Sergeant, I'm not leaving you bare."

"Would you care to explain, commissioner?"

"I'm taking half the work force, leaving the other for you to take charge of, but it won't be permanent; the curfew must be maintained, only I don't know for how long."

The sergeant seemed a little composed. He sighed.

"That makes me feel much better, commissioner, I don't mind telling you."

"Well, Sergeant, let's hope the hooligans don't return, then people can go about their business without being afraid."

"In your words, commissioner, we'll play it by ear."

"Fair comment, sergeant, and I hope it will be plain sailing."

"When are you going to inform the men who are staying?"

"All in good time, Sergeant. We have tonight's duty to manage."

It was time for dinner, and they settled down to eat. The commissioner felt the urge to express his feeling.

"You know, Sergeant, I think I could like it here; I almost wish I didn't have to return to the capital."

"But you only just got here; you haven't seen much of the locality."

"Well, let's say I liked what I saw. You see, Sergeant, I'm a country boy at heart, and where I came from, the people are friendly. I find it to be so here."

"You sound as though you're ready to move in, Mr Wade."

"One day, perhaps, Mr James, who knows?"

He was in a talkative mood, and genuinely seemed comfortable there.

"Why don't you ask for a transfer? Who knows? If you asked nicely, they might post you here."

"That's not even a probability, Mr James."

"Oh! And why not? Are you planning on returning to England any time soon?"

"No, but I think you're overlooking one thing. There is a general election, and we don't need the pollsters to tell us which party is going to win; the present administration doesn't stand a chance."

"That maybe so, but what has that got to do with the job?"

"Well, incoming administrations have a way of doing things their way, like changing personnel; it could be they'll want a new man for the constabulary."

"Much as I agree, as of now, it's all conjecture; predictions sometimes go awry."

"Mr James, you said you supported this government, but—"

"Not anymore," he interrupted. "I couldn't support a party that allowed the country to fall into such depression; everything that can go wrong, has gone wrong."

"I'm with you," said the sergeant. "This government is doomed; the country has never been in such a state, not in my lifetime."

There're a few hours before they go out on duty, they decided to take a stroll and enjoy the cool breeze. The evening was beautiful, the sun was hovering over the horizon; soon it will disappear.

"Mr James, this is what I love about life in the country. I could stroll around for hours, enjoying the scenery."

"You don't get evenings like this in England, commissioner?"

"Oh, we do, Sergeant, but it's kind of different, if you know what I mean."

"I think I do. I heard from returnees, they talked about the long hot summer, among other things."

It was about time; they were ready for duty, but the men had to be told about the new arrangement.

"Men, there are some changes to our plans. Tonight, will be the last night for Mr James, myself and some of you. The rest will be staying in the capable hands of Sergeant Maxwell. But listen, men, it's a good campaign so far, and this assignment is not permanent. As soon as we're satisfied with the situation here, you will return to the capital."

"How long do you think we'll be staying here, sir?" asked Officer Donald; he'd asked the same question once before, back in the capital.

"That, Donald, I don't know, but what I can tell you is, if the city continues to be peaceful, and the gunmen stay away, then you all will return."

There were no more questions; it was time for duty.

"Okay, men, good luck, and watch yourselves out there."

The night passed off peacefully; after breakfast, the commissioner, his deputy and the men he chose were about to leave for the capital, but to maintain good working relations, he was having one last talk with the men he was leaving behind. They gathered in the canteen.

"Men, I want to see you all back in Palma when the time is right, and I hope that will be soon."

There was a good atmosphere. To show the men he and his deputy were on the same page, he asked him to say something.

"Only this, keep up the good work, men; make yourselves and your country proud."

The men cheered to show they were in good hearts.

It was 4 pm when they set off, but there was one last duty to perform. The commissioner wanted to call on Sweetie. He was thinking, if they ever should return, and need some info or help, they could call on him.

"You did pay him, didn't you?" asked the deputy.

"Yes, but I still want to thank him; it's because of him we got One Ear."

"So, you're building bridges?"

"You could say that."

He was at his stall; the commissioner had a friendly chat while they both had a portion of his malted milk. On this hot day, it was a welcoming treat.

"Sweetie, we would like to call on you when we return, will you be here?"

"Oh yes, sir, I'm always here, it's my place of business."

He was pleased to hear him say that. They shook hands.

As for Sweetie, he knew he had forged a friendship, one that was quite lucrative to him, so far.

They took a slow drive outside the city, observing as they went.

"Mr James, I love this place; when this unrest settled down, I would like to return; but not as a policeman."

"You are a strange fellow, Mr Wade; a few weeks ago, the talk was so much different. Today, you sound as though you're ready to move house."

"As I said, Mr James, I'm not one for the city, but a place like this, yes, sir, that's my kind of habitat."

Back in the Capital

Back in the capital, Mr James went home. His wife would be glad to see him return safely. The commissioner went to the barracks to see the lieutenant. At first sight, he couldn't resist having his usual wisecrack.

"Oh look, if it isn't a boss man; I thought you weren't coming back."

"Why, Dick, you missed me that much?"

"Well, let's say I've become accustomed to you."

"Dick, your concern is touching. Get me a drink of water, and make sure it's cold."

The lieutenant summoned the hand help, and told her to fetch the water.

"Is there anything I need to know?"

"If you mean there are any killings since you've been gone, then no, I've never thought this city would be so peaceful, and I must tell you, it feels great. However, at the station, I've no idea."

"You know, Dick, I'm beginning to have a good feeling about everything, I'm beginning to see the woods from the trees."

"So, what happened in Hanover Bay, are you going to tell me, or you keeping it to yourself?"

"Good heavens, man, give me a chance."

"How much time do you need? Go ahead, spill."

The commissioner looked at him with a wry smile. "Okay, I'll put you out of your misery. So far, everything has gone well."

There was a long pause, only it was deliberate, the lieutenant's patience was running thin.

"What's the matter with you? Talk, I want details. What about the manhunt? Did you get what's his name?"

"If you mean One Ear, oh yes, we got him," he said as though he didn't care to talk about it.

"I take it he's dead?"

"Well, he didn't want to be taken alive."

"And what about Sweetie? How did he help?"

"A good man is Sweetie, a man to his word, he took us directly there."

The commissioner answered all his question. Now, he was telling him about his love for the place. The lieutenant was curious; to fell in love with the place and only being there a short time, something must have happened.

"So, are you planning on going back?"

"I don't know, but if I had my way, I would be back there in the morning."

"Something or someone must have made a good impression on you. Was she pretty?"

"You're wrong on the latter, Dick. It's the place. I would like to set up house there one day."

"Play your cards right; you never know, it might happen."

"Anyway, tomorrow, we're off to see the home secretary; there're lots to talk over."

"You said we?"

"I did, you, Mr James, and I."

"Sounds ominous. Is there anything I need to know before I get involved?"

The lieutenant was having his usual practical joke, but the commissioner snapped, he didn't seem to appreciate it.

"Involve, involve, Dick, do you think I done something illegal that I needed your help?"

"Who knows, man? You returned full of praise for the place, who knows what went on there," he said with dry eyes.

"One of these days, Dick, I swear to God." They burst into laughter. The idle chitchat was over and the commissioner was leaving.

"What time is the meeting? The usual 11 am?"

"Not this time. 2 PM, and don't be late."

Chapter 33
News of Harry

The morning after, the lieutenant went to find the commissioner. He heard the news of Harry Wells; he was on Coney Island. He was reported to be there the last time; only when they got there, he wasn't. It could be they were given false info, but these info's has to be followed up, false or otherwise.

"So, what makes you think this info is good?"

"Well, the informer sounded sincere; I can't tell you more, and we could be going on another wild goose chase."

Deputy James arrived; they bring him up to speed regarding the discussion.

"So, what should we do now, go gunning for him?" the commissioner asked.

"I think we should, we're never going to catch him if we sit wondering," said the deputy.

"That said, this place is not just down the road, it's over thirty miles offshore. It's a long way to go, again, I might add, to find he's not there."

But the deputy would like a more positive reaction from the commissioner. He stressed his previous thought; they were not going to catch this man without a few of these wild goose chases.

"Okay, Mr James, point taken. We'll send in a couple of reconnaissance. Who do you suggest, the same two as before?"

"Why not, they know the drill, I'll get them a boat," said the lieutenant.

But later that day, that arrangement was cancelled; they cast their attention to the election. There're reports of disturbances at meetings, and people were being hurt.

"I read a report about it last night, but that's not unusual; however, what is being reported is beyond the norm," said the deputy.

"Then why didn't you say? Candidates being intimidated, people getting hurt, that must not allow to happen."

"I must admit, Mr Wade, it slipped my mind; I'm sorry."

"Gentlemen, Harry is priority, but he mustn't take up all our time. We must ensure politicians are able to hold their meetings. The people are entitled to hear what they're offering, it's out duty to see that they do."

On this island, people were passionate about their politics, some even died for it. But the question was, why? These politicians never responded to their needs, once they took office; they completely forgot about their constituents. However, that could change, the opposition was receiving plenty of support, from home and abroad. Mr Mc Beam could be in the hot seat. While at an election meeting, the lieutenant was given the same tip off about Harry Wells; but by another person. He found the commissioner; he was with Deputy James; he told them what was told to him. There was some urgency about it; they agreed it should be checked out.

The day wasn't too hot but was overcast. The commissioner sends two men posing as fishermen to Coney Island. In the meantime, Deputy James will secure two boats, ready to sail, pending the report. If the report is positive, they plan to sail in broad daylight; they want him to see them. On this little isle, there's nowhere to run or hide, one can see right across, from shore to shore. It was getting dark when the reconnaissance returned, and the news was good, Harry is there, and it seems he's alone.

"How did you figure that, soldier?" asked the commissioner.

"He was sitting alone, sir, appeared to be drinking from a bottle. We waited to see if anyone comes to join him, but no one did."

"Mr James, what do you think? It's unusual for Harry to be alone, don't you think if—"

"But I don't think we should try to figured out why, Mr Wade," he interrupted. "We could be here all day."

"Listen, this could be our chance. Let's not balls it up by thinking of what he might or might not do; let's just go get him."

"I hear you, Dick, but our chances would be better if he's alone. That said, they said he's alone, let's hope that be the case."

The lieutenant couldn't understand why the commissioner was making out this fellow to be someone special; the man was only a killer.

They Sailed

It was a beautiful spring morning. The 12 men gathered, and after a short talk, they headed for the boats; they were in open water. The wind was favourable and the sea was calm; everything was in their favour. The water around the islet was shallow from a long way out; they'll have to drag the boats inland a long way. The landscape was flat, bushy with a few trees, the scenery was exceptionally beautiful. The men circled the island; they'll be coming in from all directions, and for the first time, there were three men with walkie-talkies.

They closed in slowly; the locals were not yet aware of their presence. The men with their walkie-talkies communicated, no sighting of the target. The old feelings came flooding back; he's probably eluded them once more. The lieutenant buzzed the commissioner.

"Listen, the man is here; the only place he could have gone would be out into the sea, and we would've seen him."

"Then where the hell is he?" asked the commissioner. "There're only a few people here, and we're looking at them."

But Harry was there. He'd been there for three days, waiting for them, and they walked right pass him. He had found a hiding place, up the big elm tree, a place they never looked, and watched them come ashore. He could have killed a few of them and made good his escape by using their boats, but he didn't, on account of his beloved mother. She was haunting him, telling him to give up, stop the killings and come and join her. Well, that was the story told by the faithful, and even *The Gleaner* ran an article on it, after he was captured.

He came down from the tree and standing behind it watching them, it seemed he was not ready to announce his presence.

"He's here," said the lieutenant. "I can feel his presence."

A dark cloud was gathering, and looked as though it's going to rain. There was a breeze and it was getting windier. If they were to find Harry, they needed to make it quick.

By now, there's unrest among the few locals. They'd seen it all before, men with guns on their island, and they knew why they're there, to kill their hero. The commissioner conferred with his colleagues. He didn't like the look of the black cloud, and the rain. But like the islanders, the commissioner seemed to believe the legend that Harry can make things happens. One of the locals confirmed to Mr James that he was there, but might have gone.

"Did he have a boat, mister?"

"I don't know, I didn't see one, but he could leave the island by other means," said the man.

Hearing that, the deputy didn't ask further question. This man was one of those who believed Harry could do miraculous things. The lieutenant joined him.

"If he leaves the island, it could only by boat, unless he's a damn good swimmer," said the lieutenant.

"Or someone came to collect him," Mr James said.

He's beginning to think he must have ties with the cartel if he can ship in and ship out, that's not the way of marijuana gangs. He must share his thoughts with the commissioner, but he couldn't get him on the walkie-talkie.

It was nearing 4 pm, the black clouds were building, the wind was whipping up and it started to rain. The trees were swaying violently in the wind, and visibility was poor. They'd been on the island nearly three hours; they searched high and low, and still no sign of the target. The deputy met with the commissioner and told him his thoughts.

"Mr James, whatever Harry is in, as of now it doesn't matter. If he's here we're going to find him, and Mr James, he is here, only we haven't seen him yet."

He sounded more and more like he believed the legend; Harry's got supernatural powers, and can make himself invisible.

"Mr Wade, don't tell me you believe what the locals are saying. I was of the belief you're a man with a more logical thinking. If he's here, and you seem to think so, he certainly not going to disappear, we'll find him."

Suddenly, there was a burst of gunfire. Harry announced his presence; he shot a man but only to wound him. As they moved towards the man on the ground, there was more gunfire, but no one was hit, he had no intend to.

The hunting party moved in the direction of the gunshots, but they hadn't seen him; the condition didn't allow. But Harry wanted them to see him, he hails out loud, "Here I am, lawmen, come and get me."

The sound of his voice carried on the wind was so loud, it scattered the birds. Some of the soldiers were apprehensive to continue. They didn't like the sound of his voice. But the deputy re-assured them, there's nothing to fear, it's the wind, it increases the echo.

There was another burst of gunshot, but it appeared it wasn't aimed at anyone. Now they spotted him; he was now standing in front of the cluster of bamboo, this clump of bamboo covered a wide area; and it casted a dark shadow. The commissioner was told to take him alive; the government wanted to make an example of him. However, there's no chance of that, Harry came here to die; either they kill him, or he kills himself.

The hunting party closed in; Harry was in their sight. He was standing there brandishing his weapons, a rifle in one hand and a pistol in the other. "Hold your fire," the commissioner ordered.

But the lieutenant didn't like the command. The man is there to be taken, why wait?

"What're you waiting for, commissioner?" he asked. "Give the order."

But the commissioner was persistent, wanting to carry out the government directive.

Suddenly, there was another burst of gunfire; one soldier was hit, but not fatally.

The lieutenant was angry; a man was hit needlessly. Harry was there to be taken, instead the commissioner wanted to talk with him.

"That's a dumb move, man; let's get this son of a bitch before he kills someone." A thought shared by Deputy James, but he was not going against the commissioner.

The commissioner's action baffled everyone. Apart from the deputy, Harry stood there with weapons in hand; he's an open target, but the commissioner won't give the order to take him out. It's an awful day. No one wanted to be out in this weather, unless one had to. The commissioner took a few steps forward, visibility wasn't good, and the bamboo casted a giant shadow.

"Harry Wells, lay down your weapons, and you won't be killed. You've got my word!"

"Come on lawman, are you too yellow for a fight?" But it appeared the commissioner had difficulty seeing him. He put his hands over his face for better visibility.

Then there was another round of gunfire, but this time over the commissioner's head. He raised his hand to the troops, a signal to hold their fire.

"Are you going to give the order, commissioner, or should I?" asked an angry lieutenant.

"I'll ask him to surrender one more time, Lieutenant." And he did, but Harry responded by shooting on the ground by his feet; the shot hit another soldier, he screamed lying on the ground.

Deputy James was equally anxious regarding the commissioner's actions; he knew Harry will never surrender, but he two tried to follow the government directive. With no loud hailer, the commissioner put his hands to his mouth. "Harry, put your weapon down and walk forward."

"If you want my gun, policeman, come and get me."

He took two steps forward, and with a pistol in one hand and a rifle in the other, he opened fire. One soldier screamed; he was hit. The lieutenant had enough. He's not standing for anymore of commissioner hesitation. He gave the order. "Fire." Bullets rained in on the target and continued before the lieutenant called cease fire. The commissioner remained standing on the same spot, looking somewhat bemused. The lieutenant was angry, three men were shot, and he was not pleased. They move in to survey the damage; they were astonished to see what they found. Harry was still standing; held upright between the crutches of bamboos. His rifle was on the ground, but the pistol in his hand, his head hung with blood streaming.

"I saw him fall," said the commissioner, "how did he manage to get back up?" He seemed baffled, his thought was of the folk lore, but the others weren't of the same thinking.

"He's dead alright," said one soldier after looked him over.

The Lieutenant displaying an angry feature, asked. "Did you expect him to be alive, soldier? He must have been shot over thirty times."

The few locals came to look. They stood in awe but said nothing. Deputy James checked the weapons and reported his finding.

"Mr Wade, you'd be surprised to know, Harry's weapons were empty, and he was out of bullets."

"Of course, he was," said the lieutenant. "He used them all up, otherwise, he would do more damage. Three men who shouldn't have, is being hit, and it could be avoided." His comment was a dig at the commissioner.

"How are the men, Lieutenant? Are they badly hurt," he inquired.

"They'll live, but it could have been worse," he said in an unforgiving manner.

"Well, go ahead, lieutenant, blame me; maybe I deserve it."

The lieutenant however has no time for the blame game; he knew the commissioner was following orders.

"No need to look back, man; what's done is done, you were only following orders."

Deputy James rose to the commissioner's defence. He was told to carry out a function by his commander in chief; he was only following that order.

"Dick, from time to time, our boss will tell us to do things. It may be unpleasant, or darn right impossible, but we obey that order."

"Quite so, but one can see that certain situation is impossible, there's an old saying, it's no use trying to force water up a hill. Trying to take Harry alive was a folly, he was never going to allow himself to be taken, unless we clobber him over the head, and that was never going to happen."

The commissioner was looking a little gloomy; probably rueing his action, he knew it could cause many lives. But the lieutenant, calmed down, now he's all forgiving.

"Listen, man, why did you make yourself an open target? Why he did not shoot you, I do not know."

"Sorry, Dick, I should know better; we're the ones in the line of fire, in any situation, I should assess it before take action."

"So, what do we know, man?" asked the lieutenant; eager to show there are no hard feelings.

"We done here, we take Harry and go home."

They were back on an even keel, but the commissioner seemed to be in a sombre mood; probably thinking he should show more initiatives.

"What the hell is the matter with you, man? In whatever way the job is done, it's done, there's no need to beat yourself up about it."

But he felt the need to apologise for his action, and he do so without reservation.

"Okay, but don't you go dwell on it," said the lieutenant. "We're in the business of killing; at times, we or the men are going to get killed too, no one is dead, hurt but not dead."

Mr James was impressed with the lieutenant; he sees a different side to him, but what he saw is born out of friendship.

"Dick, good heavens, man, I didn't know you're a realist. I must tell you, you surprise me."

"Err is to human, Jamie; from time to time, we all fall foul of it."

Mr James smiled wryly but didn't continue; he knew the lieutenant's comment was for the benefit of the commissioner.

Now Deputy James felt obliged to explain his feelings.

"Mr Wade, at times one has to disobeyed orders, even if it's from the commander in chief."

"Lessons learnt, Mr James, but I must tell you, I'm almost sorry Harry's dead."

"Damn fool, English man," said the lieutenant.

"I'll pretend I didn't hear that, Dick."

"Try to understand, man, Harry led us a merry dance for so long, maybe I didn't show it, but at times I relished the challenge."

"Listen to yourself, man, it's a ridiculous thought; I do hope you're not getting delirious."

But the commissioner explained. Harry ran the country ragged, but he kept them on their toes, a talking point to faithful and the non-believers alike. In that regard, he and his deputy were singing from the same hymn book.

Hearing that, the lieutenant threw his hands up in the air; an action of disbelief.

"I never thought I would live to see the day two policemen regret catching a killer."

"Don't be so melodramatic, Dick," said the commissioner, "it's the challenge, it gives one that impetus to rise to. Let's face it, Harry Wells was not only clever, but daring too. I knew we would catch him eventually, but now we have, it almost doesn't feel right."

"Listen man, that kind of talk is one I don't care for. Harry was a cold-blooded killer; the man killed people, or have people killed. You're talking about him as though he was some kind of Robin Hood. Well, let me tell you, he took from the poor, but never give them a damn thing."

"You know, Dick, he could've killed many of us today, but he didn't. Have you considered that?"

"Probably pissed off with killing; what do you want me to do? thank him? Well, don't hold your breath."

"Another thing, Harry gave himself up. He came here to die. It's almost heroic, wouldn't you say?"

The lieutenant screwed up his nose and sucked his teeth, something the locals do when someone said something preposterous, or talks nonsense.

"I need to get back on the mainland; the air is getting foul around here," commented the lieutenant.

"You've got no imagination, Dick," said Deputy James, "but one day, you'll understand."

"My heart bleeds, in time I'm sure you two will find another Harry Wells to admire."

The civilian who he shot died later; the lieutenant was quick to point it out.

"The man he killed could be a grass, and you know what I think about grass."

"You need to get your priorities right," said the lieutenant. "The police force operates largely depending on informers; your words, remember?"

"Mr Wade, you're not going to convert Dick. He's got a mindset that's different from ours."

"I gather that, Mr James, let's go home; we're done here." They loaded up their dead cargo and headed home.

Chapter 34
Back on the mainland

It was late that evening when they returned to base; no one on the mainland was aware Harry is dead; at least so they thought. The men were told to remain tight-lipped until the commissioner speaks with the home secretary in the morning. Looking in the newsagent, *The Gleaner* was carrying a headline about Bannon, Mr James bought a copy and read aloud for the benefit of the others. "Bannon was found dead in his cell early this morning; he hanged himself." The commissioner looked a little bemused, he reached for the paper and read for himself, then paused to think.

"Mr James, I think there's an irony here. The same day we killed Harry, Bannon hanged himself, wouldn't you say?"

"Whatever the irony, Mr Wade, we don't have to bother anymore about either, good riddance."

"Is that good news, Dick, or is that good news?" the commissioner asked.

"Very good news. I wish more of them would kill themselves."

They continue to the office, and there they wrapped up proceedings.

"Gentlemen, we're all tired; I'll see you back here in the morning at 10."

The Story Broke

On his way to his office the morning after, he was stopped and asked about the killing. It seemed someone from the island broke the news. *The Gleaner* was slow in getting hold of it, but the radios were broadcasting it. People stopped to listen to radios in shop windows. Mr James arrived. He too was asked of the killing.

"News about Harry is all over town."

"Yes, I was stopped and asked about it. It was wishful thinking on our path, Mr James, news like this could never be kept under wraps for long."

Miss Scott buzzed. The home secretary was on the line, but he didn't take the call, he told her to tell him he'll call him back shortly. There're a few loose ends to tie up with his colleagues, but the lieutenant hadn't arrived yet. Not wanting to keep the minister waiting too long, he asked Miss Scott to get him back.

"Good morning, commissioner, isn't it a great morning?" he asked, sounding in a rapturous mood.

"You think so, minister?" he asked, thinking he's got the news about Harry.

"Come, come, Mr Wade, haven't you seen the paper?"

"No, not yet; what is it saying?" he asked, expecting to be congratulated.

"Mr Wade, Bannon is dead; he hung himself early yesterday, isn't that wonderful news?"

"That is good news," he said, pretending to be ignorant regarding, "I thought you would be pleased, Mr Wade, but you don't sound like it."

"Oh, but I am, minister; another killer we don't have to bother about."

"So, commissioner, tell me about Coney Island, I hope it's mission accomplished?"

Realising he hadn't heard the news about Harry, and didn't want to break it to him over the phone, he hoped he won't be thinking he should be told sooner.

When he told him, there was a long silence; the minister must have paused for thought.

"Are you there, minister?" he enquired. The minister responded with a question, but in a doleful manner.

"Mr Wade, are you saying you've got Harry Wells?" he asked as though he needed re-assurance.

"Oh yes, we got him all right, except he's dead."

He went silent again, perhaps thinking of the threat made to him and his wife; it was believed to be Harry, even without proof.

"Are you all right, minister?" he asked again, aware he could be deep in thought.

"Yes, Mr Wade, I'm quite alright, and as you might gather, quite relieved." There was trembling in his voice.

The commissioner was sensitive to his plight; now with the threat removed, he probably needed time to reflect.

"Could we meet later today, Mr Wade, about 4 pm?"

"I don't see why not, minister." They hung up. This conversation was on speaker for the benefit of the deputy.

"Mr James, I have nothing but sympathy for that man. I wouldn't be surprised if he was to shed a tear or two."

They went to the mortuary to see Harry even though they only put him there the evening before. It was the commissioner's idea; the folklore said Harry had supernatural powers, he probably wanted to see if he was still dead. Arriving at the mortuary, the deputy made a sarcastic comment.

"Harry is still here, Mr Wade, he hasn't gotten up and walked away."

"You know, it would be great if this man was a decent human being; at times folks need a hero."

"So true; unfortunately, they chose a killer."

The commissioner gazed over the body, whatever his thought, he kept it to himself. When they returned, a reporter was waiting. He was from *The Gleaner*. He didn't wait for them to enter before he started asking questions.

"Commissioner, how did you kill Harry? Did you have to shoot it out?"

"Give us a chance to come in, Jack, and one question at a time. Now, which you want answered first?"

"Have you got Harry?"

"Yes, we got him. He's dead."

"Was there a shootout?" he asked excitedly.

"Yes, we couldn't take him otherwise, and before you ask, Jack, yes, we wanted to take him alive, but he didn't want to."

"Did you try balking to him, commissioner, and how hard did you try?"

"If I say yes, are you going to believe me, Jack?"

"Well did you, commissioner?"

"Yes, we tried, but it appeared he came to die, but before he did, he was going to kill one last time."

Mr James interjected.

"The man was a merciless killer, Jack; write that in your column. It might change the mindset of those who adored him."

That was of no interest to Jack. He wanted to sensationalised the story, he would like to hear heroic thing about Harry, but he got none.

"What do you mean he came to die? Harry wouldn't do that."

"Why, Jack? I didn't know you knew him that well," replied the commissioner.

"I didn't, but I don't think he would've given himself up. Why would he want to do that?"

"But I didn't say that, Jack. I said he was ready to die."

He wasn't satisfied. That's not what he wanted to hear, so he turned to the deputy.

"Do you think he was ready to die, Mr James?"

"Certainty, he was asked to lay down his weapon, but he chose to attack, so, tell me, Jack, are you sorry Harry is dead?"

"Mr James, I'm asking the questions. What you tell me, I write for the benefit of the public, so, how many times was he shot?"

"Many times. One shot couldn't have taken him down, a silo of bullets did." "Listen, Jack, when an outlaw aims a gun, one doesn't assume he's going to shoot; one shoots before he does, don't leave that out."

"Is that the truth, commissioner?"

"What do you want, Jack, for us to lie to you?"

"No, just the whole truth, and did he say anything before he died?"

The commissioner didn't respond; neither did his deputy, so Jack repeated the question.

"Nothing I care to mention, Jack."

He wasn't convinced; he believed they were hiding something, but what he really wanted to hear was, Harry lived up to the folklore.

"What are you hiding, commissioner? If Harry said something, the public needs to know."

"But why, Jack? It's only the words of a brutal killer, and we don't want to make a hero of him."

Of course, Harry did say something, but should he tell it to the press? They confer, and then decided to relate.

"Yes, Jack, he did say something."

His eyes lit up excitingly, expecting to hear wondrous word Harry said.

"Here I am, lawman, come and get me; he even called me yellow."

"That's it? And nothing more?"

"Isn't that enough, Jack, or do you want us to make up stories?"

"No, commissioner," he said as though he was disappointed. "I just want to hear everything he said."

"We have told everything, but it seems not enough."

The lieutenant arrived just in time to hear the commissioner's last words.

"Good day, gentlemen; isn't it a beautiful day? Hello, Jack, what are you doing here?" he asked sarcastically. But they had history, they crossed sword before.

"Is there anything you would like to tell me regarding Harry Wells, Lieutenant?"

"I should think not, Jack. I'm sure the commissioner filled you in."

But he was insistent, wanting to hear the lieutenant's version.

"Did Harry say anything before he died?"

"If he did, Jack, I didn't hear."

He was not satisfied, but that's all he was going to get. The commissioner looked at his watch; he had other business to deal with.

"Jack, you will have to excuse us, time beats us."

He got to his feet looking somewhat dissatisfied.

"I hope we'll talk again soon, commissioner, I have more questions."

"Of course, Jack, you have a good day now."

They settled down to discuss the situation before they met with the minister; the government wanted to put Harry's body on display, to serve as a deterrent.

"I don't like it," said the deputy, "it's unethical and immoral, even if it's Harry Wells."

"I'm with you, Mr James; I hope they reconsider," said the commissioner.

"What do you think, Dick?"

"It depends on how they'd do it. Harry is dead, but his legend lives on. Putting his body on view might be immoral. In fact, it's darn right diabolical, but if it serves the purpose intended, then it's worth it."

"I agree with the thinking, Dick, but not the principles. The country is riddled with greedy unscrupulous people; seeing a dead body isn't going to change their mindset."

However, since the report that Harry was dead, there was an uneasy calm in the country. Many refused to believe he was dead, there's a crowd hanging around the mortuary, wanting to see the body. Yet, apart from his pictures in the paper, most never saw him.

It was nearing 3 pm. Leaving the lieutenant, the commissioner and his deputy sets off for the home office. When they arrived, the minister was reading the paper, and looking quite pleased.

"Gentlemen, I must commend you on a job well done; it took a long time, but you got the job done."

"Thank you, minister, but where do we go from here regarding the body? Is it the government's intention to put it on display?"

"That was the intention, but there's a rethink and the idea has been shelved."

"Thank God for that," said the commissioner. "Now then, minister, we must have him cremated soon. There're people propping up at the mortuary, wanting to see his body."

"Then I'll get the ball rolling the moment we finish here. We don't want this to lead to any form of demonstration."

"Thank you, minister. The sooner we put Harry away, the sooner we can move on to other things. The matter is police special, is there any news regarding?"

"I spoke with the PM, and it's a no go."

"Did you explain to him the seriousness of the situation, minister?"

"Commissioner, it seems you have doubts of my ability to explain a situation, but I can assure you, I did."

"I wasn't thinking that at all, but I wonder if the PM aware that in the districts; there're no police presence. Without the soldiers, the success we enjoy could never been achieved."

"He's aware, but one cannot make blood out of stone. The country is broke, and so is the government – not my words, commissioner."

"So, about the men at Hanover Bay, they'll be needed back here, and when they do, the gun-happy hooligans could return. What happens then?"

Mr James wasn't satisfied. The minister should do more; his assurance of what he's done wasn't half enough.

"Mr Walker, I think you should have pointed out to the PM the reason for vandalism in these cities; the lack of police presence. So, we can't afford police officers, surely, they can afford specials, they don't cost half as much."

"I've done all I can; perhaps it's time you gentlemen talk with the PM."

There wasn't anything more to be said. The minister didn't seem too concern, in time the commissioner will be ask for an audience with the PM regarding.

"Gentlemen, let's be honest, in a week's time you probably will be dealing with someone else. I think it would be more appropriate to save any further question for whoever it may be."

They couldn't believe their ears; the election is young but the minister is talking of defeat. His job is to do what he can for as long as he can, but it seemed he threw in the towel before the count.

"If that's your last word, minister, I won't ask anything more of you. We'll say good evening."

They leave thinking this could be their last meeting with the minister.

Chapter 35
Janet Visits

Back at the office, there was a surprise awaiting them. As they walked through the door, Miss Scott approached them; she was smiling, and in a whisper, she spoke, "You've got a visitor, commissioner. Mrs Nelson waiting to see you."

He was aghast. He looked at his deputy; it was a look of dis belief. "What do you suppose she wants?"

"That, Mr Wade, you have to ask her," he said with a twinkle in his eyes.

"She's got a Gaul coming here. What the hell does she want with me?" he exclaimed.

"No idea, sir, she said she must speak with you, if she has to wait all day."

"She said that, did she? Right, where is she now?" he asked angrily.

"She's in the waiting room, sir."

"OK, Miss Scott, gives me five minutes, then show her in. Then call the doctor, tell him there're dead bodies in my office," he said furiously.

Miss Scott was left amazed, taking the commissioner's comment literally, she asked. "What was that, sir?"

"Ignore that last order, Miss Scott, I'm just mad at that bloody woman."

"Of all the gall, that woman has got some balls coming here. Can we arrest her, Mr James?"

"What for? Even though we know her crime, we've never caught her at it. I don't know about her balls, but she's got brass," said the deputy flippantly.

"She probably wants to see her lover's body. Why else would she be going here?"

"She couldn't be that bare-faced now, could she?"

"Well, since we can't arrest her, and like many of the locals, she probably has doubts about the body in the mortuary; she's probably come to make sure."

"Do we have to prove anything to her? I hope there's nothing in the law that said she has a right."

"No, and there's no law either saying she can't. It's left to the authority's judgement."

"Then to hell with her, she can go fly a kite."

Knowing her history and her link with Harry Well, his emotion was getting the better of him. He would like to arrest her, locked up and throws away the key.

"Mr Wade, before the emergence of Harry Wells, we knew she and her husband were in cocaine business. She probably still is; we couldn't prove it then; and we still can't. That said, she can come and go as she pleases; and even if we could prove her to be guilty, we can't touch her."

"That, Mr James, is a damn shame. All we can do is stand and watch them use the country as a dumping ground for their drugs, and making themselves rich. The onus rests with the government, and they do nothing. Let's hope we get a new government; one who will take a stand against these criminals."

Miss Scott sends her in; she enters, looking full of confidence.

"Well, look what the cat dragged in," commented the commissioner.

"And good day to you too, Mr Wade," she replied smiling.

"It's commissioner to you, madam. Only decent people refer to me as such." She ignored his comment. She's not there for a slanging match.

"Hello, Mr James, long time no see. I see you're back in the old routine, well good for you."

"Quite so, Janet, I hope you're not disappointed."

She was still standing, well, she's not going to be offered a seat, and she wasn't expecting to.

"Say your business, Janet, and leave. The stench in here now is getting fouler."

"I would like to see Harry's body," she said as though she knew she had the right.

"Why? To make sure he's who we said he is? Well, you can't, you just have to take our word for it."

"No, I would like to see his body; I need to pay my respect and say goodbye."

But while he remains aggrieved, Janet was cool calm and self-assured, and that enraged the commissioner even more.

"So, when can I see my friend's body, commissioner?"

He didn't respond immediately; he took time to gather his thoughts. In his rage, he must remember he's the commissioner of police, and behave likewise.

"You can't, there'll be no viewing."

"Is that your answer, Mr Commissioner?" she asked sarcastically.

"That's my answer; take it or leave it."

"Mr James, is there any reason why I can't see Harry's body?" she asked calmly.

Of course, he's not going to oppose the commissioner; in matters like this, they have to appear one.

"Janet, we certainly didn't expect to see you here; tell me, why do you want to see the body? and don't tell me you want to say one last goodbye."

"That's exactly why, Mr James, and I don't think it's an unreasonable request. Do you?"

"Come on now, Janet, you want to make sure the man in the mortuary is Harry Wells, isn't that the truth?"

"You said it, Mr James, not I. I just want to say farewell to a friend."

"Well, there's no viewing, but we can give you a description, and Janet, if you're under any illusion that we've got the wrong man, then dream on."

She looked at the commissioner. Her posture was calm and assured, even though she thinks they're not going to allow her to see her lover's body.

"So, you've got your man, commissioner, then why are you mad at me?"

"Janet, I don't like you, and I don't like your kind. You live on your big estate with plenty of money, but you and your kind are scums, so don't you come here posing like a decent citizen."

She was hurt but she's not going to show it, and she won't be intimidated either.

"Tell me, commissioner, is it the law that I can't see my friend's body, or is it your own personal vendetta against me?"

She deserved an answer, but she was not going to get one. The commissioner held nothing but contempt for her. Deputy James had had enough, and would like to end what was a confrontation.

"Janet, you'll have to excuse us, but you can take your case to the home secretary, if you so wish."

"I might just do that, Mr James."

He got up and moved to the door; she followed, but before her exit, she had one last dig at the commissioner.

"You have a good day now, commissioner, and you're always welcome at mine."

But the commissioner wouldn't be drawn; he wouldn't give her the satisfaction of a reply. Deputy James ushered her through the door; she left without knowing if she'll ever see her lover's body. However, if she took the deputy's word and see the home secretary, the response would be the same, the commissioner will tell him his decision on the matter, and he would act accordingly.

"Mr James, that woman has got some nerves walking in here asking to see the body of her partner in crime; what woman does that? She brings out the worst in me, and I don't like it."

"That's alright, Mr Wade, we're only human. You react the way you feel."

The lieutenant turned up, he's full of zest, with a cigar in his hand, but it was not lit.

"What the hell you doing with that. Have you started smoking?"

"Showing off, man. I see this movie once, and—"

"Yes, I probably saw it too," Interrupted the commissioner. "Pull up a chair."

He seated himself down, put the cigar in his mouth then removed it and asked, "So, how did the home secretary take the news? Was he pleased enough to offer you some kind of accommodation?"

"He was pleased, alright, but there was something strange about the things he said."

"Things like what? He didn't believe your story?"

"He believed us alright, but then came the discussion regarding police specials; he showed little or no interest."

"Are you sure it wasn't your imagination? Or it could be he was tired."

"Of doing what? No, I don't think so, there was a lack of interest. He talked shortly that we'll be dealing with another home secretary and—"

"What the hell he meant by that?" interrupted the lieutenant.

"Dick, do I have to draw you a picture? Think, man, people go to the poll in a few days. This administration is doomed, and with that, he washed his hands of his responsibility."

"He wasn't much of a home secretary anyway," commented the lieutenant.

"Come on, Dick, give the man a break; he was thrown in the deep end. He was doing his best, even though his best wasn't good enough."

"So, now there's no Harry Well to chase. What do we now, boss?"

"Well, don't rest too easy, boy," he said facetiously. "have a lot of We policing to do, these parishes that short of policemen, we're going to see that the Politian gets through their business uninterrupted."

"Is that so? And how are you going to do that? are you going to do your own recruitment?"

"Don't be naïve. For the time being, we'll use the resources we got – your soldiers."

The lieutenant puts away the cigar. He reaches for his spearmint. He unwrapped it but didn't put it in his mouth.

"Aren't you forgetting something, man? The soldiers are for the army?"

"No, I didn't forget, but without them, we would be over run."

The lieutenant needed be told, he knows, but at time he has to made a point just for the hell of it.

"So, you think we're about to get a new home secretary, do you?"

"Not only, but a new administration, so prepare yourself. You could be looking for a new job."

The commissioner was leaving. He took his stuff he doesn't usually carry.

"I'll see you here tomorrow at 12 noon, Mr James, and I will be waiting, and Dick, don't be late."

As he was about to exit the door, he remembered.

"Oh, Dick, you couldn't guess who came to see me today."

"You're right, man, I couldn't guess. Who was it?"

"Only Janet bloody Nelson."

"Janet Nelson called on you!" he exclaimed alarmingly. "What the hell for?"

"She wanted to see Harry's body. I'll tell you more in the morning, good evening."

"Wait up, man!" he exclaimed anxiously. "What did you tell her?"

"Got you thinking, didn't it? I'll tell you tomorrow, I'm off."

"A damn bad habit, man; you begin to tell someone something then stop short."

"It will keep you thinking till tomorrow, Dick, good evening."

Chapter 36
The Surprised Visitor

On Tuesday, the PM paid an unexpected visit to Police Headquarters. Miss Scott saw him coming and alerted the commissioner. He was with Mr James. It was quite unusual. What on earth could be the cause for him to be making an unannounced visit. However, since the emergence of the general election, members of this government had been acting strangely; some saw their future as not being in government – i.e. the home secretary.

"Miss Scot, as soon as he arrives, will you buzz me, please?"

"Mr James, isn't that a surprise, the PM turning up unannounced? Why do you suppose he's making such a visit?"

"A strange one indeed, and I hate to speculate why."

As he entered, she didn't wait for him to greet her. She was first to the task.

"Good day, prime minister, please come in. Is there anything I can do for you?" Naturally, he was quite polite.

"Good day, Miss Scott, yes, you could tell the commissioner I would like to speak with him."

"Yes, sir, I'll tell him you're here."

She buzzes and does as she was told; and the commissioner came out to meet him.

"Good day, prime minister. This is a surprise. I trust there's nothing untoward that brings you here?"

He was about to respond, but the commissioner didn't wait. He asked him in. As he entered, Mr James stood to greet him; they exchanged words.

"Prime minister, I have the feeling this is not a social call; what can I do for you?"

"Commissioner, you might think this is most unusual, but I would like to see Harry Wells' body."

The commissioner immediately becomes curious about his motives. He never saw Harry in the flesh, why does he want to see him now he's dead? Does he want to gloat over the body of the man who plagued his government throughout? And most certainly, to cost him the election? The question remains, but only he knows the answer.

"Sure, prime minister, we can go see him together if you don't mind."

"Thank you, commissioner, I would like that." His voice was low and his appearance was that of a man who knows what future lies ahead.

They were about to leave, but before they did, he made a statement, anticipating what they'll be saying after his visit; he was making it known to them.

"I know you'll be asking why do I want to see Harry's body. I'll tell you, gentlemen, curiosity."

"Think nothing of what we may or may not say, prime minister. The reason for doing what you're about to, is your and your business alone."

He was complimentary, trying to let the PM feel a little less perplexed. At the crematorium, the undertaker took him inside. The commissioner didn't accompany him, thinking he probably wanted the moment alone. After a short while, he emerged looking bemused, but the commissioner wasn't going to ask any question. At times, one is better left to their thoughts. However, his curiosity got the better of him, and he asked. "Is everything alright, prime minister?"

But realising it was a dumb question, he quickly tried to redress.

"As you see, prime minister, he's no different from any other man; only more dead, thank God. He won't be doing any more damage to the country."

"Damage, commissioner? The damage had been done; he's dead but we're left with the consequences."

His reply was that of a broken man; Harry and his kind ruined the country and his administration, and he won't be the one to put it right, even if he could. On their way back to HQ, there wasn't much in the way of conversation; the mood was sombre. The commissioner tried to find words of comfort, but it was of no use.

"Commissioner, I know you've got a busy day ahead, so I'll say goodbye, and thank you."

"Don't mention it, prime minister, and you have a good day now."

In conversation with Mr James, he expressed his feelings.

"Mr James, that is a broken man. I almost feel sorry for him."

"But why? He made his bed, he presided over a crooked administration, and the result is what we're struggling with."

Wednesday, Deputy James was the first to arrive at Headquarters. Miss Scott presents him with a copy of *The Gleaner*. He pauses for a quick read.

"It seems there's going to be some changes around here, Miss Scott."

"Changes, Mr James? By whom?"

"You haven't read the paper, Miss Scott?"

"No, sir, not yet; I haven't got around to it."

"The opposition. The opposition, Miss Scott. If they win the election, they'll be making plenty of changes."

"I wonder what changes they would make; I hope it wouldn't affect my job."

He didn't respond. Something caught his eye, so she asked. "What kind of changes?"

"Well, they're saying they'll burn the entire marijuana plantation."

"Oh my God, they can't do that, Mr James, could they?" she asked frightfully.

"If they're the government, they can, and I hope they do. This action should've been taken a long time ago, but this government lacked imagination."

"So, you think that would be a good thing?"

"Sure, like other issues, the government was told to act, but they did nothing. Now look where we're, living in a broken country."

"I think that is going to cause a whole lot of trouble, don't you think, sir?"

"You could be right, but if this government hadn't lost its way, this is the sort of action they should have taken. The polls are all saying the P W P is going to win, and I'm hoping they're right," he read on.

"This is interesting," he said aloud. "They would be going after the cocaine cartel too, but how?" he asked himself.

He paused to look at Miss Scott. Perhaps thinking about what he had just read.

"I hope they're not going to bite off more than they can chew."

"What do you mean?" she asked.

"We haven't got…" He paused again; and it was a long pause.

"Oh, but this is interesting. They'll be asking Britain for help, this is music to my ear, Miss Scott; another thing this government should have done. I hope I live to see the day; I would like to cheer from the roof top. I'll tell you, Miss Scott, it'll be a very long time before this People Independent Party forms another government. All this they should have done; they burned their bridges."

The commissioner arrived; he was looking nonplussed. They said good morning as he entered. He returned the compliment but not verbally. He raised his hand in acknowledgement and went through to his office. Deputy James went in after him, on observation, he asked, "Mr Wade, did you sleep at all last night?"

"Does it show that much, Mr James?"

Miss Scott entered. She was quick to notice too.

"You seem awfully tired, commissioner, would you like a cup of coffee?"

"Yes, thank you, Miss Scott, make it black and strong. I couldn't sleep at all, Mr James, no matter how many sheep I counted," he jested.

"Of course, you know why."

"No, Mr James, but I'm sure you're going to tell me."

"You took the work home with you; only you didn't leave it in your briefcase."

"Tell me something I don't know; anyway, I would like to discuss Security, but the lieutenant should be here. Why the hell isn't he here?" He was grumpy.

The lieutenant arrived almost immediately after his name was mentioned.

"Dick, you must have heard your name called," said the deputy.

"I didn't, but what's new? You fellows can't do without me."

"Don't flatter yourself, and you are late," said the commissioner.

But immediately, the lieutenant noticed his appearance, and with his usual zestfulness, he commented.

"What the hell's the matter with you, man, didn't you go to bed last night?"

The commissioner shuffled himself about uncomfortably. In reality, he was feeling rather lousy.

"The next person says that to me, I'll turn and go straight back to bed."

"That's another thing. How long are you going to live at that hotel?" he asked.

"That is one hell of a good question, Dick," said the deputy.

"Mr Wade, if you're planning on staying with us, and I hope you are, then I suggest you get yourself a proper home. A hotel is only memory accommodation."

"Gentlemen, before you start planning my future, I suggest we start planning for the next few days. Polling day is only two days away, and this is when we spread ourselves thin. We should have two officers at each polling station, but we can't meet that obligation. So, you know this situation better than I, and from what I heard, election night can be quite rough. That said, let's hear some ideas."

There was a moment of silence. Miss Scott entered with coffee for the commissioner, and asked, "Is there anything more I can do for you, commissioner?"

He didn't want anything more. She returned to her desk.

"I've been thinking about it, and I came up with an idea; an idea that I think could lighten the workload without involving the soldiers. It's a long shot, but I think it's worth a try."

"Go ahead, Mr James, let hear it," said the commissioner. He had a long pause as though he'd forgotten his lines.

"How about ask for volunteers? I believe there're people out there who would support law and order, even work with the police."

"Jamie, your faith in human nature is touching, but that, my friend, is a non-starter," said the lieutenant.

The commissioner appeared thoughtful; he fiddled with his pen, looking pensive, still not having recovered from his bad night.

"At first thought, I think it's a good idea, on second thought, if anyone comes forward, and it's a big if, can they be trusted?" he asked.

"Mr Wade, when you arrived here, people were almost at war with the constabulary; attitudes change, not much, but changed nevertheless, thanks to you. Now we need their help. Let's ask them; they might say yes."

"Okay, Mr James, let's do it. how do we go about asking them? We need them for the day after tomorrow."

"Now there you have a problem," said the lieutenant.

The commissioner came up with a solution. One he hoped would work. He'll contact the radio station and ask them to put it on air, and *The Gleaner* too.

"Assuming there're volunteers, what are you going to tell them?" asked the lieutenant.

"The truth, we'll tell them the truth; the constabulary is asking for their help, to work alongside police officers," Mr James concurred.

"Perhaps I should run it by the home secretary before telling it to the media."

Mr James doesn't think he should bother. He believes the home secretary couldn't give a damn.

"Mr Wade, with all good intentions, that idea serves no useful purpose. At the last meeting; the home secretary showed no interest in what supposed to be his duty. You should hold your question for the next person, whoever he may be – his words, remember? I don't think he would thank you for telling him."

Well, even though he didn't wholeheartedly agree with the deputy, he knew he was right, and so did the lieutenant.

"Okay, Mr James, on your heads be it, we'll proceed as planned."

He didn't wait for the talk to end; he contacted the media.

"Gentlemen, it's all systems go, and if by Thursday there are volunteers, we'll need someone to talk to them."

"I'll do the honours, Mr Wade, and I know we'll get volunteers."

"Jamie my man, I wouldn't hold my breath," said the doubtful lieutenant.

He took out the cigar he was carrying around. He held it between his fingers with no intention of lighting it; he was just being stylish.

"Is there any other business, gentlemen?" He was getting to his feet.

"Why, are you going somewhere? And what's with you and that damn cigar?" asked the commissioner. "Sit you ass back down, there's plenty to discuss."

"I was thinking about the men on duty at Hanover Bay. If we get no volunteer; for one night only, we could take some of them away, leaving three to guard the city."

The lieutenant had misgivings, he didn't like the idea; he rolled the cigar between his fingers as though he intended to put it in his mouth. The commissioner gave a glare, then smiled wryly.

"You know, Dick, you looked damn peculiar with that cigar. Let's hear what you think."

"Bad idea, man. In towns and cities; that's where the looters, pickpockets and all the bad people are heading; they're not hanging around the districts. The men should remain there; in fact, we should strengthen the forces in all those places."

"You're right, Dick," said the deputy, "at the last election there was trouble, but only in towns and cities. As I remember, two people were killed in Pen Hill, and many were hurt; some badly injured," said the deputy.

"I stand corrected, gentlemen. Of course, your knowledge of past events will have a bearing on what we do at present."

"Okay, so we know what we're up against; we'll fortify the towns and cities, depending on the man power. On Friday, we'll need three drivers to transport the men to their various destinations, will you see to it, Dick?"

"Sure thing, man."

At the Office

Friday, the commissioner was late getting to his office. He was expected to be joined by his colleagues; he was in for a surprise, but a pleasant one. Approaching his office, the place appeared to be under siege. Miss Scott waved to him from the window, as he approached; people were quick to greet him, but without thinking of what was discussed, he asked, "what's going on here, Miss Scott?"

"These are your volunteers, sir; they been waiting for quite some time."

In amazement, he paused to think. "Well, blow me down, Mr James was right."

About the same time, the lieutenant arrived, thinking it was some sort of demo. He asked, "What's going on, commissioner? Who are these people?"

"They're the volunteers who want to be policemen; we asked them to, remember?"

He was in awe as the commissioner was.

"I don't mind telling you, I never thought I would see the day when people of this country wanted to support the police, and all for free. The damn deputy was right."

"That's exactly what I said," commented the commissioner.

"So, what happens now, man, what do we do?"

"We go talk to them; we have to talk to them, don't we?"

"Yes, but what do we say? There're too many of them. We don't need them all."

"We've been through that, Dick; remember, we tell them the truth."

Mr James arrived. If he was surprised, he wasn't showing it; after all, this was his idea.

"Mr James, these are the volunteers; but we don't need them all, what are we going to do?"

"Pick the ones we need, Mr Wade, what else can we do?"

"Then, will you do the honours? After all it's your idea."

"Okay, so how many do we need? About 30?"

"That should be enough, Mr James, unless you think otherwise."

"No, 30 is a nice round number. I'll get right on it."

The volunteers were about fifty-five strong. Whatever he was going to say to them, he'll have to choose his words carefully. They were are eager to serve, but some were going to be disappointed. He was speaking from the window of Miss Scott's office.

"Good folks, it's great to see you all; when we asked for volunteers, I had my doubt no one would come. Now I'm ashamed, I should have known you'll never let your country down. However, some of you are going to be disappointed, but don't be dismayed. The ones who don't get chosen today, we will be needing you some other time."

It wasn't an easy task. No one wanted to be left out, but he did it quite well. Of course, he had an advantage; he was well-respected. His reputation as a detective stood him in good stead, even outside the capital, as he had discovered. The commissioner was awfully pleased; this was partly the result of his effort since, he arrived here.

"Mr James, this country should be so much better, and you know what, I believe it's going to. As soon as we get a better government, a government that's got the people's interest at heart. We'll not only have a better country, but better people; proud and patriotic people."

"Whatever happens to a country, Mr Wade, it largely depends on the kind of government in office. It should be a great accolade for one to serve one's country. These people came, answering the call, it shows they cared."

"You may not have long to wait, Mr James, if the polls are right, and I hope they are, we'll be having a new administration; they might be the ones to change things."

"I hope so, Mr Wade. This country has too long been run by men of greed, deception and lack of imagination."

This political chat was over; they got back to the matter in hand. The ones chosen; the deputy asked them forward.

"These're your men, Mr Wade, they would like to know their duty."

Standing next to his deputy at the window, he spoke to them.

"Gentlemen, we're asking you to work alongside police officers, tomorrow and probably beyond, helping to maintain law and order. Can we depend on you?"

There was a shout of yes from everyone, even those who weren't chosen. He whispered to the lieutenant. "Dick, isn't it wonderful, this is what one gets when he puts in the effort."

The talk was over. Tomorrow they'll be sent on their different locations.

"Dick, we'll need the transport for noon tomorrow, will there be a problem?"

"No, man, it's being taken care of."

Before the recruits leave, he gathered them to brief them on what they're up against. But facing them, he didn't speak for a short while; there was a frog in his throat, and a little tear too. He wiped his eyes.

"I'm sorry, men; some dust gets in my eyes." He was lying of course, it was his emotion; he couldn't contain himself.

"Men, most of you will be going far out of town. There're people at meetings causing disruptions, you'll be there to control the situation, and when this assignment is over, I hope you'll be wanting to join the constabulary."

There was whispering among them, probably some would like to join right now. The day continued to be pleasant, a typical summer's day, tomorrow, the people went to the poll, and Harry Wells was to be cremated. The men were prepared for what could be a difficult day.

Chapter 37
The Cremation

Crowd gathered at the Wilbur crematorium; they wanted to see Harry's body. But these were those who voted already; they had the evidence, a finger dipped in red paint. The law enforcers standing be, they were hoping the cremation goes off peacefully. But that was wishful thinking. There were people from the Harry Wells fan club, they wanted to say farewell to their hero. When told they couldn't see the body, they became restless; now they were not asking, they were demanding it. Proceedings was drawn to a halt; the official who wasn't already inside wasn't allowed to enter.

They were adamant about their demand, but they won't gate crash the chapel; places like these they held in reverence.

The commissioner was notified about the crowd demand before he arrived. Now he must talk to them. But he had to tread carefully. He didn't want to destroy the rapport he had built up with them. He didn't approach them, he went to find Deputy James; he knew they held him in high regard, and with them both, he was hoping they'll be able to calm the situation.

They planned a course of action. The commissioner will speak first, but the plan was for both men to stand together.

They wanted everyone to see them, so, they stood on a pile of bricks; it was adjacent to the chapel.

"Ladies and gentlemen," he shouted, "can I have your attention, please?"

They adhere to his call, but one man who anticipated his intention; shouted.

"Commissioner, you're wasting your time, we want to see Harry's body, and we're not leaving until we do"

"Who said that?" he asked, raising his head to see.

A burley fellow walked forward; it could be he was the man who spoke.

"I did, commissioner; we want to see Harry's body. We want to pay our respect," he spoke respectfully.

The commissioner thought it wasn't an unreasonable request, and thought they should comply. Of course, his thinking went beyond that – refuse and they could have a riot on their hands, and that would destroy the trust they have in him.

"Mr…" He paused. "What your name?"

"Reed, commissioner, but you can call me Will."

He had a whispered discussion with Mr James, and they decide on a course of action. They talk with Will. He asked him to come closer. The three men conferred, and Will was in agreement. Standing on the pile of bricks, he spoke, and this time, there was no interruption.

"Listen folks, it's a good thing you're here for. We respect your action; however, you all won't be able to see Harry's body, but four of you can."

There were grumbles and whispers among themselves, but no one spoke. He waited to see if there's any decent, but there was none.

"Does everyone here knows Mr James?" he asked. The response was positive, some were even asking him (Mr James) if he's well. Deputy James got up on the pile of bricks and continued the commissioner's theme. But firstly, he thanked them for asking after his health.

"Folks, you know me and you know I wouldn't lie to you. The commissioner and I, we're acting in accordance with the government's directive. Your friend, Will here, he fully understands the situation, and I'm hoping you do too. We may not agree with the ruling; but such is the law. However, we're going to bend the law a little. We're going to allowed four of you to go inside, and pay your respect on behalf of all; will that be satisfactory to everyone?"

They didn't much like the idea, but out of respect and perhaps realising that's the best offer they're going to get, they accepted. He thanked them for their co-operation.

Will chose three others, and accompanied by the undertaker, they went inside. It was a little less than five minutes since they were gone, but the crowd grew impatient, they wanted to hear about their hero. They returned, and Will got on the pile of bricks, but before he could speak, people were asking questions.

"Is it Harry, tell us?" Shadowed by the other, he spoke.

"We saw him, it's Harry, alright." Probably like many others, he had doubts.

"Did he say anything?" some asked.

He paused, probably thinking of the question. "No, but he was smiling."

After answering all their question, he and the others retired back to the crowd, leaving the stage for the law men.

"Good people, we thank you for your cooperation, and remember, if you have any complaints, you come and see us."

With nothing further to add, they withdrew quietly. But the crowd didn't disperse; they sat quietly waiting for the cremation. Moments later, the bell began to toll, signalling it was over, Harry Wells was cremated. There was one among them, could be a pastor, he asked them to bow their heads in silent prayer. Some were in tears, but for the authorities, they breathed a sigh of relief.

Back at the office; against what his colleagues thought, he rang the home secretary to tell him the news. This was certain to be the last conversation regarding governmental matters.

"Mr Wade, you're a good man, I always find you to be so. I hope a day will come when we will meet over the dinner we never had."

"I hope so too, minister, so let's keep our options open."

"I wish you well on your operation tonight, Mr Wade, now, I bid you good day, sir." It sounded as though he was saying his last goodbye. But however, he took the news, he feels better for telling him.

Counting the Votes

It was eight o'clock and some of the polls had already closed, and soon the counting began. All around the country, there was an air of anticipation; they were expecting a new government. In various parts of the country where the results were early, there were disturbances; the votes were not going the way of the PIP. At Bryson town, there were ugly scenes reported; Mr Harper lost his deposit, and wasn't satisfied; and was demanding a recount. When his demand was denied, his supporters stormed the podium, but they were quickly overpowered. The police along with help from both sides of the spectrum dealt with them mercilessly. In all parts of the country, the PWP were winning; things were not looking good for the government. There were thirty-two seats in total to be counted, and the PWP looked set to take at least twenty-seven.

The disturbance continued, one of which was in the capital. The commissioner with his five men rushed to the scene; one man dead, the other badly injured. When the result was announced, fight broken out between supporters, one pulled his gun and shot the two men. He tried to get away but he couldn't, so he took shelter in a store. The people were furious. The dead man was well known, he canvassed for the winning candidate.

The commissioner had to think and fast; the people wanted revenge. In some ways, he was gratified to see the people's reactions, but an overzealous mob could cause many more casualties. He pleaded to their better nature, asking them to allow the police to handle the situation. They stood back watching, they were not going anywhere. One man who was the brother of one of the injured men, confronted the commissioner and told him, if they don't get him, he will. A bold talk, the man is only armed with a machete.

Isn't it illegal for a man to be carrying a weapon even at this time of the night? You may ask. Not at all. A machete is a working tool; and is not classified as a weapon; every family has got at least one.

The commissioner got his men together; two of whom were volunteers; he told them his plan. He would like to avoid further killings, but he knew the score; the gunman held up in the store wouldn't hesitate to kill again. He pleaded with him to throw out his weapon and come on out, but that was to no avail.

The gunman fired a few rounds. It appeared to warn them off, but by doing so, he shot another person, a woman. The commissioner was concerned about the storeowner and his family. He hasn't got his two colleagues to confer with; they're in other parts of the country. He had a brainwave, and got the men together.

"Men, this is what we'll do: we're going to draw his fire, we'll fire and keep firing; but not in the store. He'll be shooting at us, and when he's out of bullets, we'll rush him." And so it was, in a short while, the shooting ceased; the shooter was out of bullets. They moved in fast. He was cornered. Two lawmen grabbed him, but he pulled a knife, and with rapid thrust, one lawman got stabbed. The other didn't hesitate. He shot the man several times; he fell to the floor dead. The commissioner was just in time to see him gasp his last breath.

"He stabbed Mike, commissioner, I had to shoot him."

"That's alright, officer, you did right."

Looking at the wounded officer, his condition wasn't good. The commissioner took him in his car and rushed him across town to the hospital, he'll be given priority. He returned to check with the family of the store; shaken but they were fine. He then checked with the woman that was hit; she was badly hurt and needed treatment. He gave his car to officer Hylton to take her to hospital. He was given a note to give to the doctor, that way she'll be treated urgently. This was the commissioner's way of building trust with the public.

It was past midnight, and things settled down somewhat; the votes were still coming in, but it was not good news for

Prime Minister Young. The PIP was swept aside, even he (the prime minister) lost his seat, and the country rejoices. All over this island paradise, there was dancing in the street, many of whom were supporters of the PIP. *The Gleaners* appeared to align themselves with the new administration; they were singing their praises. When the final count was announced, twenty-nine seats went the way of the PWP. In his speech to the nation, Prime Minister Mc Bean commented. "Our country is not at war, yet all over the island people being killed, it's got to stop. The drug barons, whether they're in cocaine or marijuana, will be driven out; we're taking our country back." And the people rejoiced.

Chapter 38
The New Government

Three days later, the commissioner and his deputy were summoned to parliament house. They were to have talks with the new prime minister. He particularly wanted to talk with Mr James; a man he knew well, and held in high regards. He knew he was a member of the other party, but as a detective, they shared the same ideals in regard to law and order. However, what he didn't know, this time round the ex-detective changed parties.

Thursday morning and the two men arrived; they were greeted by Miss Dillon, the prime minister's secretary. She greeted them both, but a special greeting was given to Mr James even though they had never met.

"Won't you take a seat, gentlemen? I'll tell the prime minister you're here."

In a quick while she returned, followed by the prime minister.

"Good day, gentlemen," he said, greeting them warmly with handshakes, and then escorting them in.

He was full of beans; appeared energetic and rearing to go.

"Make yourselves comfortable, gentlemen, I don't know if you been told, but I'm the new prime minister," he said facetiously. "I'm sorry if you're disappointed, but I'm sure in time I will grow on you."

They noticed his exuberant, so Mr James rose to the challenge.

"Prime minister, I'm not disappointed, not yet. There's an old saying, 'the proof is in the tasting'. I haven't tasted anything yet."

"Well said, Mr James, and I'll try to do my best in the kitchen. You know, Mr James, I always admired your work, and I know we shared a lot in regard to law and order. I hope nothing has changed in that regard."

"Prime minister, if one is sincere in their belief; their principles will never change, regardless of their politics."

"That's good to hear. I was sorry when you resigned from your post, and I understood your reasoning; too many bad apples, however, I was pleased when I heard you returned."

"Thank you for your kind words, prime minister. I'm pleased to be back; however, I have Mr Wade to thank; he's the reason I'm back."

The commissioner sat quietly observing and listening. it was like two old friends renewing acquaintances. The prime minister was pleased to hear that of the commissioner. He held him in high regard too.

"Commissioner, whatever methods you've used to get this gentleman back in the constabulary, more power to your elbow."

"It wasn't too difficult at all; he didn't put up much of a fight."

With all the prime minister's kind words, they're waiting anxiously to learn why they were summoned. Their curiosities running wild.

"Gentlemen, it's for a good reason I've asked you here, and I'm hoping neither you nor I will be disappointed."

They gathered that much, but it didn't make the wait any easier. He continued, but it was more like making a speech, and a lengthy one too. Then finally.

"Gentlemen, you've been the servants of the country, and I would like you to continue being servants of the country, but in other capacities. That said, I would like you, Mr Wade, to take over at the Home Office. It's a non-portfolio position of course, but I'm sure you'll do a good job there, and I have my fingers crossed you'll accept."

The commissioner looked at Deputy James. Their eyes meet; but nothing said. However, the meeting of eyes spoke volumes, the commissioner's words came back to haunt him. In Hanover Bay, he'd suggested that new administration had a way of changing personnel; he wasn't thinking of himself.

"Mr Wade, I would like your answer now, as you know, I'm in the process of forming a cabinet, and there's no time to lose."

The commissioner sat up straight. If he was feeling isolated earlier, he wasn't now; he must make a decision.

"Prime minister, I'm greatly honoured and surprised, but the position you're offering, I have no knowledge of."

Mr James cleared his throat rather noisily; it was done for the benefit of the commissioner. His words were that of the ex-detective when he was offered the position of deputy commissioner. The commissioner read the sign; he smiled as their eyes meets.

"However, prime minister, if you're confidence enough to offer me the position, how can I refuse? It will be an honour to work in your government and serve the country."

"Then, Home Secretary Wade, welcome. I wish you well, and have no doubt you'll excel in your new position."

Mr James rose to his feet to congratulate the new minister. "Mr Wade, you're going to make a fine home secretary. Congratulations." They shook hands.

The prime minister buzzed his secretary; there was a moment of silence while she took her place at the table.

"Take a note, Miss Dillon. The new home secretary is being named. He's Mr Wade."

After she noted it, she stood, and with a beaming smile, she congratulated him.

"You don't know me, commissioner, but…" She paused, realising that wasn't what she should have said. She rephased. "I should have said, home secretary, congratulation, sir."

"That's alright, Miss Dillon, this thing is new to me too."

Mr James waited anxiously to learn his fate. He had the feelings he was going to be offered a position. He didn't have to wait long.

"There's another appointment I need to make. Who will take over at the constabulary. If things were different, I would've liked it to be me. However, the man I would like to take over, is you, Mr James. The word, please, doesn't come easily, it's goes against the grain, but in this case, I'm making an exception; please say yes."

He was just as surprised as the commissioner was; he's only been a deputy commissioner for a short while, his rapid rise up the ranks will take some time to comprehend.

"Prime minister, you have surprised me and made me feel quite humble. When we were summoned here, I for one didn't know what to expect. As you know, I was a supporter of the other party, however, this time round I didn't support them, how could I? That said, how could I refused? But I must tell you, sir, I'm lacking in experience."

It was only a flattery comment; the man was perfect for the post. Apart from the new home secretary, no one was more suitable.

"Mr James, there's no doubt in my mind you're the right man for job. You're a noted man to the public; the country will be pleased."

"Well, sir, I can't think of a job I'd rather do, and I will do my best for the constabulary, the government and the country."

The new man at the home office was quick to respond.

"Prime minister, he's perfect for the job, but you have beaten me to the punch."

"May I ask for what, home secretary?"

"It was my intention to ask Mr James to be my deputy; now I have to look elsewhere."

"I'm sorry to hear that, home secretary, we all got our problems."

There were moments of laughter.

"Then I know where you'll be look," said the new commissioner.

He was thinking of his old friend, the lieutenant. They congratulated each other on their new positions. They didn't drink a toast on this occasion; it will kept for another time.

Later that evening, the new home secretary met with the lieutenant; he was posing an unusual beaming smile. The lieutenant noticed. *It is un-like the man, something must have happened,* he thought.

"Is everything alright, man? I know something happened. Are you going to tell me about it?" There was no need for the lieutenant to ask. That's why he's here, to tell him of his appointment.

"What's the hell you on about now?" he asked with little interest.

"Me, Dick, you're looking at the new the home secretary."

"If this is a joke, man, it's not in good taste."

"Who's joking? The prime minister offered me the post, and I accepted."

Discovering he was serious, he was as amazed as the home secretary was when the post was offered.

"So, when did this happen? Why wasn't I made aware?"

"Not too long ago, and it came as a surprise. I came directly here to tell you."

The lieutenant scratched his head and brushed back his curly black hair. His mind was at work. What else happened, he was not aware of.

"Well, if what you're telling me is true, and I hope it is, congratulations, you earned it. We should celebrate."

"Yes, we'll certainly have a drink at some point, thank you, Dick, and I hope I won't disappoint. There's something else, perhaps I shouldn't be telling you, but let's say I can't help myself."

"If it's a secret man, don't tell me; I'm a blabbermouth."

"No secret, it's about Mr James. He would want to tell you himself, but he's the new commissioner of police."

"Jamie, he's the new commissioner?" he asked, looking startled. "Well, it couldn't have gone to a better man."

Mr Wade cleared his throat noisily.

"Oh, present company not included." They laughed.

"So, Dick, have you ever considered leaving the army? I could do with a good deputy, and while you're thinking about it, consider this: with you and me at the home office, we would make one hell of a team."

"I'm not thinking about it, man. I'm not moving, unless they kick me out. Anyway, we'll still be working together; the army is only another wing of the constabulary – your words, remember?"

"Well, I didn't think you would, but I had to ask."

"Thanks for asking, man, I'm sure you'll find the right candidate."

A few weeks later, the lieutenant was summoned to a meeting with the prime minister. There he was put in total control of the army. Some ten months on, it looked like a new dawn; things were looking so much better.

The prime minister had stood by his promise, in collaboration with the US, the men came, and with helicopters, they burnt the entire marijuana plantations. The farmers could only stand and watch their cultivation go up in smoke; the aroma carried a long way on the wind. If one wasn't a smoker of the stuff, one could get intoxicated. The government didn't stop there. They were now in talks with the British; asking for help to fight the cocaine cartel. Less than a year on, and money was returning, and perhaps most important, the returnees, they were coming back in numbers. The tourist trade was gathering momentum. One of the world's most popular pleasure destinations was once again open for business, the good times were back.

Mr Wade

Then what about Mr Wade, the import from England, some five years ago? Well, Home Secretary Wade is one of the most popular men in the country. His good work at the constabulary had paid dividends, and the good people of the country weren't slow in showing their gratitude. At the next general election, he stood as the candidate for the PWP, the seat had changed hands at the last election, but Home Secretary Wade increased his majority. He's well established in the adapted country, and his good work continues alongside his long-time colleagues. Six years on, and with good thinking, hardworking honest men, Mr Mc Bean's government has put the country on a firm footing to prosperity and stability. On the high seas, the British are at war with the cartel, and the good news is, they're winning that battle.

Mr Wade is now living in Hanover Bay, the place he fell in love with some years ago. Three years before he was voted into office, he returned to England, but only to say goodbye to his kin folks and collect his wife and only son. Some years later, he was a proud grandfather; Mark had married the foreign minister's daughter, she bore him a son. Mr Wade, a man approaching retirement, is enjoying life with his family.

End